The Winter of Apollo

by

Valeria Reece

Copyright © 2022 Valeria Reece

ISBN: 9781915889515

All rights reserved, including the right to reproduce this book, or portions thereof in any form. No part of this text may be reproduced, transmitted, downloaded, decompiled, reverse engineered, or stored, in any form or introduced into any information storage and retrieval system, in any form or by any means, whether electronic or mechanical without the express written permission of the author.

This is a work of fiction. Names and characters are the product of the author's imagination and any resemblance to actual persons, living or dead, is entirely coincidental.

The views expressed in this work are solely those of the author and do not necessarily reflect the views of the publisher, and the publisher hereby disclaims any responsibility for them.

Chapter 1

England, 1885

She was running… running… but her legs began to burn, as if there was a fire inside her bones, finding its way through her skin. She looked down at her hand, which was covered in blood. It was too much, and her strength was starting to wane. It was so dark!

She tripped over a tree root and fell headlong on the grass. The pain was unbearable, but she had to continue, even if she had to crawl her way across the lawn. She took a deep breath and tried to continue, when suddenly her hand found a large hole in the ground, maybe a rabbit hole? The soil was damp, so perhaps she could make it bigger, and hide in it. Too much blood, but she now had some hope, as some of the soil at the edge collapsed away when she pulled at it, revealing a much wider tunnel.

She crawled into the darkness, then with her other hand and enormous effort, she started to pile the earth up to close the entrance around her refuge a little, so nobody would find her. At least she felt safer, and perhaps her wound would stop bleeding. Hopefully the light of dawn could bring strength and healing. Gently, she touched the little golden owl on her delicate necklace, then after a deep breath, she closed her eyes…

The present day, Athens, 1888

Kate opened her eyes abruptly, realising she was breathless and soaked in sweat. Her disturbed sleep woke Andrew. It was a nightmare, again.

'What happened, Kate? I will get you some water,' Andrew said anxiously, and when he was about to get up, Kate held his hand and said,

'No, thank you. I am fine, it was just a nightmare. Please, hold me, and I will be fine.'

Gently, he held her to his chest and hugged her, caressing her hair and face softly.

'You see? Love is the cure for all ills!' she exclaimed, smiling.

'Why not add happiness? Some people love, but are unhappy,' Andrew replied.

'You are absolutely right. Let's make a list of essential feelings to heal the soul whilst the body recovers. What do you think?' Kate asked.

'I have no doubt about it. Without you I would not have survived when we were attacked by those brigands last year,' Andrew replied, cuddling her tightly.

She lifted her head, seeking his lips, then kissed him passionately without noticing that the first sunlight came through the door of the balcony, reminding them that they would have a busy day ahead.

After breakfast the couple left the house by carriage, discussing their commitments whilst making plans.

'What arguments are you going to use to persuade them?' Kate asked.

'Every card I have in my pocket, including Anthony and Myra if I have to,' Andrew replied in good humour.

'Hmm... do you think that is a good idea? Anthony's bad reputation precedes him.' Kate laughed.

'Exactly what I want. They will be tempted precisely because Anthony is brilliant as an archaeologist, therefore everybody wants him as an ally and under their control, rather than working in competition against them,' Andrew stated, smiling.

'Especially with Myra around. She can make enough trouble to shake the Parthenon to get what she wants,' Kate added.

'Not more dangerous than you, I would say.' He laughed at her serious face.

'Could you let me go down here in the market? I would like to buy the last fruits of the autumn. They are still quite sweet, don't you think?' Kate asked Andrew, trying to change the subject.

'But it's quite a long walk to the school from here,' Andrew objected, concerned.

'In the winter, we will regret not having enjoyed the good weather for an invigorating walk' Kate replied decisively.

'You are right, but I will go with you. You cannot go around alone, without me or Thomas,' he responded.

'But you will be late for the meeting,' she complained, adding, 'I promise you that I will buy the fruits and go straight to the school; no walking around,' she said.

'Sure?' Andrew asked.

'I promise, from my heart!' she replied honestly.

The carriage stopped, so after a kiss, Kate said goodbye to her husband then walked to the little market to buy fruits. After tasting a couple, she made her selection and bought enough for the next few days.

It was not a particularly sunny day, and although they were on the cusp of winter, the weather was very pleasant for the end of autumn; everything indicated that the winter would be a little milder this year than usual.

The air in the market was laden with the delicious aroma of fruit, spices and other exotic smells. It was as if time had stopped and she was trapped in it, with a voice from the distant past addressing her, and her alone. Kate was completely absorbed in her thoughts when a strange, deep voice brought her back to the present. An old woman, sitting in a wooden chair a few feet from the British School of Athens, spoke:

"*Listen to my words!*
Nowhere is Panacea seen,
But where the sunset meets moonrise,
Hyperborea!"

But suddenly she got up and left, while Kate, not knowing what to say, remained standing there looking at the woman until she disappeared from her sight.

After a momentary hesitation caused by those strange words, Kate shrugged her shoulders and entered the school immediately as she had too much work to do to ponder what the woman meant. Inside, Thomas was standing wringing his hands, clearly agitated.

'Miss Tiverton, sorry, I mean, Lady Katherine, thank goodness you have arrived,' he said.

'What is the matter, Thomas? Did anything happen?' Kate asked, worried.

'Something very peculiar happened,' he replied, looking a little pale.

'Well, I think that I know you enough to deduct that something really important happened. So, tell me, what was it?' Kate demanded in a kind tone.

'A couple of hours ago, a lady came to the school and asked to speak with Lady Katherine Enfield. I told her that today you would be a little late, and I offered to help her, but she said that it was a personal matter and she would return later,' Thomas detailed.

'Never mind, Thomas; if it really was important she will come back for sure, don't worry about it,' Kate replied, before heading to her office.

However, it wasn't long before the lady returned, and when Thomas entered the room agitated, Kate knew that the mysterious lady had come back.

'Lady Katherine, she is back, and she brought a carriage full of boxes and chests; I think that she is going away,' Thomas alerted Kate.

'Calm down, Thomas, don't worry. Let's see what this is all about,' she reassured him.

Kate walked to the entrance hall, certain that the mysterious lady would be the same one who'd addressed her in Greek outside the school earlier; however, she was entirely mistaken.

'You are younger than I expected, but if you have the same passion my father had for ancient history, I think that I am in the right place,' the lady declared in a friendly tone when introduced to Kate.

'What is your father's name?' Kate asked, trying to be convivial and to establish a conversation.

'Sir Joshua Egerton. I am his daughter, Mary Egerton,' the lady replied.

'Oh... this is a great honour, how wonderful!' Kate beamed. 'I know your father by reputation – one of the greatest Hellenists of our time. My husband and I were talking about him recently. We wanted to go to Corinth to meet him personally; perhaps he could give a lecture here, at school, for the British post-graduates next summer?' Kate said, very pleased to make the acquaintance of the eminent scholar's daughter.

'Unfortunately, my father had a stroke. He died three weeks ago, but he survived long enough after the stroke to assert his last wish,' she informed Kate.

'I am so sorry to hear about your father. It is undoubtedly a big loss for the academy. My husband will receive this news with great regret for not being able to have the honour of meeting him in person,' Kate stated, sad at the bad news.

'I was not wrong either, his work will continue here in this school, for certain. His last wish was to donate his entire library and notes to the British School of Athens, and he asked me for something in particular, and of a great importance to him. Amongst the boxes outside there is a leather trunk in which he placed certain selected books inside; manuscripts and notes, which should be submitted to you only. He was certain that you would continue his life's work. Here is the key to the lock.' She handed Kate a small silver key, whilst Kate was recovering from the unexpected news.

'Would you join me for a cup of tea, Mary?' Kate asked, hoping that the lady could stay longer.

'I am sorry, but my mother and I are catching a ship to England in a few hours' time. We are moving back home, and I still have some other commitments before our departure,' she explained politely.

'Please send my condolences to your mother; the British School will give your father's library a place of honour here. I will keep you informed about the development, as this is a very new school, but we are full of ideas and hope to turn it into an important centre for learning, and reference for research in ancient Greek history and language,' Kate assured her.

'Thank you, Katherine, I appreciate that,' she replied soberly.

'Please, call me Kate, and I am very thankful. Have a safe journey.'

Mary smiled and bade goodbye, so whilst Thomas carried the boxes to the library, Kate watched her enter her carriage and leave.

After a long day, Kate felt tired, but at the same time pleased to have so many important books and manuscripts in front of her; it would take days, though, to check everything before she could start a proper catalogue.

She was wondering if they would have everything finished before next summer when the post-graduate students would arrive. After all the excitement of the day, she finally had a moment to relax, which enabled her to focus attention on the leather trunk, which contained Sir Joshua's mysterious research. So she called Thomas.

'Thomas! Could you ask Michael to help you to carry that leather trunk to my carriage? I need to take it with me, because it has to do with Sir Joshua's personal research. I must study his notes as soon as possible,' Kate asked.

'Yes, Lady Katherine, we will do it now,' Thomas replied.

'I will finish early today, so you can close the school after I leave, and go home if you like,' Kate said.

'Thank you, my lady,' Thomas replied happily. He was probably as excited as her, at the arrival of more books; she had noticed how enthusiastic he was for reading, leaving no doubt that ancient history had claimed another soul for its retinue of subjects. When they finished, he attended to closing up the school, and Kate went home with the precious documents.

Having arrived home, whilst the servants were organising the removal of the leather trunk from her carriage, Kate went to the kitchen and asked Amalia, the cook, to send tea to her room, rather than the study. Kate was very curious about Sir Joshua's research, so it was with considerable expectation she got the key and opened the trunk to see what treasures lay within.

The inner lid of the box had some writing in Ancient Greek on it and Kate was able to translate what seemed to be the title of the text – *The Winter of Apollo*. That sounded unusual as she had never in her academic life heard of Apollo being associated with winter. It was always the opposite – *Apollo as bright as the sun*; *Phoebus Apollo*. Whoever had written that achieved their goal, because Kate could not hold her excitement any longer and went to the studio quickly. She grabbed a Greek dictionary and ran up the stairs towards her bedroom again to start the translation, which was not especially difficult:

"*The voice in the temple*
A benevolent spirit have,
And beautiful body,
And great knowledge,
The herald proclaims!"

That was a very unusual text, perhaps a fragment of another. She no doubt would be unable to determine its proper meaning until she examined the entire contents of the trunk. All of the books had marked sheets quoting ancient authors concerning a very specific subject – *medicine*. She started to make notes of the names – philosophers, poets and geographers. They were all there, and in addition to the references to historical people, several sheets were marked with the name of mythological deities: Apollo, Artemis (his twin sister), Asclepius (his son), and the Hyperboreans.

It was a tiring day, and Kate's mind started spinning, so a little rest and a cup of tea with a bite to eat would invigorate her to continue later, she decided.

Whilst closing the trunk, Kate noticed a little sound coming from the balcony. Perplexed, she walked slowly towards it. On the way she picked up Mr Bear, who was sitting comfortably on her dressing table, then, cuddling him very tight, she sat on one of the chairs of the balcony. There, as if waiting for Kate to appear, was an owl, perched on the railing. Kate smiled and said,

'You were always there, weren't you?'

Kate closed her eyes with her toy bear in her arms, and didn't notice the time passing until a soft voice called her.

'Kate…'

She opened her eyes and smiled when she saw Andrew standing by her side.

'What time is it?' she asked.

'Late, I am sorry. I didn't intend to miss our tea, but it was a tough day,' he apologised.

'Never mind, what was their decision?' she asked, though from his expression it didn't feel like good news.

'Bad news, I am afraid. Due to the hostilities between Greece and Turkey, the French School of Athens decided to postpone the excavation of Delphi for a couple of years. They will limit the number of foreign teams as well. We have hope that King George, being our Greek ally, will intervene in our favour and include a British team as observers,' Andrew explained, feeling helpless and annoyed by these developments.

'I am so sorry, you were so excited,' Kate said, a little disappointed, then added, 'But I noticed a certain sparkle in your eyes whilst you were speaking, evoking from the past a certain young boy, eager for adventures, and you know by now that you cannot exclude me, don't you?' she teased him.

'Oh, don't worry. I would never exclude you from this one,' he replied, enjoying delaying the news.

'Oh, please, stop the suspense; you are killing me!' She smiled.

'If you insist… I received a letter from Britain, from my friend, Lord Henry Tollemache. He is a mathematician and amateur astronomer. We might call him an "Antiquarian", as he likes to dig as a hobby. You may remember him from the Jubilee last summer. He didn't stop dancing with Diana,' Andrew reminded her.

'Please… tell me… he didn't marry Diana, did he?' Kate laughed.

'Exactly! And he has invited us to a triple celebration in Wiltshire. It seems that he could not offer his bride the sumptuous ceremony she deserved when they married, because of Sir John's death. Therefore,

She is taking the opportunity to kill three rabbits with a single shot. We were invited for a week-long celebration at their manor house there in Wiltshire, and to share with him some archaeological experiment or other,' Andrew explained.

'And... what is the third? Tell me, please,' Kate pleaded.

'Christmas, my dear. What do you think about a proper English Christmas?' Andrew asked, curious for her answer, whilst not sure himself if it would be a good idea.

'I think that Diana deserves our solidarity,' Kate replied. 'She might be quite sad about losing her father. I miss him very much too; he was like a father to me,' Kate said, with genuine sadness.

'Indeed, he was a great man, and I miss him dearly.' Andrew nodded. 'However, knowing Diana, it was perhaps inevitable her mourning would not be excessive. She might be quite eager for a big party,' Andrew replied maliciously.

Suddenly, Andrew's attention was caught by the leather trunk next to the dressing table, which had a couple of books opened on top.

'Where did that trunk come from?' he asked.

'Do you remember Sir Joshua Egerton, the Hellenist?' Kate asked.

'Yes, why?' Andrew frowned.

'He died, and his daughter is moving back to Britain with her mother. They came to the British school to donate his entire library to us, before they left. That trunk was sent to me specifically. It was his last wish, his daughter said,' Kate explained.

'Another dreadful loss, unfortunately, and I didn't have time to know him personally.'

'I know,' Kate said, and trying to be positive, she added, 'That trunk contains some very intriguing material – books and manuscripts he had collected, detailing how the ancients treated sickness and diseases; some of them talk about the plagues, like in Thucydides. There is a consensus that they had a purely religious and mythological view; however, Sir Joshua didn't completely agree and he went much further in his notes. He introduced a third element to the body and the soul – the mind,' she explained.

'Did he think the Greeks already distinguished mind from soul?' Andrew asked, interested.

'Far beyond the Greeks, Andrew – the Hyperboreans.'

'Oh... Kate. Hyperborea was a myth, you know that,' Andrew teased her.

'I know, I know. However, Sir Joshua listed some of the authors and their references to Hyperborea – *The land beyond the Celts, where the North wind blows, with a stone circle temple.*'

'If the Celts were settled in Gaul, then *the land beyond...*' Andrew said thoughtfully. He was interrupted by Kate.

'According to Diodorus Siculus – *An island not smaller than Sicily, with a stone circle as the temple of Apollo.* Does it sound familiar?' She asked excitedly.

'Wait a moment, what are you trying to say – Apollo resided in a stone circle in Britain, before even the Celts and the Greeks?' Andrew asked, without believing a word of her theory.

'You might not accept the words of the poets, but what about the philosophers, historians and geographers, even Pythagoras himself? They all mention the stone circle temple in Hyperborea.'

'Fine, fine, I understood. What did you say about Pythagoras just now?' Andrew asked, interested.

'Plato and Socrates were both influenced by Pythagoras, and Plato said that "knowledge about geometry" was essential to join his academy,' she argued. 'Do not forget, it was inscribed above the doors of his academy – *No one unversed in geometry shall enter here*, eh?'

'That doesn't explain why Pythagoras, Apollo and medicine are related, unless you begin to believe in transmigration of the soul, like Pythagoras,' Andrew interrupted her humorously, but trying to make some sense of the network of facts.

'Don't laugh at me, this is very serious research; it is scientific and evidence based. By the way, I didn't have time to read all the manuscripts, addendums and notes. I don't even know if Sir Joshua finished his research. This might be the reason why he sent it to me; perhaps he wanted me to find the answers?' Kate defended herself.

'Do you believe in coincidence, Kate?' Andrew asked enigmatically.

'It doesn't happen, not in science, Andrew,' Kate answered decidedly.

'In his letter, Lord Henry mentioned that he has organised a three-day trip to Stonehenge for us, as part of the celebrations, to check his theories, not just with archaeologists, but with mathematicians and astronomers as well,' Andrew informed her.

'Stone circle!' Kate exclaimed, excited.

'So, we both will have fun, I suppose. If I remember correctly, Henry Tollemache has advanced theories which infuriate prominent academics, much because he is not an academic himself,' Andrew explained, and hurried on. 'Anyway, we have to get ready. If we are lucky we could find tickets for the ship to Malta next week' Andrew tempted her.

'Malta? Next week? Are you sure? Why Malta?' Kate asked, excited, throwing herself in his arms.

'Because I know Dr Bartholomew Walker, and he is excavating in Malta at this very moment. He found artefacts which are particularly interesting, and according to his theory some of them could be used to record or teach about the movement of the stars. He is also trying to get permission to excavate a few stone ruins, which in his opinion were stone temples. He is a little mad, but you don't have problems with mad people, do you?' He laughed.

'I don't like the joke, but I forgive you, if you tell me more about our adventure,' Kate asked, eager to know what plans he had in mind for them.

'From Malta I will take you to Paris, to see the National Museum of Natural History, and meet the director, my friend Professor Maurice Legrand. Perhaps we might extend our trip to Brittany to visit the ancient stones at Carnac, if he has the time. How does it sound?' he asked, smiling.

'You mean that we are going to cross France by train? I never went to France.' Kate was over the moon at these suggestions.

'So, it will be our honeymoon. We didn't really have one yet.' He laughed.

'Oh... goodness! I have so much to do. I will have to send this trunk to England by ship.' Kate started making plans.

Andrew enjoyed seeing her as excited as a child, running from one corner to the other of their bedroom, picking important bits and pieces up, forgetting things, dropping others on the floor in a hurry. Before he left, Andrew turned at the door and added,

'It will also be a great opportunity for you to get to know our estate in Wiltshire, Lady Enfield.'

'Our home... We have a home in England!' She was absolutely thrilled, and could not contain her excitement.

'Yes, we do – Enfield Manor, my dear wife.' Andrew laughed and left the bedroom to head to the kitchen to get some food and a cup of tea.

Kate was in quite an agitated state the next few days, busily making notes of everything not to forget, things to do and people to contact.

'I notice that you are too quiet, and you have a sad face, Thomas,' Kate said.

'I will miss you, Lady Katherine,' Thomas replied.

'It's just for a month. Anyway, I am counting on you to look after the school in our absence. If we train an assistant junior when we come back, we will take you next time, how does that sound?' Kate tried to encourage him.

'Yes, Lady Katherine, I will look after this school like it is my own precious home,' Thomas assured her, quite enamoured at her words.

'By the way, did you dispatch the leather trunk to England?' she asked, trying to remember whether she had forgotten anything.

'Yes, Lady Katherine. I did everything you asked on the list,' Thomas confirmed proudly.

'So, we might go home earlier today; our ship departs tomorrow morning, and I don't think we forgot anything,' Kate concluded with a deep sigh.

'You forgot me!' Andrew exclaimed, entering the room.

'Oh, Andrew, I forgot our tea, I am so sorry, there were so many things to check,' Kate apologised.

'Never mind. May I steal you from this school for a wine in the tavern opposite?' Andrew invited her.

'You can go, my lady, I will check all the doors and windows before I leave.' Thomas encouraged her.

'Thank you, Thomas, have a good evening,' Andrew said, grabbing Kate's hand before she had time to find any excuse to stay.

Later, at the tavern table, Andrew asked about Kate's progress in her new research.

'Have you been reading about Apollo and the Hyperboreans?' he asked.

'Always, between one job and another; did you know that Apollo had a son – Asclepius, the god of medicine?' Kate asked.

'No, did he?' Andrew raised an eyebrow.

'Yes, and his son had five daughters, and one of them – Panacea – had the universal remedy, to cure all ills,' Kate answered, bright eyed, then continued. 'Importantly, they all lived in Hyperborea, including Apollo, who stayed in Greece for a short time in the summer, at his oracle in Delphi, then he left to Hyperborea for the winter. I think the myth of Apollo and his son is much older than the Greeks.'

'So, your theory is that Greek travellers actually came to Britain and learned from the Hyperboreans, and later they built a temple to Apollo in Delphi?' Andrew asked.

'This was what Sir Joshua thought, but I have to search for more. There are some gaps and spaces in his research that I need to fill.' She nodded.

'We might have an opportunity to fill the gaps with Lord Henry during this trip to Stonehenge; and what about Pythagoras?' Andrew asked.

'I am not sure yet, but I have the feeling he was related. Apollo, the healer, was also the god of music, and Pythagoras developed the musical tune theory. Pythagoras was certain that the sun, the moon and the planets' movement produced harmonic sounds. Perhaps the soul, or the mind, could reach through music some kind of balance and harmony with the body.'

'Interesting.' Andrew nodded thoughtfully; then, changing the subject, he asked her,

'By the way, are you ready for our travel tomorrow? We shall pass this winter in England,' Andrew teased her.

'I don't mind the weather, as long as you are by my side to keep me warm,' Kate replied with a glint in her eyes.

'I can arrange that easily,' he responded, in the tone of a willing accomplice.

The next morning should have started early and organised, but Kate and Andrew, being always late, left some arrangements for the last minute, therefore they had to run to the Piraeus to catch their ship, blessed, though, for having Thomas's lucid and practical mind, always ready to take them out of their constant plight.

'Have a safe journey, Sir Andrew, Lady Katherine. Everything will be fine here, and when you return you will find most of these books catalogued, I promise you.' Thomas said goodbye, more than a little sad at their departure.

'Oh, Thomas, don't be sad, you will have so much trouble with Anthony and Myra that you will not have time to miss us,' Kate said optimistically.

'Perhaps you will have so much trouble with those two that you will end up blaming us for leaving you behind,' Andrew added, laughing.

'Stop, Andrew, don't make things more difficult.' Kate barely finished speaking when she was interrupted by the hoot of two eagle owls which flew and landed on the ship's mast.

'Even your birds don't want to stay here with me.' Thomas tried to make a joke, but at heart he was indeed a little worried at the prospect of being alone in Greece with Anthony and Myra.

'The owls want to spend the winter in England, I suppose. Do you think they eat fish? If they don't we might have to feed them,' Andrew said, whilst examining the two birds in the ship's mast.

'How many times do I have to tell you two that I don't have any birds?' Kate complained, knowing they would never stop teasing her about those owls.

'But they might have you, which don't change anything,' Andrew stated. However, the ship's whistle made him stop the joke and rush. 'Come on, Kate, it is time to go.'

Kate looked around, remembering the day she arrived in that port a little over a year ago, with her dreams and a great love within her, big enough to make her follow that man wherever he had to go, until the end of her days.

Chapter 2

Kate suddenly realised that the Mediterranean was always beautiful, even with winter so close. Like Greece, Malta could be sunny, whilst the sound of seagulls searching the shore harmoniously filled the gap between the waves breaking on the sands.

From the deck, Kate was watching the ship circumnavigating Malta, making their way carefully around that rocky coast to the dock at Valletta's Harbour, one of the most important ports of the British Empire, coveted for millennia by those seeking commercial ascendency in the Mediterranean.

Andrew helped Kate down the stairs; then, whilst she was standing next to their luggage, he went to try and get a carriage to take them to the Grand Hotel. He came back twenty minutes later, so pleased that one might imagine he had found some hidden ancient treasure. Without knowing the place, or people, it was not easy to do business, as it was extremely difficult to understand the local dialect, which since Roman times was a mixture of various sovereign languages that over the centuries played important roles in the lives of the inhabitants. He felt very fortunate to be able to find an English-speaking native and arrange transport for them and their luggage to their hotel.

The carriage stopped in front of the Grand Hotel, which was not very impressive really, most likely not as comfortable as the ones they were accustomed to, but a sense of adventure and the quest for the unknown are powerful drugs, able to seduce many a soul and to transport them far beyond their safe zone – a small price to pay though, the couple agreed, as long as they were together to unveil the mysteries ahead.

Whilst they were both observing the hotel's servant take their luggage from the carriage, somebody shouted,

'Andrew? Andrew Enfield?' The voice immediately caught Andrew and Kate's attention.

'Arturo! What are you doing here?' Andrew asked, surprised, and a little embarrassed for not having introduced Kate immediately.

'I am sorry, this is my wife, Katherine.' He smiled, bowing slightly.

'*Una bella signora.*' The stranger kissed her hand.

'Kate, this is Arturo Bonnici – a very eminent Italian Architect,' Andrew explained.

'It is a pleasure to meet you, sir,' Kate greeted him, smiling back.

'Well, you are the last person in the world I thought I would meet here in Malta at the moment. Are you on holiday?' Andrew asked.

'At the moment I feel like an island, surrounded by water everywhere, and waiting for a flood,' the Italian replied, mysteriously.

'That's a strange observation, sir, as we are on an island, and not a particularly large one at that,' Kate stated, trying to determine the meaning behind his enigmatic words.

'Lady Katherine, you will feel the same, when you realise that you are in a *piccolo posto* without help, where nobody understands a civilised language, and they are determined to make you leave, by swimming if necessary,' Arturo replied politely, evidently vexed.

'Do you need any help? Is something troubling you?' Andrew asked, similarly perplexed by his friend's statement.

'Andrew, you are British; perhaps you could help me to find who is in charge of this island?' Arturo begged.

'The Maltese government, I dare say,' Andrew responded, matter-of-factly, if not entirely helpfully.

'And where is it, because I am surrounded by the British Navy?' Arturo asked, in a hopeless tone.

'If I am not mistaken we are next to the Treasury of the Order. Certainly somebody inside can give such information;' Andrew suggested.

'It is *a perdita di tempo*. I was there for more than an hour, and they were useless,' Arturo replied disconsolately. 'I wanted to find the police to arrest a madman, and nobody would help me. I never went to a place in my life which had no proper police department. It seems that the Royal Navy has to solve everything. The problem is – the navy says they cannot arrest civilians; they are here to protect the borders and the sea, I suppose. So who is going to protect us on the island, eh?' Arturo was clearly very annoyed.

Andrew looked at Kate, who raised an eyebrow slightly but said nothing. Andrew asked Arturo to go inside the hotel, as the servant who was helping them with the luggage was waiting to take them to reception. After they checked in and were sure their belongings were taken to their room, the trio left the hotel and went directly to the treasury, hoping to find someone who might assist Arturo.

After ringing a bell and waiting a couple of minutes, an attendant arrived; however, when he saw Arturo, his face dropped, and before they could say anything, he complained,

'Oh, no. Not you again. How many times do I have to tell you that we are not the police, and we cannot arrest people, especially British subjects,' he directed at Arturo. Upon hearing this, Andrew intervened.

'Excuse me, sir, what happened, and why are there no police officers available?'

'Who are you, sir?' the attendant asked politely when he realised that Andrew was British.

'Sir Andrew Enfield, and this is my wife, Lady Katherine Enfield. This gentleman is my friend, Arturo Bonnici, a respected Italian architect, very well-known in Europe. My wife and I had just arrived when we met him, but he seems to be desperate and in need of assistance,' Andrew explained, doing his best to engender some sympathy.

'I am sorry, sir, but we are an island, which has been over the centuries, a stage of confrontations between many nations since Roman times, so you have no idea how many French, Spanish, and Italians come here every single day to make complaints against each other. Thank God we now have an Executive Council under British jurisdiction, to restore some order,' the attendant explained, a little annoyed.

'I told you! They are *inutile*,' Arturo snapped, equally annoyed, attracting a hard, cold stare from the attendant.

'Please, Arturo, stop with the insults.' Andrew tried to appease the spirits.

Kate observed the situation quietly, certain that a fight would have started between the attendant and Arturo had it not been for Andrew's presence and patience.

'Did this gentleman explain what he wants, Sir Andrew?' the attendant asked, smiling, indicating Arturo. By his demeanour it was apparent that the attendant knew exactly what the problem was, and that it might not be something he could or would be able to help with.

'It would be helpful if you tell me what is going on, so I might try to help,' Andrew replied, eager to resolve the issue as quickly as possible and without further conflagration. He would much rather be enjoying a glass of wine in a restaurant or tavern with Kate than watching two grown men bicker.

'This gentleman had an argument, a very big argument, I should emphasise, with an important and well-connected British archaeologist, I might add. Your friend Mr Bonnici wants us to arrest him,' the attendant explained, examining his neat finger nails in a show of detachment.

Andrew had learned not to doubt his instincts when they alerted him to problems ahead, and he was already very suspicious of what was to come.

'I am here as an urbanism researcher. You know what my work is about, don't you Andrew?' Arturo asked.

'Yes, indeed,' Andrew confirmed, waiting for an explanation.

Then Arturo turned to Kate and addressed her instead, hoping to garner more sympathy.

'Lady Katherine, I have been working on a new architectural project for years, which made my travel to Malta crucial, to see the stone ruins of the Ancient Maltese *civilizioni*,' Arturo explained. Then, realising he had perked Kate's interest, he continued,

'After visiting many cities and farms in England and France, I made serious and important *conclusioni per il futuro*, if we want to solve the problems that come along the progress and technology of our *civiltà.*'

'Your point of view is based on the concept of the evolution of society, if I am not mistaken?' Kate asked.

'Hmm... well, there isn't exactly an agreement about *questo punto*, dear lady, but at least there is almost a consensus that city and factories are creating a social *problema,* which is inevitable, given our history, I have to admit,' Arturo explained.

'How can Malta contribute to your research, Mr Bonnici?' Kate asked, now genuinely interested.

'The ruins of *Hagar Qim*!' Arturo announced, a too little grandly, holding up his index finger to emphasise his words and with obvious pride, as if by the mere statement they would understand his point, which seemed to imply that he himself had discovered some important architectural, archaeological or sociological fact that nobody else was aware of.

'What? We know hardly anything about that archaeological site. They only started excavating quite recently. I do know the archaeologist in charge, and he hasn't "discovered" much yet,' Andrew interjected, somewhat doubtfully.

'Do you know Dr. Bartholomew Walker, sir?' the attendant asked Andrew.

'Of course! I met him years ago in Cambridge. I haven't seen him for ages, but at that time he was over the moon with the financial support he was provided to excavate these ruins,' Andrew told them; then he asked his Italian friend, 'What is your problem with Dr Walker, Arturo?'

'Dr Walker thinks Mr Bonnici is an Italian spy,' the attendant interjected, before Arturo had the chance to speak. Then he gave Arturo a sidelong disdainful glance from head to toe, making implicit his opinion of the Italian.

'*Questo è un assurdo!* These idiots see spies everywhere, like ghosts. Could anybody explain to these "local people" that spies are the product of their imagination? They confuse science with politics.' Arturo was indignant, indeed on the verge of incandescent as he defended himself, raising his hands up as if he were praying to the gods. Andrew tilted his head and seemed to take a pause to think. Whilst upon hearing and seeing this, Kate sought to temper the Italian's indignation by providing him with a valve to let off steam.

'I am curious as to how any stone ruins might contribute to your urbanism project, Mr Bonnici,' she asked, hoping to learn more about her new acquaintance, whilst defusing the situation.

'Ah... ha! That is my point – religion was the crucial factor in ancient *civilizioni*; it is the central element from which *il tutto* emanates culturally, socially, and politically,' Arturo explained. Then, after a brief pause, when he adjusted his waistcoat and recovered some of his demeanour, he continued.

'I intend to re-create a perfect "Greek state", without making the same mistakes they made in their "Golden Age", when a plague killed a third of the Greek population, even after they had acquired great knowledge of philosophy, mathematics, geometry and astronomy; it is crucial to understand the role of gods, seasons, and unexpected setbacks of nature, which should be responsible in their view for the hunger, misery and collapse of their *civilizioni*,' Arturo concluded, whilst the attendant, after a deep sigh, began to examine some miscellaneous papers he had on his counter.,

Kate then asked Arturo, 'Do you mean you believe that future generations should expand their cities, integrating manufacturing, agriculture, social and cultural issues?' She was deliberately feeding his ego to calm him down.

'Bravo! Finally! Somebody *capisce la mia lingua*!' Arturo exclaimed, evidently very pleased with himself, and simultaneously relieved to find an accomplice who understood his perspective.

'But this is obvious, don't you think?' Kate said, somewhat surprised.

'Not as obvious as it sounds, Lady Katherine,' Arturo began to explain, after casting a challenging look at the attendant, who studiously ignored him. 'Ordinary people,' he emphasised, 'tend to get stuck to old concepts and even superstitions, sometimes,' Arturo explained haughtily.

'Well,' Andrew interjected, 'I know that my wife doesn't like the word "coincidence", but we are here to visit the ruins at Hagar Qim, and I intend to speak with Dr Walker tomorrow.

You are welcome to go with us. Perhaps he might be more flexible this time, although I cannot give you any guarantees,' Andrew suggested, not completely convinced about Arturo's intentions, as his arguments to support his research didn't make too much sense.

'Andrew! Lady Enfield! You two have saved my life. *Grazi!*' Arturo clapped his hands together, beaming as if he had won some important prize.

'Don't be so melodramatic, Arturo,' Andrew implored, disregarding his friend's excess, then asked, 'Where are you staying? Would you like to join us for a wine in a tavern later?'

'*Mi sento incantato.* I am staying in my cousin's Palazzo Fontana. By the way, I was in charge of the Palazzo's construction a few years ago. Giovanna and her husband are very influential people in Italy. Do you know them?' Arturo asked, quite proud of himself.

'I remember reading something about them at that time, but if you excuse us, Arturo, we will meet again later at the tavern; meanwhile, we have to get our things ready for our trip to Hagar Qim tomorrow.' Andrew and Kate excused themselves and left.

Then Arturo glowered at the attendant before leaving and heading off in the opposite direction. Andrew was relieved that they were all on good terms and the incident had de-escalated. He was a little worried about what Dr Walker's reaction might be when they arrived at his archaeological site with Arturo, *the spy*, but he could imagine.

The tavern's atmosphere was very cheerful, as all taverns are in this world, especially when most of the costumers were British sailors, Royal Marines, some Italian businessmen, French sailors, Spanish merchants, and a gaggle of locals; an eclectic crowd in an island in the middle of the Mediterranean, where everything that could happen, really does happen.

'Tell me Andrew, why you and Lady Katherine are going to visit that madman?'

Arturo asked them. Andrew ignored his comment and explained.

'Kate is doing research about a possible relationship between the ancient Greeks and the stone circles of Britain,' Andrew began, knowing that Kate would not be able to resist talking about it.

'I visited a few of those stone circles when I was in Britain,' Arturo replied. 'As well as the rows of stones in Brittany in France, "*menhirs*", I think they say. They are all very impressive *costruzione*, eh? They defy our knowledge of engineering, no?' Arturo asked.

'I am very interested in your project, Mr Bonnici, thinking about how those ancient civilisations had their lives revolving around divine designs. The religious aspect determined their architecture and life,' Kate said.

'*Infatti,* my dear lady, and of course those stone circles and rows must have had the same importance to people's lives. But what do they have to do with the ancient Greeks?' Arturo asked, shaking his head, at a loss to find a connection.

Kate looked at Andrew, then explained, 'The stone circles in Britain were mentioned by Greek travellers long before the great Greek mathematicians and philosophers. It is my belief that much of their mathematical and astronomical knowledge was assimilated from those trips to the North *"to an island not larger than Sicily, far beyond the Gaul's, with a stone circle".*'

'*Ma questo è straordinario!* It could be Malta!' Arturo exclaimed, suddenly excited.

'I think that geographically, at least, Malta is a little far south, don't you think?' Andrew asked, laughing and taking a sip of wine.

'Are you sure?' Arturo asked, disappointed, looking dejected.

'I am afraid they called it Hyperborea *"Beyond the North Wind and Gaul land"*,' Kate answered confidently.

'Who can beat the British? In the end they win them all; *Brindiamo* to the Greek gods and goddesses to intercede on our behalf tomorrow, when that mad British archaeologist starts to attack us.' Arturo raised his glass, laughing, followed by Kate and Andrew, who exchanged concerned looks.

With the prognosis of a difficult situation ahead, the toast to the gods the night before was not sufficient for the god Helios to manifest himself in favour of Kate and Andrew, and although it was not raining, without sun, the weather was warning of unexpected change. However, for Andrew and Kate the weather was never an issue really, thus it was with a cheerful and willing spirit that the three companions embarked upon their journey to Hagar Qim, hopeful of having some questions answered.

The archaeological site was located on the other side of the island to Valletta, in the direction of the southwest. Because Malta was a small island, though, they only had to travel nine miles, and try as much as possible to observe the beauties offered to their sight, knowing that some of the island secrets would not be attainable.

Malta had a steam train line, but it crossed the centre of the island heading north, giving them no choice but to hire a horse-drawn carriage, which was waiting for them in front of the hotel, ready to take them wherever they wanted to go.

'Did you bring your compass, Kate? I could not find mine,' Andrew asked her, before clambering aboard.

'Yes, I have mine,' Kate answered, wondering why he always lost his compass and notebooks, and other odds and ends. He could be very absent minded sometimes, about the little things.

'Great, we cannot waste any time,' Andrew said; then he told their coachman to make haste for their destination.

After two stops along the way to rest the horses and take some refreshments, the travellers arrived at Hagar Qim. The coachman left them at the site, agreeing to return after a few hours.

They didn't know if Dr Walker had received their telegram informing him that they were due, but this was the price to pay for not using mail pigeons any more. The three of them were examining the site of the ruins with great interest, when the air was split by the terrific sound of a rifle retort and a bullet whined when it ricocheted off a rock near to where they were standing. All three of them scuttled to take cover behind rocks, trying to come to terms with what had just happened. Andrew, to Kate's dismay, suddenly stood up, holding his hands up in a gesture of submission. Kate watched, wide eyed, without knowing what to say; however, Andrew seemed to think he was unlikely to be targeted.

'Andrew, please get down. He will kill you,' Kate hissed from her kneeling position just a few feet from him.

'Don't worry, Kate. I know what I am doing,' Andrew replied, firmly, whilst Kate looked at him, quite astonished.

'Bart, it's me! Andrew, Andrew Enfield. Stop shooting at us old chap, put your rifle down. I am here with my wife, Lady Katherine Enfield. She is keen to meet you and see your work here,' Andrew explained very calmly.

'Andrew? Andrew Enfield? What the devil are you doing here with that disqualified Italian spy? He doesn't fool me,' Dr Walker shouted back from his unseen vantage point.

'We don't know yet, but we mean no harm, trust me. We don't have any weapons in any case,' Andrew insisted. There was a moment's pause, then Dr Walker stood up, with his rifle lowered now, not so sure about what to make of things.

'What do you want, Andrew? Because I know what this Italian spy wants,' Dr Walker asked gruffly.

'My wife and I are here for the day, only to clarify some questions she has about the ancient civilisation of Malta and their stone ruins. We thought you might help us? Mr Bonnici here was added to the expedition at the very last minute,' Andrew replied.

'What are you doing, Andrew? He is going to kill me,' Arturo complained, his voice trembling.

'He will not kill you, if you don't do or say anything stupid. You have to tell us the truth, otherwise I cannot help you. So, think about it, whilst Kate and I go up and speak with Dr Walker, will you?' Andrew said.

'Bart, I'm coming up there with my wife, so you can explain to us what is going on.' Andrew spoke.

'Come on up, Andrew, and bring your good lady with you, but if that spy tries anything, I will shoot the blighter,' Dr Walker replied seriously, but very politely.

The couple climbed the rocks together and were received with a welcoming smile and cheerful demeanour.

'Andrew, I am pleased to see you. I didn't think you would be tired of the Balkans so quickly. Perhaps this beautiful lady has something to do with it, eh?' Dr Walker asked, laughing.

'I would say she is everything in my life really, good or bad,' Andrew replied, laughing when he saw Kate's glower of reproach.

'That is not fair! What is Dr Walker going to think about me? I am not a trouble-maker, sir,' she said to Dr Walker. 'It is quite the opposite. I have to rescue him, frequently.' Kate pointed at Andrew.

'Don't worry, Lady Katherine, I know your husband very well,' Dr Walker reconciled, winking at her.

'Please, call me Kate,' she said.

'As long as you call me Bart,' Dr Walker replied, then continued. 'Now, tell me, what are you doing here, and with him?' He nodded in the direction of the still cowering Italian, who, fairly justifiably, was in fear for his life.

'Not before you tell me what is going on between you and Arturo,' Andrew insisted.

'Ha! That spy! He is an Italian spy, don't be fooled. He is working for the government in Sicily. They want to take Malta from the British,' Dr Walker said quite furiously.

'Everyone wants to take Malta from the British, Bart. This is nothing new,' Andrew tried to explain, but he was interrupted by his friend.

'Seven years ago the Italians made an alliance with the Austrians and Germans; now they decided to not interfere if their allies didn't solve their border problems with France. How long will it be before the Italians decide to invade Malta with the help of their allies, hmm?' Dr Walker complained.

'You cannot fight every Italian that comes to this island, Bart. Arturo is an architect, and a very respectable one at that. He really is doing some research; that is all,' Andrew protested.

'No, he is not! He is mapping the whole island, and I would not be surprised if the Italians made an agreement with the Austro-Hungarians to take over Malta. You did similar work in the past for the Crown; you know how these things work. But I will not allow them to take my temples,' Dr Walker stated vehemently.

'Temples? What temples?' Kate asked suddenly intrigued, eyes bright.

'Yes, my dear, "temples",' Dr Walker confirmed.

'How can you be so sure?' Kate asked, excited.

'There aren't many certainties and guarantees in this life, Kate, but from the things that came up in our excavations so far, I am certain about temples. Come with me and have a look.' Dr Walker invited them to enter a large stone chamber which by the look of the inside, was being used as the archaeologist's headquarters, with personal belongings, camp bed, tools, papers, and even an improvised stone table.

'This is impressive, Bart! No wonder you are worried about an invasion. They can set up a post here and monitor the whole southwest of Malta from this position,' Andrew joked.

'I didn't show you everything. Come on and look at this.' Then Dr Walker took out from behind his improvised bed a cloth with something wrapped inside – it was a piece of pottery, carefully inscribed with interesting patterns and shapes; then he asked, 'What do these carvings remind you of?'

'Reminds me a little of a compass, don't you think, Andrew?' Kate answered, surprised and excited to see the little relic.

'Indeed so. How old do you think it is?' Andrew asked, curious.

'It is difficult to say. But I think it is older than the Celts, and certainly more ancient than the Romans or Greeks,' Dr Walker answered thoughtfully, before continuing.

'These drawings represent, in my opinion, the movement of the sun, and I would not be surprised if I find in future excavations artefacts related to the moon's movement, perhaps even the stars; who knows what they were capable of? I am still in the beginning, but apart from some small chambers that could be used as dwellings, some of these stone circles might be temples, with their entrance determined by the movement of the sun, which I am still observing to confirm. That is my theory.'

Dr Walker hardly finished his words and a voice behind them exclaimed, '*Bravo, dottore!* You confirmed something I have been thinking for quite a while.' After Arturo said that, he noticed Dr Walker move to pick up his rifle. He was about to run when Andrew positioned himself in between the two of them.

'Let's stop this stupid quarrel. Bart, you are safe here, trust me. You cannot go anywhere in this island without bumping into sailors from the Royal Navy. Perhaps you can see them from here, so assured, let's behave like scientists, shall we?' Andrew scolded the two of them.

'You, you Italian spy… if I catch you touching my stuff I will feed you to my snakes,' Dr Walker warned Arturo.

'Snakes, you have snakes?' Arturo panicked and clambered onto a rock.

'Of course, they are everywhere here, it's an island; did you forget that?' Dr Walker replied with an air of superiority. His words made Kate open her eyes wide, but she immediately relaxed when Dr Walker winked at her.

An English gentleman, archaeologist or not, can withstand the lack of comforts, the cold, the heat, other unexpected situations, snakes even, but they never miss tea time which, even though making use of a small and rudimentary stove, that important ritual was honoured by being served in authentic English porcelain, not the terribly expensive sort, but certainly appropriate. Reluctantly, Dr Walker, who didn't want to be impolite in front of Kate, offered a cup of tea to the Italian too, and after sitting next to her, he took the time to ask,

'Tell me about your research, Kate, and what do you intend to find in the stone circle.'

'I am following Sir Joshua Egerton's research. He believed that Greeks from the Bronze Age visited Britain, and were inspired by the stone circles they saw there, which in my opinion were temples as well,' she explained.

'So, are you saying the Greeks learned geometry and astronomy from the Britons to build their "*tholos*"?' Dr Walker asked.

'What is a "*tholos*"?' Arturo asked completely lost.

'I told you that he is a spy. How could an architect not know what a "*tholos*" is? I will throw him to my snakes,' Dr Walker stood up, as if he intended to get something, at which Arturo panicked, left the chamber and ran amongst the stone ruins shouting, 'He is a madman! *Lunatico, posseduto dal diavolo!*'

Kate and Andrew exchanged looks, then she asked her companions,

'Why do they think we British are mad?'

'I don't know, but I am inclined to agree with Bart that he might be a spy. The location of these ruins is crucial for monitoring most of the island. On the other hand, these temples functioned as observatories where the priests of ancient societies could read divine designs through the stars,' Andrew replied thoughtfully.

'I told you "Don't trust Italians". Anyway, I don't think we are safe here at this site any longer. We might move some important things away. Kate, I entrust this piece of pottery to your care. Please, guard it with your life.' Dr Walker wrapped the pottery with the fabric and handed it to her.

'Oh my goodness, what if something happens to me?' Kate complained, concerned at being held responsible for somebody else's treasured artefact.

'Don't be silly, nothing can be worse than an Italian invasion,' Dr Walker quipped confidently. Below the site, near the entrance through the stone walls that led into the field, Arturo was gesticulating and having a conversation with the coachman who had returned with their carriage.

'Kate, are you ready? We had better catch up with that Italian in case he leaves without us.' Andrew turned to his friend. 'Take care of yourself, Bart, and don't get in trouble, eh? You should go for wine in Valletta sometimes; maybe get married. It will do you well, am I right, Kate?' Andrew asked, smiling.

'He is right. You need someone to rescue you from trouble,' Kate replied humorously.

'I might visit you two in England at some point, when I have found the answers *"which are still buried, but not dead"*,' Dr Walker said enigmatically, and although Andrew didn't understand the meaning, Kate didn't have any doubt about it – it felt like an echo of the past following her in each step. He was a *Guardian*, she felt certain. What she could not understand was why those Guardians decided to place such a weight on her shoulders.

They met Arturo down near the entrance to the site, complaining about the "mad archaeologist" and the delay.

'I refuse to stay on this island a day longer. I have to go back to Europe, to Italy. I need to be in touch with civilised people, not in a rocky fortress surrounded by British buccaneers.' He looked around anxiously, as if he half-expected to be thrown into the Mediterranean without mercy.

'We don't have pirates anymore, Mr Bonnici.' Kate tried to calm him down, holding back a laugh.

'What is the difference with the Navy around?' Arturo asked, which made Andrew laugh.

'I shall introduce you to a friend from Cambridge, who certainly would invite you for a wine in a tavern to calm you down,' Andrew said.

'Oh no, not Sir Richard, please! That gentleman has serious problems. Thank God he is thousands of miles away,' Kate interrupted, hoping he was not in their plans.

'By the way, Lady Katherine, now that we are safe, could you please clarify my curiosity – what does *"tholos"* mean?' Arturo asked.

'Oh, just some ancient Greek circular buildings, that's all,' Kate replied, feeling sorry for the Italian, but at the same time finding difficult to believe that an architect didn't know that.

After a long day and miles of travelling through Malta's countryside, Andrew and Kate were tired and really without any enthusiasm to go out for the evening. An early dinner would be ideal, with perhaps a bottle of wine in their bedroom, watching the sea, beautiful as it was, even in winter. If there weren't words to say, their thoughts could be found in the temples of Malta or Greece; and why not in the stone circles that defied time and so many civilisations that crossed there, just like the waves of this *"water between so many lands"*, the Mediterranean, that defied and took away from its shores all those who, like *Odysseus*, tried in the past to master its stormy waters.

Chapter 3

Leaving Malta behind was like carrying nostalgia with you – the last wine that was not drunk; the streets that were never visited; the feeling that the time was faster, and you were definitely late. Kate wondered if Andrew was feeling the same. He put his arm around her and together in silence from the deck of the ship, they watched the island recede further and further away until it disappeared completely on the horizon. On the other hand, why should she care about Malta, when she had Andrew and the Mediterranean around her, the only place she wanted to be? She smiled and they left the deck for a cup of tea in the ship's galley.

After a few days enjoying the convivial atmosphere on-board ship with the other passengers, and partaking of the wonderful sea air, they arrived at the busy port of Marseille in southern France. They didn't have to wait long for a carriage to take them to catch their train to Paris. Fortunately, the entire route was furnished by the *Compagnie des Chemins de fer de Paris à Lyon et à la Méditerranée* (otherwise known as *PLM*), making their journey rather less troublesome than had they been travelling through France in any other direction.

The rail trip across France on those elegantly furnished carriages made for a wonderful change from the high seas. The metronome-like rattle of the tracks as the train steamed its way through rural France was comforting somehow, whilst the smell of steam and hot oil coupled with the occasional shrill whistle from the locomotive was excitingly different.

Andrew and Kate watched as the beautiful French countryside rolled past – fields full of brown cows, haystacks, scare-crows, horses, busy farm workers, little market towns and orchards. Crossing old wooden bridges across gorges brought all the passengers to the windows, to stare at the view and hope the bridge didn't collapse. It was a perfectly lovely adventure for a young couple very much in love.

The food in the dining cars was very good, if a little predictable and limited in scope, but the wines and champagne more than made up for the delicate sauces and small portions which Andrew eyed suspiciously and disdainfully. At one meal he ordered a beef steak. It was perfectly good, but rather small, perhaps just six ounces or so, and when he asked for another the waiter raised his eyebrows in amazement, insisting that the steak was perfectly cooked, and that the chef had never had a single complaint about his steaks. Andrew confirmed there was nothing at all wrong with it, indeed it was perfectly good, but it was simply too small for his appetite, and as he had enjoyed it so much he would rather like another. The waiter did not appear to be convinced, but returned within a few minutes, muttering under his breath, putting a large steak on the bone at least two times the size of the previous in front of Andrew.

'*Le chef* sends his apologies, *monsieur*. He hopes you enjoy this one. He has cooked it perfectly, he assured me,' the waiter intoned, in a heavy French accent. He then bowed over-zealously, turned on his heels and was gone. Kate couldn't constrain herself a moment longer and let out a loud and sudden laugh, making the other diners turn to see what was causing such amusement. They were too polite to stare though, and being unable to determine the source of the laughter, as Kate lowered her gaze and examined her plate studiously, they resumed their dining and conversation; then Kate smiled at Andrew.

'That waiter's face, Andrew. These French are so proud of their food. When you asked for another steak I rather thought he might faint.' She grinned. 'I expect the chef is a dictator and the waiter was terrified of taking something back.'

'Well, I'm hungry,' Andrew defended himself. 'We might be on a train, but I don't see why the portions should be any smaller at the prices they charge.'

'You're right, of course, but it was ever so funny, and now you have a rather huge steak. Will you be able to eat it all?' She laughed. Andrew raised his nose slightly then with an elegant flourish, daintily he began to cut the beautifully cooked piece of beef and finish his dinner. Kate accepted his offer of a bite, and nodded.

'Excellent steak, I have to agree.' She smiled, pleased to see that he was happy. They drank the wonderful wine together, raising their glasses, whilst Andrew polished off his steak. When he put down his knife and fork, the little waiter appeared almost miraculously by his side.

'Was the *côte de boeuf* acceptable, *monsieur*?' he asked very politely.

'Indeed it was most excellent, thank you,' Andrew assured him. There was in any case no evidence left of it on his plate except the T-bone itself. The waiter smiled genuinely and picked up their plates, quietly balancing one expertly on his sleeve, rather than stacking them.

'Would *madame et monsieur* wish to try a dessert?' he asked.

'Oh, I might. What do you recommend?' Kate asked cheerily. The waiter turned and looked to see if anybody might overhear, then in a lowered voice explained,

'*Madame*, I must be honest. The deserts here are not exceptional. In my opinion, the fruit is best.' He smiled.

'In that case, may I have strawberries and cream please?' Kate asked.

'Of course, *madame,* perfect.' The waiter smiled, turning to Andrew. '*Monsieur*?'

'Oh, nothing for me, thank you, I couldn't.' The waiter nodded, smiled and left.

Kate and Andrew had just finished the bottle of red wine they had ordered when the waiter returned. He made a tiny bow, then deftly placed a little plate of raspberries and cream in front of Kate before heading off to another table with their main course.

'Something lost in translation, my dear.' Andrew smiled as Kate looked at the raspberries instead of the strawberries she was expecting. She laughed.

'Oh well, they look rather lovely, and he's such a sweet waiter.' Kate smiled, then ate them cheerfully.

Thus they enjoyed a beautiful journey, criss-crossing the French countryside up through Avignon, on to Lyon; then Dijon, changing at Montereau for the final leg to Paris. Kate was now getting excited at the prospect of visiting the famous museum in Paris, and whatever other sites their short stay would allow them to visit.

The Museum of Natural History was far bigger than Kate had expected. It is a fact that museums should be proud not only of their collections, but of their architecture as well, since the history behind each window and door that adorns such buildings adds beauty and harmony to the already arranged elements of seduction, inviting those outside to the mysteries hidden within those walls.

After Kate had properly appreciated the facade of the building, she started examining some interesting artefacts displayed inside wood and glass cases close to the entrance, whilst Andrew was trying to find his friend, who had answered his telegram confirming, before the couple left Greece, that he would be waiting for them.

Kate could not help noticing an extremely old gentleman in uniform, apparently a curator of sorts, who was ambling around the entrance with the aid of a walking stick; he seemed to be enjoying the movement of people coming and going. A few people stopped and asked him questions, which filled Kate with admiration for the dedication the gentleman seemed to have for his job.

Whilst she was observing the old man, Andrew came back with his friend, an elegant man in his late thirties, perhaps early forties – hard to tell – who was wearing a very expensive suit, and who had a big, stylish moustache.

'Lady Katherine Enfield, what a great pleasure to meet you finally.' The gentleman greeted her in perfect English, though with a distinctly Parisian accent, apparently delighted to see her.

Andrew introduced him,

'Kate, this is Professor Maurice Legrand – the director of the museum.'

'*Enchanté, monsieur,*' Kate greeted him, smiling.

'*Une belle dame.* Come! We must go for tea and cake, and a chat,' he declared, escorting them to a little café just a short walk away. They were quickly seated by an attentive waitress at a little table with a white marble top adjacent to a large, plate-glass window from where they could watch the world going by, whilst enjoying the relative quiet atmosphere of being off the street.

'So, this is your first time in Paris?' the professor enquired of Kate, then continued. 'Andrew told me that you studied at the University of Boston. Quite a determined woman, I must say, to face such a journey and to go to study in a distant land; I admire your tenacity in achieving your goals.' He smiled.

'No journey is too long when the goal is worth it,' Kate replied cheerfully.

'So, this most interesting couple wish to know about the Locmariaquer Megaliths in Brittany, uh?' Maurice asked, enthusiastically.

'I was told that the museum has a partnership with a British archaeologist who is here to excavate the Carnac Megaliths,' Andrew explained.

'Hmm... hmm... yes, indeed. His name is Zachariah Taylor, a difficult man, without commitment,' Maurice complained, turning suddenly to look at the figure of the old man who Kate had seen earlier in the front of the museum, who entered the café. The old gentleman had not seen them yet, but when Maurice stood and waved him over, inviting him to sit, Kate noticed that the older man tried to move away but was restrained by Maurice, who insisted he join them.

'Professor Chevrand, this is Sir Andrew Enfield, an eminent archaeologist, and his classicist wife, Lady Katherine Enfield. They are going to visit the Carnac Megaliths in Brittany,' Maurice informed his acquaintance.

'What?' the old professor asked loudly, producing a small decorated silver ear-trumpet with a perforated grille, the better to listen to Maurice.

'Enfield, I said, and his wife, Lady Enfield,' Maurice repeated, exasperated.

'What?' Professor Chevrand asked, again.

'Oh, never mind, sit down and have a tea with us,' Maurice said, defeated but undeterred.

Professor Chevrand somewhat grudgingly sat down, with the ear-trumpet in his hand, waiting for his drink. Meanwhile, another gentleman who entered the café noticed the little group and approached them most enthusiastically.

'Andrew! Maurice, and Chevrand as well, what an unexpected meeting!' the gentleman exclaimed.

'Emile, you sound much more cheerful than the last time I saw you. This is my wife, Katherine. This is my friend, Emile Marcel, Kate,' Andrew introduced them.

'*Charmé*, madam,' the gentleman greeted her, delighted.

'*Enchanté, monsieur*,' she replied in turn, smiling.

'Hello, Chevrand, how are you doing?' Emile addressed the old fellow, holding back a laugh.

'What?' Chevrand asked, holding the ear-trumpet to his ear.

'Never mind.' He turned to Andrew. 'So, you married a Greek goddess, did you, Andrew?' Emile joked, making Kate blush.

'One of the most dangerous goddesses in the entire Pantheon, I must say,' Andrew replied, laughing.

Suddenly, one of the museum security guards in a dark blue uniform interrupted them and approached Maurice, asking him to come immediately to resolve some urgent problem in one of the museum chambers, not leaving Maurice any alternative but to excuse himself and leave; he gave his apologies.

'I will meet you later at the restaurant for the dinner, so we can plan our travel tomorrow. *Enchanté*, Lady Katherine.' Maurice left after kissing her hand.

The director had barely left when Chevrand put the ear-trumpet on the table with a sigh of relief, whilst Emile started to laugh.

'Thank God! I'm so glad he left,' Chevrand declared. 'I wouldn't be able to drink my tea in peace without him moaning about museum bills, decreasing funds, and complaining about everything imaginable.' He smiled at Kate. 'I really must apologise for my rude manners, my dear. Fortunately, old age allows us to select what really matters and what can be discarded or ignored. We should not waste time with unimportant frivolities, should we? Don't you agree?' Professor Chevrand asked, looking for sympathy.

'Don't answer, Lady Katherine, otherwise you will become, like me, an accomplice to his cheats; he is a very artful man,' Emile intervened.

'Please, call me Kate. By the way, you can hear us very well, *monsieur*?' Kate asked, faking disapproval.

'It is just a tiny lie, don't worry about Maurice. He is a politician – lies are in his daily agenda, trust me.' The old man explained his subterfuge.

'Old age, uh? You are almost a mummy, Chevrand,' Emile complained.

'I will be ninety next week, and I can hear anything better than you can,' the old man informed him.

'What is your area of research, Professor Chevrand?' Andrew asked, curious, not being acquainted with his name.

'I work with the restoration and preservation of artefacts, amongst other things; you have to be versatile when you work in a museum. I personally catalogued most of the artefacts at this museum.' Professor Chevrand answered proudly. 'They had been badly recorded previously.' He smiled.

'How interesting!' Andrew replied. 'Kate and I work at the new British School of Athens, just opened last year. We are expecting our first post-graduate students next summer. They are all archaeologists but, as I was told, one of them has a great interest on classifying pottery according to their use in Ancient Greece,' Andrew said, feeling lucky to be having such an interesting conversation with an erudite and superbly qualified gentleman, who no doubt knew much about pottery and how it should be properly dated and recorded.

'Ah, this is the point – we are talking about "function",' Professor Chevrand stated categorically. 'I have always had a weakness for chemistry and the production of colours from pigments and their various origins, trying to detect when they were first used.' He took a sip of tea and bit on a hard little biscuit on the saucer. 'Twenty years ago I went to Egypt to look at the collection of artefacts at the National Museum; I later went to Greece as well with the same purpose. From my analyses I concluded that shape, size and colours could be related to the use they were originally put, such as storing oil, wine or grains; however, we cannot discard the aesthetic appeal that the use of colour or any other adornments add to the object, which incorporate a new function – the gift.' He was very animated and clearly knew a lot about ancient pottery and how it was made and used.

'It is not fair to say that a "gift" is simply an object to cause delight and pleasure,' Emile interrupted, in a slightly argumentative, but kindly, tone.

'Oh, there you are, shoving politics into everything you see,' Professor Chevrand replied.

'Of course, it is inevitable. Your "aesthetic appeal" is intrinsically related to the economic and political aspect of the relationship that involves those who give and those who receive the gift; from the moment you receive the gift, you are in debt,' Emile explained.

'The academy will never be the same now these damned sociologists decided to suspect every good intention. Don't listen to Emile, my dear. He is frustrated because he failed to be a good artist. Now every art object is political – music, painting, dance, you name it.' Professor Chevrand took his revenge.

'What about charity?' Kate questioned, confused.

'Oh… quite observant,' Emile chirped. 'There is an implicit agreement between the beggar and the helpful person – the beggar smiles and says "thank you", whilst the helpful one leaves with his conscience clean and his soul saved,' Emile explained.

'If there is no salvation for those who do charity, imagine where those who use gifts as bribery will end up?' Professor Chevrand laughed.

'What about the ancient pharaohs? Do you think the Egyptian gods were jealous when they saw kings being buried with all those objects with the purpose of enjoying them in the afterlife, not bothering to take any gift-souvenirs to the gods?' Andrew provoked, laughing.

'That's it! Jealousy! Andrew, you solved the Egyptian mystery of the "Cursed Mummy". When you see a mummy going around trying to find its sarcophagus to finally rest in peace, like Chevrand here, it is because the gods didn't allow him to join them with all his paraphernalia,' Emile joked, and everybody laughed.

It was a very pleasant afternoon tea, much like they all should be, with friends, croissants, dainties and animated conversation. After saying goodbye to their new friends, Andrew and Kate went for a walk around the museum to appreciate its collections, and to see if they could establish some connections with departmental staff, for future partnerships and expeditions.

They couldn't ignore that the days in this late part of autumn were shorter, and it was better not to linger too long, due to their dinner later with Maurice. So they returned to their hotel to get ready for the evening. After a couple of hours, Kate and Andrew headed to the restaurant, La Tour D'Argent.

There was nothing to complain about Paris, which was very pretty and alive at night with its inviting bistros and restaurants. Coincidently, when the couple were a few yards from the restaurant entrance, Maurice arrived and was about to enter when he spotted them. He waited at the entrance and started talking with Andrew, when Kate turned and noticed on the other side of the street a very large black dog staring at her, sitting on its hind legs amongst the trees on the path along the River Seine.

Kate was fascinated by the dog's narrow gaze directed at her, without moving a muscle until the moment she heard Andrew's voice. In a fraction of a second, she had turned to her husband, but when she looked back at the dog, he was no longer there; he had vanished into the darkness of the night, whilst a cold breeze gave Kate a sudden chill. She waited for a few seconds to see if the dog would come back, but Andrew called her to come in, so she went inside to enjoy the splendid decor, food and atmosphere in that elegant restaurant.

The next day started quite early. Kate was looking forward to their journey across the countryside of northern France by steam train, especially as it should not take more than five hours, with the final leg of the journey to be covered by horse-drawn carriage because the railway did not yet go further than Rennes.

The journey to Brittany was a pleasant detour. First class was very well appointed, with the dining car exquisitely furnished. They enjoyed an excellent chilled local white wine with a lovely *Quenelles du Brochet*, freshly baked baguette with luxuriously creamy butter from Normandy.

After lunch, Kate was sitting, enjoying the conversation with Andrew and Maurice, but perhaps due to the hundreds of miles that she had covered in a little over a week since leaving Greece, a soft laziness embraced her, making it impossible to keep her eyes open until, with a sigh, she surrendered to tiredness and let herself be carried away by the swaying rhythm of the locomotive, steaming its way across the frosty fields of France, whilst the distorted images were being left behind.

She was woken suddenly by a loud noise – there was fire everywhere. The train had stopped, and looking out of the window, she could see a large black dog, which to all appearances seemed to be the same which had stared at her in Paris at the entrance of the restaurant the night before. It could not be? She put her hand flat on the glass of the window, leaning close to see passengers jumping from carriages, trying to escape from fire, but when she turned to look for Andrew, she heard a voice calling her.

'Kate, wake up! We have arrived at Rennes in Brittany. Now we have to catch our carriage.' It was Andrew, with a soft and gentle voice, then she realised everything she had just experienced was nothing more than a bad dream. Not like any other she had experienced, but a bad dream just the same. She breathed deeply and smiled at her kindly husband, whose smile and reassuring voice lifted her out of that dark place into the light.

Holding Andrew's arms as they walked, Kate smiled to herself at the warm feeling of being protected by him; but she was not smiling just because of the sense of protection that he inspired in her – his aftershave could trigger beautiful memories and desires, even after a nightmare. Thankfully she was not a woman of her time, hampered by chains made by the morality and the religious customs others wrapped around themselves like shackles. She was free to love and dare to go wherever her great beloved goes, and feel what she deserved to feel.

'The trip was quicker than I expected,' Kate joked.

'You, you big lazy one. You slept the whole way after lunch,' Andrew reproached her, laughing.

'That is not true; maybe halfway, I would say,' Kate contested.

'Whatever my beloved little Kate says. By the way, where is Mr Bear? I haven't seen him for a while,' Andrew asked, changing the subject.

'Why? He didn't desert us. Mr Bear is always with me, in my bag, having a well-deserved little rest, I dare say,' Kate answered, whilst Andrew gently kissed her forehead.

'I feel safe with him around, did you know that?' Andrew confessed.

'But I do his job most of the time, not him' Kate protested, smiling.

Andrew didn't give her the opportunity to say more and he kissed her, but quickly, before Maurice came back.

'I am sorry to intrude,' Maurice said from behind, having approached unnoticed, 'but our coach is waiting for us.' He was a little embarrassed.

'Andrew, have you sent Dr Bartholomew's pottery direct to our house in Wiltshire?' Kate asked suddenly when she remembered the ceramic map that the archaeologist had given her in confidence to keep, before leaving Malta.

'Don't worry, my dear, what would you do without me to remind you of the small details, eh?' Andrew joked, adding, 'It is very safe, and on its way to England.'

Kate breathed a loud sigh, feeling quite relieved, and said, 'Thank God! I had completely forgotten about it.'

Their carriage was a pretty little affair, with a flat roof, black painted brass lanterns either side of the driver's seat, quite comfortable, with dark burgundy-coloured velvet seats, velvet swagged curtains and glass windows that could be lowered to let in fresh air. The horses were very handsome, whilst their uniformed driver seemed very much a gentleman himself, such was his attire and composure. It was very exciting for Kate, and as comfortable as any coach travel could ever be. The two-day trip from Rennes to Vannes, passed relatively quickly; the weather was fine, with blue skies and sunshine, frosty mornings and frosty fields. They stayed at little coaching inns on the way, simple hostelries, but welcoming and charming enough, if the food and accommodation was somewhat rustic.

As they neared Vannes the excitement at the prospect of seeing the Menhirs and stone rows of Carnac created an air of anticipation in the carriage, whilst Kate often spied glamorous grand French *chateaus* and sprawling medieval *anoirs* as the rural countryside changed to something resembling a more English land than the France they had previously traversed.

They arrived at their destination late in the afternoon of the second day, the medieval walled town of Vannes. They were booked into a pleasant enough hotel, which had comfortable beds and a warm lounge with a crackling fireplace and oak panel walls. It was not all that different from the hotels of England, except that everything was distinctly French in style, whilst the voices were not French, but Breton, and the people seemed altogether unlike the Parisians and southern French Kate had previously encountered. It was a lovely place to stay and they were warmly welcomed by the owner, a fastidious gentleman with a bulging moustache, a brightly coloured waistcoat and an infectious laugh. He was honoured to have such esteemed guests at his humble provincial establishment, and keen to provide the very best service he could muster.

The next day, after a hearty breakfast, they got their coachman to take them to Locmariaquer. Kate and Andrew were not prepared for what was waiting for them – a complex of megaliths and ancient stone structures ready to carry their imagination to a place back in time, who could know how many thousands of years in the past?

They expected to find Dr Taylor at the main site at Locmariaquer, as agreed, but apart from a little boy who passed by carrying a basket of carrots, there was no sign of the archaeologist. Maurice decided to ask the boy for his whereabouts.

They were speaking in French, but because of the distance and strange Breton dialect, Kate could not understand exactly what they were saying, until the boy pointed with his arm to what seemed to be the direction they had to take to find their friend.

Maurice was apparently somewhat angry, but after he asked the coachman to take them to another destination, he climbed back in the carriage and explained.

'I apologise for the *contretemps*, but it seems that our doctor changed his mind and has been excavating another site without informing me.' Maurice was visibly annoyed and agitated.

'Do you know which site it is?' Andrew asked.

'Dr Taylor is a very eccentric and wilful man, very difficult to deal with. Sometimes he infuriates me, I am sure he takes a certain pleasure in so doing,' Maurice explained, grumbling.

'I hope it doesn't testify against us as well. We British are not *all* eccentric and difficult to deal with.' Andrew tried to calm Maurice down, whilst Kate was equally eager to know if the next stop would be fruitful, or whether some game or other might be playing itself out.

Far in the distance, when the travellers were approaching the site, they could see the silhouette of a man wearing a white linen shirt and a pith hat, whilst near him a young girl was sitting making notes in a little journal with a pencil, which made Maurice very annoyed. When the archaeologist noticed the carriage approaching, he somewhat grudgingly stopped what he was doing and came over to them, addressing Maurice in a very serious tone.

'Where are they, Maurice?'

'Who?' Maurice was in doubt about what he was saying.

'Not "who"... "what"! Where are my supplies?' the Englishman insisted.

'Hmm... hmm, let's be civilised first, Zach,' Maurice interrupted, trying to calm him down.

'Don't call me Zach until I get my supplies, or I will find other sponsors for partnership. I know dozens who would love to get their hands on this site,' Dr Taylor replied seriously, before addressing the couple, when he apologised.

'I didn't mean to be rude. My name is Zachariah Taylor. I know it is a very strange name, but who knows what was going on in the minds of my parents when I was born.' He shrugged to himself, as if his forename had in the past been the subject of derision or interrogation.

'My name is Andrew Enfield and this is my wife, Katherine. We have a particular interest in what you are researching here,' Andrew greeted him.

'It is nice to talk with people who speak the same language, especially if they are academics without numbers and money on their mind,' Zachariah said sarcastically, looking Maurice from head to toe.

Maurice didn't like the insinuation and retorted,

'Could you tell me what you are doing here?' He waved his hand, indicating the ground around them. 'You should be at the stone structures of Locmariaquer, not here with these... these... rocks.'

'They are all stones, Maurice, and in fact these are more important than the others,' Zachariah counterattacked.

'But not so interesting for tourists,' Maurice complained.

'Do you see?' Zachariah addressed Andrew and Kate, and added, 'We are in front of one of the most important discoveries for astronomical science, and he only thinks about money and tourists.' He grimaced at Maurice.

'Please, what is so important here with these stones?' Kate asked, excited.

'Not before Zachariah tells me what that *mademoiselle* is doing here,' Maurice interrupted, pointing to the girl.

'That is my... assistant. When I realised that you abandoned me without food, tea, a proper bed for the winter, and equipment, I decided to accept the offer of help that lady kindly offered me,' Zachariah replied.

'But she could be working for our competitors,' Maurice complained.

'No, she is not. Her purpose of helping is genuine, and she lives down there – can you see her house? She gave me a room, food and fire for the winter, whilst you didn't send me even a croissant. She makes croissants every day. You French think that we English don't feel cold, so you left me here to freeze in the winter. Now shut up! I want to know more about my English visitors.' Zachariah addressed Andrew and Kate, who were quietly observing the discussion between the two men.

'Why are you so interested about these megaliths in Brittany?' Zachariah asked, in a friendly and civil tone.

'We were invited to a sort of experiment in Britain, and it has to do with the stone circle in Wiltshire,' Andrew explained.

'Stonehenge! Tollemache's research, eh?' Zachariah asked, suddenly attentive.

'Yes, indeed. He invited us. Kate is particularly interested as she is in charge of other research, connecting these ancient stone circles to the Greeks,' Andrew vouchsafed, turning to Kate, knowing she would want to explain. She immediately obliged.

'Sir Joshua Egerton sent me his notes and books about a possible connection between Britain, the stone circles and the Hyperboreans. We think that Stonehenge could be an old Temple of Apollo with his Oracle, and his son Asclepius, the god of medicine, as well; the Greeks used to call them Hyperboreans – *those who live in an island not smaller than Sicily, beyond the Celts, with the stone circle*,' Kate explained.

'I am quite interested about their connection with Pythagoras,' Andrew added. 'It seems to me likely that the mathematician came to Britain and developed some of his theories from the contact he had with the Hyperboreans.'

'Then you couldn't have chosen a better place to start. Brittany has thousands of megaliths, not exactly like the stone circles in Britain, but after I saw the one in Wiltshire, I am absolutely certain that the structures there and here belong to the same period, possibly built with the same purpose,' Zachariah said, excited at what they had just explained.

'*C'est magnifique!* Apollo and the Greeks here, in France! This will attract tourists from all over the world,' Maurice exclaimed excitedly.

'Don't start to distort things, Maurice. You only think about numbers. Didn't you listen to them? Hyperborea is "beyond" Gaul, not "in" Gaul,' Zachariah reproached him.

'How old do you think these ruins are?' Andrew asked.

'It's hard to say, but the Romans referred to them as being as old as the Celts; I think they are much older,' Zachariah replied.

'What is your theory about these megaliths, Zachariah?' Andrew asked.

'It's Zach, but only for friends,' he replied, looking at Maurice disdainfully; however, the French was not paying attention any more, as he sat on one of the stones and started making notes and calculations in a little notepad.

'Come with me, I want to show you something.' Then the archaeologist turned to his assistant, Sophie, and asked, 'Could you prepare us tea, my dear? They will be in heaven with your beautiful croissants.' The girl smiled happily at his compliment, gathered her dress and left, heading to her house to prepare lunch for the visitors.

'I am seriously thinking about marrying her,' Zachariah confided. 'You will understand "why" after tasting her croissants; but I must say she is a good assistant as well, very pragmatic; she organised all my notes, do you see?' Zachariah said, resting his arm on Andrew's shoulder with an air of complicity.

'I couldn't be more supportive. Life ties us to what is most dear, in circumstances that are often unexpected,' Andrew replied, looking at Kate, who was absorbed and examining some standing stones near the carriage. The coachman was feeding the horses with oats from little sacks and talking to them as if they were old friends.

'Lady Katherine, this stone you are examining has a crucial role in what I am about to show you.' The three of them left

Maurice with his calculations, heading to what seemed to be a group of stones arranged as if forming an angle of ninety degrees.

They walked over to the stones, and when they reached a specific place, Zachariah asked them to look in three specific directions from where they stood and explained.

'We are in one of the four corners of a perfect Pythagoras rectangle. I have measured it dozens of times and I have no doubt about it. I started measuring the distance between those stones repeatedly, for days, and by chance I noticed a certain constancy in the movement of the moon; then I decided to redo the measurements last year, trying to understand what I was observing, and that is the reason why I stopped my research at Locmariaquer and concentrated all my efforts here, at the Crucono Stones.' He indicated the stones around them with his hand, before continuing with his explanation.

'The diagonal dividing this rectangle of standing stones into Pythagorean triangles is aligned with the midsummer sunrise, but the two shorter parallels of the rectangle are aligned with the moon's movement, without any shadow of a doubt. Sophie has been taking notes for me – great assistant, I must emphasise.' Zachariah nodded to himself.

'...a moon calendar?' Andrew asked, not quite believing what he had just heard.

'Precisely! They built these structures oriented by the movement of the moon, with certain knowledge of astronomy. However, because my research is still ongoing, who knows what else will come up? Maybe it was not only the moon and the sun; did they map constellations as well? Who knows?' Zachariah said, excited, and paused.

'Look! Sophie is waving. Our tea must be waiting for us,' Zachariah announced happily, grabbing his bag.

'Do you think Monsieur Legrand saw her waving? He didn't seem to have noticed,' Kate asked, worried.

'Who?' Zachariah asked, then he laughed and continued. 'His name is not "Le grand", is "L'Enfant", but he doesn't like to be called "the child", which is the translation for "L'Enfant";

he prefers to be called "Le grand" – The Great, like Alexander – Maurice The Great.' He laughed.

'He never told me that,' Andrew said, a little surprised; then he laughed, whilst the three of them walked to Sophie's house.

In the end, Sophie decided to go and collect Maurice, who was engrossed in his calculations and notes about the site and its prospects for the future. Meanwhile, Zachariah showed his fellows several drawings he had made, and talked more about his ideas and theories. He knew that Maurice was not inclined to give money for the expedition, but only to take whatever he could from the research, so he confided in Andrew and Kate.

'You might have a surprise when you come back next time. I am thinking of founding a proper museum here; I know that I will have sponsors for this project, so everything we have in these sites in Brittany will not become just a little tiny collection in one of the National Museum chambers in Paris. If they stay here, the Carnac Megaliths will be the prime star,' Zachariah said, his eyes bright, taking a large bite from a freshly baked flaky croissant.

Sophie and Zachariah invited Kate and Andrew to spend the night, with good wine and a delicious homemade dinner of roast duck with a lovely sauce and garlic potatoes. They were trying to be polite and extended the invitation to Maurice; however, he was eager to leave the place, with its rustic hospitality and lack of sumptuous comfort to which he was accustomed, so when the coachman knocked on the door to take them back to the rail station, he was definitely relieved.

On the other hand, Kate and Andrew, despite the temptation and the possibility of discussing some of Zachariah's theories in front of the fireplace with a glass of wine, didn't come prepared to spend the night. However, there was no doubt they would include Brittany in their plans for next year, perhaps after the summer, when the post-graduate students returned to Britain.

The carriage left, and although Kate felt the same feeling of nostalgia she'd experienced during their departure from Malta, the smell of freshly baked croissants in the little leather bag that Sophie gave to her was enough to guarantee their return, possibly soon.

Chapter 4

Whilst Kate knew it was impossible to stop time, or even slow it down somewhat when we are happy; and although she knew, like all of us, that happiness is not eternal, she didn't want to think about the future. She was there in England again, but this time with Andrew, thinking that maybe common sense might be wrong, and "forever" may exist. At that moment at least, Kate didn't care about anything else as she was determined to enjoy her honeymoon, which thus far had been pretty perfect.

Andrew and Kate were standing on the platform at Dover Station, waiting for the call to get on the South Eastern Railway train which had pulled up, when Kate told him her thoughts.

'I cannot wait to see Enfield Manor,' She beamed, excited at the prospect.

'Didn't you enjoy our travels in France and Malta?' Andrew asked, worried that perhaps she had not enjoyed their trip as much as he had himself.

'Of course I did! You should know that, don't tease me. Apart from our travel to Greece last year, when we met again after so many long years apart, this is quite the most fantastic time of my life,' Kate replied, smiling.

Their conversation was interrupted by the loud, shrill whistle from the locomotive, accompanied by a release of steam from around the wheels; the engineer was informing the waiting passengers they were readying to depart.

'Time to board.' Andrew picked up his little brown attaché case and they climbed onto the first-class carriage near the front of the train. Although these branch line coaches were much smaller than the ones they had used in France, it was comfortably furnished and quite adequate, if not quite as grand.

Later, as the train trundled along the tracks, they ate ham sandwiches, which Kate produced from a wax paper parcel she had bought at the station, and enjoyed swigs of Leney's excellent ginger beer from a stoneware bottle, whilst making plans for their trip to Wiltshire.

'How old is Stonehenge?' Kate asked.

'They used to think the Celts built it, but there is still no consensus,' Andrew explained. 'Some researchers think it might be much older. The notes in Sir Joshua's research will very likely fan the flames of the controversy.' Andrew was enjoying the fact that the academy would be shaken by the new theory. He continued.

'If Apollo was an all-encompassing god – healer, oracle and sun deity; the patron of music with his lyre and a warrior with a bow; as his origin is not certain, perhaps he was the "only" god of some civilisation, later absorbed by the Greeks, than the Romans,' Andrew vouchsafed thoughtfully.

'His twin sister Artemis is his female counterpart, associated with the moon,' Kate added.

'Good to have something to think about.' He smiled. 'We might find the answers in the texts Sir Joshua collected, possibly hidden in another kind of riddle; he seems to have been very fond of riddles,' Andrew remarked.

Kate suddenly became very pale and fell silent. Andrew noticed her change of demeanour.

'What happened, Kate? Are you feeling unwell?' he asked, wanting to know what came over her.

Kate looked at him, speechless, because at that very moment she remembered something she had recently read. It was as if the whole atmosphere around this research was being orchestrated intentionally, in order to involve her in something much wider than she'd initially expected. She had the feeling of being left in darkness much of the time, but every now and then she would be allowed to collect small clues that the Supreme Light, feeling sorry for Kate, would allow her to catch and gather them to make sense; with such a feeling, she looked at Andrew and answered,

'I don't know yet, but there is something I read and made a note of to decipher later; it is in my notebook, in my bag in the locker near the exit. Give me a minute and I will get it.' Kate looked at him for a second, kissed him softly on the cheek, then with a smile she left to get her little book.

Andrew knew that something didn't seem quite right; however, he sat quietly, watching Kate walk away towards the baggage locker. Suddenly, an ominous feeling overwhelmed him and without knowing why, he stood up, intending to go after her, but he had barely taken two steps when the train started to shake vigorously, accompanied by a deafening noise. He shouted out her name and tried to run after her, but was thrown to the floor violently.

Andrew had no idea how long he was unconscious; it might have been just moments, though nothing mattered for him except Kate. He had to find her, but he found himself in the middle of a mess of distorted chairs and tables and steel and wood and bodies. Whilst he was trying to get up, an explosion threw him back to the floor again, and this time he lost consciousness completely.

Her eyes were closed but Kate could hear noises around her; people screaming, others shouting, and although it was nearly winter, she could feel warm air rushing over her. Somehow she was lying on the cold, damp ground. Slowly, she opened her eyes to try and make sense of what was happening. The cabin where she was supposed to be was in flames, but she was on the grass near the rails, apparently thrown out of the carriage, together with parts of the train. Kate was still too close to the blaze, though, so she tried to move to get away, but she was stuck under a piece of twisted metal and some burning wood from the cabin, which was going to be catastrophic for her if she could not escape.

Her efforts to escape from under the debris were in vain, her long skirt was caught on something and she was almost overcome with the pain of being crushed. She felt strangely tired; her vision began to blur, and she was just on the brink of losing consciousness when a little hand touched her face. Kate opened her eyes and saw the silhouette of a young girl against the light from the fires, which made it difficult to see her face. Gently, the young girl held Kate's hand and started to pull her from under the debris. There was a sudden huge explosion and Kate instinctively closed her eyes, clasping her head in her hands to protect herself. The debris she was under was thrown away violently, and when she looked to the girl, trying to speak, the girl put a finger to her lips to quieten her.

'Shhh... *Panacea*, the sun will meet the moon,' the young girl said. Kate noticed a delicate golden chain hanging from the girl's neck, adorned with a small gold pendant in the shape of an owl; then she closed her eyes and lost all consciousness.

When Andrew opened his eyes, he found himself beside the tracks, with other people sitting or sprawled next to him; some of them were injured but not seriously. He could see a group of passengers about a hundred feet away, talking with police officers and railway staff. Andrew stood up quickly and tried to run towards them to find Kate, but he realised his right leg was bandaged and the pain made him limp.

Andrew asked about Kate everywhere, but nobody could give him any precise information as everywhere was chaos, with fire, smoke, and terrible noises from people who were in shock, or distress, and others who were badly injured.

Andrew looked back and recognised the train car where he and Kate had been – it was in mangled pieces and what was left was ablaze. In mounting angst and desperation, he tried to walk towards it, struggling with his injured leg; then he felt his heart begin to beat quickly in his chest when he approached the wreckage and realised the magnitude of the calamity. He was able to identify by sight some of the passengers from their carriage who were on the ground, some groaning in agony, others yet unconscious, whilst police constables and other passengers were trying to help them. He searched amongst them for Kate, fearing to give up hope; he had to keep looking for her, and find her alive.

There was no sign of Kate, but through the gaps between the wreckage of the train he could see the other side of the tracks. Andrew walked quickly towards one of them and crossed the track, standing still on the other side, anxiously looking around, trying to find her.

For a moment his heart froze, as he could not feel it beating when he saw her, lying on the grass without moving. Those fractions of seconds lasted for eternity, and he remembered what Kate once told him – that only one in love knows what eternity means; however, in despair, he thought – those lovers who lost their beloved one experience the terrifying side of eternity. From hell to heaven he was taken, though, when he glimpsed a small movement of her hand, filling his heart with hope and bringing him to life again. He ran to Kate, shouting,

'Kate, Kate, I'm here!'

Andrew embraced her and held her in his arms, hugging her and crying when he realised that she was not fatally injured.

'Oh Kate, Kate, my little Kate…'

'Mr Bear… Where is Mr Bear?' Kate asked in a whisper.

'Don't worry, my love, he will find us, don't worry…' he replied, cuddling her, without making sense of his own words.

The two of them stayed there, lying on the floor, without care about anything, until two policemen approached them with blankets, as it was getting dark, and although the heat of the train on fire warmed the air, it was winter and the evening was approaching.

A couple of hours later they were taken to a carriage which was supposed to go to the nearest infirmary, but Andrew declared,

'We are not seriously injured, and we would rather go to another place where we could rest until tomorrow. Some of the other passengers need more medical attention than we do.' Andrew helped Kate to get into the carriage.

However, another policeman approached them and said,

'Excuse me, miss, a young girl asked me to give you this. She said that it belongs to you.' The policeman had Mr Bear in his hand.

'It is Mr Bear! Please, where is she? She saved my life,' Kate asked, looking around desperately, whilst the policeman looked back in the direction he'd come from, trying to find her as well; then he gave up, shrugged and said,

'I can't see her, I'm sorry. She must be amongst the other passengers; I will let you know when we find her.' He headed off to attend to another couple who were clearly in distress – the lady had broken her arm.

'Thank you for your help, sir,' Kate said in a whisper, cuddling Mr Bear. Andrew nodded and thanked him too. Then Kate looked at the devastation around her with the feeling that there was nothing she could do at that moment but accept what she was told to do to avoid creating more problems for those who already had enough.

Andrew and Kate were taken to an inn and when the carriage arrived, the owner came out to greet and help them to their bedroom; upstairs they found a bath ready, and the owner's wife was there to guide them.

'Sir Andrew, Lady Katherine, we were told what happened and to expect you. I left some nice clean clothes for you to sleep in, and if you leave your clothes outside the bedroom door, I can wash and dry them for tomorrow, if it suits you.'

'Thank you, we will,' Andrew replied quietly, nodding approval.

Andrew prepared a bath for Kate, who was looking through the window, very quiet.

'Your bath is ready, so too are your clean clothes.' Andrew approached and hugged her.

'Thank you, I'm fine, don't worry. I cannot stop thinking about that young girl. Do you think perhaps that I imagined everything?'

'We don't know what our mind may do under extreme stress; on the other hand, she sent you Mr Bear, so she was definitely real, though I cannot imagine how she found Mr Bear,' Andrew tried to console her.

'But Mr Bear never left our cabin at any time. Therefore, if she found him, how did she know he was mine?' Kate questioned, confused.

'Maybe you asked for him in delirium, and when she found him, she linked the facts,' Andrew replied confidently.

'You may be right; who knows what our mind can do when our body gives up, and our soul cannot find any comfort,' Kate said enigmatically.

'I will help you, we both need a rest,' Andrew replied, trying to help her to undress for her bath.

It was not easy to sleep with so much noise downstairs in the bar. Like Kate and Andrew, many other passengers were taken to the inn, but not everybody was willing to rest in their rooms; talking might be the only way some people can relieve their trauma and anxiety.

They woke very early the next morning, and although the owner and his wife insisted they stay and rest for another day, they were determined to keep to their schedule, so politely thanked them for their hospitality, which would be generously rewarded when they got home.

Later, when they arrived in London, Andrew was informed of the details of the accident. It was in the evening paper. The train had been carrying eighty first-class passengers and thirty-five second-class passengers; tragically, the boat train to London had derailed because the man with a red flag, who was supposed to signal that there was engineering works on the tracks, was not positioned far enough away for the train to be able to stop in time, resulting in ten deaths and forty badly injured. Most of the passengers were in shock.

It took a few days for Andrew and Kate to finally arrive at Enfield Manor, in Wiltshire, as they had to stay in London for a couple of days to get their luggage, which was sent separately from Greece and which took some time to reach them.

Nothing could have prepared Kate for the splendid view from the stone gatehouse whose cast-iron gates opened to welcome and guide them through that beautiful landscape, where lakes, lawns, streams and meadows were harmoniously brought together, mingling almost three hundred years of loving attention from gardeners working for that single estate.

'It is so beautiful, Andrew! Look at the swans in the lake! I can imagine how beautiful the flowers must be in the gardens in the spring,' Kate exclaimed, spinning like a child, making small turns around herself, as if she was dancing.

Andrew could not stop laughing, as only Kate could see the world colourful in the winter. He decided to introduce her to the servants and show her the interior of the house.

Kate greeted all of them enthusiastically, then walked through their home, looking around attentively at all the details – the ceilings, the beautiful carved woodwork panels, elegant paintings on the walls; the magnificent stairs to the first and second floors.

Andrew held her hand and took her to the east wing of the house, naming the members of his family portrayed in the paintings.

'This wing of the house has not been used for more than a hundred years. I thought that you would not mind living in this part with me. The other wing was used by my parents and family, when they were alive, and it was always too busy with many friends, people coming and going. My parents had a very busy social life,' he explained, then added,

'The great thing about this bedroom is that it is the biggest in the house; and it is isolated from the routine of the estate. I always preferred this area, as you can see the woods and the hills from the balcony. Do you see the stream there?' Andrew pointed at a little stream enthusiastically.

'Yes, I do! It is so quiet here, I can hear the birds,' Kate replied, very pleased.

'Behind that door, there is a small room with a table and a comfortable chair. Later I can ask the butler, Matthew, to put a small cupboard for you to keep your notes. I cannot offer a better place for reading and research, as the other parts of the house are quite busy and noisy.'

Then Andrew pointed at another door in the opposite direction.

'I have my little studio as well. It is the only way to get peace to work,' he explained.

Andrew held Kate's hand and kissed it, asking, 'Do you like it?'

'I completely feel at home,' she replied, smiling.

Andrew then took her to show what would be her studio, and when they opened the door, they had a surprise.

'The leather trunk is already here; it arrived before us!' Kate exclaimed, smiling.

'No wonder, with all the trouble we had,' Andrew declared, adding, 'I want to show you the library, come on...' he grabbed her hand, like a little boy running for a cake.

'Wait, please.' Kate stopped and looked around to find her bag; then she opened it and took Mr Bear out and placed him on the bed, telling him,

'Look after that trunk, Mr Bear, there is something important about it that I cannot remember, but give me time and I will.'

Kate could not be happier. They were both running from one room to another, like children playing, leaving the servants astonished and standing still without knowing what to do, until Kate made a fool of him and hid under the stairs, leaving Andrew calling for her.

'Kate, where are you? Come on, show yourself or I will not show you our gardens...' She did not respond, so he said, 'I will bring scones for Mr Bear...' Then one of the servants helped him by silently pointing under the stairs.

'This is not fair!' she complained, then asked expectantly, 'Did I hear you say something about scones?'

'Yes, you did. I asked them to make some especially for Mr Bear,' Andrew replied, grabbing her hand and heading to the lounge, where they enjoyed a scrumptious afternoon tea with mouth-watering freshly baked scones, beautiful butter and home-made jams of gooseberry, strawberry and damson, whilst tea was served in exquisite cups and saucers with gilded rims.

Later that day, after dinner, Andrew excused himself as he had letters and administration to sort out before his meeting with the estate manager the next day. Kate took the opportunity of reading some manuscripts in her studio, as something had been bothering her since the accident with the train; and she suspected the answer was in that trunk.

Before she had dispatched it from Greece, she had carefully copied the text inscribed on the leather on the underside of the trunk lid, so that she could read and analyse it during their journey; however, her copy had disappeared in the train wreck and fire, so it was with considerable relief she knew that the original was still here, waiting for her. She felt very fortunate for having shipped that precious heavy trunk to England separately, otherwise everything might be lost forever.

'*I used to think that Fate didn't exist, not in science, but I have to think more about that later*,' she thought to herself.

She opened the trunk and sat on the chair, staring at that inscription for a while. Suddenly she remembered Andrew's last words on the train, before she stood up to look for the text in her luggage.

'Riddle,' he said; 'perhaps a secret clue...' Kate whispered thoughtfully; and as if by magic, the key to the puzzle jumped out at her – discarding articles and interjections, the key of the riddle would be in the letters of the first noun in each verse. They were part of an anagram formed by the first sound of '"*phthegma*"; the second of "*eynoikon*"; the third of " *kallon*"; the forth in "*megalen*" and the last in "*keruks*". Those letters formed the word "*phylaks*", which means "Guardian" in Greek.

"*The voice in the temple is
a benevolent spirit,
and beautiful body,
and great knowledge,
the herald proclaims!*"

'Was it possible that Sir Joshua was one of the Guardians as well?' Kate wondered. Talking to herself in a whisper, she recalled,

'Sir Christopher told me last year that some of the papyri of Alexandria were not burned by the Romans, but were taken and hidden in Greece. Only a handful of "Guardians", as well as I, knew the secret location; but after the earthquake in Greece, the best thing to do was to pretend the location was lost forever,' Kate tried to establish a link between the Guardians and important secrets and mysteries of the past.'

She recalled that Sir Christopher had also said that the Guardians knew each other, which meant that Sir Joshua knew about her. What she didn't understand was why he sent his research about Stonehenge to her. Perhaps the Guardians protected more secrets than she had been informed? She was determined to find the link between Sir Joshua's research into Stonehenge, and the Oracle of Delphi.

A few days later, standing outside at the bottom of the steps at the front of the house next to a carriage, Kate was admiring the facade of Enfield House, waiting for Andrew to finish his last instructions for the administrator. A few minutes later he turned to Kate and said,

'Everything is done. Now we can leave for Diana's celebration. What are you looking at?' he asked curiously.

'I cannot stop admiring our house; I got a warm feeling when I was in the garden, looking at the estate parkland. Do you think that it has to do with happiness? I mean, happiness makes everything perfect, doesn't it?'

He held her hands and kissed them, and before helping her into the carriage, he said with shining eyes,

'It is more than that, Kate – happiness can make you feel alive.' After they were comfortably sitting, he asked the coachman to leave.

Although the weather was fine at the start of their journey, they were in Britain, whose weather's unpredictability never disappoints, and torrential rain provided a path full of mud and surprises ahead.

Andrew and Kate were absorbed in a conversation about archaeology when the carriage stopped abruptly. They could hear people's voices outside, and they seemed to be rather annoyed about something.

'Bernard, do something. We cannot stop and be standing around here in this weather. It is getting cold,' Charlotte exclaimed furiously.

Bernard was outside the carriage, nodding his head when he realised that not only the coach but also his boots were stuck in the mud.

'Damn!' Bernard cursed, a bit upset. The carriage behind his similarly stopped, and another passenger, his friend Peter, joined him and tried to help, since his own carriage could not pass. It didn't take long for the jammed carriages to create a considerable congestion on the wet road, as gradually other carriages, which seemed to share the same destination, arrived and joined the queue.

Andrew and Kate were behind Peter's carriage, and they were watching the scene, trying to think of a way to solve the problem, when they were both caught by surprise at the sound of a very familiar voice behind them.

'Andrew, Kate! What a pleasure to see you again! Thank goodness this winter will not be as cold as I expected; not when Lady Katherine Enfield is around, I suppose,' Sir Christopher Lidstone, the magistrate from Devon, exclaimed enthusiastically, smiling from the window of his carriage.

'Oh! Not you again, Sir Christopher! Why does everybody think that I am "trouble"?' Kate replied, faking indignation.

'Are you cursed, Kate?' Andrew asked, adding, 'Because I have the feeling that you do attract trouble, I must admit – first the train, and now this mud,' Andrew joked.

Suddenly, their attention was caught by a woman's scream.'

'Ahh...!'

'Oh my God, now Bernard is in real trouble,' Peter declared, lighting his damp cigarette with some difficulty.

The watching ensemble were aghast with the situation because Bernard, trying to make the carriage lighter, had asked Charlotte to get out, but when he tried to help her, he ended slipping and falling with her in the mud, pulling her to the ground with him.

'I knew it! We are still cursed by your ghost eagle-owls, Lady Katherine,' cried another well-known voice coming from the fifth carriage, which was stuck behind all of them.

'Sir Richard! What are you doing here? And how many times do I have to tell you that I don't have any birds, much less eagle-owls,' Kate exclaimed, rather annoyed.

'I shall be civilised first and introduce you to Dr Augustus Turner. He is an astronomer and member of SPR – the Society for Psychical Research.'

'Oh... another astrologist; do you interpret oracles as well?' Sir Christopher joked.

'I am not an astrologist, I am an astronomer!' Dr Turner replied, slightly annoyed.

'I am not so sure. I read about your research in "paranormal" something – energy, perhaps?

'It is true, Chris, he is a serious researcher and was invited by Lord Henry Tollemache, for his celebration at Stonehenge,' declared Sir Richard Wilson, a professor from Cambridge who was trying to convince his friend, the magistrate.

'I am not only an astronomer, I am also a paranormal investigator, and what I do is pure science, since my job is to demystify psychic phenomena that people insist on calling ghosts.' Dr Turner defended his position.

'We have a kind of disagreement, Chris, as I joined the Ghost Club of Cambridge, at Trinity College,' Sir Richard explained, continuing in a whisper to Sir Christopher, 'I think that Dr Turner was sent to spy on me.'

'You... what?' Sir Christopher exclaimed, quite shocked, adding, 'I cannot leave you alone for a moment, or you end up making mischief.'

'Chris, you should keep an open mind. Arthur Conan Doyle is an active member of the Ghost Club; Charles Dickens was one of the founders of the club. Poor soul, unexpected death, and so young...' Sir Richard intoned with great sadness, sighing.

'No wonder, writing ghost novels. I would die from a heart attack if I saw a ghost,' Peter, who was still trying to light his bedraggled cigarette, interjected.

'Don't worry, Peter, Chris is just jealous because he was not invited to be a member of the Ghost Club,' Sir Richard suggested, trying to tease his friend; then added, 'Perhaps if you offer Conan Doyle some ideas to enhance his character "Sherlock Homes" in his next novel, he could be very grateful.'

'Are you mad, Richard? I am a magistrate, and "he" should be the one to come to me, seeking advice for his character... what is the name of his character? Sherlock... something?' Sir Christopher said, outraged.

'Don't be a pedant, Chris, you are just jealous!' Sir Richard said, laughing.

'My dear fellows,' Bernard interjected, 'please, excuse my filthy clothes and humble appearance, but it seems that when the coachman and I tried to push the carriage forward, a "ghost" insisted on pushing it in the opposite direction. With the support of other hands, we might send "the ghost" to Limbo,' Bernard suggested, almost to the point of begging, but with good humour yet.

'I don't think that ghosts can move things, do you, Chris?' Sir Richard whispered to his friend.

'Depends on what entity we are talking about,' replied Sir Christopher.

'Ghosts are not entities. To be an entity they would have to have an independent existence,' Dr Turner stated confidently, overhearing them.

'I thought you investigate ghosts?' Sir Christopher asked, confused.

'I am an atheist who believes that we have a powerful energy around us, which could perhaps be under the control of our mind,' Dr Turner explained.

'Don't utter such blasphemies. This is blasphemy! There is no ghost amongst God's creation; and you, whoever you are, are a heretic!' announced a new arrival, who had parked his carriage some distance away, at the rear of the queue.

'Reverend St Clair! God was never as requested as in this adverse moment!' exclaimed Peter, who added, 'I can hardly imagine how and why you ended up here, but if praying does not help, it certainly will not hinder our task,' Peter stated, smiling at the sight of the vicar.

'We are wasting time! Come on, let's push that carriage before the mud dries.' Andrew took the lead, heading towards the first carriage, which was stuck.

'Peter, I simply will not get out, I cannot dirty my dress. Diana will be mortified when she sees a bunch of dirty people ruining her carpets,' Ellen, Peter's wife, stated, from the window of the second carriage.

'Never mind, my darling, you stay where you are. We don't know what the ghost's taste is like; it may not like the colour of your dress,' Peter responded, following Andrew and Bernard to push the first carriage.

'Shall we offer to help, Chris?' Sir Richard asked, fearing to get dirty.

'My fellow Richard, I start from the principal that two hands are few, and six is a very good number; if they add to the equation the other coachmen's hands, it will be crowded for certain, leading possibly to an incident even bigger than this one before us,' the magistrate explained calmly.

'What do you mean by "bigger incident"?' Sir Richard asked, confused.

'My experience at court shows that for each prosecution witness, the defence arranges two more. Therefore, if our ghost becomes intimidated, he might bring his macabre acquaintances to help,' Sir Christopher replied categorically.

'Do you mean "cause and reaction", Chris?' Sir Richard asked.

'Sir Christopher, Sir Richard, I am shocked to hear your blasphemies about ghosts. You should remember that we serve God, not ghosts, especially you, Sir Christopher, as a magistrate. You judge with the Bible on your table in the court as a symbol of truth and faith,' the vicar exclaimed, slightly put out.

'Wait a moment! Are you talking about mind, or soul?' Kate asked slyly, trying to stoke the fire.

'Soul!' said the vicar,

'Mind!' said the magistrate.

'Ghost!' insisted Sir Richard.

The vicar, the magistrate and the professor simultaneously responded.

'The Soul never lies! It is an extension of God!' The vicar declared.

'But I have witnessed many nasty perpetrators' minds perjuring blatantly with their hand over the Bible,' the magistrate argued, not to be so easily dismissed.

'Don't forget that the senses of our "body", especially that of sight, which can cause a trick in our mind,' the astronomer, who was so far observing the discussion intervened, and added,

'It is possible for the body to be moved by the depths of unconsciousness, and therefore, lie unintentionally.'

'I told you, Chris, this is science,' Sir Richard reiterated proudly.

'Ahh...' several voices interjected.

Suddenly, a flurry of shouts drew their attention back to the trouble with the stuck carriage, a sight which made Kate hold a hand over her face at the calamity she witnessed unfurl before her. Everybody looked on, wide-eyed.

Chapter 5

'We should have stayed at Enfield and declined this invitation. Look what's happened,' Andrew complained, covered in mud and quite upset.

'And miss this celebration? Never! It is getting better and better.' Kate laughed, watching Andrew, Peter and Bernard trying to brush the mud off their clothes; an impossible task, whilst their hands and faces were even dirtier.

'What did I tell you? The ghost's revenge! He probably called his macabre companions and threw everybody in the mud. But they will survive this experience, trust me...' Sir Christopher added, laughing.

'As long as Lord Henry Tollemache has good wine in his cellar, they will indeed survive, I suppose,' Sir Richard replied maliciously.

'Don't worry, Richard, I have known him for years. You could not wish for a more distinguished and exquisite wine cellar, you will see,' Sir Christopher replied in a whisper.

'What did I hear? If you are talking about alcoholic orgies, I can assure you that Lady Diana Tollemache would never allow it,' the vicar intervened.

'That is new to me,' Peter commented, in a whisper to Bernard.

'Who is this vicar, and what is he doing here? He seems to know everybody. I cannot conduct my experiments with negative electromagnetic waves from his brain around,' the astronomer, Dr Turner confided in Kate.

'Don't worry, he is always around, and only God knows why; but as a minority, I assure you,' Kate answered, leaving him to try to pacify her husband's spirits.

'Can we go now, Bernard? I am getting rather bothered, and I need a bath to wash off all this mud,' Charlotte, whose dress was completely caked with mud, demanded impatiently.

'Peter, how can you be so sure that our carriage will not get stuck in the mud like Bernard and Charlotte's?' Ellen asked her husband in a concerned voice from the window of her carriage. Hearing this, all of the passengers from the five carriages in the queue became quite agitated at the prospect, but after a momentary silence, Andrew took the initiative.

'Everybody, listen! Get as many stones and bits of wood you can lay your hands on, so we prevent another coach from sinking. I suggest that all passengers cross on foot carefully, to reduce the weight of the carriages whilst preventing anyone from getting trapped inside.'

There was a sudden bustle as people alighted from the coaches and the men-folk started gathering what wood and rocks they could find from the adjacent hedgerows. The ladies were hitching their skirts up and tentatively making their way forward, avoiding the worst of the mud.

'Kate, I will carry you,' Andrew announced.

'Oh no, I will not take the risk. I saw what happened to Charlotte; I will walk with my own legs, thank you,' Kate replied.

'Oh, come on Kate, don't be stubborn and make things worse,' Andrew snapped, picking Kate up to carry her, but when they had crossed halfway to the grass verge, he slipped, and together they fell into the mud.

'Is this your idea of safety? Never touch me again, Sir Andrew Enfield!' Kate shouted, very upset with her husband.

'This is bad luck. Where are your eagle-owls, Lady Katherine? You might need their help. We have a long journey ahead,' Sir Richard asked jokingly.

'I don't have birds, and I am not cursed. Andrew might be the cursed one, not me,' she replied, similarly annoyed with Sir Richard.

At that very moment though, two eagle-owls crossed the sky towards the north, leaving some of the passengers speechless, until Sir Richard broke the silence, saying seriously,

'I might submit your case to the Ghost Club in Cambridge. It is very peculiar, Lady Katherine, very peculiar indeed...'

It took more than an hour for the rest of the coaches and passengers to circumnavigate the muddy section of road, before finally continuing their journey towards the long-awaited celebration.

Although Andrew and some of the others were not in a good mood, the rest of the journey ended without any incident, and together, as if it was a great religious entourage, the carriages were parking behind each other in front of the steps of Lord Henry Tollemache's magnificent mansion.

As soon as they were informed of the arrival of the guests, a welcome committee of servants lined up outside at the bottom of the stairs, with the Lord of the House and his distinguished and beautiful wife at the top to welcome them.

It is a fact that old age combined with wealth provides a greater sense of humour, with less care for convention and etiquette. If it is not a consensus, at least it could be said with regard to Lord Henry Tollemache, who was trying in vain to disguise from his wife his amusement upon observing the muddy retinue. In contrast, a look of disgust took hold of Lady Diana Tollemache, when facing that terrible sight.

'Welcome, everybody! Our British unpredictable weather proved relentless this time, I am afraid' Lord Henry greeted them, smiling; then proceeded, 'I am pleased to say that my dear and beautiful wife Diana has designated a maid or a valet to each one of you, to make your stay as pleasant as possible, hoping, as I can see, that you soon forget this long journey; they will take you to your rooms, so that you could have a… quick recovery?' Lord Henry announced, attempting to disguise his merriment.

Whilst Diana was greeting her guests in silence, Lord Henry could not be more enthusiastic.

'Andrew! Oh my goodness, how happy and grateful I am for you to have accepted my invitation. It was a long journey from Greece, I must say, wasn't it? And you might be Lady Katherine Enfield!' Lord Henry kissed her hand.

'Please, call me Kate,' she said.

'Enchanted, my dear Lady Kate,' he replied, bowing.

Kate could not help addressing Andrew in a whisper.

'Lady Kate reminds me of little cake,' she said.

'I know, and I didn't like it at all,' Andrew answered, still in a bad mood.

'Chris, you are late! I was waiting for you two days ago; we have so much to catch up on,' Lord Henry greeted the magistrate.

'I am sorry, Henry, we were short of staff, but I am sure that you will not deny me the "Crème De La Crème" from your famous cellar,' the magistrate replied with the wink of an eye.

'It is waiting for you, my dear friend,' Henry reassured him, beaming.

'You might be Mr and Mrs Price? My dear wife is very fond of you... and you two as well, Mr and Mrs White,' he declared upon seeing the couples.

'We would never miss this celebration, as our last one was in Greece months ago; I remember that Diana seemed to have enjoyed it immensely,' Peter said, with a little hint of irony in his voice.

'Of course I did. It was when I met my dear Henry, after I had survived that tragic trip to Eleusis to hunt a treasure that never existed,' Diana replied sarcastically.

'I have no doubt about that – special moments always follow tragic events,' Peter added ambiguously, smiling.

'You might be Dr Augustus Turner from Cambridge, astronomer amongst other peculiar specialities?' Lord Henry asked. 'I am very pleased that you accepted my invitation. You will be surprised by my new theories about British astronomy,' he hinted.

'I am honoured and pleased for being invited, thank you. However, I would like to clarify that some events can turn out to be fraudulent, and conclusions easily fabricated, if the investigations are not strictly and scientifically proven; the university made it clear of this when they assigned me to represent them at this commission,' the astronomer riposted.

'What happened between these two, Richard?' Sir Christopher asked his friend in a whisper.

'You know how the academy behaves towards antiquarians. Lord Henry has both prestige and wealth, which he used to "buy" permission for digging as a hobby,' Sir Richard explained.

'How did you get an invitation, Richard?' the magistrate asked, curious.

'Because Conan Doyle and I are both members of the Ghost club at Trinity College, in Cambridge. I told you earlier about it – the club encouraged the academy to include me in Augustus' commission, so I could investigate some strange events at the George Hotel, where we are going to stay on our trip to Stonehenge.'

'You cannot be serious about this, it is nonsense! Does Dr Augustus Turner believe in ghosts as well?' Sir Christopher asked, intrigued.

'No, he is an atheist, as he said. He follows John Ferriar and Samuel Hibbert-Ware's theory that physiological explanations could account for all paranormal phenomena.'

Suddenly, their gossip was interrupted by Diana's exclamation.

'Reverend St Clair! Thank you for coming. Only you could brighten my muddy day,' exclaimed Diana, clearly delighted.

'Lady Diana, I am honoured to have been asked to bless your marriage… ah… a little late, I am afraid,' the vicar greeted her politely.

'So, do come in as I can't stand watching my drive covered by mud from the carriages' wheels.' Diana hurried the vicar along.

Later that evening, the guests began to leave their rooms, heading to the reception to meet their hosts. Usually, preparation and expectation are the essential condiments of a great party, and although the recipe had failed during the earlier travel, the guests did now at least attempt to remedy the situation by making the most of that strange celebration.

'Are you still angry with me, Kate? I am so sorry,' Andrew begged, knocking gently on the bathroom door.

'You should be, because you keep insisting on treating me as a child…' Kate replied, opening the door.

'I was only trying to be a gentleman and keep you from getting your shoes dirty,' Andrew apologised.

'…and made things ten times worse,' Kate added.

'What do you think if I try to redeem myself later in this room, in a private celebration, between you and me only, and a bottle of champagne that I hid in my luggage to make for you a surprise, if Mr Bear gives us permission, of course?' Andrew hinted, inviting her.

The strategy worked as Kate, now with the bathroom door wide open said,

'Mr Bear told me that he will have an early evening,' Kate replied, taking a quick glance at her toy bear on the dressing table.

Andrew smiled, happy as a child, holding her hand and kissing it, before they both headed to meet their hosts.

When they arrived in the reception room, Lord Henry was about to introduce another two guests.

'My dear visitors and friends, I am delighted to introduce you to my nephew Albert Tollemache, who I consider as a son, as nature has not graced me with one yet…' Lord Henry intoned wistfully, giving Diana a peculiar glance.

'Diana? A mother?' Bernard whispered to Charlotte, Ellen and Peter, trying to find in a hurry his pipe in his pocket.

'Diana never stops to surprise me, I must say,' Peter commented ironically, lighting a cigarette.

Lord Henry continued.

'I also want to introduce you to my nephew's fiancée, Miss Mary Abington, who recently arrived from our ex-colony in the West,' he said, with a certain disdain; and as soon as he saw Andrew and Kate at the entrance, he left his nephew and fiancée, and addressed them enthusiastically instead.

'Andrew, Lady Kate, I want to introduce you to Dr Adrian Gruber.'

In one of the back corners of the reception room, Dr Augustus Turner confided, annoyed, to Sir Richard and Sir Christopher,

'It was just what I suspected – that German!'

'He is not German, he is Austrian,' Sir Christopher corrected him.

'Even worse, these Austrians are Arianists. They think they are better than anybody else. 'How could they be better than us British?' Dr Turner complained.

'You're right, Augustus, their food and wines are awful. Don't forget that we have cider, and nothing can be compared with a full English breakfast,' Sir Richard added.

'We are not talking about food and drink, Richard. We are talking about "thoughts and mind". The Germans have very good philosophers, I have to admit, but I don't know anything much about the Austrians,' Sir Christopher said.

'We British have scientists, mathematicians, and a greater empire than theirs,' Augustus said adamantly.

'Anyway, let's indulge ourselves with a superb wine, to appease our minds in the face of the unusual,' Sir Christopher suggested, changing the subject as he was getting annoyed with the scientist and his morbid ironies.

'What do you mean, Chris?' Sir Richard asked, worried.

'That I have a bad feeling about this celebration, my dear fellow,' Sir Christopher replied thoughtfully.

'Please, don't tell me that Lady Katherine is involved? Not again,' Sir Richard begged.

'Hope not, my dear fellow, hope not,' Sir Christopher said, in almost a whisper.

Henry Tollemache, Andrew, Kate, and Dr Gruber continued their discussion.

'I apologise, my dear friends, I will return to you in a few minutes, as my dear wife claims my presence, and I simply must attend,' Lord Henry excused himself.

After he left, Dr Adrian Gruber addressed Andrew.

'Sir Andrew, I have been reading your articles about the religious conflict in the Balkans, and I wonder if you would agree with me that a rational mind, free from the imprisoning chains of a punitive entity, would make a better judgement about things related to our real world; religion should be an instrument of control that we, as intellectuals, should use to restore order, nothing else,' Dr Gruber suggested.

Kate, who was outraged with that sort of statement, decided to intervene, but Andrew, knowing his wife, took the initiative to prevent her from creating a conflict.

'I am sorry, Dr Gruber, but I never wrote anything that could possibly suggest that a group of people were more qualified to govern than another; it is quite the opposite. In antiquity, the Greeks created democracy, where any citizen could not only vote and decide the daily life of their community but could also become the leader himself. Unfortunately those who, as you said, were fortunate to become leaders found it extremely difficult to detach themselves from the position of power, whilst the illiterate were easily manipulated. What I emphasised in my articles was that education should be extended to anyone, and most of all it should be separated from religion, to prevent God from being held responsible for men's decisions.' Andrew paused, then continued.

'People should use Faith to comfort themselves in the face of adversity and death, as well as for charity. Not every illiterate is poor, but those who are know better than us what they need to survive. Therefore, they should not only be heard about their needs, but have access to education as well, to learn a peaceful way to claim what they need, instead of going to foolish and meaningless war,' Andrew finished.

'Well said, Sir Andrew. I finally found, apart from Lady Diana of course, somebody in this room who is not an atheist,' the vicar stated, approaching them.

'And who are you?' Dr Gruber enquired pompously, in his austere Austrian accent.

'Reverend St Clair, confidante and close friend of Lady Diana Tollemache. I am here to bless her marriage,' he vicar answered, with clerical authority.

'A little late, I suppose. They married months ago,' Dr Gruber replied ironically.

'By the way, Dr Gruber...' Kate brought back the discussion. 'Who do you think should be chosen to govern the rest of us? Not philosophers, I hope, since they were not able to save Greece from tyranny in the past. It took more than two and a half thousand years for Greece to be independent again,' Kate stated.

'Hopefully, Lady Katherine, you are not suggesting that women should be in command. They already have too much to supervise at home, including the duty of providing healthy and adequate descendants for their family,' Dr Gruber rudely replied, but was interrupted by Miss Mary Abington, who approached them.

'We were not properly introduced, Lady Katherine, but Lord Henry told us about your interest in the Oracle of Delphi. You did your doctorate in America; perhaps you didn't notice that we are a very religious country,' the young girl said, in a soft, lilting voice.

'I have nothing against religion. My PhD was a scientific analysis of politics and religion in Ancient Greece. I agree with my husband that religion should not be used to take advantage from the poor, or illiterate,' Kate replied, surprised with Miss Abington's point of view.

Meanwhile, Diana approached and asked the guests,

'Hopefully you approve of your rooms? Were the maids and valets suitable for you?' Diana smiled, feeling rather grand.

'Diana... I mean... Lady Diana Tollemache, you have amazing talents, a true Pandora's box,' Peter said ambiguously.

'What is Pandora's box?' Ellen asked her husband, confused by Peter's statement, but Diana intervened, trying to prevent Peter from making more trouble.

'Pandora was the most beautiful mortal creation of the Greek gods. She had all the talents that a woman could wish,' Diana informed them.

'Unfortunately, Pandora had a box containing, amongst other things, all the evils that a man could ever wish,' Peter replied, having some fun.

'Next time I invite you and Charlotte don't bring your husbands, as they don't know how to behave in front of a proper lady,' Diana stated, disgruntled, before she turned on her heels and left them standing.

'I didn't say anything,' Bernard said loudly to Diana as she walked away.

Charlotte waited until Diana had left, to avoid her friend hearing what she was going to say to her husband, and Peter.

'Can you see what you and Peter did, Bernard? Now she will never invite us again. Look at this magnificent mansion. She is younger than me by only one year, and she has married twice.'

'... and getting richer...' Peter intervened, laughing.

'Don't put ideas in your mind, Charlotte. I am worth more alive than I am dead,' Bernard replied, feigning a worried expression.

'I don't think she is lucky, he is twice her age, perhaps more,' Ellen said disapprovingly.

'You misunderstand Diana. She doesn't like to be married; she likes to be... "a widow",' Peter explained, laughing.

'...which is not a bad idea,' Charlotte added pointedly examining her husband Bernard from top to toe.

Meanwhile, Lord Henry was regaling his gathered guests again.

'My dear friends, before I invite you to embark upon our exquisite dinner, carefully prepared and organised by my dear wife I must add, I would let you know our agenda for the next few days. I booked the whole George Hotel in Amesbury for three days, so we may visit the stone circle called Stonehenge, where I will expose my theories about the ancient Britons. We shall be prepared to leave tomorrow by lunch time, and I suggest you take your notebooks, compass and other research equipment; the rest will be provided at the hotel, which was carefully supplied with a generous cart of wine. You can be certain that you will not be disappointed.' He smiled cheerfully.

Kate could not avoid thinking that amongst all divine creations, nothing can usurp the highest seat designated to the banquet. Certainly it was created knowing that even words – which in consensus were considered to be the greatest human achievement – became dumb and empty of meaning, until the last bit of meal was enjoyed, and the last sip was taken.

'Let's toast the Queen!' Lord Henry raised his glass.

'To the Queen!' Everybody stood and toasted.

Later whilst they were drinking liqueurs, Dr Turner approached his host.

'Lord Henry, I am not sure if I fully understood your intention about this trip to Stonehenge. That is a private land, and as far as I know, you don't have permission to dig there,' Dr Turner asked.

'Who is talking about digging tomorrow? We are going to witness the celestial movement above us, like the ancients did before us.' He smiled. 'Our conclusions will not be "fabricated", as you suggested earlier – they will be observed empirically,' Lord Henry replied.

'I do hope you are not suggesting that an old stone circle could conceal any kind of scientific knowledge? The people who built it were barbarians; pagans who used to make sacrifices to who knows what,' Dr Gruber insisted.

'You cannot call them barbarians. There is evidence that they had an advanced way of thinking, possibly prior to the Greeks,' Kate argued.

'Perhaps we should go to the lounge for a glass of liqueur, don't you think, my dear?' Diana interrupted, addressing her husband.

'I don't think it is a good idea you expose Sir Joshua's research at the moment, Kate; not until we could prove his theories.' Andrew advised his wife in a whisper.

'Prove what?' she asked. 'There is nothing to prove. The authors were very clear in their texts. Nothing could be a greater testimony of the truth than the words of the ancients themselves. This is the problem with archaeologists – they don't value words. They think that it is necessary to find concrete evidence.'

'I am on your side, Kate. We have to take into consideration that those texts passed through God knows how many subjective translations until they reached us. Historians, geographers might be influenced by their own religion, regurgitating elements of some oral tradition; the images they could have used as allegory might be part of their own beliefs,' Andrew argued.

'I find very interesting what you just said.' Lord Henry's nephew, Albert, who was behind the couple, intervened and added, 'I admire my uncle for his tenacity in seeking the truths of the past. He thinks that there is much more to be discovered behind the words in those books, such as in the Bible,' Albert explained confidently.

'You are going too far, Albert. It is a fact that what is in the Bible cannot be substantiated, because believing in its words is an act of faith. Some words in the Bible could even promote healing with the simple act of being repeated,' retorted his fiancée, Mary Abington.

'Uh... Andrew... I am going to speak with Sir Christopher as I didn't have the chance yet, not since we arrived.' Kate excused herself and quickly left her husband with that strange couple.

'Kate! A refreshing sight is the best antidote to fatiguing words; but I have to admit that you yourself do not seem to have had a pleasant experience after dessert,' Sir Christopher whispered to her.

'I am afraid not, Sir Christopher. What is going on with these people? It seems that Lord Henry has a most peculiar sense of humour, gathering inside the same walls people who would be prepared to kill to defend their point of view,' Kate declared, somewhat annoyed.

'Including you, my dear Kate?' Sir Christopher replied humorously.

'Including myself, I have to admit,' she responded with a mischievous smile, then added,

'When Miss Abington talked about the Bible, I suddenly remembered where I heard those words. I think that she is a member of the Science of Christ's Love in America, which proclaims that the material world is evil and sick. In their doctrine, healing can only be obtained by God's words, so, in their ideology, when you accept that this world is not real, so will it be whatever your illness is, and people are led to deny any kind of medicine or medical treatment. Tell me how this kind of thinking differs from the Ancients, three thousand years ago?' She smiled.

'Fortunately, my dear Kate, age makes you lazy and selfish, and although I am in complete solidarity with you, I cannot help thinking how good this wine is... Henry!' Sir Christopher exclaimed when his friend joined them for a chat. 'I was just telling Kate how we are fortunate to be able to enjoy small pleasures of life – like your wine,' Sir Christopher exclaimed, in a whisper though, to Kate and Henry.

'You are right; let the *words from the past remain buried for a while, after all they are not dead*,' Lord Henry replied with a wink of an eye for Kate, who, suddenly speechless, watched him move away, to greet another group of guests.

Since Kate left Greece, she felt herself immersed in a mysterious atmosphere which could be compared to a rug, revealing gradually its unusual patterns as it unrolled. Unlike Penelope, who sewed her rug during the day, and unravelled it at night to stop time, Kate yearned to finish it to find out where it intended to take her.

'Sir Christopher, I think...' Kate addressed the magistrate beside her, but to her surprise he was not there; like Lord Henry, he had disappeared.

'Would you like a wine, Lady Katherine?' a servant asked her.

'Yes, thank you,' she answered, taking a glass from the tray.

Those words from Lord Henry sent Kate back in time, to months ago in Greece. She was so excited at meeting Andrew after so many years, and being part of his archaeological expedition full of surprises, though some of them turned nasty later, she had to admit.

Kate knew that finding the original papyrus with Aeschylus' tragedies was crucial to prove her thesis that real democracy in Ancient Greece started one hundred years before, with Solon, and ended with his death, instead of with Pericles, as scholars attested.

Kate never imagined that she would discover part of the Alexandrian Library, whose papyri were saved by a Greek librarian from being burned by the Romans; an incredible secret carefully kept by those called "Guardians", whose duty was to protect the knowledge contained in that library. Were they right in believing that knowledge hidden in those papyri should be denied to everyone?

Kate knew Sir Christopher was one of the Guardians, but she didn't expect that Lord Henry would be one as well, but those words *"the past is buried but not dead"* left no doubt that he knew everything about it, as did Sir Joshua, who trusted her to the point of leaving her his precious research about the stone circle and the Hyperboreans.

'May I invite you for a glass of champagne in a private celebration upstairs, Lady Katherine?' Andrew came and held her hand, waiting for her answer.

'We shall never waste a bottle of champagne, so I will grant you a truce, Sir Andrew,' Kate answered with a smile.

Chapter 6

Kate was lying in bed with her head resting on Andrew's chest, thinking how happy she was for being able to follow him wherever fate would take them. She sighed deeply, catching Andrew's attention as he had been completely absorbed in gently stroking her long hair.

'Why such a deep sigh, Kate?' he asked.

'Because I am happy, and I wonder what fate is planning for us tomorrow,' Kate replied, trying not to be too obvious, as only Mr Bear could really know the intensity of her feelings for that man she loved so much, from the very beginning when they first met.

'Don't worry. Henry knows what he is doing. He has always lived his life as if it was a theatre, with him in the lead role of course. A strange couple though, I must say, as Diana has never previously accepted only playing a supporting role in anything,' he mused.

'I lived close to Diana my entire life and I could never judge her personality with as much precision as you just did. I couldn't pay her much attention really, as I was in a race against time, with other priorities in mind,' Kate hinted, teasing him.

'What do you mean?' Andrew asked.

'I had to cross the Atlantic to get the qualifications that nobody in England wanted to give to a woman; then I had to come back before you chose some other assistant. Fortunately I arrived when there was only one applicant for the post, and it was quite easy to get him out of the way. You should have seen Sir Richard's face – I swear he wanted to kill me.' Kate laughed.

'What about John, your tutor?' Andrew asked, pretending to be angry.

'He hatched the plan with me from the very beginning!' Kate explained, smiling.

'So I didn't have a chance from the beginning, eh? I see...' Andrew said, defeated; then he kissed her.

Meanwhile down in the wine cellar, Bernard addressed Sir Richard.

'Richard, you couldn't have been more efficient in your new role of entertainment organiser. This is the most exquisite wine cellar that I have ever seen,' he declared.

'It takes time to develop certain skills, my dear fellow, and we are getting better with age, like the wines here in this cellar,' Sir Richard replied proudly.

'I wonder why Dr Gruber is so quiet...' Dr Turner asked Sir Christopher, speaking intentionally loudly, which did not go unnoticed by the Austrian doctor, who, upon hearing those words, straightened himself preparing for war against his rival, but was immediately interrupted by Sir Christopher.

'As a magistrate, I must establish some rules here. For example: from now on I declare this cellar a sanctuary, where Baccus, Liber or Dionysus, whatever name or nationality you assign to the god of wine, will be our dearest host in making us enjoy the nectars in his temple.' Sir Christopher tried to calm the two rivals.

'You cannot be serious, Sir Christopher. I refuse to share the same space as a pagan god,' the vicar objected.

'It was merely an innocent metaphor, Vicar,' Bernard intervened reassuringly. 'By the way, what are you doing here?' Bernard asked him, intrigued, lighting his pipe with a match.

'I am here to ensure that you and your friend Mr Price do not go overboard, as your wives make generous contributions to our parish,' the vicar replied imperiously, then asked, 'By the way, where is your friend, Mr Price?' seeing he was not present.

Meanwhile, upstairs in Peter's bedroom...

'I don't understand, Peter. Why do you have to meet them now, to discuss things that you will do tomorrow? It sounds redundant,' Ellen asked, confused, adding, 'Does it have to do with Pandora's Box?'

'I am afraid, my dear, it has to do with other gods,' Peter answered, putting cigarettes and matches in his pockets.

'Oh, please, tell me what gods?' Ellen insisted.

Back in the cellar...

'Augustus, I don't understand why you are so particularly upset with the Austrian doctor; I don't agree with many academics from Cambridge, but in the end we all dine at the same table and, most of all, we drink the same wine,' Sir Richard addressed Dr Turner in a whisper, pouring wine into an elegant cut lead crystal glass.

'I once wrote an article suggesting that we have different human races today because we are derived from different origins. In fact, I was trying to persuade Darwin that he too, deep inside, was a polygenist as well,' Dr Turner explained.

'Oh... and what happened? Did Darwin read your article and say anything?' Sir Richard asked, curious as to Darwin's response.

'Well, he never wrote back to me, but this Austrian read it, who knows how he got access to my article – and he said that he was certain that "the British descend from monkeys", whilst he and his fellows descend from Scandinavian Hyperboreans,' Dr Turner replied, before being interrupted by a loud voice coming from the direction of the stairs.

'Did I hear the Hyperboreans being mentioned?' Lord Henry enquired, enthusiastically.

'Could anybody tell me who the hell these Hyperboreans are?' Bernard asked. 'By the way, does anybody know where Peter is?' he enquired, worried by his good friend's absence.

'I am here! Last, but not least,' Peter replied, not less enthusiastically from the bottom of the stairs, close behind Lord Henry.

'Ah! All of my dear and honourable guests are here,' Lord Henry exclaimed, laughing loudly, whilst sitting and asking the two servants who arrived with him to bring more wine, cheese, crackers and other delicacies.

'Why did you take so long, Peter?' Bernard asked, relieved to see his friend.

'My wife was curious about certain aspects of ancient Greek mythology, so I had to explain some of their myths to her.' Peter justified his tardiness.

'I didn't know that you were an authority on mythology,' Sir Christopher sniped maliciously.

'I am not. I only know a couple of myths – about Aphrodite and Hades,' Peter responded.

'I know about Aphrodite, but who is this Hades? I never heard of him,' Bernard said.

'I decided to do some research a while ago, when I started to contemplate death and mortality, and where we might go afterwards. Then I read about this fellow, Hades, who seems to be the god of the underworld. However, I learned that the place is in complete darkness and full of ghosts, with no matches for my cigarettes, so I gave Greek mythology up, and I decided to reaffirm my faith in Christianity,' Peter answered with conviction, lighting a cigarette cheerfully.

'Well done, Mr Price, a lost soul returns to God's arms, and in expiating your sins Heaven will be waiting for you,' the vicar declared proudly.

'Who said anything about Heaven? I'm looking forward to going to Hell mentioned in the Bible to fulfil my needs, if you please.' Peter corrected the vicar, laughing out loud at his own joke.

Rubbing his hands, Lord Henry announced,

'Well, gentlemen, let's postpone the wives and Hyperboreans for tomorrow. This evening we are just simple sinners, unable to resist a good wine, dainty delicacies and a good game of cards. By the way, who has the cards?' He asked.

The next morning began very quietly, and when Kate and Andrew opened the lounge door where the breakfast would be served, nobody else was there. Somewhat surprised she addressed Andrew.

'I am not sure if we are in the right room. What do you think?' she asked, but before Andrew could say anything, he was interrupted by Diana, who had just arrived.

'Yes you are, and I will kill my husband for that.' Diana was evidently quite upset at something. Then Ellen, Charlotte and Lord Henry's nephew's fiancée Mary entered the lounge together.

'Diana, I am so sorry, Peter had nightmares last night, but he will be here soon.' Ellen excused her husband, rather embarrassed.

'Peter is the nightmare, Ellen. I never understood why you married him,' Diana replied tartly.

'Don't waste your time trying to answer, Ellen,' Charlotte intervened. 'I have been asking myself the same question about me and Bernard, unsuccessfully, for some time,' Charlotte advised her.

'Would anybody like a cup of tea?' Kate intervened, pouring some for herself.

'I would, please,' Andrew replied, and added, 'Look, Kate, scones! Oh, Victoria sponge sandwich cake too, my favourite.' Andrew was trying to change the subject and the sight of crumpets, scones, toast, muffins, cakes, a variety of jams and creamy butter was sufficiently enticing to change the demeanour of all present.

Minutes later, other guests started to appear for breakfast, some in a good shape, others not. Curiously, they came gradually, in small groups, and Kate suspected that age makes us better able to judge our limits; or perhaps the body becomes accustomed to excess. Whatever the explanation, Sir Christopher, Sir Richard and the two rival doctors entered the lounge with cheerful expressions on their faces, very eager for breakfast. Apart from the usual "Good morning" and a quick comment about the lovely weather, they hurried to the table of food and drinks to partake of the wonderful array that greeted them.

The next group came alone, but no less enthusiastically.

'My dear and beautiful wife, look at the weather. The sun has come out to celebrate us!' Lord Henry exclaimed, kissing Diana amiably.

Diana didn't smile, but did offer her cheek for him to kiss.

'Oh, come on, dear, we didn't drink too much.' Lord Henry tried to prise a smile from his wife, and he was half successful, when she decided to give him half a smile.

Minutes later, Peter, Bernard and Lord Henry's nephew, Albert, entered the lounge for breakfast, together.

'Peter, I am so pleased that you have recovered from your headache.' Ellen smiled, then addressed her friend. 'You should have seen him earlier, Diana. He looked so poorly,' Ellen said, trying to apologise for her husband's slightly grubby and dishevelled state.

'I don't think he was "poorly" just because of his mood. Did you check your husband's pockets today?' Diana asked ambiguously.

'Don't worry, my dear; you can be certain that our guest was not unlucky yesterday,' Lord Henry replied a little enviously, but then added, suddenly excited, 'However, it was just the first night.' He smiled.

'Diana, I have to congratulate the cook. These are the best scones I have ever tasted in my life,' Kate exclaimed, hoping to change the subject.

'Thank you, Kate. Emma has an incomparable talent. I never need to worry about the menu. She is completely in charge of the kitchen. Actually, I don't have to supervise anybody here, as everybody knows what to do; consequently, I have more time to dedicate to my dear husband,' Diana replied proudly, tilting her head and smiling sweetly at him.

'I have to say, Henry, you have a wonderful estate here, with some truly remarkable stone circles and barrows,' Andrew said. 'It's very promising for research, perhaps even for excavation? I wonder, why did you decide to conduct your research at Stonehenge?' Andrew asked.

'It is a waste of time, Andrew,' Diana interrupted. 'I tried to persuade him as well, but it seems like he takes great pleasure in defying Sir Edmund Mulgrave.'

'Who is that?' Bernard asked, his interest piqued.

'He owns most of Amesbury, and Stonehenge of course,' Sir Christopher interjected, since Lord Henry's face made it clear that he was not comfortable in talking about the senior aristocrat from Amesbury.

'That is one of the reasons I invited you for this celebration, but unfortunately I cannot tell you precisely why until we arrive at the George Hotel for dinner, later this evening,' Lord Henry explained, recovering some of his earlier enthusiasm.

'What time are we going to leave?' Albert asked his uncle.

'We are not going, are we?' Albert's fiancée Mary asked, hoping they weren't.

'Hmm... well, I think we are, aren't we, Uncle?' Albert asked, creating a little discomfort amongst the guests in the lounge, due to the young woman's disapproving reaction.

'You know how I feel about this pagan temple made of stones.' She glowered at Albert, and asked, 'You don't have anything to do with this research, do you?' Mary enquired.

'Well said, Miss Abington. They were not only pagans, but barbarians as well, making all sorts of arcane ritual sacrifices,' the vicar stated as he entered the lounge for breakfast.

'Oh my God, human sacrifices?' Ellen was shocked.

'Where were you, Vicar? You are the last soul to arrive for breakfast; unless you're adept at some kind of mystic Christian fasting?' Peter asked.

'I was praying for the pagan souls in this house not to be tempted to practise obscene pagan rituals, Mr Price,' the vicar responded, annoyed at Peter's slight.

'Not even libations? I wonder if we should take a couple of bottles of wine for libations; this will not do any harm,' Sir Richard whispered to his old friend Sir Christopher.

'Enough!' Lord Henry interrupted. 'This nonsense is just a myth created by the Romans. There aren't any pagan souls, human sacrifices, or any other kind of barbaric rituals at Stonehenge,' he assured them.

'Whatever you have in mind, I hope you don't drag my Albert there too,' Mary said cautiously.

'My dear Mary, my nephew Albert is a Tollemache, so you should start to get used to the Tollemache tenacity in the search for Truth, and the development of Knowledge. As I said yesterday, I may be gifted in future with a son, and I have to leave to him (God willing), or her, an important legacy,' Lord Henry replied, before turning to Diana and looking for her support. 'Isn't that right, my dear wife?'

'Yes, my dear,' Diana replied amiably, noticing Mary's hostility.

'We were not deaf yesterday. He does expect to be a father,' Charlotte confided in Ellen.

'Remarkable!' Peter exclaimed loudly, having a bit of fun at Diana's expense.

'Anyway, we shall delay our departure for another hour, due to our late night yesterday, I am afraid. However, everything else will remain according to the schedule,' Lord Henry stated imperiously, standing up with his wife and leaving the room in a hurry.

With a concerned look, Kate whispered to Andrew,

'Did you get all your equipment ready yesterday?'

'Hmm... no, did you?' Andrew asked, suddenly realising they were not properly prepared.

'...no,' she replied, wide-eyed.

'Hmm... err, if you excuse us, we have to go and get ready.' Andrew coughed then stood up with Kate, and they too left in a hurry.

'Come on, Mr Bear, be quick or you will be left behind.' Kate put her little treasured friend inside her bag.

'Did you see my compass, Kate?' Andrew asked, sounding worried, looking under the bed.

'No, but I have mine if you don't find yours,' she replied, running from one corner of the room to the other, dropping some papers on the floor. 'My papers, I mustn't lose them. Do you have any books to put in the suitcase? I must lock it and ask your valet to take it downstairs,' Kate said, whilst Andrew was looking for his compass.

'Found it!' Andrew exclaimed, holding his compass up. 'I need to take these two books as well. I will call the valet.' Andrew gave her the compass and the books.

Meanwhile, Sir Christopher was sitting in a comfortable chair in one of the reception rooms, drinking a cup of tea with the door open, admiring the busy servants and maids coming past up and down in a hurry, carrying suitcases, umbrellas, shooting sticks and other paraphernalia. A couple of minutes later, Sir Richard joined him in the reception room.

'Thank goodness I am not a woman. I am going to take just one suitcase and nothing else,' Sir Richard stated, sitting in a chair opposite his friend, whilst his valet took his suitcase to the carriage.

'Well said, Richard, we already carry the weight of our age; we don't need anything else to delay us,' Sir Christopher replied with some satisfaction.

Suddenly they heard people arguing loudly in the entrance hall; so they turned to watch what was happening.

'I told you, I refuse to be humiliated by this stupid girl. I want her out of my house. Did you see the look she gave me when you talked about a son? She thinks that I cannot be a mother. How dare she look at me like that!' Diana exclaimed.

'Mary is just a silly girl, obsessed with her Science of Love, or whatever they call it in America.' Lord Henry tried to calm his wife.

'I'm warning you, I will kill this girl if she crosses the line again, and I will kill you if you try to defend her,' Diana promised.

'I will try to bring Albert back to reason, darling. Let's enjoy our trip,' Lord Henry appealed to his wife, smiling and trying to make light of it.

'The only thing you know how to do is smile for everyone,' Diana said furiously, turned on her heels then walked off, leaving her husband standing alone in the hall.

Sir Christopher and Sir Richard looked at each other wide-eyed, without saying a word, after seeing the scene in the hall.

It didn't take long for Dr Turner to turn up and join the two of them.

'Sir Richard, Sir Christopher, I would be very pleased to be able to share with you the quietness of this reception room,' he smiled ironically, and entered. 'If Lord Henry doesn't know how to control his own private life,' he confided, 'how could he control an important scientific experiment, hoping to obtain reliable results?' He asked, then continued,

'An experiment requires key features to obtain control of the cause and effect of relationships, and careful measurement of each step of the process is essential. It seems to me that Lord Henry did not make an accurate measurement regarding the age difference between himself and his wife, which sadly may compromise the experiment, leading to a disastrous result. A scientist should devote his life to the Academy and forget mundane issues; I am here not as a judge, but as a demander, who will not allow an antiquarian to share the same roof as devoted scientists, and throw almost a thousand years of academic research into the sewer; not whilst I am alive...' Dr Turner was very animated.

'Are you spiteful because Lord Henry's prestige and wealth carries sufficient weight to obtain permission from Queen Victoria to make astronomical experiments at Stonehenge; a permission which you were unable to obtain?' Sir Christopher teased the doctor.

'You two, "Knights of the Queen", listen to what I have to say – you will live long enough to see your noble names and this monarchy falling from grace in this country,' Dr Turner spat.

Sir Richard and Sir Christopher were astonished by their opponent's public display of ferocious animosity; but didn't have time to reply, as the astronomer got up and left just when another fight started in the hall; this time between Lord Henry and his nephew.

'You cannot do that Uncle Henry!' Albert cried, 'She is my fiancée, and her family is politically influential in America. As a lawyer I have a promising career in politics there, and I will not let you interfere; not because of your "beautiful wife",' Albert shouted, and also left his uncle standing alone in the hall. Lord Henry only noticed his audience when he glanced at the door of the reception room, and with the warmest of smiles, he approached Sir Christopher and Sir Richard.

'Gentlemen, the heat in this house could cook a pheasant today!' He declared cheerfully, adding, 'The winter, which is about to start, was supposed to be cold my dear fellows, but in this country not only the weather, now even the seasons have become unpredictable. I think that I will follow your suggestion, Richard, and take a few special bottles of wine for libations at Stonehenge. Do you agree?' Lord Henry asked, searching for support.

'Libations? I thought you were an atheist, Henry?' Sir Christopher took the opportunity to joke, before his friend Sir Richard had any opportunity to answer.

'We shall not exclude anybody from the party Chris, be they pagans, Christians, atheists – they can all come, because it will be a glorious day for British Astronomy,' Lord Henry exclaimed enthusiastically, determined not to allow any mundane or religious issue divert him from his experiment.

'Bravo Lord Henry, even the ghosts will appreciate your generosity,' Sir Richard smiled, remembering the exquisite cellar.

Meanwhile, Diana walked quickly towards the other end of the house, then, checking to see she was not being observed, she took a key out of her pocket and opened a door. There was an old sofa inside and a table with two drawers; a few wooden cupboards and old curtains. The room was full of dust, which made Diana cough a little. Quickly, with another key, she opened one of the table's drawers and took out a rectangular wooden box, without noticing that the door was not completely closed.

Whilst she was looking inside it to check its contents, a voice from the door announced,

'Finally, Pandora decided to open her precious box!' Peter exclaimed ironically, whilst smoking a cigarette.

Taken by surprise Diana closed the box quickly, glowering defiantly at Peter,

'What are you doing here, Peter? You should be getting ready to leave. I... I don't have time for you,' Diana said, trying to appear casual.

'And steal from Ellen and her maid the pleasure of putting several dresses in the suitcases, then taking them out after choosing different ones, God knows how many times?' Peter replied, having fun with Diana's discomfort.

Trying to be cordial and change the subject, Diana decided to tease her friend.

'What do you think about my house?' She preened.

'Big. With a dreadful scheme of decoration, I must say; but I wonder if you are going to be married long enough to show your husband your good taste? Your first husband was not that lucky,' Peter replied, trying to hold the laugh back.

'You remind me of Henry with his strange sense of humour, or perhaps in your case it is just a lack of heart...' Diana retorted.

'That is not fair, I do have a heart, and it was broken for the second time when we received your letter informing us about your sudden marriage. To be honest I found it rather bizarre, and too soon, especially after our memorable adventures in Greece last year; but knowing you as I do, I recovered quickly, to be ready when you come to old Peter and cry on my shoulder, feeling sorry for your boring life,' Peter defended himself, responding to her provocation with good humour.

'You should take advantage of the abundance of scientists in this house and declare that you are going to donate your body to science after you die,' Diana said, 'Maybe dead you will worth more, if they could find anything useful inside you.' Diana smiled sarcastically.

'Hmm... I don't think that's a good idea, especially if I die before you.' Peter replied,

'Imagine if they manage to open the box with our memorable moments, it could ruin your chances for your next wedding, as I am not sure that Henry Tollemache will be the last one.' Peter grinned. 'By the way, what is your plan for this trip? I tried to picture you measuring things and looking at the stars with telescopes, but you are not romantic enough to fit the role. It is more appropriate for Andrew and Kate, don't you think?' Without giving her the chance to reply he asked, 'Tell me, how many evils are inside that box, my dear Pandora?' Peter laughed.

'The only evil in my life is you Peter, and I don't know why I keep inviting Ellen, knowing that you are like a haunting shadow chasing after me.' Diana sniped.

'A somewhat macabre thought, but it makes Stonehenge even more promising, don't you think?' Peter said, laughing, making Diana even more agitated, so she pushed him out of the room, closing the door behind her, leaving Peter chuckling to himself whilst she, carrying the wooden box, left him standing alone in the corridor.

Sir Christopher and Sir Richard were about to leave the hall to walk to their carriage, when Dr Gruber turned up evidently a little upset.

'I am sorry to bother you two, gentlemen, but I was just told that Dr Turner and I will share the same carriage. Lord Henry is notorious for his unconventional behaviour and his bizarre sense of humour,' he sighed; then continued. 'Perhaps he is willing to get rid of one of us during this trip to Stonehenge? I don't think it is safe to get too close to a man who thinks his grandfather was a monkey. I was thinking of asking Andrew Enfield and his wife to welcome me in their carriage, but that didn't seem to be a good idea either, as his wife is even worse than Dr Turner, with her ideas about a woman with a brain… I mean… a mind, like us.' Dr Gruber explained, not noticing the exchange of looks between the two old fellows, especially Sir Christopher, who in fact disagreed with them regarding Kate. However, this time Sir Richard took the advantage to reply, before Sir Christopher could say anything in her defence.

'I perfectly agree with you, Dr Gruber. Women should not be allowed to exercise their brains with academic issues, they are emotionally unfit. However, such emotional hearts might play an important role, as we have to admit they often exceed their talents if focusing on dancing gracefully, playing pianoforte masterfully, or speaking French with a sweet and soft accent. Unfortunately, most men don't listen to experienced voices.'

'I thought you hated women, Richard,' Sir Christopher intervened, outraged.

'I don't hate them, I just think their true talent is lost when they set out to do what they weren't cut out for,' Sir Richard said, without realising that Kate was behind him, listening to everything.

'You may have to ride to Stonehenge, Richard, if you are not careful what you say,' Sir Christopher warned, worried for his friend.

'You should be ashamed of underestimating the value and contribution of women to society and science, Sir Richard,' Kate fumed. Then, addressing Andrew she added, 'It is your fault, Andrew, from the moment in Cambridge last year that you tried to prevent me joining your expedition to Greece.'

'My fault?' Andrew asked, astonished for being involved in a discussion that he didn't know how started, and "why" he was involved, so he added, 'You are the stubborn one here, you don't know how to listen to other people's advice, often acting impulsively, without...' he was interrupted by his wife.

'Without asking for permission? Is this what you mean, that I should ask for permission to do anything I want?' Kate glowered, then turned heel, leaving them standing in the reception.

'I think that we four will have to travel in the same carriage, as I don't think Kate will allow Andrew to accompany her, I am afraid,' Sir Christopher complained, annoyed at his companions.

'Oh... no,' Sir Richard exclaimed.

'What's up, Richard? It is not the end of the world, we can have a nice conversation to help time pass quickly,' the magistrate soothed his friend.

'I am not worried about the space in the carriage. Look!' he said, pointing, 'Those two eagle-owls again, and they seem to be taking the same direction as us,' Sir Richard explained, a little spooked by their presence.

Chapter 7

Alone in her carriage, Kate was watching the people outside chattering excitedly when she realised that even though winter had just knocked on the door, the temperature outside was surprisingly warm, not dissimilar to the temperature inside Diana's grand house. She shivered a little, as some people could take pleasure from watching how people lose composure for crumbs, or plead for more than they would ever be able to keep. However, this party had not even started, so why not just enjoy for now the thrill of going into the unknown? That was, perhaps, the spirit of all the guests, including herself, who shared the same excitement in that great retinue of carriages that left that day for the George Hotel in Amesbury.

Sir Christopher was not wrong, as usual, in predicting other people's behaviour, as the four gentlemen did indeed have to share the same carriage on that trip, which fortunately would not take more than a couple of hours, if that.

Kate tried, as a way of appeasing her temper, to read and take some notes whilst travelling, which proved to be difficult, due the poor condition of the road. She decided to close her book and look at the passing landscape through the carriage window, thinking about Sir Joshua's research and Hyperborea.

'Oh... I feel so much pain and the wound is bleeding again, but I must run, I cannot stop.' Then, falling on the grass, she cried, 'Even with this unbearable pain, I must keep going; I can still crawl... I might have a chance to escape... as long you never leave me...' She paused for a moment to touch the delicate necklace around her neck.

Breathing hard, Kate suddenly woke up. It was that nightmare again, and now she was certain there was something important in that dream, but what was it? What was so important, and at the same time so well-hidden deep inside her mind? Even though she did everything to recall, it was in vain.

Kate knew that it must be related to something she had seen recently, whilst no matter how hidden in her mind it was, she would unravel the enigma; that mystery would not perpetuate itself forever. She would find the answer.

With such promising weather, it didn't take long for them to arrive at the George Hotel. The guests' excitement was huge and sufficiently contagious for them to accept that they were on their own – their servants and maids were not invited to the party, probably because the hotel was not big enough; therefore they had to deal with their heavy luggage themselves.

'Do you think all those suitcases were really necessary?' Sir Christopher asked Sir Richard, indicating the growing mountain of cases being unloaded from the carriages.

'Bernard, stop smoking your pipe and carry our suitcases upstairs, before somebody takes them by mistake,' Charlotte ordered her husband.

'My dear lady, how many times do I have to tell you that we have three servants to take your luggage to your bedroom?' a miserable deep voice interrupted Charlotte.

'Did you see that, Bernard? This man is addressing me, instead of you. You are so useless,' she said.

'But you seem to be the one in charge of the luggage. This might be the reason why he addresses you; I am not saying anything,' Bernard replied, smoking his pipe calmly.

'Andrew, are we in the queue?' Kate asked, trying to establish good terms with her husband and leave behind the recent hostility.

'I don't know. Is there any? Well, we have two options: skip the queue and carry our luggage up, or join Sir Christopher and Sir Richard at the bar and have a drink,' Andrew suggested, hoping that Kate might agree with the second option.

'Maybe you're right. It is winter, and instead of carrying our luggage we should go to the end of the queue and give an opportunity for those servants to earn a good tip. Let's join Sir Richard and Sir Christopher for a glass of wine,' Kate enthused, trying to convince herself that their laziness was for a good cause.

'You are a sweetheart when you agree with me, did you know that?' Andrew laughed.

'Don't start. It was the weight of your books. The bags are too heavy...' Kate said, trying not to lose the battle.

'My books? You brought Sir Joshua's entire library,' Andrew replied, smiling.

'You are prejudiced, like all husbands, thinking that all extravagances emanate from their wives, and never from themselves,' Kate replied, approaching the two old fellows at the bar.

'I am sorry, but we were told that this bar is a sanctuary, therefore married couples are not allowed. However, we may deign to consider your case, if you have already overcome your quarrel,' Sir Christopher smiled.

'Yes, we have. A glass of wine now is essential to deal with the crowd in the hotel reception,' Andrew cheerfully responded.

They laughed, reinstating the good atmosphere amongst the four travellers, and after a few hours, everybody seemed well accommodated in their rooms. The rooms were a little on the small side, with old furniture, whilst parts of the building dated back almost two hundred years, and it was not exactly pristine. Something else was bothering Kate, though, but whatever it was she had the strange feeling that it would not take long to be revealed.

'What happened, Kate? You have been unusually quiet this last hour,' Andrew asked, noticing her introspective mood.

'Nothing, it is just a bad feeling. It might be because I am hungry,' Kate replied, not completely convinced.

'Me too, and I can't help thinking that we should have stayed at home. Perhaps excavating other archaeological sites closer to home is not a bad idea for next summer, what do you think?' Andrew asked whilst getting ready for dinner, not noticing that she was getting closer quietly, trying to catch him by surprise; and indeed she succeeded when she jumped and hugged him, shouting,

'That's a wonderful idea, I will be so happy!' she exclaimed.

'So, this is a perfect plan for next year then,' he agreed, and kissed her.

Later, Andrew and Kate arrived at the dinner lounge, taking the table that was assigned to them, and for the first time Kate had to agree with the prevailing opinion amongst the guests that Lord Henry had a peculiar way of dealing with people, or at least with his guests. This notion was reinforced when she realised they were about to share their table with Dr Turner and Dr Gruber – a certain recipe for disaster, knowing the four of them had very different opinions on controversial issues. However, she had to give credit to their hosts, who treated their guests to an exquisite dinner with unquestionably excellent wine, which fortunately (or unfortunately) delayed the controversial conversation for after dinner and the toast to the Queen. Lord Henry stood and addressed his gathering.

'Dear guests and friends, let's toast to the Queen, who played an essential role in enabling this event.' He raised his glass – 'Her Majesty, Queen Victoria!'

Everybody stood and raised their glasses and toasted the Queen (though some were disinclined, they thought they better had anyway). After everybody had sat down again, Lord Henry began to explain the reasons why they were there.

'My dear guests and friends, I know that you all may be curious about our presence here, at this time, on this particular day in the middle of nowhere,' he began, receiving a cold look from Mr Clark, the hotel's owner, who was standing at the door and didn't like to hear that his hotel was considered to be "in the middle of nowhere".

When Lord Henry was certain that he had the room's full attention, he continued.

'According to my calculations over the last nineteen years, tomorrow, late in the afternoon, it will be the winter solstice, which means that we will watch the sunset on what will be the shortest day of the year. The big surprise, though, will be the moon, which will rise in alignment with the setting sun tomorrow, appearing through the stone circle – to be more precise, from exactly where the Heel Stone is located,' Lord Henry declared proudly.

'I didn't understand anything,' Ellen complained to Charlotte in a whisper.

'Shhh... me neither, but the food was lovely. Let's see if they give some sort of explanation; perhaps we might ask Diana later...' Charlotte replied, whispering.

'Apart from the fact that the Celts liked to see the moon and the sun together in an alignment, what is the usefulness of this?' Dr Turner enquired of their host.

'Who said anything about Celts? I am an antiquarian, and my knowledge is subsidised by almost half a century of observation and accurate calculation. I can tell you with absolute certainty that Stonehenge was built long before the Celts came to Britain,' Lord Henry answered confidently.

'I told you that he was too old for her,' Ellen whispered to Charlotte again.

'Although I have been careful with my calculations, I have invited Sir Andrew Enfield, an eminent and famous archaeologist, to definitively confirm the measurements I made at that site,' Lord Henry announced, glancing at Andrew with a friendly smile.

'What exactly are we going to measure, Henry?' Andrew asked, trying to clarify his role in that event.

'You will be very proud to join me tomorrow, Andrew. There are four Station Stones set inside the henge, and according to my calculations, they form a precise rectangle, in which the tall Sarsen Stones form such an extraordinary circle.'

'And what were they used for?' Bernard asked, lighting his pipe.

'This is the reason why I invited Doctor Adrian Gruber...' Lord Henry explained.

'Oh no, this Ger... I mean... Austrian, again,' Dr Turner complained in a whisper, whilst Lord Henry added,

'Dr Gruber is a well-known anthropologist, linguist and geographer, and apart from his polemic and extremist theories about Aryanism, I think that he can be more useful if he contributes with his knowledge about religion and rituals.'

'You will have to provide much more evidence than just a few stones surrounding a rectangle,' Dr Gruber replied, challenging Lord Henry.

'Oh yes, I will, and if you want material evidence, you will have it too,' Lord Henry confirmed, adding,

'Years ago, Colt Hoare on the summer solstice noticed towards the southwest the alignment of the sunrise with the Heel Stone – at that time he didn't have the calculations that I have, so he didn't include the moon in his experiment. He followed the alignment until it reached a barrow, which is called Sun Barrow, and he excavated it.' Lord Henry paused and addressed his wife, in a theatrical way.

'My darling Diana, do you have the box?' he asked.

'Yes, my dear,' Diana responded, standing and presenting him with a small wooden box.

'Remarkable, Diana, always remarkable!' Peter said, ironically.

Lord Henry took the box as if it contained the Crown jewels and carefully opened it.

'This is what he found in the Sun Barrow, ladies and gentlemen.' Diana's husband displayed the two objects kept inside: a small dagger with a golden hilt, and a golden disc.

'It is impossible! This dagger and the golden disc disappeared almost fifty years ago,' Dr Turner intervened, adding, 'Colt Hoare didn't have any heirs. When he died, all his belongings and properties were sold in auction, and nobody has seen the dagger and the disc since then.'

'Nobody but me,' Lord Henry exclaimed proudly, beaming at the surprise on their faces.

'Tomorrow it will be the winter solstice, and if my calculations are correct, and I am certain that they are, we will observe the moon rise and sun set in perfect alignment with the Heel Stone; and if we face the northeast – if my calculations are correct – I am certain that we will find a barrow, which I will call "Moon Barrow", and who knows what can be found therein, my dear fellows?' He was positively beaming.

'Do you have a hunch?' Peter asked curiously.

'Yes, indeed, we shall find an important and wealthy warrior skeleton, or perhaps a priest, with a dagger and a lunar calendar disc...' Lord Henry replied enthusiastically, excited with people's interest in his theory.

'In gold or silver?' Ellen interrupted him, excited.

'Maybe both, Mrs Price. The Moon Barrow is supposed to be older and bigger than the Sun Barrow, and we have evidence that places where gold or silver was not in abundance, the ancients, like the Greeks, produced a metal called "electrum" – a mixture of gold and silver – which would be most fitting considering the conjunction of sun and moon, don't you think?' he replied.

'Henry, I am quite certain that the purpose of building the stone circle was not merely to indicate burials of powerful people from their communities; it might have been a place for other activities – religious, most certainly,' Andrew suggested.

'Lord Henry…' Kate interrupted, attracting looks of reproach from some of the guests. Kate was not the type of woman to be intimidated by a silent crowd, so characteristically she continued, noticing from the corner of her eye that Andrew was looking at her with a wicked smile, knowing that it was time for her to introduce an even bigger controversy to the discussion.

'Oh my dear Lady Kate, as I heard before you came, your presence would bring precious contribution to our research.' Lord Henry was delighted to have people who were actually interested in what he was doing.

'I am certain that you know… I am sorry… knew, Sir Joshua Egerton…' she began.

'Indeed, a great loss for all of us,' Lord Henry said, putting his hand to his left breast and lowering his head momentarily, theatrically.

'It is a very polemic subject, I am afraid, but his last wish was for his research to be continued after he died. He made sure his notes and books reached me safely.' Kate paused, waiting for some reaction, but her audience were silent. The ticking of an elegant clock on a fireplace could be heard. So she continued. 'In his notes, Sir Joshua attested that the stone circle… I mean… Stonehenge, might have been the venerated location of an oracle; in fact, two oracles – one being considerably older than the other,' Kate said.

'Interesting!' Lord Henry exclaimed, then asked, 'What else did he say about it?'

'I would say that he discovered a very definite connection between Stonehenge and the Greeks, more specifically – the Oracle of Apollo at Delphi,' she paused, looking around at the blank faces staring back at her. 'There are written testimonies from ancient Greek geographers, historians, mathematicians, and philosophers confirming that the Apollo myth of Delphi, placed the god in Greece only for a short period in the summer, then he left every year to Hyperborea *"an island with a stone circle beyond the land of the Celts"*,' she explained.

'I must say – Joshua was always very perceptive, and with unquestionable taste, my dear, when he chose you for a disciple,' Lord Henry declared triumphantly.

'I refuse to believe that to understand the birth of our civilisation we have to be here in the middle of nowhere, listening to a mad and senile man, and... a woman,' Dr Gruber said loudly.

'Who is the senile man?' Lord Tollemache enquired furiously.

'My wife has qualifications that you certainly would never be able to obtain, Dr Gruber,' Andrew claimed, equally furious at this outrageous outburst.

'There isn't any evidence pointing to Britain as Hyperborea. That civilisation was based in Scandinavia, the origin of a supreme and intellectual race, quite different from the rest of humanity,' Dr Gruber added, himself quite agitated.

'Wait a moment! I didn't say that the Hyperboreans were better than anybody else. They were probably farmers, with the same worries as us about the weather, crops, their health and peace.' Kate defended her point of view, receiving nods from amongst the guests who were upset at the Austrian's insults.

'They could probably have developed some basic astronomy, watching the movements of the sun and the moon, perhaps stars and constellations, like the Egyptians and Babylonians did.' Andrew hurried to defend Kate's hypothesis.

'Now I am completely confused, Charlotte,' Ellen complained, being interrupted by Peter, who explained in a whisper,

'It seems that they disagree about the way to observe the sky and predict the weather, my dear.' Peter tried to keep it simple.

'I don't think that they will come to an agreement, Peter, especially about British weather, which is the reason why we have always to carry a coat and umbrella, don't you agree, Charlotte?' Ellen whispered confidently.

'Of course, what they are trying to achieve is definitely nonsense. Even fishermen cannot predict the weather,' Charlotte agreed, whilst Peter and Bernard looked at each other.

'Lord Tollemache, are you jealous because British archaeology is much more advanced in Egypt? Are you trying to belittle the great findings and theories of our scholars, diverting attention to a pile of rocks in the middle of nowhere?' Dr Turner said defiantly, and continued. 'It took almost forty years to establish the British School at Athens, and now you want to diminish the value of the Greek contribution to our culture and science, trying to attract support for your private experiment to... to this place?'

'Wait a moment! This "nowhere" has a name, did you know that? You would be surprised at how many dignitaries have stayed here in my hotel; amongst them the Duke of Wellington himself after the battle of Waterloo,' Mr Clark, the owner of the hotel, intervened, very upset.

'We are not disputing supremacy over science, or disparaging one civilisation over another. Science speaks for itself from what is discovered and developed.' Andrew tried to compromise and to cool the discussion.

'This is the crucial mistake you all make!' The vicar intervened as prepared for war, and continued. 'Science fails where only God has the power to triumph. You are confused in thinking that the sun, the moon, and pagan gods have the answers for your questions, and in the end you will all be wrong, like the Egyptians and Babylonians were before you. When we think we have gotten the cure for an illness, evil throws us another. That is the reason why other civilisations perished, and ours will do as well if we continue to seek in worldly things the explanations that only faith in God can provide,' the vicar concluded.

'I agree with you, Reverend St Clair, this material world is full of death and illusion, and only God can provide healing, because He is Mind, and He will come to you if you let your mind faithfully focus on love and truth,' Miss Abington intervened in favour of the vicar.

'We agree with her, don't we, Charlotte? Only God knows how the weather will be like tomorrow, and if we pray with contrition, we will have a very sunny day,' Ellen declared, whilst her husband, Peter, discreetly lit another cigarette.

'Bravo, bravo, Vicar! I can see that you have ardent followers, and before you steal the other guests' support, let's do a libation to God, and pray for good weather tomorrow because, if it rains, there will not be sun, moon or stars for our experiment,' Lord Tollemache interrupted, hoping to prevent more religious discussion where it had no business.

'What did I tell you, Peter? British weather is unpredictable and only God knows better,' Ellen reassured in a whisper proudly.

Suddenly, a commotion that began in the reception hall came closer and closer, until a deep and thunderous voice announced at the entrance to the dining hall,

'Where is he? Where is he? Where are you, TOLLEMACHE?'

'What are you doing here, Edmund? This is a private celebration, and you were not invited. To be more precise, I booked the whole hotel, and you are not welcome; anyway, you have your inn.' Tollemache was furious and upset at this interruption and invasion of privacy.

'You, you diabolic specimen. What did you promise to the Queen to make her give me an ultimatum, eh?' Sir Edmund Mulgrave insisted, beetroot-faced.

'I didn't promise her anything,' Lord Tollemache responded. 'Her Majesty is extremely perceptive, and most interested in seeing the wonders of Britain being spoken around the world.' Lord Tollemache smiled at Sir Edmund ironically.

'You must have promised something to make her threaten to take my knighthood if I didn't allow you on my land, whatever stupidity you intend doing there,' Sir Edmund snapped, getting a reaction from most of the people in the hall.

'Oh...' exclaimed several voices in unison.

'Amesbury is mine, and so is Stonehenge,' the uninvited guest complained.

'Not for long, if I prove my theory, and Her Majesty buys Stonehenge for the Crown,' Lord Tollemache threatened him, full of himself.

Kate whispered to Andrew,

'Do you think she will?'

'I think the situation is getting out of control,' Andrew replied, quite worried.

'I will curse you, Tollemache, and you know I mean it,' Sir Edmund threatened, but he was immediately interrupted by another man in a very expensive suit, who entered the hall carrying a large canvas sack.

'Oh, Joseph, I am glad that you made it!' Lord Tollemache exclaimed, happy to divert attention from Sir Edmund.

'Oh no, not another "Sir"... I mean... another knight of the Queen,' Bernard complained to Peter in a whisper.

'A little late, Lord Tollemache, but here I am; and how many times I have to remind you that my name is James, not Joseph?' The mysterious man returned the greeting.

'Oh, it is just about letters only. My dear fellows, I introduce you to Dr James Baker. He is an archaeologist, an ethnologist to be precise, with a vast research concerned with human evolution.' Lord Tollemache introduced him.

'What kind of evolution are you talking about?' the vicar interrupted.

'This one, sir,' Dr Baker answered, opening the sac on one of the tables, revealing several skulls.'

'Oh, my God, he is a murderer!' Diana fainted, collapsing in her chair.

'Poor Diana,' Peter stated ironically, knowing that Diana was faking.

'He is going to kill us all, Bernard. Do something, he might be a cannibal; what did he do with the rest of the skeletons?' Charlotte asked in panic.

'Albert, you have to choose between me and your mad uncle,' Mary Abington declared to her fiancé vehemently.

'This bizarre celebration is getting even more fascinating,' Sir Christopher whispered to Sir Richard.

'As long as the skulls don't start to levitate,' Sir Richard replied, pouring more wine into his glass.

'I thought that you were a member of the Ghost Club in Cambridge,' Sir Christopher questioned.

'I never saw a skull without the rest of the skeleton, and Sir Arthur Conan Doyle will agree with me that this is very peculiar, because our ghosts are normal... whilst this... this situation is quite bizarre,' Sir Richard replied.

'You, you thief of tombs, have been stealing from my barrows all these years. I have no doubt about it. I will tell the Queen everything, and she will hang you two, Tollemache,' Sir Edmund shouted, in shock at the sight of the skulls, and quite enraged.

'Not before I personally denounce these two heretics to the archbishop and watch them burn in a public square,' the vicar declared.

'I am afraid they will have to burn most academics, especially Darwin.' Kate laughed to Andrew, who put his head in his hands and said,

'I knew we should have stayed at home. This is a circus. We still have time to get the carriage and leave this place before things get any worse, Kate.'

'Oh no, I refuse to leave. I want to see the end of this story,' Kate said.

'It will end tragically, as they are all mad, trust me,' Andrew insisted.

'Do you know how much a skull is on the black market, without tax?' Bernard asked Peter, whispering.

'Let me see... if we knew the price of the whole skeleton, we could have an estimate of the skull separate from the body,'

Peter suggested thoughtfully, then addressing the unexpected guest, he asked,

'Excuse me, how many skulls do you have?'

'About seven hundred,' Dr Baker replied.

'Seven hundred? You stole seven hundred of my skeletons?' Sir Edmund enquired, outraged.

'Who said that only you have barrows in Britain? I have to say that most of them are in a better condition than yours,' Dr Baker replied.

'Ah... ha! So you did excavate my barrows, otherwise how could you possibly compare the quality of the skulls?' Sir Edmund asked furiously.

'Excuse me, if you don't mind me asking, why do you collect skulls?' Sir Christopher asked. 'As a magistrate I need to know the perpetrator's motive to analyse the relevance of the crime... I mean... the *act per se*, and its contribution to the empire,' Sir Christopher interjected, less for knowing the extent of the crime than for the perverse desire of further heating the discussion.

'Exactly! We don't want to come across skeletons without skulls hanging around, unless if it could be considered a paranormal activity, which I doubt, as ghosts don't have skeletons, am I right, Dr Turner?' Sir Richard asked in a worried tone.

'My research will prove that different humans came from different races,' Dr Baker interrupted with authority, before Dr Turner had the chance to answer.

'Oh, another polygenist. So, do you want to prove that British skulls are bigger than the Scandinavian's?' Dr Gruber asked sarcastically.

'The size of the skull doesn't mean it has an advanced brain.' Dr Turner tried to make a point, as he objected to Dr Gruber's and Baker's theories.

'I will find my skeletons and if they don't have skulls, I will kill both of you, Tollemache, and from now on I will curse you as I did before, and you will end up like the others,' Sir Edmund declared, and left the hall furiously.

'I didn't understand. What did he mean with "like the others"?' Sir Richard asked, whilst the hotel's owner, who had quietly observed the argument, took the lead to explain, with his peculiar grave tone of voice.

'Two years ago, seven antiquarians started excavating barrows around here. They were looking for gold. They decided to do it hidden in the dead of night, as they didn't want Sir Edmund to know. They claimed that the man would never give permission, but in fact, they didn't want to share their finds with him.'

'Did they find any gold?' Diana, who had fainted, suddenly recovered to hear the rest of the story.

'Yes, indeed. At least that is what others say out there; however, no one had ever seen this gold. Later, when Sir Edmund heard the gossip about the violation of the barrows, he went completely mad, and cursed all of them.' He nodded seriously.

'Oh my God, how did he curse them?' Ellen asked in panic.

'He told them they would burn in hell in less than a year, and would not have any opportunity to spend the gold,' Mr Clark said in a sinister voice.

'What happened to those thieves?' Sir Richard asked, after a big sip of wine.

'For six months the body of each antiquarian was discovered here and there, all but one – the leader of the group, who disappeared without a trace,' Mr Clark replied, with a cold voice and a colder demeanour. He was deadly serious; a hush went around the room and only the ticking of the clock on the mantelpiece disturbed that silence.

'This seems to me to be a typical case of greed, in which the perpetrator becomes blind to the risks of the "profession" and doesn't see the step forward, or below, I don't remember which one it is,' the magistrate suggested.

'But I remember very well – he didn't see the step below, and he went to Hell,' the vicar interrupted.

'Did God witness the man kill the other six, Reverend?' the magistrate asked.

'Of course! Tell me one thing that happens in this world, that God doesn't see?' the vicar insisted confidently.

'The vicar is right. God sees everything. The poor lad lost his head,' the hotelier confirmed.

'He went mad?' Bernard asked, wide-eyed.

'I would not be surprised, if he started distributing gold round there,' Peter added, smoking his cigarette.

'No, you are all wrong. He actually lost his head... I mean to say... weeks later, his headless corpse turned up at the foot of a tree that people here used to think is sacred; the tree's been there for more than a thousand years, they say,' Mr Clark informed them.

'...and what about the treasure?' Peter enquired.

'It was never found,' Mr Clark replied.

'...and what happened with the head?' Sir Richard asked, scared.

'Neither found,' the hotelier replied, shaking his head, whilst the guests turned and looked at Dr Baker, the collector of skulls, who immediately began to speak in his own defence.

'I had nothing to do with it. My skulls are older than that,' he explained.

A morbid silence again fell on those present, whilst the owner left the dining hall with a strange smile on his face. A few moments later, Andrew broke the silence.

'Well, Lord and Lady Tollemache, after such an impressive dinner, full of surprises, if you would excuse us, it is time for bed.' Andrew grabbed Kate's arm and pulled her discreetly, since she seemed to want to continue listening to the discussion.

'It's too early, Andrew,' Kate complained.

'No, it is not, and we have a tough day tomorrow, trust me,' Andrew whispered to her, and reluctantly, she left with him and they returned to their room.

Back in the hall, Lord Tollemache was talking with Dr Baker whilst examining the skulls. In the other hand, Diana, who was frustrated and annoyed because nobody had noticed her faint, composed herself and joined Ellen and Charlotte, whilst Peter and Bernard were busy discussing their plans.

'Do you think that the whole head is worth more than just the skull?' Bernard asked.

'Of course, Bernard, I am sure that eyes and brain put the price up,' Peter confirmed.

'I will not allow you to buy and sell heads. They have souls which belong to God, Peter,' Ellen opposed him, annoyed.

'Don't worry, darling, I will only negotiate the evil heads.' Peter tried to calm her down, with a tender smile.

'Ellen, if he will only sell the evil heads, you could start to advertise your husband's head, because he is the chief of evils. Why don't you consult your solicitor? You might become a very rich widow,' Diana said sarcastically.

'What you had just said is not very Christian, Diana. I agree that evil heads might be valuable, but Peter is not actually evil.' Ellen defended her husband.

'Why don't I try it first? Just to see if Bernard dead would be more useful than alive,' Charlotte said to Diana, loud enough for her husband to overhear.

'You will be disappointed, my dear Charlotte, I am not evil, and I am worth more alive than dead,' Bernard said, smoking his pipe, and continued, 'By the way, Peter, how many "Sirs" we have here?'

'Let me see… Sir Richard and Sir Christopher; Sir Andrew and Sir Edmund have just left; and an earl; why?' Peter asked, curious.

'The Queen might be accepting applications for knighthoods; maybe we should apply, don't you think? We have been contributing to the empire's economy for years,' Bernard suggested.

'We don't have to write on the form anything about the goods we brought from Greece last year, do we? I didn't pay tax on that, did you?' Peter asked, a little worried.

'No, but we should fill the application forms in together to avoid contradiction,' Bernard said.

'Peter, will I have to call you "Sir"?' Ellen asked.

'Don't worry about it, Ellen, the most important thing is that you will become a "Lady",' Peter replied, trying to tease Diana.

'Like Diana?' Ellen asked, excited, looking to Diana and Charlotte.

'Finally, Bernard, you decided to be useful,' Charlotte declared, getting excited at the prospect.

'Sir Peter and Sir Bernard? Unbelievable!' Diana shook her head.

'Why not? Anybody can be a "Sir" nowadays,' Peter added, delighted with the results of his provocation.

'Nothing coming from you and Bernard surprises me, Peter,' Diana replied sarcastically.

'Hopefully you will increase your contribution to the parish, when you are knighted,' the vicar addressed Peter and Bernard.

'Well, that rather depends on whether you enlighten me or not, vicar,' Bernard replied provocatively.

'What do you mean? I am on a mission, and I don't have time for your silly things tonight,' the vicar warned him.

'It is just a simple question – if it is too late to save the body, as in my case and Peter's, isn't the vicar's duty to save the souls for God?'

'Wait a moment, I am a little bit confused here. Is God willing to save our minds or our souls?' Peter argued.

'The soul, of course,' the vicar replied.

'But Miss Abington stated eloquently that God is Mind and the power of Mind can heal, therefore God-Mind heals the body, which doesn't leave any space for the soul, does it?' Peter intervened.

'Not exactly...' The vicar tried to speak, but he was interrupted by Mary Abington.

'Yes, he is right. *Science of Christ's Love* assures the power of God-Mind over this world full of lies and evils,' she said authoritatively.

'I told you, there is a misunderstanding here,' Bernard said, and addressed the magistrate. 'Sir Christopher, could you please clarify a complex situation. What does the law judge: the soul or the mind?' e asked.

'The law is clear – if the perpetrator is condemned, we incarcerate the whole lot,' the magistrate replied eloquently.

'What do you mean with "the whole lot"?' Sir Richard intervened, confused.

'The body with all his companions and accessories: the soul, the mind, the evil, etc,' Sir Christopher replied.

'But the soul belongs to God, doesn't it, Vicar?' Peter asked.

'Nobody has any authority to arrest the soul, only God... I mean... God doesn't arrest souls, he saves them,' the vicar informed them.

'Even if the soul is in the body of a perpetrator?' Peter asked, confused.

'Exactly. The wolf and the lamb are both creatures of God.' The vicar defended his position.

'What has a wolf got to do with the vicar?' Ellen asked, completely confused.

'Don't worry, darling, it was just a metaphor,' Peter tried to explain.

'Oh, no, metaphors again, this one is very complicated,' Ellen complained.

'I don't know anything about the soul, because the *Science of Christ's Love* deals only with mind and evil, and Mind is God, therefore you cannot arrest the Mind,' Miss Abington intervened defiantly.

'I am getting so confused, Peter. I don't think there is space for so many things – soul, mind, evil; at least not in my brain,' Ellen complained, looking for support.

'Don't worry, my darling. Apart from evil, you can choose one of the others to be your accessory, and you will be fine,' Peter comforted her.

'He's right, Ellen, your husband is the only one who has evil for company,' Diana added, bored with the direction of the conversation.

'This is not fair, why does everybody blame evil for everything? God is the one who gave free will to men, not evil,' Peter complained.

'Are you sure that evil can be arrested? He seems to multiply here, there...' Bernard asked the magistrate.

'Couldn't you just arrest the soul and mind and let the poor body make an appeal for the next life?' Peter interjected.

'Something is not quite right, Chris, too many accessories. Are you sure about the "whole" perpetrator?' Sir Richard asked.

'Enough! This is a very complex trial, I must say to you once and for all: since the body cannot be hung more than once, we shall give the body the right to choose which accessory he wants to take with him,' Sir Christopher declared.

'Impossible, you cannot hang God's souls,' the vicar complained.

'Yes, we can, if it is the last wish of the body before he dies; and if the perpetrator's body wants the soul with him, we shall allow it. Don't forget that God gave man free will,' the magistrate confirmed. 'By the way, where does this *Science of Christ's Love* come from?' he asked.

'From the United States of America, proposed by Mrs Mary Caroline Thompson, who says that only God-Mind exists, and because the material world doesn't, all illnesses are not real,' Miss Abington answered with evident conviction.

'I knew that this could not be an English science. Our former colonists are not very bright, don't you think, Diana?' Lord Tollemache turned and asked his wife.

'You should ask the magistrate to arrest your nephew's fiancée for ruining our tipple celebration,' Diana complained.

'Oh, she didn't ruin it. Edmund did, because he was not invited to come to our party,' Lord Tollemache said, upset with the way the dinner party had ended.

'You see? I told you to not defend her, and I warned you before, I will kill you and her as well, if you try to take her side instead of mine,' Diana reminded him.

'I am not defending her; I just don't think that religion is the main problem. Prestige, honour and money are the things that really keep the world going, or at least they contribute heavily to make life take different, and unexpected, turns,' Lord Tollemache responded.

'This is your problem, Lord Tollemache,' Dr Gruber intervened. 'You think that your British titles and money make you better than us intellectuals and scientists, but you are not. What I witnessed here tonight confirmed what I have been trying to prove for years: that my countrymen and I are descended from a different race from that of the British.'

'What do you mean with "different race", Dr Gruber? We all descend from Adam and Eve?' The vicar interrupted him.

'I am sorry, but I must intervene, because Austrian wine is not at all good, therefore your race isn't perfect or superior than other Europeans, as you proclaim. Even Greek wine is superior to Austria's,' Sir Richard stated vehemently.

'...and what about British wine?' Dr Gruber defied him.

'Hm... I don't think that wine should be a polemic issue about our origin as Adam and Eve ate apples, not grapes,' Bernard interjected, and added, 'That is the reason why God got so angry, because He thought the cider was His alone. We British grow apples, not grapes.' Bernard smiled at the Austrian.

'I told you before that some translators of the Bible didn't specify the fruit,' the vicar corrected.

'This is insane! You British are insane, and you should all burn in Hell,' Dr Gruber declared, got up and left furiously. Once he had gone, the occupants of the room noticed another noise growing louder by the minute. It transpired to be Dr Turner, who was deeply asleep and snoring loudly.

'Well, my dear guests... the remaining ones... at least, I think that we have had ample entertaining this evening, so my wife and I should have a rest and prepare for tomorrow.' Lord Tollemache announced, smiling as usual. Then he lifted his wife's hand and kissed it gently, leaving the dinner hall with her, followed by the others, who suddenly realised how very late it was.

Chapter 8

'It is so cold and dark. He will never find me... Please, hurry, I am dying.' Kate took a deep breath, for what she thought would be the last time.

Suddenly she woke up, sweating. As ever it was a great relief when she woke from her persistent nightmares. In them she was waiting for Andrew, but he never came, thus she died, cold and alone.

It might be the wine or the tiredness of the travel, Kate thought to herself, noticing she was very thirsty. Quietly she got up, then looked at Mr Bear, who seemed to reproach her.

'Shhh... don't make any noise, I only need a glass of water, and I will be back soon. No, I don't need your help, and I'm not afraid. I have experienced worse darkness before, you know that,' Kate said to Mr Bear in a whisper. Then she left the bedroom, leaving Andrew, who was equally tired from the journey, deep asleep.

Kate could not complain about the George Hotel, as even "in the middle of nowhere" the corridors and the hall were lit by gas lamps hanging on the walls, making it much easier to walk without carrying a candle. She didn't know what time it was but the hotel was in complete silence, apart from a creaking floor-board under the carpet. Kate had to admit that winter always gave her the impression that the light of the day had to ask for permission to come out.

The silence didn't last long though, as Kate heard a strange noise from a floor below. She thought that some of the guests must be still awake, but as she reached the top of the stairs she could see near the bottom a black dog looking up at her, and it was snarling. After a few moments she realised that it seemed to be the same black dog she had seen in front of the restaurant in Paris. It could not be.

Whilst the dog was snarling at Kate, she noticed he had very peculiar eyes, which were a mixture of red and orange colours, as if from a smouldering fire. Strangely, Kate felt attracted to the dog, and she could neither think properly nor run away; she found herself unable to move, whilst everything around her seemed to move gradually from front to back. Suddenly the dog stopped snarling and began to whine, sitting on his hind legs and staring at her, like the time she saw him in front of the restaurant in Paris.

Kate started descending the stairs as if hypnotised. Then, when she was halfway down, after a vain attempt to hold on to the railing, a strange vertigo overcame her, and she closed her eyes and fell.

The silence in the middle of the night was disturbed by the noise of her fall, which was loud enough to wake up some of the guests, including Andrew, who, realising that Kate was not beside him, shouted her name loudly, 'Kate!'

He jumped out of bed and ran out of the room with a dreadful feeling that something awful had happened to his wife. When he reached the top of the stairs, he saw Kate at the bottom and began shouting her name desperately until he reached her side. He cradled her in his arms, greatly relieved to see that she was breathing, now gradually regaining consciousness. Gently he carried her to a comfortable sofa nearby in the reception and began to examine her to see if she was injured.

'What happened, Kate? Are you hurt? Do you need a drink?' he asked anxiously.

'Yes, please, I wanted some water. I'm sorry, I didn't want to wake you,' Kate replied, more than a little embarrassed when she realised that some of the other guests were standing around watching, still in their night-clothes, equally worried about her. Gradually a small crowd gathered around Kate and Andrew, amongst them Sir Christopher and Sir Richard, proving again that age makes you tougher as they were both in great spirits in spite of how much they had drunk earlier that night.

The owner of the hotel and his daughter Eleanor were there as well, and they both looked at each other suspiciously.

'Lady Katherine, what happened to you?' Eleanor asked in a worried voice.

'I think that I slipped on the stairs, maybe. Do you have a dog here? I mean... a big black one?' Kate asked.

Eleanor looked to her father, raising an eyebrow, and replied,

'No, we don't,' definitively.

However, the hotelier corrected his daughter immediately.

'Well, it depends on which dog you are talking about,' he said.

'Don't be silly, Dad. Please, forget what he said... he... he's getting old,' his daughter interrupted him.

'What dog are you talking about?' Sir Richard asked, clearly worried by this conversation.

Meanwhile, another three guests joined the unexpected meeting in reception – Dr Turner, Lady Diana and Peter. Fortunately, most of the guests seemed to be sleeping deeply in Morpheus' arms, since people react differently to a good quality wine.

'Could anybody explain what happened here?' Dr Turner insisted authoritatively.

'Do you see this leg here, Doctor?' Mr Clark asked, tapping his leg three times with the knuckles of his hand, leaving no doubt that it was made from wood.

'I told you, Dad, don't be silly,' his daughter implored.

'I think that we deserve an explanation, immediately. I don't want to waste my entire night in this reception,' Diana demanded.

'I bought this hotel two years ago at auction. Since then I regret every minute of my miserable life,' Mr Clark began to explain.

A sudden gust of wind interrupted him and blew open a window which was not locked properly, sending a cold blast of winter air inside, unsettling the guests. Eleanor went and closed it, double-checking the latch was firmly seated. Mr Clark then continued.

'This hotel belonged to a man called Adam Fairfax. "Mr Fair", people used to call him round here. He was a proper gentleman and very discreet. He had a wife and daughter, and he used to walk his dog in the field every day, as things in the hotel were usually very calm, people told me.' After a pause to relight his pipe, he resumed his tale.

'One day, a couple of guests came down for breakfast and waited for him or his wife to come to the reception, but after an hour waiting to no avail, they took it upon themselves to look for the owners. The two guests were petrified, though, when they found the body of Mr Fairfax's wife in the kitchen – she had been murdered by stabbing.' He paused and looked around his audience whilst they took this in. 'They continued the search for him, but found nothing – not him, nor his daughter, nor the dog; all three had completely vanished. The police came and searched everywhere, but turned up nothing.' The hotelier tamped his pipe and sucked on it. Once it was burning satisfactorily again, he resumed.

'Time passed, and the search for the rest of the family was getting cold. Not only could they not locate Mr Fairfax and his daughter, the police were also unable to locate any relatives.' Mr Clark paused again, aware of being the centre of attention of such a distinguished audience, who were listening wide-eyed and aghast; he continued.

'After a year of intense searching, no one was able to find him or his daughter's whereabouts, nor a relative to inherit the hotel.'

'...and the dog?' Sir Richard asked, wide-eyed.

'Nor he,' the owner replied.

'Then they put the hotel up for auction, and I bought it, as I had been looking to change my business for years. People used to say that his dog was seen hereabouts, sometimes barking, sometimes whining. Rumours that the hotel was haunted started to circulate, and the locals insisted that the black dog was searching for his missing owner.'

'Superstition, pure superstition,' interjected Dr Turner, adding, 'Silly stories are common amongst country folk. Old inns like this one are often the target of imaginative minds, no doubt fuelled by ale and brandy.'

'How dare you call my hotel an inn? It's registered as a hotel, and I pay tax accordingly. I told you earlier – the Duke of Wellington stayed here, after Waterloo.' Mr Clark was outraged by the sleight. Then Sir Richard intervened to defend the hotelier.

'I am not so sure, Dr Turner. In my experience I can say hand on heart that there is often something tangible behind such superstitions.' He nodded slowly, as if that lent gravitas to his words.

'Mr Clark, I think I can confirm that I saw Mr Fairfax's dog. It was down there, near the stairs, with firelight in his eyes, looking straight at me,' Kate divulged in almost a whisper, knowing that no one would believe her; then, she added, 'Everything seemed so real. It's very hard to accept that I was delusional.'

'You are very tired, Kate, we all drank too much at the dinner,' Andrew comforted her. 'I think that a cup of cocoa will help you recover, and when we wake up tomorrow, we might go home after breakfast. I am quite sure that Lord Henry will understand if we have to leave,' Andrew added.

'Excuse me, Mr Clark,' Sir Christopher chimed in, 'you didn't tell us what this story has to do with your wooden leg.' He was interested to know the whole story, especially concerning the grisly murder of Fairfax's wife.

After a long draw from his pipe, the owner glanced to his leg with a disgusted look and continued.

'It happened six months after my daughter and I moved here. I used to laugh when people talked about the ghost dog. I didn't realise that I was cursed when I bought this hotel; anyone who bought it would be cursed, and I was the unlucky one.'

'Only the buyer is cursed, or guests as well?' Sir Richard asked, feeling a little unruffled.

'I think that Lady Katherine might answer that question, sir,' the hotelier replied, then resumed, 'As I said, six months after we moved here, I was at the top of the stairs lighting the gas lamps when I heard that unmistakable noise – it was him, staring at me from down there, snarling with fire in his eyes. I lost my balance when I saw him coming up towards me, and that was the last thing I remember, because when I woke up days later, they said that my leg was badly broken. It affected my circulation in such a way that they had to amputate, due to gangrene.' The owner finished his tale, and the atmosphere around the crowd of guests became extremely morbid, with one looking to another without having the courage to be the first to say anything, until Dr Turner said,

'Lady Katherine, I am afraid that fertile minds often let their imagination run wild, and their unconscious plays tricks on them. As you all know I am a member of the Psychical Society, an experienced scientist who specialises in paranormal activity.' His audience was listening intently, so he continued. 'I can state categorically there is always a rational and logical explanation for such events, which are often mistakenly attributed as being religious in nature and macabre by those without... I should say... a superior mind. Although women are not gifted with a rational mind, I implore to your good sense to accept that what happened to you tonight was probably caused by gas poisoning from the lamps; it can cause hallucinations, even death,' he explained confidently.

'Hallucinations?' Kate said in a whisper, looking to Andrew, not at all convinced; however, as a scientist, she knew she should at least consider this possibility.

'Yes. It seems that we have in this hotel a potential case of collective hallucination, instigated no doubt by Lord Henry earlier, I dare say,' Dr Turner confirmed.

'That is enough Doctor Turner, thank you. You have had your stage for your criticisms and to make your point. Kate needs to rest for our journey back tomorrow,' Andrew growled at him.

'Wait a moment, I'm not going anywhere. With or without hallucinations I have a mission to accomplish – important research was entrusted to me and I intend to continue it; I owe it to Sir Joshua,' Kate argued, then, she stood up and addressed everybody.

'I apologise for waking you. I'm feeling much better now, and I'm very lucky as I didn't break any bones tumbling down those stairs. If you don't mind, I will go back to bed,' Kate said, heading to the stairs, followed by Andrew, who didn't like to be contradicted but could do little when his wife had made her mind up about something.

On the way towards the stairs, Kate's attention was caught by a small picture hanging on the wall. She stopped to examine the photograph of a man with a black dog, and a woman sitting with a young girl beside them; Kate could not help but ask,

'Is this the late Mr Fairfax and his family?'

'Yes, Lady Katherine, they are,' Mr Clark answered. Kate looked at it for a moment, intrigued. She nodded, then continued up the stairs to her bedroom, deep in thought – there was something very peculiar about that photograph, but she could not say what it was. She hoped she would be able to work out what was so bothersome about it.

Seeing that Kate appeared to be relatively recovered from her fall, people gradually began to disperse. The last people to leave the reception apart from the hotelier were Diana and Peter. After a brief thoughtful pause, Peter addressed Mr Clark.

'I would like to invite Lady Diana for a glass of wine, if your bar is still open.'

'Yes, sir, the bar is never closed when one of us is around,' he replied politely, but added, 'I will get you a bottle of wine, but we will have to leave you to your own devices, because we have to wake up at the crack of dawn to serve breakfast. Lord Henry wants to leave early for the stone circle,' the owner sighed.

Diana was quiet and somewhat hesitant, but ended up accepting the glass of wine that Peter offered her. After the owner and his daughter left the bar, he said to Diana,

'I have to admit, my dear, that "Lady Diana Tollemache" is an eminently suitable title for you, and I have to say this one is much better than the first; at least he has sense of humour and an exquisite wine cellar. This means that you are refining your taste with age. When is the funeral, by the way?' Peter provoked her.

'I wondered when you would start your insinuations and ironies. I knew that you would not disappoint me,' Diana replied sarcastically.

'Oh, come on, Diana, you cannot see yourself married to him for very long, can you? In five years I imagine you knocking on my door, desperately looking for old Peter,' he replied, smiling.

'Don't be silly, I have never knocked on your door,' Diana retorted, grimacing.

'No, you didn't,' Peter nodded. 'There is always a first time for everything, though. You know me, I am a believer, and I never lose hope. At the same time I know you very well, and you always have a card hidden up your sleeve,' Peter added, whispering the last.

'You...' Diana started to protest, but he interrupted her.

'No, please, don't tell me. You know how I love your surprises,' Peter said, stubbing out his cigarette; then he took the last sip of wine from his glass, before leaving Diana alone and annoyed in the reception.

Meanwhile, upstairs,

'Are you feeling better?' Andrew asked Kate, who was lying on the bed with her head on his chest.

'Strangely, I feel like I was reborn, somehow,' Kate replied, smiling at him as if nothing untoward had happened.

'Do you have any idea how serious what happened downstairs was? You could be dead now.' Andrew was annoyed because she seemed not to take it seriously.

'Yes, I know, but I didn't, and I will be very upset if you decide to pack everything and go home,' she replied.

'You like to get into trouble, don't you?' Very well, we will stay, but you can be sure that I will keep you in my sights all the time from now on.'

'Do you think that I am cursed?' she asked, teasing him.

'You love to provoke me, don't you? Let's get some sleep; I have a bad feeling about tomorrow.' He cuddled her, and they fell asleep in each other's warm embrace.

Breakfast the next morning was very decorous, though people were quietly discussing the events of the previous night. Some of the guests had been entirely unaware of the incident as they had been sleeping soundly and hadn't heard a thing. Some regretted, though, not being downstairs to listen to the hotelier's macabre story about the black dog, and judging by the nature of the chatter, Kate realised that some of them were not really interested in the astronomical experiment at Stonehenge.

However, everybody was indebted to their host Lord Henry, as he was footing the entire bill for their hotel stay, as well as expenses and transport costs, so it would not be polite to deny him the audience he wanted, but Kate would not be surprised if there was a desire amongst them crying out for rain in order to ruin the day and halt his experiment.

Curious about the weather, Kate approached the window and could see a patch of sky – it was clear and unusually pleasant for winter. British weather, though, was so unpredictable, and rain might arrive later, leaving no option but to abandon the experiment. She sensed the guests were eager to be back at the hotel by evening to see if the black dog would make another appearance, if the ghost had not yet finished his job.

Although Stonehenge was less than two miles from the hotel, the ladies decided to use carriages – offered by Lord Henry, who spared no effort to get as many supporters to Stonehenge as possible for his endeavour. In their wisdom, Sir Christopher, Sir Richard and the vicar, with the excuse of looking after the equipment, claimed a lift in the carriages which were full of tents, and most importantly, wine and hampers of food, intended to sustain the guests for the duration of his experiment at Stonehenge. Happily for all concerned, this would coincide with the no less glorious British afternoon tea-time.

Scientists and other onlookers decided to take advantage of the good weather to walk to Stonehenge, using the opportunity to take measurements, observations and important notes along the way, as well as enjoying a chat with their fellows. Kate thought it prudent not to walk, following the events of the night before, so she travelled in a carriage. As she drew near the monument, she was enthralled by the landscape that was gradually unravelling in front of her. Nothing could prepare her, though, for the sight of Stonehenge, which left no doubts about

Sir Joshua's research – that fascinating megalithic monument had an important reason to be there, she was absolutely certain.

Servants had been hired to set the tents up and carry things from one place to another, and they buzzed around like busy bees. Whilst the ladies were sitting and chatting, Kate walked around Stonehenge, going to the centre of the circle, completely absorbed with Sir Joshua's ideas and her own. It was incredible how they all came together in her mind, depicting the picture of what Stonehenge's original purpose could have been.

Kate was surprised how time passed so quickly, and when Andrew found her a few hours later, he was very thirsty and terribly excited.

'Henry was right, Kate. Would you make me a cup of tea? You will not believe it, but those four station stones not only make a perfect rectangle, they also form two Pythagorean triangles, like the four stones in Brittany; the stone circle fits perfectly inside the rectangle, and they all share the same centre. What do you think of that?' he asked, smiling like a little boy in front of a cake shop window.

'Are you certain?' Kate asked whilst pouring tea in his cup and handing him a sandwich, which suddenly became the most delicious sandwich he had ever tasted in his life, probably due to the fact that he hadn't eaten anything since breakfast. Coupled with the exciting news, such a combination could not be more pleasant.

'Mostly certain, whoever built this had an incredibly advanced knowledge of astronomy and geometry. It makes me wonder what could have happened to break the continuity, or its development,' Andrew said.

'Please, don't say that in front of the vicar, or he will try to convince everybody that it was God's punishment for our boldness.' Kate laughed.

After they had eaten their sandwiches together, they sat on two small wooden folding wood and canvas chairs inside one of the tents to discuss their theories. They had barely begun their conversation when Lord Henry joined them, equally excited.

'So? What do you think?' he asked, anxious to hear their opinion.

'Well, the alignment of the sun and the moon with the "Heel stone" is still to be investigated, but so far I must agree with you about the three perfect geometric forms here: one circle, one rectangle forming two Pythagorean triangles – all three with a common centre.' Andrew pointed to the place where the centre might be.

'...and you, Lady Kate?' Lord Henry asked.

'Such precision could not be coincidence. Although the purpose was probably religious, we cannot ignore their knowledge of geometry; if you prove the alignment of the sun and moon later, we might witness their astronomical knowledge as well,' Kate declared.

'Tell him, about Sir Joshua's theory,' Andrew encouraged her.

'His hypothesis, and I am inclined to agree with him,' Kate explained, 'is that a temple belonging to a moon goddess was built first – represented by the rectangle formed by the station stones. Later, they built the stone circle inside the rectangle and dedicated it to another god, one related to the sun. Sir Joshua believed they were designed for Artemis – Apollo's twin sister, and Apollo and his oracle, respectively. That is the reason the station stones and the Sarsen circle share the same centre – they were intrinsically related.'

'So you both agree that the rectangle formed by the station stones seems to be older than the stone circle?' Lord Henry asked them.

'Yes, it might be,' Andrew confirmed, nodding.

'Did Joshua believe that the Greeks visited Stonehenge and were aware of the native knowledge of geometry and astronomy?' Lord Henry asked excitedly.

'Since the construction of their temples, especially the one dedicated to Apollo in Delphi seems to have started not earlier than eight hundred BC, everything suggests that Stonehenge is older,' Andrew concluded optimistically.

'So we are the Hyperboreans!' Lord Henry exclaimed proudly; then he announced, 'I cannot wait to see the face of those two silly scientists out there.'

'Lord Henry, wait, please, I think there is more than that...' Kate interrupted him.

'Yes? Please tell me, Lady Kate,' Lord Henry encouraged her, sitting on a chair next to her to hear more, as it seemed there was much more to be known about the stone circle than he expected. Kate had to refrain from laughing, as she knew that Andrew was getting irritated with Lord Henry calling her "Lady Kate"; then she continued.

'Sir Joshua also believed that Pythagoras visited this site at some point, perhaps when his enemies destroyed his school and killed most of his disciples. He might have escaped and left Greece in a hurry. Historians are contradictory about his death – some say that he escaped with his family and a few disciples; others say that he was killed in the attack; in fact, nobody knows precisely what happened to Pythagoras, and some of his theories were attributed to his disciples, not to him,' Kate explained, then continued.

'If he escaped to Britain, the people who lived here, the Hyperboreans, might have developed his understanding of the equilibrium between soul, mind and body, I would say.'

'Yes, indeed, and if I am not mistaken, the Pythagoreans also believed in transmigration of the soul after death,' Lord Henry agreed.

'Herodotus and other historians referred to Asclepius, Apollo's son, the god of medicine who, according to the myth, lived in Hyperborea with his five daughter...'

'That's very interesting,' Lord Henry exclaimed.

'Pythagoras or his disciples also developed the musical theory concerning the tones and harmony that we still use today. Don't forget that Apollo is the god of music and patron of the nine Muses,' Kate concluded, caught by surprise by an exclamation behind her.

'Fascinating, Lady Kate,' Sir Christopher said proudly. 'Joshua Egerton, wherever he is now, certainly not in Paradise according to the vicar, would be proud of you two,' he stated, referring to Andrew and Kate. Sir Richard, who was with him, nodded agreement.

'I didn't understand what you said about transmigration of the soul, Lord Henry,' Sir Richard asked in a concerned tone.

'Although the theory did not originate with Pythagoras, he firmly believed that the soul was reincarnated in another body after death, and along with it "the mind",' Lord Henry explained. 'According to him, knowledge would be saved and transmitted, hibernating and transmigrating who knows how many times. Hundreds of years, perhaps thousands would pass, and that "knowledge" hibernating in somebody's soul would surface at the right moment, in the right place,' he explained.

'Did he say anything about ghosts?' Sir Richard enquired.

'Oh no, I refuse to talk about your ghosts, Sir Richard,' Kate snapped. 'Don't forget that Dr Turner gave a very reasonable explanation yesterday, and I am inclined to agree with him – it was the poisonous effect of the lamp's gas,' Kate reproached him.

'So what about your birds, the eagle-owls, are they an optical illusion as well?' Sir Richard insisted.

'He's right, Kate, you might consider the possibility…' Andrew teased her, but she interrupted him, now furious.

'Oh, you as well? I know what your problem is – you two cannot accept a female scientist. You have to find something irrational to link to me. That way you can depreciate my merit.'

'Ah, so that is the reason why you don't want to admit that those birds follow you, am I right?' Andrew provoked her again, laughing.

'I will not listen to your silliness, Sir Andrew Enfield,' Kate declared, leaving the tent, followed by Andrew and Sir Richard, whilst Lord Henry and Sir Christopher stayed behind.

'What a temper! I like that! A man could never be bored in such company.' Lord Henry laughed.

'Oh, this is nothing. You haven't seen her in action yet,' Sir Christopher said, nodding his head, agreeing with his friend.

'Do you think that she understood my words the other night in my house, Chris?' Lord Henry asked.

'Oh yes, indeed; she is a very discerning girl, Henry, and I can't think of anybody more qualified for the difficult task of being a Guardian of Alexandria's Library. I am worried for her safety though, as she seems to like the danger that the unknown is sometimes tied to,' Sir Christopher replied in a concerned tone.

'I don't blame her, Chris. Don't forget we had the same spirit when we were younger. You cannot imagine how I felt when I was told about Professor Regina Davis' death, in Greece last year. I never forgot her spirit and enthusiasm. I had a crush on her, did you know that?'

'Have you met her before?' Sir Christopher asked, surprised by his friend's confession.

'Of course, she was one of the most intelligent people in this world. But she would not marry me, she was married to her job; a wise choice, I must admit,' Lord Henry said nostalgically.

'Indeed, my friend, indeed,' Sir Christopher agreed.

'Does Kate remember where Alexandria's Library was buried?' Lord Henry enquired, giving the impression that he wanted to know more about that episode.

'No, she doesn't. According to her, when the fanatic Ottoman killed Regina in the cavern, there was an earthquake, and she was the only one to escape. After trying for hours to find the way out, she was thirsty, tired and confused; completely lost indeed, and she doesn't remember the direction she took as she was blindfolded when she first arrived at the cavern before the incident,' Sir Christopher replied.

'Well, maybe she doesn't then,' Lord Henry said quietly.

'Do you think? She has some knowledge of navigation, and she also has her own compass. Anyway, the sky was clear that Greek summer night. In my opinion, Kate would be the last person in the world to get lost,' Sir Christopher suggested.

'Do you think that she is testing us?' Lord Henry asked.

'She may not trust any of us which means she is taking this job seriously. We have to keep an eye on her – don't forget that we are her Guardians,' Sir Christopher reminded them, a little worried.

'Does she know that Joshua Egerton was a Guardian?' Lord Henry insisted.

'She might know, being intelligent the way she is,' Sir Christopher replied.

'What about Andrew, how much does he know?' Lord Henry asked.

'I suppose he doesn't know anything, otherwise he would have come to me, not only with questions, but also furious that we involved his wife in this dangerous affair, don't you think?' Sir Christopher asked.

'It is a shame. Andrew would be a great addition to our Order, and he would know how to look after her, making our job a little easier. Do you remember last night? We both had an idea after dinner how people, even those with significant academic qualifications, are intolerant to new ideas, or completely blind to the "truth",' Lord Henry replied, sad and disappointed at the same time.

'Unfortunately, Andrew would be blind to the importance of our endeavour, and afraid that she might be in danger. Who knows what he might do? That is the reason why I am certain she didn't tell him anything. She might want to protect him, I suspect,' Sir Christopher explained.

'Regina, Joshua and John, we are running short on our Order, Chris. What is happening with this world? There is so much intolerance, anger and hatred; we were supposed to get better after these millennia, don't you think?' Lord Henry complained.

'We are heading for a war, I'm afraid,' Sir Christopher stated.

'Oh yes, I have no doubt; unfortunately, another one which makes our job even more difficult. From time to time, fanatics and madmen are always burning words of wisdom.'

'…as well as the wise men who wrote and gave meaning to those words, my dear fellow,' Sir Christopher added sadly.

'Kate is right, it is better to forget for a while that the contents of the Library of Alexandria still exist; better buried than dead. We shall not lose hope, though,' Lord Henry insisted confidently.

'Hmm… I am certain you haven't; getting married again has rejuvenated you. You seem twenty years younger,' Sir Christopher teased him.

'Definitely! Let's enjoy the last few years that we have ahead, if we have them; and don't forget that today is the shortest day of our yearly cycle, and we must get ready for the most important event in recent astronomy,' Lord Henry declared in a theatrical tone.

The two of them left the tent and headed towards the mysterious event that was to unfold in Stonehenge itself.

Chapter 9

Despite the fact that the people involved in the event were unable to reach a consensus on which deity – god or goddess – would be responsible for the clear late afternoon, whoever was in charge didn't disappoint. The shortest day of the year gradually unfolded in a glorious mixture of light blue and light purple, whilst the cold sun graced them with its majestic presence and light, even in the midst of winter in that green land.

Being called to take their places as spectators and witnesses, the guests positioned themselves around the immense stone circle to see the promised show. However, whilst some were looking towards the sun and others waiting for the moon to rise, the expectation for the two celestial protagonists' performance was momentarily disturbed by the bizarre appearance of a procession of men dressed in rustic white, hooded, woollen cloaks, walking sombrely towards the centre of the stone circle with candles cupped in their hands.

Without knowing what to look at – up or down – the crowd turned to their host, who at first appeared to be frozen in time, whilst the blood drained from his face. Gradually, Lord Henry was overtaken by an incandescent indignation, then outrage, when he recognised the man who was at the head of this strange group.

'Mulgrave! What are you doing here, and why are you dressed like this?' Lord Henry shouted furiously.

'I am the Master Priest of the United Ancient Order of Druids (UAOD). This is my land, and I will do what I want,' Sir Edmund Mulgrave replied defiantly.

'Wait a moment, the druids meet here on the summer solstice, for the sunrise, and we are here at the winter solstice, for the sunset,' Lord Henry replied emphatically.

'You are talking about the Ancient Order of Druids (AOD). We are dissident. We split and formed the United Ancient Order of Druids, and now my order has more members than the other. We even have members from the United States, and throughout the Empire,' Sir Edmund replied, and then turned to his friends:

'Come on, druids,
Let's honour the Sun-God who is leaving us,
earlier than ever today;
a light that blessed our land and crops...'

Suddenly, Sir Edmund, in disbelief at what he was seeing, paused mid-sentence when another group of people marching in single file approached from the opposite direction. They were clothed in quite exquisite expensive-looking black velvet hooded cloaks, lined with deep red silk, and carrying lit black candles. Catching the attention of everybody present, the new group approached at a slow pace, in step as though marching.

Before Lord Henry could say anything, Sir Edmund, outraged, shouted loudly,

'Georgiana! What are you doing here? I told you if you came here I would arrest you and... and... whoever your companions are. By the way, why are you using this diabolical cloak?'

'We would never wear cheap cloaks like you,' she retorted. 'I am a Larkhill. Lady Georgiana Larkhill, don't forget that,' she stated pedantically.

'Oh, but you have to answer to me, Georgiana. What are you doing here in the middle of my experiment, with these... these ridiculous costumes?' Lord Henry demanded, almost possessed.

'I am the High Priestess of the Ancient Order of Female Druids (AOFD), and we are here to honour and celebrate the moon, when it rises,' she proudly replied.

'Look, Ellen, do you see the woman who is following the High Priestess?' Charlotte asked, intrigued.

'Yes, she looks like the hotel owner's daughter, Eleanor, I think,' Ellen replied, not so sure.

'Yes, that's it, Eleanor is her name. She is a druidess as well, which means that anybody can join the order, I suppose,' Charlotte confirmed.

'Oh my goodness! She is not a Christian...' Ellen exclaimed.

'I am sure she is not, dressed in a black cloak like that,' Charlotte replied.

'I am a little confused. Which one is important today? I mean... which one we are worshipping today – the sun or the moon?' Ellen asked.

'We are not worshipping anything or anybody, Ellen. We are here to witness my husband's scientific experiment,' Diana declared. She was upset because the two strange groups of 'druids' stole the show from her husband.

Charlotte was determined to tease Diana, so she shouted over to her husband,

'Bernard, what does the guide say about worship here today?'

'We don't have a guide, I'm afraid, but you have given us an important idea for a project,' Bernard replied.

'I'm sorry, Charlotte, but I'm still confused – if we have moon in the summer, why did we come in the winter?' Ellen asked. 'It's quite cold, don't you think?' she added.

'I don't know. The moon might be very busy in the summer, I suppose,' Charlotte replied testily.

'We might suggest that Diana books the place in advance, so it isn't overcrowded next time,' Ellen suggested.

'The only thing I know is that I am getting very cold, and so far I didn't see anything interesting. I need a warm cup of tea,' Charlotte replied, then shouted to her husband again,

'Bernard, do something, bring me a cup of tea, will you? I'm so cold.' She waved at him.

'Are you thinking the same thing as me, Peter?' Bernard asked quietly, raising an eyebrow whilst lighting his pipe.

'Yes, indeed, we will make a fortune, I am certain. If we discuss this project with Sir Edmund, we might secure him as a partner, and... who knows? We might get a knighthood for contributing to the economy of the empire! We could have some souvenirs made to sell with the tickets as well,' Peter replied thoughtfully.

'A tent offering tea and cakes would be very elegant and distinctive, don't you think?' Bernard suggested.

'Indeed, and mulled wine in the winter would be a treat; but our prices must be fairly steep, because Sir Edmund will not want commoners around,' Peter agreed optimistically.

'Mr Price! Mr White! I will not allow you to make part of this pagan scandal staining the Christian soil of England. I profess that everyone who does will burn in hell, and I warn you two not to be part of this,' announced the vicar.

'Reverend St Clair,' Bernard responded, 'we could set up another tent to sell Christian souvenirs, and little Bibles and things. It will be a charity tent for those who have seen the pagan ritual and then need to come to you to ask for absolution,' Bernard tried to persuade the Vicar.

'We could double the money, perhaps by offering some kind of purification afterwards for those who were concerned about visiting a pagan place,' Peter chirped up. 'You would be famous "The vicar's Purification Tent at Stonehenge". Your parish would be very wealthy, trust me,' Peter tried to seduce him.

The vicar gave this idea some thought for a moment or two, then insisted, 'I would have to choose the souvenirs, and the decoration of the tent; I wouldn't want anything overly permissive,' the vicar mused.

Meanwhile, the High Priestess went over and addressed Sir Edmund, who was outraged.

'Don't threaten me, Edmund! What do you think the Police will say when you ask them to arrest the Queen's cousin, eh?' Lady Georgiana replied; then turned to Lord Henry. 'This is a sacred place, and a much older goddess was worshipped here. This temple belongs to Mother Earth from whom all living creatures were born, and from the darkness of their mother's womb they will come to life for the first time, under the moonlight,' Lady Georgiana declared, as if she were making a prophecy.

'Wait a moment – why the light of the moon instead of the sunlight?' Sir Edmund asked doubtfully.

'Because from the dark womb it is important that all creatures come to see the moonlight first, to unveil the secrets of the night and darkness, preparing their souls for justice and love. So they will not go around doing stupid things, for example: succumbing to men, or pagan gods' appetites,' Georgiana replied sarcastically.

'Could anybody tell me how much longer I have to listen to such stupidity and superstition?' Dr Turner asked impatiently.

'Albert, I will never forgive you for dragging me to this diabolical place,' Miss Abington declared. 'It is full of insane people, possessed by devils,' she complained, completely shocked at what was unfolding.

'You have to understand, Mary, I am his next of kin. It is my duty to be here. I don't want him to disinherit me,' Albert whispered to her anxiously.

'Andrew, this temple seems to be much older.' Kate nudged him. 'I have no doubt they worshipped a female goddess in those ancient times,' she whispered in his ear.

'You might be right. Maybe we should excavate some other stone circles to obtain more evidence,' he replied, then Kate added,

'If the Greeks came to Britain in the Bronze Age, they were probably inspired by what they encountered here; the temples of Apollo and Artemis in Greece later were a kind of extension of the myth, instead of a new version of it,' Kate added.

'Don't forget that Artemis is connected to the moon and to all animals, trees and nature as a whole.'

'Yes, indeed,' Andrew agreed thoughtfully.

Suddenly, Lord Henry looked up at the sky, which was insisting on not giving up the sunlight, battling the infant light of the moon that started to claim its place with the sun on the celestial path.

'Look, the Moon! She is here as she promised. Let's all share this moment with our celestial fellows and their alignment,' Lord Henry, who was standing next to the Heel Stone with Andrew and Kate, announced, absolutely delighted, claiming everybody's attention.

'Did you make a wish, my dear?' Peter approached Diana, whilst everybody was looking at the events in the sky.

'Why do you always have to bother me, when I am... I am... busy?' Diana replied, pretending she didn't care and to be engrossed in the movement of the sun and the moon.

'Because I know when you are bothered. Anyway, looking at the sky was never your cup of tea. I know that you prefer what is here on Earth, where you can reach out and take it,' Peter replied, then continued. 'However, I am not an insensitive man, so in advance I offer you my condolences for your loss, just in case any god or goddess complies with your wish to be widowed,' Peter whispered, with an ironic smile.

'Let's toast the Queen, the sun, and...' Sir Richard raised his glass of wine, but stopped suddenly, with a strange face.

'Oh, no, those eagle-owls again...' he exclaimed, when two very large birds swooped down and perched on top of the Great Trilithon, which was situated in the innermost arrangement within the great circle.

Everybody looked over to their host when they heard Lord Henry call out, 'Yes, let's toast the birds! They are creatures of the night, and they are looking at the direction of the alignment of the sun, the moon and the "Heel Stone" there!' he shouted, pointing.

After observing and acknowledging the peculiar alignment, Andrew thought to himself for a few moments, then addressed Kate.

'If his theory is correct, and I am certain of that now, there were originally five pairs of Sarsen stones surrounding what may have been an altar in the centre of the circle,' Andrew explained.

'Did you say five pairs of stones inside the circle surrounding the "altar"?' Kate asked suddenly; then explained, 'According to the myth, Apollo's son, Asclepius, had five daughters, each one related to a specific step of the healing process. 'Oh my goodness!' She smiled. 'I think you have unravelled part of Sir Joshua's riddle. If we place Apollo and his oracle here, we might be in Hyperborea, where pilgrims used to come to consult the oracle about their illness,' Kate said excitedly, before continuing.

'What intrigues me is that although the ancient texts mention Apollo and his son Asclepius, the role of Apollo as the healer and the voice of the oracle are widely known, but the myths don't actually specify the role of Asclepius...' she said.

'I have to admit that it is very intriguing. It makes sense that Apollo being an active god in all domains might be situated here; along with Artemis, his female counterpart, sovereign of the night and the moon, protecting nature. I don't see how Asclepius might be associated with Stonehenge though.' Then Kate continued, delighted with her Eureka moment.

'Unless... perhaps the role of Asclepius was to prepare the patient's soul for imminent death, as of course not everyone could be cured.'

Meanwhile, Sir Christopher whispered to Sir Richard, very concerned, after overhearing what Kate was saying,

'Fascinating, Richard, Kate has just gotten herself into real trouble.'

'Extraordinary Lady Kate. We are in Hyperborea, just like Herodotus and Hecateus wrote *"An island not smaller than Sicily; the Land beyond the Celts."* Where else could Apollo and his son be placed? It was only much later the Greeks built the temple of Apollo in Delphos – not so rudimentary as this ancient temple; after all, the Greeks were master builders with a proper sense of beauty; but everything must have started right here, in Hyperborea. You are definitely right,' Lord Henry agreed, very pleased at this turn of events.

'Are you out of your mind?' Dr Gruber shouted. 'Hyperborea cannot be associated with such a rudimentary pile of stones, with a couple of owls on top. I refuse to accept it. We all know that Hyperborea was in Scandinavia, and it was from there that all knowledge and Greek culture were derived.' Dr Gruber was outraged.

'Perhaps if we forget the owls... these two birds may be here merely by coincidence,' Peter suggested ironically, lighting a cigarette.

'Well done, Peter, let's forget the owls and make some libations for all gods and goddesses, so none of them will be jealous,' Sir Richard agreed, finishing his glass of wine in one gulp.

'Lord Henry, where is the evidence?' Dr Turner interrupted. 'As I expected, your disqualification and lack of material evidence will be motive for laughter amongst academics. The astronomical event is quite insipient. You are just a senile antiquarian clamouring for attention, nothing else,' Dr Turner announced imperiously.

'Who is senile, eh?' My experiment hasn't finished yet! Today I proved that this stone circle was built taking into consideration the movement of the sun and the moon in alignment with the Heel Stone; if the purpose was also religious and medicinal, that enhances my theory. However, the biggest issue is this – what will we find if we follow the northeast direction indicated by this alignment of celestial spheres, the stones, and... the owls, of course?' Lord Henry asked mysteriously.

'We shall not demerit the astronomical event we saw here this evening by trying to connect it with any supernatural phenomenon, with or without owls,' Andrew interjected, adding, 'The sun and the moon were perfectly aligned today with the Heel Stone, so I am certain that if we follow that direction we will find a barrow dedicated to somebody who seems to have been very important to the people who were here long before us.' Andrew tried to calm everybody down.

Lord Henry was not particularly interested in the other scientists' opinions, as his ego and determination followed Andrew's instinct. Meanwhile, Kate ran to the tent where her papers, notes and books were hidden in her suitcase, but was intercepted by Eleanor, the hotelier's daughter, who was the second druidess.

'Be careful, Kate Enfield, you are walking a very dangerous path. Don't let your curiosity take you too far, attracting the wrath of nature,' she growled, giving Kate a withering look.

'What do you mean by "dangerous"? My interest is not related to any religious belief on my part,' Kate replied, then added, 'It is purely scientific and historical. I don't believe in gods and goddesses surrounding us, about to act. I am here to study an ancient culture, especially the way they treated their illnesses, diseases and fears.' Kate spoke categorically, without a shred of sympathy for that kind of superstition, then, having found what she wanted, she left the strange girl standing there alone in front of the tent.

'Come with me, my druidesses. The moon is fully risen now. It is time to pray to nature.' The high priestess was calling her followers.

'We have no strength without your light.
Facing the darkness and fear itself
is a challenge that only
You, Mother Nature, and your Love
can make us overcome...'

Meanwhile, on the opposite side of the circle, Sir Edmund Mulgrave called his followers to continue their prayers to the sun. He turned and loudly addressed them,

'You blessed our land and crops with your light;
We pray for your return with the dawn,
To bring us your strength and...'

Suddenly, their prayers were interrupted by a strange noise that caught the attention of everybody, including Kate, who was crossing the stone circle towards Andrew and Lord Henry. They were abruptly surprised by a speech, which although spoken in English, only Kate was able to understand, as the crowd was petrified in face of the bizarre spectacle unfolding.

'Oh my God, it is Ellen! What happened to her? I cannot understand what she is saying,' Charlotte cried.

Kate moved slowly towards Ellen whilst Peter, who was already next to her, was trying in vain to wake Ellen up from what for him seemed to be a kind of trance, as she intoned,

'Earth, Mother Earth!
And you, Apollo of the dawn...
You destroyed me...
With an evil at home.
Stabbed by a dagger set by greedy hand,
The Lord is killed.
He falls by treachery!'

Ellen paused; then continued, horrified,

Again the agony...
With a dread pain...
That racks my soul.
A monster of the earth...
No man, nor woman
Would fit such comparison.
Again a dagger poisoned by wrath.'

Ellen uttered those words with icy eyes and a ghostly face, without moving a single muscle of her body, and she did not react at all to Peter's words.

'Ellen, darling, please wake up. It is me, Peter! We are all worried about you. Are you cold?' After saying that to her, he turned to everybody else, pleading,

'We need to take her back to the hotel. She doesn't seem very well.'

'It is Cassandra!' Kate said anxiously, receiving anguished exclamations from everybody from all sides.

'Who?' asked Charlotte.

'What?' said Lord Henry.

'Oh no... more ghosts!' Sir Richard cried.

'Silence, let Lady Kate speak!' Lord Henry declared.

'I am sorry, but I recognise those words and verses – they are from Cassandra's speech in Aeschylus's Tragedy,' Kate explained, worried about the content of the speech, knowing its meaning and danger.

'Who is this "Cassandra"?' Diana asked, confused.

'I am sorry, my dear, but according to the words I heard, she didn't seem very lucky, a bit like Pandora,' Peter told her, quite concerned.

'Cassandra was Agamemnon's concubine, and when he came back from the war against Troy, bringing her as a war trophy, his wife killed them both. I have to say, though, it is very strange, because the speech is not precisely identical... I mean... the words were chosen from the old verses to reconstruct new ones, with a slightly different meaning from the original text,' Kate tried to explain.

'I'm sorry, Kate, but it doesn't make any sense to me, whatever was said before, or after,' Diana complained, then shouted, 'Where is the vicar? I want him NOW!'

'I am right here, kneeling, praying with contrition for the moment this bunch of heretics started this clowning, defying Almighty God. But He is powerful, so despite them, He will save Mrs Price's soul,' the vicar declared confidently.

'Don't forget to save her mind as well, because she knows how to use it sometimes,' Charlotte added, worried about her friend.

'It is getting late and cold, and we are all very tired. I suggest we return to the hotel for a nice dinner and exchange our thoughts, whilst Mrs. Price recovers from her nervous breakdown,' Lord Henry announced.

'Excuse me, Lord Henry, but I don't think it was a nervous breakdown. It seems more like a poisoning to me, followed by hallucinations. Perhaps someone tried to poison her?' Peter suggested.

'Does anybody have a motive to poison Mrs. Price? Do you remember anything that could have instigated some kind of revenge against her?' Sir Christopher the magistrate asked, keen to learn more about all possible facets of this strange case.

'Not that I remember. Aside from some neighbours' jealousy of her beautiful dresses, my wife doesn't have any enemies; it is a considerable wardrobe, though,' Peter said thoughtfully.

'What about supposed friends with dubious intentions? Sometimes friends are worse than enemies, trust me,' Sir Christopher stated.

'I think this is a little difficult to know, don't you think?' Peter asked ironically.

'I have a rational explanation for what we had just seen. Mrs. Price suffered a self-induced delirium – some fear, or perhaps a desire to kill was asleep in her unconsciousness, then it surfaced, due to stress,' Dr Turner postulated.

'I don't think my wife has any hidden delusions for any kind of violence, especially against me.' Peter defended his wife.

'I would not be so sure, Peter. Ellen has probably been planning to kill you for ages, to become a rich widow, without title, I am afraid. Anyway, nothing is perfect, even murder.' Diana very publicly had her revenge on him.

Quiet and worried about being the next victim, Bernard edged slowly away from his wife Charlotte, who glowered at him from head to toe, with a furrowed brow.

'As a magistrate, I must say we shall first determine whether, during the trance, she personified the victim, who was about to be killed with her lover... I mean... the unfaithful husband, or whether she spoke as witness to the act itself, perhaps a servant, who was observing the scene' Sir Christopher ruminated.

'I disagree, Chris. Perhaps she personified the murderer... I mean... the wife, who regretted the gruesome act when she saw her husband dead, and acknowledged her vile and disgusting act; she even compared herself to a "monster",' Sir Richard opined.

'I think you British read too many novels. When you fill your minds with silly ideas you end up being your own victims, taking your country to the same abyss,' Dr Gruber declared. 'That is the reason why, when I return to Austria, I will ensure that British literature is banned from our schools. Superstitions and vile acts are not educational for the mind.'

'But it is "good food" for the soul,' Sir Richard added, smiling, with another glass of wine in his hand.

'How dare you complain about British literature whilst being here in my land? Remove this Austrian villain from my sight NOW!' Sir Edmund shouted, and went after the Austrian ready to punch him, but was held back by Andrew and Bernard.

'It is your fault, Henry. I will have all of you arrested,' Sir Edmund threatened everybody, then left the stone circle with his group of druids.

'You little worm, you were always very pompous and boastful. Look around and see what you did – you completely unbalanced our beautiful refuge of energy,' Lady Georgiana growled at Lord Henry. 'But it will not stop here, because Mother Earth gives life, and takes it whenever she wants to restore order. I will not allow you to desecrate what was buried and veiled by Earth.' She shook her fist at Lord Henry, then left the stone circle with her group of priestesses, heading off in another direction. The bemused onlookers watched the two processions of druids stomp off across Salisbury Plain, not entirely sure what it was all about.

'I agree with Lord Henry,' Sir Christopher stated. 'It is getting cold, and a nice warm dinner will help us recover from the events of this evening, as well as giving us the energy to solve Mrs Price's riddle, I mean, helping us to determine who possessed her – the concubine or the wife,' he suggested, discreetly excited by the challenge.

'There is no case, Chris. We all know that Agamemnon and his lover Cassandra were murdered by his wife, with the support of the husband's cousin,' Sir Richard stated.

'I am not that certain, my dear fellow. Kate herself said that some words, and even entire verses, have been changed. Maybe that could be a warning of what might yet be to come?' Sir Christopher explained, concerned.

'Pagan infidelity, unfaithfulness, disloyalty. Sodom and Gomorrah!' the vicar exclaimed, still kneeling, but with hardly an audience, as everybody had decided to get their things quickly, so as not to miss the carriages which were getting ready to leave.

'Come on, Vicar, would you like a lift? You might miss the dinner if you keep waiting for God's answer,' Bernard asked him, whilst heading towards Sir Christopher and Sir Richard's carriage, as he was not so sure if it was safe to share the same carriage with his wife Charlotte at the moment – he didn't want to end up murdered too.

Inside Andrew and Kate's carriage, the couple exchanged glances until Andrew, who was intrigued, broke the silence.

'Do you think it is possible that Stonehenge is so old that it could be an early oracle of Apollo, the Healer, built as a temple to cure illnesses – the place in the winter where Apollo went to, when he left Greece?' Andrew asked, although his question actually sounded more like a statement.

'Stonehenge might be even older if, in its origin, this monument was dedicated to a mother-goddess, which could be associated with Artemis; but nobody, especially old academics, will accept it; you know that, don't you?' Kate asked, smiling back at her husband, finding the whole thing very exciting and academically stimulating.

'Why have I just detected in your words that little satisfaction you usually express when contradicting scholars, hmm?' Andrew teased.

'I have absolutely no idea what you are talking about,' Kate replied, feigning false naivety, which made Andrew laugh.

'This is not fair, Andrew, what else do you need? Sir Joshua had been doing this researching for more than thirty years. Lord Henry finds it absolutely plausible; and what about Herodotus, Pythagoras, and...' Kate tried to defend her ideas.

'I know, I know,' Andrew interjected, 'I am not disagreeing, but we have to be very careful with those dates. If we don't get material evidence, we cannot prove it; so it will be our opinion against their solid tradition. We need to get some allies first,' Andrew suggested thoughtfully.

'What do you mean "allies"? Who are you thinking about?' Kate asked, curious.

'Do you remember Arthur Evans?' Andrew asked.

'Of course, the spy,' Kate replied, laughing.

'Don't say that. You don't know anything,' Andrew corrected her.

'Don't you think that I am stupid. You, Anthony and Arthur were all spies in the Balkans. You three have been spying for the British government for almost a decade. How do you think he became an expert in the conflict in that area? I read all the articles he wrote for the Manchester Guardian.'

'Oh, I didn't know you followed his career as well,' Andrew said, a little jealous.

'You don't have any reason to be jealous. I had to follow his footsteps to hear about you. As a reporter, he was in the newspapers every day, and you weren't. How could I know where you were?' Kate explained with a sweet voice, then told him, 'I panicked when I knew you were both arrested by the Austrians; everybody seemed to want to arrest you two – the Russians, the Turks. They didn't think you were archaeologists; they suspected it was just cover. You didn't make my life and Mr Bear's life easy, didn't you realise?' Kate scolded him.

'I'm afraid it was the other way round, Kate. Arthur Evans and I volunteered for those political missions to obtain easy access to archaeological sites. What we really wanted was to excavate, and send the artefacts to Britain to study,' Andrew excused himself.

'Oh goodness, and you were complaining about Anthony and his "dubious activities",' Kate exclaimed indignantly.

'I didn't sell anything like Anthony did... or perhaps is still doing, who knows?' Andrew defended himself and continued. 'Anyway, what I was trying to say is that Arthur is an expert on Greece. He has been collecting data about the Mycenaean and Minoan civilisations. We should contact him as his opinion is very important to us.' Andrew paused thoughtfully, then continued.

'I recall that Arthur was inclined to believe the Minoans worshipped a very old mother-goddess, but he didn't begin his excavation there yet, to confirm his theories. If he is correct, the Greeks didn't import Apollo from Bronze Age Crete, so it is likely that their contact with Apollo's myth was from the northwest, *"the island beyond the Celts"*. Did you know that his next step is to get permission to excavate Mycenae and Crete?

We might be invited. What do you think?' Andrew tried to tempt her.

'As long as you don't get yourself into trouble again; for example, by getting arrested. I cannot keep saving you from Ottomans, Russians, and who knows whatever other enemies,' Kate agreed, delighted, whilst teasing him at the same time.

They were both excited at the prospect of this new endeavour, but it was time to rest a little, and pray for a nice quiet dinner, so they stared through the glass of the carriage window to observe the night closing about them, as the sun had now disappeared.

The moon was full and bright for a winter night, and as the carriages got closer to the hotel, the celestial light danced with the trees and bushes, covering the land with shadows, then immediately revealing it, like the rhythm of tired eyes, closing and opening successively, after a busy day full of surprises. For most of those involved, the day was very exciting; for others, quite terrible, even sinister. However, nobody could deny that Apollo's name was ever mentioned as much as in that strange winter in a land so far from Greece, and from the Olympians.

Chapter 10

The atmosphere in the room during dinner was very cheerful, perhaps because some of the guests' spirits needed a rest after an event-filled day, or maybe because of the difficulty of resisting the pleasures of such an exquisite menu, carefully planned and executed by Lord Henry's chef and his servants; the earl spared no effort in providing an unforgettable dinner to seal the end of an important day.

Nobody doubted that tomorrow would provide more surprises, and conflicts between vain egos fed by jealousy, arrogance and vanity. Perhaps that explained why some of the wiser guests, after a liqueur and a quick chat, decided to retire to their rooms shortly after dinner to recharge their minds, bodies, and souls.

Kate was walking with Andrew towards the stairs, but when she passed in front of the wooden wall next to it, she again seemed to be hypnotised by the hung picture of the former owner, Mr Fairfax, and his small family. Some of the other guests, as well as the new owner, Mr Clark, and his daughter, also noticed Kate's interest in the picture, so they stopped what they were doing to look at her, to see if she had anything to say. Kate still could not understand what was so important about that photograph to attract her attention so strongly, then after a few seconds, Andrew asked,

'What happened, Kate, are you feeling well? You seem to be miles away.'

Kate finally grew aware of the people around her, curiously waiting for some sort of explanation for her strange and unusual behaviour, but in almost a whisper she could only say,

'There is something strange about this picture, something that I have seen before, but I will not give up; I will remember…' Then she turned to Andrew and they climbed the stairs to their room.

Meanwhile, in the dinner hall, Sir Christopher tried unsuccessfully to wake Sir Richard, who was sitting on a comfortable burgundy velvet-covered chair, fast asleep and snoring lightly. After a while, Sir Christopher decided to leave his friend be, thinking that Sir Richard would not at all mind being left alone; he could find his own way to his room later, or perhaps in the morning.

Kate was sitting on a large comfy chair next to the window, cuddling Mr Bear and looking out at the sky, which had clouded over. After putting more wood on the fire, Andrew washed his hands and face in a bowl with water next to the wardrobe; he looked at Kate, who still seemed to be miles away, so he approached and crouched in front of her.

'Would you tell me what is bothering you?' he asked her gently.

'There is something buried deeply in my mind, but I cannot remember what it is; something related to that picture. Perhaps my recent "accidents" helped to bury it deeply in my mind,' she said thoughtfully.

Andrew sat in a chair and gently made her sit on his legs, as if she was a child.

'You are cuddling Mr Bear; do you think he is going to protect you?' he asked, smiling, with his arms around her waist.

'No. He is only helping me think about it. He said that it is your job to protect me now that he has retired.' She laughed.

'We shall find a companion for him, perhaps those two owls outside who never stop staring at me. I don't think they trust me, do you?' He tried to cheer her up.

'You have a very strange sense of humour, Sir Andrew. You like to tease me during my most difficult moments,' she answered formally, faking annoyance.

'Difficult moments? You attract train accidents, gun shots in Greece, fall down staircases, ghosts...' He would have continued, but she interrupted.

'Yes... yes... I know, it's all my fault.' She was a little too defensive.

'No, it's not, I'm only joking. Did I tell you how much I love you? I can't lose you,' he said, then kissed her, gently but passionately.

Later, when they were in bed, snuggled together under a beautifully decorated patchwork quilt and he was caressing her hair, he asked,

'Do you remember the Crucono Stone in Brittany and Hagar Qim in Malta?'

'Yes, of course, why?' She turned to look at him.

'Now I have actually seen them, and Stonehenge, I cannot stop thinking they are all related, somehow. As you said before, there are no coincidences in science. I find it difficult to believe that three places with flourishing societies could share so many similarities, without having some contact with one another' Andrew mused.

'I have been thinking exactly the same thing,' Kate agreed. 'If Marseille is an old Greek colony, and lies on the obvious route between Malta and Brittany in such perfect alignment, the Greeks could not have ignored the ancient stone ruins in their path,' she added.

'They might all have been temples with shrines inside for worshiping the gods. However, those stone ruins in Malta and Brittany, and here at Stonehenge, seem inextricably linked with the celestial movement of both sun and moon,' Andrew said, and continued. 'I have no doubt that the purpose of those stone ruins was religious, but after I have witnessed such an interesting experiment today it is almost certain that these stone circles might be one of the oldest celestial calendars in the world. However, how could they be so precise?'

'If we are in Hyperborea, perhaps this could be the origin of the myths of Apollo and his son Asclepius, the place from where the Greeks derived some of their knowledge of astronomy and geometry,' Kate wondered, adding, 'Not only the myths, but actually a very ancient oracle which provided healing as well...' she wondered.

'As they observed that the sea's waves were affected by the moon's movement around the Earth, it is likely they thought it could interfere in their health as well,' Andrew suggested.

'Arturo Bonnici would be in heaven at hearing this. A unique stone building, where mathematical and astronomical knowledge coupled with religion could be used to heal,' Kate exclaimed, excited by their discussion.

'Don't forget the music; after all, Apollo is the god of music and Pythagoras developed the sound of the spheres' theory and linked it with the movement of the planets.' He nodded.

'It does make sense, considering we witnessed today how the ancient people cared about the moon's movement around the horizon, and Stonehenge. I cannot wait for tomorrow!' She smiled excitedly.

'Henry did not explain any details of his research. He loves mystery, I have to say; and knowing him as I do, we can definitely expect more surprises ahead,' Andrew said, worrying himself a little.

Later, in the silent dinner hall, Sir Richard was suddenly woken up by his own snoring, then when he realised that everybody else had gone, he stood up, stretched, and in a little pain from his arthritis, walked towards the stairs, but something didn't seem quite right. He sensed a presence behind him, and when he turned to look, he saw a large black dog with fiery eyes staring at him. Wide-eyed, looking aghast at the hound, Sir Richard started walking slowly backwards, whilst the dog advanced towards him slowly and growling. The dog seemed about to leap at him so he crossed his arms in front of his face to protect himself. Backing off, he stumbled backwards, crashing violently against the wooden panelling, which under his not inconsiderable weight creaked briefly, then splintered and broke as he screamed. He collapsed onto the floor of a little chamber which was hidden behind the wall, a secret place unknown to anyone.

The silent night was shattered by the crash and sound of wood breaking from downstairs. Along the various corridors of the hotel, doors were opening, with frightened people wondering about the source of the scream and crash. When they noticed somebody moaning, a group of guests led by Andrew hurried to the stairs to see what was happening, whilst Diana shouted, loudly and furiously,

'For heaven's sake, how many people have to fall down these stairs until somebody starts using their brain and takes the precaution of fixing whatever is broken?' She was angry. 'I refuse to spend another night in this place, to be woken up in the middle of the night with a noise like that.'

'It was not the stairs; somebody broke the wooden wall down here,' Andrew shouted back as they went to investigate where the noise came from.

'Whoever did it chose the wrong time to refurbish the hotel,' Peter said acerbically.

'Bernard, do something. Use your brain, if you have one. I am too tired, and I want to sleep,' Charlotte complained.

'Richard, are you alright?' Andrew asked Sir Richard, discovering him still on the floor in that little recess, amidst broken wooden panelling.

Sir Richard's eyes suddenly opened wide and he let out a loud shout.

'Arghh...!' He put his fists up as if to defend himself from something.

Sir Christopher, who had followed the little troop of inquisitive guests, worriedly enquired,

'What happened? Has he broken any bone?'

'No, he shouted because there is a cadaver here. Actually, there are two,' Andrew replied, trying to help Sir Richard to his feet.

'Two cadavers? Fascinating!' Sir Christopher exclaimed, adjusting the belt of his elegant and expensive velvet robe, as if preparing for an investigation.

'A human body, possibly a man, and a dog's body,' Andrew replied, more than a little surprised at what they'd discovered.

'Adam Fairfax and his dog, surely; and all this time we thought that he'd killed his wife for some reason, and escaped with his dog and daughter.' Mr Clark declared, astonished, whilst his daughter, Eleanor, stood silently next to him.

'I'm sorry, Mr Clark, but there is a ghost dog here, and it came back to claim his skeleton, you can be certain about it,' Sir Richard stated in a wavering voice.

'Another delusional case due to the lamp gas and a bump on the head,' Dr Turner stated categorically, then added, 'I would say that whatever you intend to report about your experiment, Lord Henry, it cannot be supported by such a bunch of delusional witnesses. I rather suspect that tomorrow night, we will probably have a case of collective hysteria in this hotel, a very frequent collective reaction in this type of case; let me see... Lady Kate, Mrs Ellen Price, and now Sir Richard...' Dr Turner said, but was immediately interrupted by Kate.

'How dare you call me hysterical?' Kate shouted back furiously, whilst Andrew, smiling, folded his arms and whispered to Sir Christopher proudly,

'I love this part. Do you know that she is half-Greek?' He grinned, indicating his wife.

'Indeed, Spartan blood, if I am not mistaken,' Sir Christopher whispered back, nodding, whilst admiring the unfolding scene.

'You fat academic prototype!' Kate shouted at Dr Turner. 'I will report your intolerable behaviour to...' but she was interrupted by Lord Henry, who had arrived with Diana.

'Calm down, my dear, leave the report to me. Don't be surprised if Dr Turner finds a letter from Cambridge sending him to the borders of the empire when he gets back home.'

'Is this a threat, Tollemache? Because I warn you...' Dr Turner could not finish as he was suddenly interrupted by Sir Christopher.

'Enough!' he shouted. 'From this moment forwards, I am the authority here. We have a murder case. Possibly a double murder, if we take into consideration the man's wife, three years ago. I will begin this enquiry properly, early in the morning, so I advise you all to go back to your rooms, now.'

'But these bodies are three years old. I was not here at the time,' Peter complained.

'I am not talking about you, Mr Price, but we have some very suspicious scientists here; some who prowl around looking for skulls, others looking for treasure, and aristocrats fighting each other because of their experiments. I would not be surprised if the cadaver, I mean the deceased,' he said, correcting himself, 'was caught in the middle of this quarrel,' the magistrate declared.

'Are you trying to insinuate that my husband is a murderer, Sir Christopher?' Diana asked, outraged.

'Poor Diana, this is not the type of publicity she wanted to be involved with,' Peter whispered to his friends, who were staying very quiet.

'Diana, I am a magistrate, a subject of Her Majesty, and it is my duty to find the murderer of Mr… What was his name?' Sir Christopher asked.

'Adam Fairfax,' the hotelier replied miserably, then added, 'I told you I was cursed; it will start all over again. Now we have two murders.' He sighed.

'Three, don't forget the dog; we don't want his ghost getting upset with us for being neglected,' Sir Richard corrected.

'Possibly four, unless you think that a twelve-year-old girl could kill her parents, and the dog, then escape,' Kate corrected, dusting off the little family picture, which had been hanging on the wooden wall that collapsed under Sir Richard's weight when he collided with it.

'You're right – perhaps four then, that's all, no more bodies,' Sir Christopher agreed.

'I will call the police…' Mr Clark added.

'I represent the police,' Sir Christopher informed him.

'But you are not in your jurisdiction, and I still have to call the police,' the hotelier insisted miserably.

'Whatever. I will see you all in the morning,' Sir Christopher declared.

'I am sorry, Sir Christopher, but immediately after breakfast Sir Andrew and I have to go to Stonehenge to follow the trail left by the sun and moon's alignment; and the birds, of course,' Lord Henry informed him categorically.

'I don't mind, anything that the sun and moon have witnessed in the past does not interest us in this case; we need living witnesses. However, I strongly advise you not to come back too late, or leave the county, as you, Henry, are one of the suspects I have my eyes on.' Sir Christopher declared officiously. Diana pursed her lips, and was about to explode, then thought better of it and addressed her husband.

'Henry, I will be here with the other guests, and you can be sure I will observe this enquiry very closely,' Diana comforted her husband, followed by Kate, who addressed Andrew.

'Sorry Andrew, but I have reasons to stay here tomorrow; I will explain why later.' And, holding tightly on to the picture, Kate left to go to her room, with Andrew in tow.

For the second time, they were getting ready to sleep again when Andrew turned to Kate.

'I am not so sure that the owner is cursed. It makes more sense to me to think that you are the cursed one, don't you think?' Saying that, he had to move quickly before being hit by the pillow Kate tried to bludgeon him with. She failed, then he laughed and asked,

'Where is your sense of humour, Kate?' He grinned, waiting for another pillow, this one flying towards him.

'You will sleep on the floor tonight if you don't stop teasing me,' she said, faking an angry voice.

Andrew didn't allow her to complain again; he climbed back in bed and cuddled her, quietly soothing her.

'Our honeymoon was ruined with all these people around. We need another one, without them next year,' he promised, stroking her hair gently. Kate sighed, then she closed her eyes with a smile.

The cheerful dinner from the night before was followed by a not so cheerful breakfast. Nobody could blame the food, though, which was excellent; the chef was sending unlimited trays of plates with bacon, sausage, eggs, black pudding, fried bread, mushrooms and grilled tomato; there was tea, coffee and toast with butter, jams and marmalade as well.

Splendid as breakfast was, the prospect of a murder inquiry was never good for the stomach. Not everybody was miserable though, as there is always someone interested in this type of situation; on the other hand, some seemed entirely immune to the heavy atmosphere, whilst others were trying to give their own version of the facts.

Andrew and Lord Henry left the hotel early on horseback, heading to Stonehenge. Later, in the middle of the morning when everybody was in the lounge, Mr Clark came in and introduced a couple of strangers – one of them a tall, robust-looking fellow who was wearing a long coat; the other, equally tall but rather thinner, was wearing his uniform.

'These are Detective Inspector Parnell and Constable Parker,' Mr Clark announced loudly, and pointing at the gathered guests, he turned to the larger gentleman, then said, 'These, Inspector, are the guests of Lord Henry Tollemache.' When he noticed the magistrate approaching in their direction, he introduced him properly '...and this is Sir Christopher Lidstone, magistrate of Devon, who was in charge, until now.'

'Correct Mr Clark – he "was" in charge because I will conduct the inquiry and investigation from now on,' Inspector Parnell declared, a little annoyed at having being taken out of bed too early, and indeed just two days before Christmas Eve.

'How dare you steal from me the lead of this inquiry? Do you know who I am?' The magistrate puffed out his chest and adjusted his spectacles.

The inspector calmly indicated the owner of the hotel, and replied,

'He already told me, and you are out of your jurisdiction, so from now on I consider you a witness or a suspect, and if you don't mind, sit down please, sir.' Then, addressing the constable, the inspector continued,

'Parker, start taking down the names of everybody here. Where is the deceased?' he asked, visibly in a bad mood.

'This is the problem, Inspector. He has been dead for three years, and you might need some further relevant information regarding this complicated case, if you allow me to assist you?' Sir Christopher interjected.

'Fair enough, Magistrate, you can observe, but I ask the questions. By the way, who found the body?' he wanted to know.

'I did; actually, the dog found me... I mean... the ghost dog,' Sir Richard answered, standing up.

'What? What language are you speaking, sir?' the inspector enquired, not sure about what he had just heard.

'Don't make fun of me, Inspector. I am Sir Richard Wilson from Cambridge University. I am a member of the Ghost Club of Trinity College; my friend, Arthur Conan Doyle, sometimes discusses the murder cases in his books with me. There are rumours that he will be knighted soon, aren't there, Chris?' Sir Richard begged the magistrate for support.

'I think, Richard,' his friend replied, 'we have enough investigators here. We shall not involve Arthur.'

'Excuse me, how many "Sirs" do we have here?' Inspector Parnell asked, realising that he might have a problem.

'Enough for you to show some deference, Inspector,' Diana said in a restrained voice.

'And who are you, miss?' The inspector asked, annoyed at being interrupted.

'I am Lady Diana Tollemache, my husband is Lord Henry Tollemache,' she replied pedantically and proudly.

'I hope her title will help her,' Peter whispered to Bernard.

'And you, who are you?' The inspector addressed Peter, annoyed with his comment.

'My name is Mr Peter Price and this is my friend and business partner, Mr Bernard White. We are applying for the knighthood though, Inspector.'

'Parker, write this down. "Two applicants for knighthood who have decided to skip the queue and might have killed the deceased applicant,' the inspector said sarcastically.

'I admire your sense of humour, Inspector, but it is the first time, and hopefully the last, I will visit this county, so I have nothing to do with the deceased, as you describe him.' Peter lit a cigarette.

'Me too! And tell my wife that I am worth more alive than dead.' Bernard laughed, lighting his pipe in turn.

'Doctor Baker, if you want to buy my husband's skull I will give you a discount, as there is no brain inside,' Charlotte said to Dr Baker, loud enough for everybody to hear.

'What are these people talking about?' the inspector asked Sir Christopher.

'Variants of the same domestic theme, I am afraid; some couples threaten with poison or daggers, others threaten to sell the skull, this type of thing,' the magistrate replied calmly.

'That is news to me, and who is Dr Baker?' the inspector asked.

'I am Dr James, not Joseph, Baker,' the doctor replied.

'Do you buy skulls?' the inspector asked, intrigued.

'Not really... sometimes they are "available" on the ground, or perhaps underground...' Dr Baker replied, grimacing, a little uncomfortable.

'He is a thief, and I am very glad that you have come, Inspector Sparrow.' Sir Edmund Mulgrave intervened from the door, having just arrived and overheard some of the conversation.

'And who are you?' the inspector asked.

'Sir Edmund Mulgrave. I own almost everything around here.'

'An applicant, or a proper "Sir"?' the inspector asked, in doubt.

'What do you mean?' Sir Edmund asked.

'Forget about it. Parker, write this down, so I will not forget when they come with those forms for us to fill in with suggestions: "Her Majesty the Queen shall limit the number of knighthoods per year." It is just to make our job a little easier,' the inspector addressed the constable, and turning to Sir Edmund, he said, 'By the way, my name is Parnell, not Sparrow.'

'I apologise, but are you going to arrest this thief?' Sir Edmund asked, indicating Dr Baker.

'Dr Baker, what skulls do you usually steal?' the inspector asked.

'Only prehistoric skulls from before the Roman period, and I didn't steal them; as I said, they were "available"; no relatives claimed them yet,' Dr Baker replied.

'I am sorry, Sir Edmund, but I only arrest perpetrators in cases where the deceased died in the last fifty years; it is a technical issue, I am afraid. I will, however, report the matter to a colleague who works with this type of case, especially if the perpetrator is avoiding paying tax.' Inspector Parnell tried to calm him down.

'I didn't know that we have to pay tax on skulls,' Bernard whispered to Peter, who replied,

'Depends on the skull. We will find a way, don't worry.'

'Inspector Parnell, my name is Dr Augustus Turner, and I was here to witness a "pseudo-scientific" experiment that never happened. The gas lamp is the source of the collective hysteria around us. I've just confirmed my final diagnosis now,' he announced.

'I am not hysterical, Inspector, the ghost dog started everything,' insisted Sir Richard. 'It was because of the ghost dog that we found the cadaver... I mean... the dog's cadaver too; but both cadavers had skulls... I mean... they both had heads... no... only the skulls without brain. I am sorry, let's keep it simple – I will start again: Dr Baker didn't steal the skulls yet; the cadavers are intact, with their skulls.'

'Very well, Sir Richard, have a rest; we will keep their skulls, don't worry.' The inspector addressed Dr Turner. 'These two skulls belong to the Crown from now on; they are evidence in this case,' the inspector asserted.

'Damn you and your skulls; you can hang them in your office, if you want,' Dr Turner replied, annoyed that the inspector had confused him with Dr Baker.

'I am the one who collects skulls,' Dr Baker piped up. 'I will not touch them, I promise. However, my research depends on data. Would you allow me to measure them, for scientific data collection purposes?' he asked.

'Could you tell me, please, why the hell do you collect skulls, Doctor Baker?' The inspector wanted to know.

'I am a polygenist scientist. I measure skulls to determine the evolution of human beings,' Dr Baker replied.

'What?' the inspector asked, astonished.

'I want to prove that different human beings come from different origins,' Dr Baker explained confidently.

'...and have you proved it?' the inspector asked.

'Not yet, I am afraid; a skull with a brain would be more useful, I must admit,' Dr Baker responded suggestively.

'How many skulls do you have?' the inspector asked.

'... quite a few,' Dr Baker replied.

'Don't listen to them. They are pagans, heretics, evil scientists, thieves!' the vicar interjected upon hearing about the collection. 'They desecrate the final abode of the dead without God's permission. When they are not following the sun and the moon they participate in orgiastic pagan rituals; and now they are trying to deny Adam and Eve, with this Evolution Theory.'

'And who are you, sir?' Inspector Parnell turned to the vicar.

'Reverend St Clair, from Devon.'

'You are out of your jurisdiction, Vicar. By the way, I recall you now, I thought I recognised you. I never forget a face. I met you few years ago, in another case with a ghost dog as it happens, but that was in Staffordshire if I am not mistaken,' the inspector said thoughtfully.

'Yes, I moved to Devon after that,' the vicar confirmed, looking a little embarrassed.

'No wonder you were transferred, the whole village was praying for a ghost dog,' the inspector added, remembering certain details of the case. Constable Parker nodded, after checking a tattered little red leather-covered note book he retrieved from one of his many pockets.

'The reverend is right,' Miss Abington intervened, 'they worship the sun and the moon, instead of Almighty God.' She continued. 'There is no ghost. The Science of Christ's Love believes only in evil, and in God-Mind,' she explained. Inspector Parnell nodded without saying anything.

'Parker, are we at the right address?' the inspector asked the constable, whispering to him from behind a hand.

'Unfortunately we are, Sir. I have just checked myself, as I too was in doubt,' the constable replied, also in a hushed tone, studiously not looking at anything, or anyone in particular. It was at this point that Bernard, upon hearing Miss Abington, spoke up.

'But we agreed the other night that soul and mind are different things,' he said, 'and as far as I am concerned, I have both – mind and soul. So God cannot be the "Mind", I mean to say, "mind" is not exclusive to God. I agree, though, that He is authorised to save our souls.' Bernard defended his position.

'What about the ghost – is it part of the mind or the soul?' Sir Richard asked, not sure about where this was heading.

'I would not be surprised if ghosts were rebellious souls,' Diana added. 'Poor souls, upset with the dire accommodation in which they were placed after being saved, much as I am not satisfied with mine, in this dreadful hotel,' Diana added, exceedingly unhappy with the entire situation now.

'Inspector Parnell, I don't mind if she was a ghost, or a soul, but could you do something about the woman from yesterday?' Ellen asked.

'What woman?' the inspector enquired, but Sir Christopher intervened before Ellen had chance to respond.

'It is nothing important... I mean... it doesn't have any connection with this case.' He squirmed.

'Perhaps it does; actually, it definitely is still in discussion, if Mrs Ellen Price incorporated yesterday the ghost of the victim or the murderer at the stone circle.' Sir Richard tried to defend his point of view.

'For God's sake, is there anybody here who is sane?' the inspector pleaded, exasperated.

However, instead of a verbal answer, he heard a slow clap of hands coming from the table at the back of the hall.

'Who are you, sir?' the inspector asked, upset at the rude intervention.

'Dr Adrian Gruber.' The reply came in a thick Austrian accent.

'Are you German?' the inspector asked, suddenly interested.

'I am Austrian, and I want to congratulate the British nation for the comic scenes I have been witnessing since I put my feet in this country; no wonder they think they evolved from monkeys. When we conquer Britain, we will put all of you in a circus,' Dr Gruber declared.

'I don't like your attitude and comments, Doctor, and show more respect for my Queen as well, at least whilst you are a guest here, or I will arrest you for... for...' Inspector Parnell warned furiously, whilst the constable whispered in his ear,

'I think you wanted to say you will arrest him for offending an authority of the Queen, Sir.'

'Exactly, we are the authority here, and we don't want foreigners going around offending the Queen's subjects,' the inspector agreed, straightening his waistcoat.

'Monkeys... poppycock! Frankly! My uncle, Lord Henry Tollemache, is about to prove that we are descended from the Hyperboreans.' Albert interrupted, outraged by the Austrian.

'I think that you are a little confused about his research, Albert,' Sir Christopher interrupted. 'Your uncle actually wants to prove that the ancient Greeks came to Britain sometime in the Bronze Age, and whilst here they learned some rudiments of astronomy and medicine from the people who lived here before the Celts,' Sir Christopher corrected the young fellow.

'Enough!' Everybody shut up!' the inspector interrupted, then turned to Constable Parker. 'Constable, write there in your notebook that, thank goodness, you, the dog and I don't share the same origins as these people, and don't forget to underline "God deserted us" – I can't say I blame Him, though.'

Meanwhile, in their room, Kate was looking at the family picture in her hand, and suddenly she noticed the little necklace the girl in the photo was wearing; then she addressed Mr Bear, astonished,

'I know who she is – the girl who saved me in the train crash.' Kate stood up, put on her coat and gloves and left the room to go downstairs.

Kate had just arrived at the reception when her attention was attracted by the loud voices coming from the hall, so she enquired of the receptionist what was going on.

'What is happening in the hall?' she asked.

'The police are here to investigate the murder,' the young fellow on the desk replied.

'The police? I need to speak to them,' Kate said, then hurried to the hall, and when she appeared in the open door, the magistrate exclaimed happily,

'Lady Katherine Enfield! Finally, somebody with brains and common sense has arrived amongst this chaos.' He smiled, and beckoned her forwards.

'Now I am definitely confused – brain and soul, mind and sense,' Ellen exclaimed, astonished.

'Don't worry about it, my dear, just save the brain and leave the rest for those who like to waste time and don't appreciate the beauty of a delicious menu, exquisite wines, beautiful dresses like yours, and a little game of cards occasionally.' Peter tried to calm his wife.

'Lady Katherine? Are you able to shed some light on this inquiry?' the inspector asked Kate hopefully.

'I don't know if I can help you, but I might have some information about the girl in this photo,' Kate said, showing him the picture.

'This photo was hanging on the broken wall which, in fact, was hiding the chamber where the bodies were found,' Kate explained.

'And the girl?' Sir Christopher asked, very interested.

'She saved me during the train accident,' Kate replied.

'What accident? When did it happen?' the inspector asked.

'A few weeks ago. When my husband and I arrived from France, we took a train from Dover to London, but the train derailed…'

'I remember that accident. We read about it in the newspapers, didn't we, Sir?' Constable Parker confirmed.

'After the shock of the crash, I woke up, and I was stuck under some broken wood, right next to the train. I could not move, but suddenly this girl came and pulled me out from the wreckage.' Kate continued. 'I don't understand how, but seconds later I was free, and everything where I had been stuck was engulfed in an explosion. She saved my life. I could not see her face very well, because her body was silhouetted against the light from the fire, but I did see her necklace shining in the firelight.' Kate described the episode.

'Hmm, do you know how many people use necklaces similar to this one?' the inspector asked, not entirely convinced.

'Well, Inspector, I never saw a pendant like that before – a golden owl exactly like this one in the photo, with two red ruby eyes. Don't you think it's too much to be a coincidence? A young girl about the same age, with the same necklace?' Kate insisted, without any doubt.

'Inspector, Lady Katherine is a scientist, I would not doubt her word if I were you. I think it would be worthwhile to at least investigate,' Sir Christopher suggested.

'I am not doubting your word, my lady, but you said you could not see her face very well, and even if you did, this photo is at least three years old, thus the girl in turn would be a little older. You don't remember any other details?' the inspector asked hopefully.

'I am so sorry, but so far this is all that I remember, but I have a strange feeling that it was indeed her,' Kate replied sadly.

'Perhaps we should take into consideration the fact that you were shaken because of the accident,' Inspector Parnell suggested. 'I would not be surprised if the murderer who killed her parents, also killed the little girl and stole the necklace. I can see from the photo that it looks quite valuable.' The inspector was trying to build a mental picture of the scene with the information he had to hand.

'You may be right, but I still have hopes that she could be found alive somewhere,' Kate said. 'Perhaps she was scared by the murderer, and escaped, never to come back. We know how far a greedy man might go, especially if he thinks that somebody invaded his land,' Kate said, looking at Sir Edmund.

'How dare you accuse me of killing somebody?' Sir Edmund reacted, enraged.

'You are the one who goes around threatening people whose purpose is to contribute to science. Nobody is stealing your land, and sincerely, I hope that this young girl is still alive somewhere, as human lives are much more important than your land, sir.' Kate addressed Sir Edmund harshly.

'Calm down, Lady Katherine…' The inspector tried to bring her to reason.

'Why does everybody want to "calm me down"?' Kate complained.

'Perhaps because we are dealing with a murder case,' Sir Christopher suggested. 'I'm sorry, Kate, but we have to stick to the evidence, especially as it is not a recent event,' He said soothingly, smiling.

'I think we have had some good progress in this "lost" case, which is a good sign. Where is the owner of the hotel?' The magistrate looked around, unable to locate him.

'I am here, right behind you, sir,' the miserable hotelier replied, standing with his daughter, both observing the enquiry quietly.

'Could you bring us some tea?' Sir Christopher asked. 'I think we all deserve a good old cup of tea to cheer us up. How does that sound, Mr Clark?' the magistrate beamed, aiming to recalibrate tempers and give the police time to analyse the information collected during the first part of the inquiry.

Kate noticed the look Mr Clark gave to his daughter, and the sign he made with a nod of his head – a typical sign of authority, reaffirming the place where women without qualifications, study, or good birth would be relegated.

Later, when the guests and police officers were drinking tea and examining some freshly baked scones, they were interrupted by a lady who entered the lounge, clearly upset.

'Where is Henry? Where is Henry Tollemache?' the lady asked of the room impatiently.

'What do you want with my husband?' Diana asked impatiently.

'Don't worry, I don't want your husband, at least not alive. I heard that Adam's body was found, and I want an explanation, now,' the lady declared.

'Could somebody lock the entrance, please, to stop more people coming in?' Inspector Parnell cried. 'By the way, Parker, include in the "suggestion list" to contact the agency that provides the courier service here – they might be interested in opening a branch near us; they are quite efficient as the news runs faster in this place,' the inspector told him, then addressed the woman, 'Who are you and what is your business with the deceased?' He looked at her down his nose.

'I am Lady Georgiana Larkhill, and I didn't have any business with him. I am interested in who killed his wife. She was a friend of mine, and my druid priestess. All these years we thought she was killed by her husband. Did anybody find her daughter? She was my goddaughter,' Lady Georgiana stated.

'Lady Georgiana, we have hope that she is still alive.' Kate addressed her. 'I am quite certain that I saw her a few weeks ago, half way between Dover and London. Do you know any detail that might help us to confirm her identity – a necklace perhaps?' Kate tried to calm Georgiana down and get more information at the same time.

'Yes, of course, she had a necklace with a little golden owl with little rubies for eyes. I had a goldsmith make that owl for her when she was born. She loved it so much. Her name was Anna, and I used to tell her local stories, legends, mythologies. I always had a fertile imagination, although I didn't have children. When she was seven she asked me to call her Panacea, after one of the myths I had taught her. She wanted to be a nurse, and I had everything arranged for her to go to college when she was seventeen, but when she was twelve... that terrible tragedy... with her mother.' Georgina explained.

'It was her, Inspector! I am certain now,' Kate told him. 'She saved me. I tried to speak, but she said, "The sun and moon – Panacea." How could her parents' killer steal her owl and know about the name Panacea?' Kate said, full of hope.

'Nobody knew about the name "Panacea", it was our secret,' Lady Georgiana agreed, but the inspector interrupted her, putting up his hand.

'Could you tell me, please, where does the name "Panacea" come from? I have never heard it before.'

'It is Greek, and means *a remedy to kill all ills*,' Lady Georgiana replied proudly, and continued. 'I am pleased to help you. I can help financially as well, if it helps to find my goddaughter Anna,' she stated, full of hope.

'Don't worry, my lady, we will contact the police in Dover and London, and try to find the girl,' Inspector Parnell assured her, then turned to the constable, who in turn assured the inspector in advance,

'Don't worry, Sir, I have just written down in my notebook to contact them as soon as possible.'

'Thank you, Parker.' The inspector nodded, very satisfied.

'Inspector, I need to find my husband and bring him back, as I am certain that Andrew will corroborate my story,' Kate interjected. 'After the accident with the train, a policeman brought me one of my belongings, which was found by the mysterious girl. The officer could describe her to you, I have no doubt. My husband knows his name,' Kate explained, then addressed the hotelier's daughter, who was watching everything in silence.

'Miss Clark, would you ask one of the men to saddle a horse for me, please?' Then Kate hurried out of the hall, determined to find Andrew as quickly as possible to speak about the policeman who'd helped them after the accident.

The day was not as bright as the previous one. It was winter, and the days would be short for a while. However, the prospect of finding the girl who saved her life lifted Kate's spirits somewhat. Kate had not spent the last winter or summer in England, so she was grateful that it was not snowing. The winter this year looked quite promising and not as cold as previous years.

She was absorbed in her thoughts as she rode to Stonehenge along a lane, looking forward to finding Andrew, partly because she wanted to get out of the heavy atmosphere at the hotel, and also due to her excitement about the next step of the astronomical experiment.

Suddenly, though, she felt that something was not quite right with the horse. The strap that held the saddle seemed loose, and although in a fraction of a second she tried to hold on to the reins, her effort was in vain – there was nothing she could do, and she fell.

However, Kate didn't lose her consciousness completely; she felt a bit dizzy from the fall, but she got up and brushed herself off. Standing there, she heard the sound of dry branches being broken, like footsteps. She looked around but couldn't see anybody, so she called Andrew's name, thinking he might have returned to the hotel early and probably came after her.

'Is it you, Andrew? I am here, where are you?' But nobody replied. Then she thought it might be an animal, perhaps a rabbit, or a fox.

The weather was still pleasant, so Kate began to walk as she could see her horse farther along the lane. When she finally reached the horse, she found that the strap looked as if it had been cut, perhaps with a knife, which immediately alerted her to the fact her fall was not merely an accident; but it didn't make sense, unless this horse was meant for someone else?

Kate decided to walk back to the hotel, guiding her horse by the reins, but whilst she was checking if he was fine to walk, she heard that strange noise again, and Kate realised without any doubt that someone was approaching, hiding in the hedgerow. She turned to see who was behind her, but was right then hit hard on the head, and an intense pain made everything around her spin until she lost her balance and fell to the floor, unconscious.

Chapter 11

Andrew and Henry were walking across Salisbury Plain away from Stonehenge, in the direction indicated by the astronomical alignment Henry had discovered.

'Have you checked your compass, Andrew?' Henry asked, agitated.

'Yes, still northeast, and not a mile yet since our last stop,' Andrew reassured him, carefully examining his compass.

'There, Andrew, look! Barrows, several of them!' Henry exclaimed, pointing excitedly.

'So, if your theory is correct, those ones are very important, since they are not randomly distributed like most of the others,' Andrew observed. 'If this is the case, there is no doubt that what or who was buried there does appear to have had their privilege expressed by the alignment of the sun and the moon from the great stone circle.' Andrew turned to his companion,

'The two big questions are: why did they want those barrows determined precisely by the stone circle? Secondly, how did they build the stone circle so precisely in order to reflect the dual alignment of both the sun and the moon?'

'I don't know, but I do hope you might agree to continue with this project, and help me answer these questions,' Henry replied cheerfully.

'We will have to investigate very carefully because according to Kate, based on Sir Joshua's research, the Greeks came to Britain much earlier than we ever realised. She believes they learned their knowledge of astronomy and geometry from the people here,' Andrew explained.

'Of course, we were the Hyperboreans!' Henry exclaimed.

'What intrigues me is the stone circle,' Andrew said. 'Kate thinks that it could be an Oracle of Apollo, possibly used as a place to cure sickness. She also found ancient Greek biographers who state categorically that Pythagoras was not killed in Greece – that he came here around 500 BC, and it was here that he developed his theories of music and harmony, which were continued later by his disciples back in Greece,' Andrew explained.

'I don't see why not?' Henry nodded. 'That myth does indeed say that Apollo passed the winters in Hyperborea. Kate is right. Apollo was the god of music and Muses; he was usually depicted with a lyre on pottery and in sculptures, as you know – Apollo the Healer, and the Patron of Muses. That's it! He established an Oracle here, Hyperborea, and his son Asclepius became the God of Medicine – everything matches!' Henry was excited.

'Yes indeed – an ancient civilisation, far older than we imagined, in which medicine and religion, astronomy, music and harmony were not dissociated,' Andrew agreed.

'Well, give me an example of a religion where its believers didn't sing for their particular deity or deities,' Henry said. 'The role of music in religion might have a much deeper meaning than we supposed...' he suggested.

'I thought you were an atheist?' Andrew challenged.

'That is a very slippery path, my dear fellow... When you are old, life and death start to make more sense, and your mind instead of speaking with the world decides to go straight deep to the heart,' Henry explained, smiling.

'Maybe music has an important role, not just in religion, but also for the healing process – a balance, between mind and body,' Andrew mused.

'...You mean body and soul?' Henry corrected playfully.

'We didn't yet start to drink like the others, Henry. Let's postpone this discussion about mind and soul, for later, after dinner, perhaps.' Andrew smiled, and Henry nodded.

'This may have influenced Pythagoras in some way with respect to his belief in transmigration of the soul,' Henry said thoughtfully.

'You don't believe in transmigration of the soul, do you?' Andrew asked, startled.

'No, of course I don't, but he did, and our job here is to connect the Greek civilisation with those who came before and erected the first stone,' Henry replied, adding, 'More than the uncertainties of the future, the past is fascinating, Andrew, precisely because we have not unveiled its great mysteries, at least not yet. How boring would the world be without them?' He laughed. 'Now that we have found the barrows indicated by the Sarsen alignments, it is time to go home and enjoy our Christmas celebrations together, because I have a big surprise which will delight some, yet which others will certainly hate.' He beamed at the prospect. 'There is nothing that we can do here until we get permission to excavate these barrows. Come on, let's have a glass of wine and ride back to the hotel,' Henry insisted, very pleased with the situation.

They were nearing the hotel when Henry brought up a more personal matter with Andrew, after their long morning together.

'I am very pleased you married such an adorable and intelligent young lady, Andrew. You seem much happier, indeed, somehow younger, than the last time I saw you. Love works miracles, my dear fellow; if not younger, at least much happier.' He smiled.

'You couldn't be more correct, Henry. She is the most important thing in my life. I would follow her to the edge of the world, if it was what she wanted. I could not live without her, I must say,' Andrew replied, from the deepest corners of his heart, with shining eyes, then added,

'You, too, seem happy with your new wife. You seem like a bull with renewed vigour.' Andrew smiled, and Henry laughed.

'Diana has the beauty and soul of a typhoon, a dangerous combination, I must admit,' he said. 'However, just like life, love without risk is bland, it is not worth experiencing,' Henry explained, smiling as he got off his horse, then the servant holding their bridles took their steeds in the direction of the hotel's stable.

Inside, Andrew and Henry were immediately introduced to the two police officers, so whilst Henry was questioned by Inspector Parnell, Andrew took a quick look around the hall. Upon seeing no sign of Kate, he excused himself and went to their room, certain that he would find her upstairs. His search proved fruitless, though, so he decided to look for her outside and went to the back of the hotel. He thought she might be in the garden, given the atmosphere in the lounge didn't seem very cheerful, certainly unlikely to hold Kate's attention for long. Knowing her as he did, or at least what he was allowed to know, he was certain that she would have her little notebook, and would be deliberating over the puzzling aspects of her recent research.

After washing, he donned a clean shirt, put on his coat and gloves, just in case Kate was outside. He went downstairs quickly, checked from the door of the dining room but didn't see her, then just as he was about to leave, Sir Christopher called him over for a conversation, to which he reluctantly agreed out of politeness. Andrew was determined to be as quick as possible as it would be soon dark and he didn't want to delay the good news to his wife about the barrows.

'How was your search for the unknown, Andrew? Hopefully you brought more mysteries to entertain us? The investigation into this murder is getting nowhere; and to make things worse, scones without Devon clotted cream are quite average,' Sir Christopher said. 'By the way, Kate gave us some very important information – she finally remembered where she had seen the girl in the photo.'

'Did she? Where?' Andrew asked, interested.

'It seems that this girl, whose name is Anna apparently, was the one who helped her at that calamitous train crash. Kate recognised the necklace with the golden owl,' Sir Christopher explained.

'How bizarre! How could this girl suddenly appear, hundreds of miles away?' Andrew was astonished, then, in a hurry, 'I'm sorry, Chris, but I have to find Kate, it is getting late, and dark...'

'Wasn't she with you two?' Sir Christopher asked, surprised.

'No, why? Isn't she in the hotel or garden?' Andrew asked, concerned.

'Well, a couple of hours ago she apologised, saying she was going to meet you. It seems a little strange, if you didn't meet her on your way back. As far as I am aware there is no other logical way to the stone circle from here,' Sir Christopher replied.

'Was she intending to ride?' Andrew asked, although it was a stupid question, as she would never go walking, knowing that they were on horseback.

'Yes, indeed,' Sir Christopher confirmed.

'Strange, very strange,' Andrew mused. 'Kate always carries her compass; and there is only one route to follow. She would never get lost, I am certain. I will go and check for her in the garden.' He apologised then left, leaving Sir Christopher intrigued about her whereabouts, as deep inside he knew it didn't make sense that Kate would linger in the garden all this time, determined as she had been to find Andrew and discuss the girl on the train.

As Andrew suspected, Kate was not in the garden. After looking for her outside the hotel, he decided to ask the guests to see if anyone knew of her whereabouts; however, the search inside was in vain also, reinforcing Sir Christopher's worries that Kate had left the hotel hours earlier with the intention of meeting her husband.

Kate opened her eyes, and it took a few seconds for her to understand what was happening. She remembered she had fallen from her horse, but also that he was not to be blamed, as the saddle had suddenly slipped and she unavoidably fell off.

She was a little dazed and her vision was blurred, but gradually she recalled the sequence of events, and it seemed somebody was following her, then she bumped her head... but that was all she could remember. Where was she? Kate sat up on the grass and looked around, when a noise in the bushes behind made her turn, so it was with considerable relief she could see Eleanor bringing two horses – one of them was Kate's.

'Thank goodness you are here, Eleanor. I'm so glad you found my horse. I think I might have tripped over a stone, or a rabbit hole or something, and he ran off,' Kate said.

'Where did you find her, where is she?' Eleanor interrupted angrily.

'Who? What are you talking about?' Kate asked, confused.

'Don't think of making a fool out of me. You aristocrats think you can trick people with your false promises. You and Anna will not get me arrested, it was all his fault.' She revealed a knife she was carrying, and asked again, 'If you don't want me to kill you, tell me, where is Anna?' she snarled, threatening her with the knife, waving it about near Kate's face.

At the sight of the knife, Kate's mind cleared and suddenly she understood the gravity of her predicament. She spoke quietly to Eleanor.

'You killed her parents and the dog? Why? Was it a plan to kill the owner of the hotel so your father could later buy it cheaply at auction?' Kate asked, trying to fathom what was going on.

'Don't be stupid!' Eleanor barked. 'Do you think that women like me don't have the right to be loved and get married? My father has nothing to do with it. I always had a brilliant mind, and a normal life, until Adam destroyed my dreams and everything,' Eleanor spat, her voice full of hatred.

'Listen, Eleanor,' Kate said quietly in a calm and friendly voice, 'whatever happened in the past, it is over now. Don't do anything silly, please.' Kate tried to reason with her.

'Adam seduced me and promised that he would leave his wife,' Eleanor explained. 'He told me we would go to America and live together forever, but it was all lies, from the beginning.' She sobbed. 'His wife was a priestess in Lady Georgiana's druidic order who loved that stupid child, Anna. Lady Georgiana started inviting the family for parties, afternoon teas, and I was increasingly cast aside by him. He was fascinated with his family being invited to attend aristocratic events. I could feel Adam getting more and more distant from me,' Eleanor explained, with her heart full of angst, and then she continued, as if hypnotised by her own words.

'I remember that winter night, the winter solstice, when Adam accused me of pressuring him. He said that it would ruin his daughter's future by abandoning his family and leaving Britain to go to America with me.' Tears ran down Eleanor's cheeks. 'He told me that Lady Georgiana would never accept her goddaughter had an unfaithful and deviant father; it would ruin the family's reputation forever.'

'So you killed him?' Kate asked.

'First, I went to the kitchen and stabbed his wife. The girl was in shock and couldn't move; it was easier for me to stab her too. Then I went to the reception, and when Adam saw me coming from the kitchen, he became furious, thinking that I'd told his wife everything. I caught him by surprise – he didn't know I had the knife in my pocket. I killed him, and I had to get rid of his dog too, as it was barking like crazy.' Eleanor paused; it was as if she was in a trance, reliving those moments in the past. Then she continued.

'We used to meet in that secret chamber behind the wooden wall, you know. I didn't think twice – I opened the chamber's door and dragged his body and the dog's in. It took me a while to do that. Then I hung that picture on the wall and put a big chair next to it, to make sure that nobody would ever discover that chamber. Suddenly everything came to my mind – I decided to leave his wife and his daughter's bodies in the kitchen so everybody would think that he killed the family and then escaped.' Her eyes glistened. Kate nodded, and Eleanor continued her story.

'When I went to the kitchen, Anna had gone. She wasn't dead... she had escaped. I ran outside and looked everywhere, trying to find her, but it was getting very cold and there was no sign of her. I had to leave the search for the next day, hoping that she would appear dead somewhere, because I knew I'd stabbed her deeply. Luck was on my side, though, as the hotel had only a couple of guests who were sleeping when everything happened. The day after, Lady Georgiana came early to the hotel to take Anna for a picnic with some friends, who came to visit her. Thus it was the "Important Lady" and her two guests who alerted everyone; conveniently for me, and the good news was that she raised the hypothesis that Adam killed his wife and ran away with the girl...' Eleanor smiled grimly.

Kate, who was still sitting, noticed a stone in the track and remembered the first time she spoke with Andrew, eighteen years ago, when he had saved her and Mr Bear from Robert, who wanted to burn her toy bear. Here was another strategic stone, like the one in her past, so she grabbed it whilst Eleanor was distracted telling her story, not noticing Kate cradle the stone and hiding it in her palm.

'I wanted to stay around to find out what happened with Anna,' Eleanor continued, 'but as time passed and there was no sign of her, I presumed she must surely have died, her body left undiscovered in some rural place,' Eleanor explained matter-of-factly. She turned back to look at Kate, then continued.

'When they couldn't find any of Adam's relatives, they put the hotel up for auction and I pushed my father to buy it; he had sufficient funds. It was a good way to control the situation and to not allow anybody to search it ever again. My strategy worked until now, when you appeared here to destroy my life. Now, I need to know, where is Anna?' Eleanor insisted, walking towards Kate, threatening her with the knife.

'I don't know,' Kate replied. 'It all happened the way I said. She saved my life, and I didn't see her again. I didn't even know her name was Anna,' Kate pleaded, her eyes fixed on Eleanor's knife. She prepared to try an escape. There would be only one chance to survive this insane woman.

'Well, if you don't know where she is, I don't need you, do I?' Eleanor shouted.

Kate found herself in a desperate battle for survival. She tried to stand as Eleanor charged at her, but the girl stabbed her in the stomach. Kate's waistcoat was a thick tweed though, and as she turned to avoid the knife, her whalebone corset stopped it from cutting her deeply; luckily the injury was neither deep nor serious enough to stop Kate from hitting Eleanor on the head with a stunning blow from the stone in her hand. Eleanor stumbled to her knees on the floor, dazed and bloodied, but she did not drop the knife.

Kate didn't think twice – she ran for her life, trying to staunch the blood soaking her waistcoat. She ran as quickly as she could, whilst behind her Kate could hear Eleanor, screaming in pain but also calling out her name, vowing to kill her.

At the George Hotel, everyone could feel an uneasy tension in the air. Nobody could rationally explain the events in that place, and there was an undercurrent of hushed gossip and speculation spreading throughout the guests and staff.

'What do you think happened to Kate?' Ellen asked Diana, clearly frightened.

'Nothing, Ellen. Kate always chooses to disappear at an inconvenient time; it's in her nature,' Diana replied, bored.

'I knew her relationship with ghost-owls and ghost-dogs would be a problem at some point,' Sir Richard stated. 'Would you like another glass of wine, Chris?' he asked, offering a glass to his friend.

'Shhh... Richard, I need to know what Andrew is going to do,' Sir Christopher replied as Andrew organised things.

'Henry, I have to leave now to find Kate,' Andrew declared. 'I'm taking the two stable-hands with me. She might be wounded somewhere. Tell the inspector that I will speak with him when I get back.' Then he hurried off with the two men.

Meanwhile, Constable Parker addressed Inspector Parnell.

'How do we always end up getting involved with these supernatural situations, Sir?'

'It's your fault, Parker,' the inspector replied, annoyed.

'Mine? Why my fault, Sir?' the constable replied, taken aback.

'Why didn't you take down the wrong address? At least we would have an excuse. At the moment we are stuck here in this infernal hotel until New Year,' the inspector complained.

'Why until "New Year", Sir?' Constable Parker asked, feeling a little hopeless.

'If this crime is still unsolved after three long years, what do you think is going to happen now that we have two more bodies, hmm?' the inspector explained, extremely annoyed.

'Three, you mean, Sir?' the constable corrected, carefully.

After giving the policeman an icy look, the inspector added,

'Hopefully it doesn't start snowing, to make things worse.' He sighed, then in a gruff but friendly tone, he said, 'Come on, Parker, ask the barman for a vintage Scotch for the both of us. Actually, a double, eh?'

'Yes, sir!' the constable replied cheerfully, and hurried away.

'Inspector Parnell, would you like to accompany me to examine the crime scene?' Sir Christopher suggested.

'Well, why not? I will miss my Christmas turkey anyway,' The Inspector agreed.

'We Austrians place our sense of duty above anything else.' Dr Gruber taunted the inspector.

'The only thing more important than my Christmas turkey is the Queen. And you are not my turkey, nor my Queen; so if you don't shut up I will arrest you for obstructing the course of justice,' the inspector warned him.

'Tell me, how am I obstructing the law?' Dr Gruber replied angrily.

'For disqualifying my turkey,' the inspector replied impatiently. Then, he turned his back on the Austrian to address Sir Christopher.

'Come on, Sir Christopher, show me the crime scene.'

They left the lounge to the secret wooden room where constable Parker was waiting for them at the dining room door with their double whiskies on a little silver tray. They sipped their whisky and began examining the scene.

'Why the hell did they hide the body in here?' the inspector wondered aloud.

'That is an important question, Inspector,' Sir Christopher replied. 'It feeds my theory that it was not a robbery; nothing was stolen from the hotel.'

'You might be right. If it was a robbery and Mr Fairfax tried to resist, why bother to hide his body but not his wife's as well?' the inspector asked.

'Exactly what I wondered,' the magistrate agreed.

'Somebody wanted to incriminate him for the death of his wife, perhaps?' Constable Parker interjected, his cheeks flushed from gulping down the double whisky.

'Very good, Parker, very good,' the inspector praised him, 'However, where does the daughter fit in? I have no idea.'

Suddenly, the magistrate examined the carpet at the bottom of the wall, noticing four marks there.

'Look, what do you think these marks on the carpet are?' he pointed.

'Four "interesting" discoloured marks, I suppose,' the inspector replied.

Without saying anything, the magistrate walked to the reception looking round until he found a big chair in the back.

'Constable, could you come here and help me with this chair?' he asked.

Constable Parker dutifully obliged, and under Sir Christopher's direction, both carried the chair to the wooden wall. Then they tried to place the chair's legs exactly in the marks once left on the carpet. It was an exact match, and the four men looked at each other with puzzled brows.

'Are you thinking what I am thinking, Sir Christopher?' the inspector asked.

'I think we might have a conversation with the owner of this hotel,' Sir Christopher replied, with an enigmatic smile.

'Constable Parker, ask Mr Clark to come here, we need to speak with him,' the inspector ordered.

'Yes, sir!' He left in a hurry, hoping that he as well might have his Christmas turkey after all.

Five minutes later, Mr Clark and Constable Parker arrived back in reception, and the inspector fired the first question.

'Mr Clark, when did you buy this hotel?' he asked.

'At auction, two years ago, I told you that,' Mr Clark replied, puzzled.

'Did you know the victim?' the inspector asked.

'Which one?' the owner asked, in a worried voice.

'Any of them,' the inspector asked impatiently.

'Well, I knew the owner; I met him once. My daughter used to come here regularly. She knew Mr Fairfax's wife; they both joined Lady Georgiana's druidic order – the one for women. I never understood why, it didn't sound very Christian to me, but I didn't interfere, because Lady Georgiana is very well known around here, and nobody wants to… cross her path, if you understand what I mean? Even Sir Edmund tries to avoid her; people used to say that she is some kind of witch…' He paused, watching for some response.

The inspector remained implacable, completely unreadable, so the hotelier continued.

'I didn't believe that, of course, but trust me no one round here wants to go against a powerful lady like that; not here, not in these surroundings,' the owner said, as if trying to warn the officers.

'Did Lady Georgiana have a good relationship with the deceased family?' the magistrate asked, interested.

'It seems that the child was her goddaughter – mother and child used to go to the lady's parties. I think that she didn't like Mr Fairfax too much, but he used to go to her house sometimes, when she invited the whole family; I don't think she trusted him. Anyway, it was not my business.'

The owner wanted to get rid of them, but Sir Christopher insisted,

'Was your daughter, Miss Eleanor, very close to Mrs. Fairfax?' He looked into the hoteliers's eyes, watching for the response.

'No, she couldn't stand her. I told you – this order, Lady Georgiana and Mrs. Fairfax, they didn't seem Christian. To be honest, I didn't want my daughter to be involved with them,' the hotelier explained.

'What about the enquiry three years ago? Did the police talk to you about it?' Sir Christopher asked, intrigued.

'No, why? I didn't have anything to do with that man. I only met him once,' Mr Clark replied, whilst the inspector and the magistrate exchanged glances.

'Did your daughter have a good relationship with Lady Georgiana?' the inspector asked, digging deeper.

'No, she was always complaining that Lady Georgiana only cared about Mrs Fairfax and her child, so there was no chance of my daughter rising to a higher level in the order of priestesses.'

'Do you think your daughter resented this?' the magistrate asked, inclined to give the man more space to talk.

'Who would not be? Although I didn't like her involvement with these pagan women, there aren't opportunities for people here, especially for a woman without proper education or good birth, like my daughter; but I did everything I could to help her, whenever possible,' the hotelier replied defensively.

'You didn't touch your savings to give her any opportunities, did you?' Sir Christopher asked.

'There wouldn't be much left for us to live on if I had, would there?' the hotelier said bitterly.

'I can see that after Mrs Fairfax's death, your daughter finally had the opportunity of climbing up the ranks in the Order,' Sir Christopher observed. 'Miss Eleanor now is the second highest druidess, despite the fact that she had often complained about Lady Georgiana in the past. Your daughter doesn't seem to care about Christianity, if I am not mistaken,' Sir Christopher mused.

'Oh, that's just what I need – my daughter not only involved with those heretics, but also suspected of murder,' the owner complained, and walked off angrily, leaving the investigators in the reception.

'Do you think he could be involved in the murders, Sir?' Constable Parker asked the inspector.

'It is possible. Our killer had to have knowledge about this chamber in order to hide the bodies; someone with access to the family, with a good motive to kill,' the inspector said.

'Motive, Inspector, motive! With my experience I can tell you that we here have a case of passion, or a case involving religious belief,' Sir Christopher interjected. 'However, none of those involved seem to be religious fanatics. This order of druids is more likely a social club for bored aristocrats; passion, though, can trigger jealousy, perhaps resentment, for not being able to achieve their expectations. Hopelessness can lead you to despair and wield a dagger against the source of the pain,' Sir Christopher told them.

'...an unbearable pain in the body can be treated, but how could you treat a "soul in pain"?' Sir Richard asked, joining the three investigators in reception, with his usual glass of wine in his hand.

'Fascinating, Richard! Sometimes you surprise me by untying one of the most intricate knots in a rope,' Sir Christopher said, happy with his friend's contribution.

'Of course, Arthur used to say that even a ghost could be trapped and stuck to the crime scene, as much as the murderer. In his words, the scene is sewn with knots that often our eyes do not notice; the knots are there, though, tying the soul and imprisoning the body without chance of breaking free, unless the murderer is grabbed,' Sir Richard said proudly, not noticing that the magistrate was a little uncomfortable with his explanation, due to the exchange of glances between the police officers.

'Who is Arthur?' Inspector Parnell asked, intrigued.

'Arthur Conan Doyle. We used to discuss his books and talk about ghosts in Cambridge...' Sir Richard started to explain, but was interrupted by Sir Christopher, who hurriedly tried to save the situation.

'It is about fiction; they discuss literature because Conan Doyle writes crime novels. Have you heard about Sherlock Holmes? You know how these people are – a ghost here, a mystery there; nothing like a fertile imagination,' Sir Christopher explained.

'Hmm...' the inspector made a slight movement of the head, without being completely convinced with the explanation, then continued. 'We shall find Miss Eleanor for a few questions. Parker, bring her to the reception,' he instructed.

The two friends joined the inspector for another whisky, whilst Constable Parker went out to find Mr Clark's daughter, with his head full of whiskey, ghosts, and every kind of speculation that could arise from such a strange circumstance, on such a cold afternoon, on that distant island where the north wind blows.

Chapter 12

Kate stopped, exhausted, then looked down at her stomach, touching her waistcoat gingerly to see how bad it was. The waistcoat was crusted with blood so it was difficult to see it properly. It was hurting, though, and when she moved, blood seeped from the wound. Her other hand was sore too, grazed around the wrist and along the forearm when she had put it out to break her fall from the horse. It was not dark yet, but she didn't know where she was, and with a cloudy winter sky, she doubted she would be able to find any constellations later to help guide her. Kate decided her only option was to keep running; with a little luck, she would find some place to hide.

Exhausted and in agony, Kate stumbled to the floor, and looking to the heavens, she wished it was already night, and to be blessed with a clear sky.

'I need to find you, Little Bear. You said I would never be alone, because you would be there, always, showing me the way,' Kate muttered, breathing deeply to find the strength to keep going.

Suddenly, Kate heard the call of an owl, and for the first time she felt safe because she recognised the tree where the owl had called out from. In the branches she could see the owl serenely observing both her and that wintry landscape. Kate remembered seeing the tree earlier in the day, standing, imposing and alone in the middle of a frosty field, which a few months earlier would have been green and full of life.

Andrew used to say that only she could see colours in a grey field. She had to head south if she wanted to get back to the hotel, but considering how far it was, with night approaching and cold seeping into her bones, Kate knew that it might not be possible for her to make it back alone, and she suspected Eleanor would be following her visible footsteps in the frosty grass.

It was so cold... her legs were losing strength, and she felt so tired, but Kate wasn't the sort of person to give up. When she put her hands on the ground to stand, some turf gave way and soft soil opened up, a bit like a hole typical of those made by rabbits, or even a badger, or maybe it had been a sheep scrape? Whatever it was, it was enough to give her an idea. She didn't waste any time, and pulled at the turf to see how big it was – might it be sufficient to hide her until the daylight came again next morning? With luck, that hole could shelter her from the cold, and protect her from the dangers of the night. She had a choice: stumble on through the darkness with an armed attacker following, intent on killing her, or hiding and resting, in a place where she could have a tiny chance of surviving.

Fighting darkness was not new to Kate, and she knew it was a desperate choice, as the cold could be intense in winter at night. That saying, she had a good coat and thick gloves, which gave her hope that she might be graced with a miracle.

Whilst digging the hole, with some difficulty given her injured hand, Kate noticed that the soil was getting even softer and she wondered what made that unusual hole, since rabbits don't make their houses with such grand proportions. However, it was not time to question or understand the designs of Fate – the most important thing was to be able to get into the hole and wait for events to unfold. She cared less about what lay ahead than the immediate danger.

Kate crawled through the hole she had excavated and a sizeable chamber revealed itself to her. It was not dark yet, so the last of the daylight illuminated just enough of that subterranean abode for her to see her surroundings, if but dimly. It was with astonishment that she saw the remains of a small human body; she could see some bones mixed and scattered around a small skull. Without any other context, it was impossible to identify who was buried there, their age or gender.

A little disappointed for not being able to find any evidence, she decided to explore the low chamber, but when she was about to move away from the remains of the body, she noticed a metallic object, partially buried beneath the skull. Carefully, Kate excavated it without disturbing her resting companion. When she finally had it in her hand she was shocked to recognise the golden necklace and the owl pendant with ruby-red eyes. That little jewel gave Kate no doubt about who was there in front of her, as incredible and unlikely that might sound. In her heart, Kate knew exactly who this was – the young girl who'd saved her life once, and now the same girl, Anna, was right there, perhaps showing her the shelter and hope.

Gently, Kate took the necklace to keep as evidence to identify Anna later, if she herself could survive Eleanor. Inside that little cavity, it was not as cold as outside, and examining her wound, she noticed that it had completely stopped bleeding, her waistcoat acting like some rudimentary bandage. Kate reached over and placed her hands on Anna's bones and spoke in a whisper.

'You wanted to be a nurse, Anna Panacea. Were you in my dreams all this time, cold and wounded? Were you all this time, even before I heard your name from that old woman in Greece…? You ended up here, viciously injured, looking for healing and protection until dawn, but you couldn't make it, and this place turned out to be your sepulchre.'

Kate smiled, thinking that the Greeks would say that Zeus would not allow Asclepius to cure Panacea this time, since he was also banished from the world of the living for his audacity. Myths and religion always find a way to explain things, even the inexplicable.

Kate looked around the chamber, and with the last thread of daylight, she noticed a small carved stone figurine. It was a rudimentary statue, without any precise indication about the entity, who could be represented; perhaps that little chamber was part of a kind of place of worship, involving the people who once lived in that desolate place, Kate thought.

Kate knew the statue would remain in darkness for another millennium, or perhaps never be named at all, were it not for an object which was sculpted in stone, firmly held by one of the entity's hands.

Such sculpted detail took Kate's thoughts back to Greece, and with bright eyes Kate smiled happily, having no doubt about what she had just discovered. She knew that object was certainly the centre and the meaning of everything that might have once been part of that tomb, and although the work in stone was rudimentary, the symbol could not be anything other than a *caduceus* with an entwined snake, which made Kate take a sudden deep breath when she approached the sculpture, before she eventually uttered his name, loudly,

'*Asclepius! Sir Joshua was right. We are in Hyperborea! That means Apollo, who passed the winter in this distant land, had his oracle here at Stonehenge. Now everything makes sense. People came here for Apollo's oracle, to cure and heal their illnesses and wounds*,' she thought; and speaking to herself in a whisper,

'The owl and the serpent guided the supplicants underground, as the darkness didn't let them see. If Apollo could not heal them, Asclepius would make their passage from the living world to the world of the dead, since he himself had to make the crossing. That would explain Apollo's healing temple inside the stone circle, and Asclepius' chamber underground.'

Kate's heart was now filled with a stoic determination to survive the night, but suddenly she stepped on something that made a dry noise, so she bent down to see what it could be, and despite the scarce light which was more like a penumbra, she realised they were more human bones, or rather, fragments of bones, and some of them seemed to be parts of skulls, especially concentrated around the sculpture of Asclepius; a scene that seemed to be lost in time, as by the state of those bones they were certainly ancient, perhaps older than the Celts, whilst many other bones might have disintegrated over the millennia. Kate had no doubt that they were buried there, near the statue of Asclepius, and although the excitement was huge, she could not think properly, as she was losing her balance.

So, moving with difficulty due to the pain and cold, Kate decided to sit next to Anna's body near the entrance of that subterranean chamber. She was tired, and with her mind racing, Kate tried to scrape soil to close off most of the entrance, leaving just a little hole to get some air, and to hear someone who could be looking for her; then she said to herself,

'Andrew will come. I know he will, and we will take you back home to rest in peace, Panacea,' looking over at Anna's skull and bones.

A few minutes later, Kate opened her eyes when she heard a dreadful howl that seemed similar to that of a dog howling at the moon, but she also heard someone shouting her name repeatedly. That voice wasn't any other than Eleanor's, who sounded furious, and who was running around with the dagger in her hand.

Eleanor knew there was no way back after she had told Kate everything; she hoped, though, that Kate was mortally wounded, but she couldn't return to the hotel without finding Kate, because if she was alive the others would find her sooner or later, and she would tell them the whole truth. So, for Eleanor, it was imperative to find Kate or her body.

Tired and very cold, Eleanor paused when she saw a small pile of stones, which she thought could have been used by Kate to hide. Approaching slowly and quietly, Eleanor was certain that there was no other way for Kate to escape. Suddenly, though, Eleanor heard a strange sound behind her, which made her turn around abruptly, and with her eyes full of fury and terror, she recognised the black dog with the fiery eyes, snarling at her with equal fury – two creatures full of hate and spite met again; a reckoning determined by time, pain and memory.

Eleanor suddenly realised that his attack was imminent, and furiously, as if possessed by madness, she screamed at the dog.

'You filthy hound! I killed you once, so I can kill you again if I have to, and send you back to hell, where you should have stayed.'

The dog growled even more fiercely, baring his sharp white teeth, then, as if rejoicing from a final moment that would soon fade into the air, he gave a huge last growl before leaping up at her. Eleanor couldn't do anything to protect herself other than cross her hands in front of her face, but she lost her balance and fell to the floor where she lay still and lifeless after hitting her head on one of the sharp stones on the ground...

Whilst blood seeped from that fatal wound in Eleanor's skull, a dog's howl echoed across the plain, making Kate, from the chamber underground, open her eyes at the same time as the strange but somewhat comforting hoot of an owl somewhere out there was heard. She looked to Anna's remains and an inexplicable thought came to her mind, something that she'd heard a long time ago *"The dead return to collect what was due to them..."*. *'Maybe it is not my time yet,'* she thought to herself.

Andrew found no sign of Kate, so he was hopeful when one of the men he had hired showed him a small piece of frayed waistcoat fabric, which he recognised as belonging to Kate. The man explained he had found it not too far from Stonehenge. In a hurry, Andrew headed in the direction where they had found the fabric; it didn't matter how long the night and darkness lasted, or how cold it was – that piece of fabric fuelled his heart with love and hope, fighting away the fear of loss. They rode quickly to the area where they had found the cloth from Kate's waistcoat and spread out to try and find her.

Half an hour later, Andrew was getting desperate. Night had fallen, it was getting colder, and there was still no sign of Kate. He knew that although the weather was fairly mild for the time of year, they shouldn't underestimate how cold a winter night in Britain could be. He was determined not to fail her; even if it took all night, he would not stop looking.

Minutes later, one of the men pointed to some rocks; he had noticed a body on the ground next to them. Almost overcome with anguish, Andrew hoped it was Kate, but when the three men got closer, he immediately recognised Eleanor. She was dead. She had a pool of dark blood around her head, probably due to hitting one of the stones which also had some blood on and around it. The men's faces went white when they saw the state of her, and Andrew wondered what had happened. He thought it was not right to leave her body laying there in the darkness where wild animals might come upon it, so he instructed the two men to take her back to the hotel, whilst he continued looking for Kate. He helped them put her body on one of the horses, and let them go.

The sky was still overcast, but the temperature dropped dramatically, giving him the chills thinking about Kate alone somewhere, unprotected, maybe hurt, alone in the cold darkness; but with hope in his heart he said to himself,

'I will find you, Kate, wait for me.' In a panic, he started shouting,

'Kate! Where are you? Kate, please...'

Meanwhile, in her subterranean shelter, with her eyes half-closed, Kate was shivering, wondering if she would survive that night. Thinking about Mr Bear, she reproached him playfully, trying to distract herself from her predicament.

'I will never believe in you ever again! You were supposed to protect me, but where are you now? Probably resting comfortably in a warm bed in the hotel, and here I am, all alone. A clear sky with a lovely moon and bright stars would be very helpful, wouldn't it?'

Kate had barely finished speaking when she heard a voice in the distance, shouting her name. That beloved, unmistakable voice gave her the courage and strength to scrabble at the earth surrounding the hole as fast as she could, shouting his name,

'Andrew, Andrew, I am here!' she cried desperately from her hiding place.

Andrew heard her voice, faintly, then shouted back, as he could not see her,

'Kate, I can hear you, please, keep shouting and I will find you.'

Kate shouted as loud as she could whilst Andrew's voice got closer and closer. It didn't take him very long to find where she was, and when he saw her crawl out of the hole and stand unsteadily, he ran straight to her and embraced her cold body with his warm arms which held her tight when she, exhausted, fainted.

Carefully, he put her on the horse in front of him, whilst opening his coat, trying to cover her as much as possible to warm her up. As it was dark, Andrew did not see the blood on her clothes, and apart from the cold, she seemed fine. He took her back to the hotel, calling her name soothingly a few times, telling her everything would be alright; but for the most part they travelled quickly and silently, both grateful for such a miracle.

As they approached the hotel, he could see all the lamps were lit inside and out. He knew that Kate was tired and needed warm clothes and a peaceful fireplace. This would be impossible if he could not avoid everybody's curiosity; they were clamouring for news about their adventure in the middle of nowhere, much of it in part due to the two stablemen who'd brought Eleanor's body back to the hotel, without any explanation being thus far provided.

Andrew climbed off his horse and with help from a servant, he picked Kate up in his arms and carried her inside. Despite all the perplexed people around, he took her directly upstairs to their room. After helping her to change her clothes, he decided to get soup from the kitchen, but she held his arm gently and told him,

'No, Andrew, unfortunately, I have to go down and talk to Inspector Parnell and the owner of the hotel.'

'What? Are you mad? You need to rest. You almost died out there. What is so important that it cannot wait until tomorrow?' Andrew implored her, gravely concerned for her health.

'Please, Andrew, it is important, trust me,' Kate begged him, so he paused. Ever since they'd first met, Andrew had understood how impossible it was to stop her from doing something when she was determined to do it. Even though she had gone far beyond what she would be able to bear sometimes, at that moment he felt that Kate had something terribly important to explain; something that could have cost her life.

Meanwhile, downstairs, people were doing what they always do in this type of situation – imagining and exchanging their own theories about another strange day, full of surprises.

'Mr Clark might be right. I think he and his daughter might have been cursed,' Ellen confided in Charlotte and Diana.

'I think it is the hotel itself,' Diana replied. 'Before it ruins my celebrations, we should pray to get rid of these ghosts and go home as soon as possible, without them chasing after us,' she said.

'Lord Henry,' Dr Turner asked, 'does Miss Eleanor's death have anything to do with your experiments? I mean... some people here might think that she was the target of your deities, who emerged from the underworld claiming souls, who have forgotten the way out of this world,' he said sarcastically.

'Stop right there, Dr Turner. This is not the time for sarcasm or irony. That is a grave lack of respect for the dead!' the vicar snapped, glowering.

'Ghosts don't claim souls, because ghosts don't exist,' Miss Abington said. 'Only God can claim our souls, if they are due to be saved.' She was intent on making her point again.

'What does your Church tell you about souls that were not due to be saved?' Bernard asked Albert's fiancée, quite interested.

'Evil will claim them, naturally,' she replied confidently.

'My dear Peter, we should book an appointment with the Devil and try to negotiate a good deal for the future,' Bernard suggested to his friend, who laughed loudly.

Inspector Parnell pinched the bridge of his nose, closed his eyes and sighed, then turned to his companion.

'Well, Parker, if there was ever any hope of saving our Christmas it has now escaped us completely,' he said dejectedly.

'What do you mean, Sir?' the constable asked, rather unsure about what everybody was saying.

'Instead of finding the murderer, we were punished with another body, without knowing if it belongs to the old case, or if we are dealing with a completely new and separate one,' the inspector explained miserably. Without waiting for any reaction, the inspector took the last sip of his single malt whisky and puffed his chest up, determined to face the battle with the same weapons.

'Come on, Constable Parker, let's see if our souls are cursed as well. I would not be surprised if the Bible says anything about trading souls, but I am prepared to negotiate my Christmas Turkey,' the inspector said; then he turned to look for his colleague, who had suddenly disappeared. Then he said aloud to himself, 'Where the devil is Parker, the moment I need him most? Never mind, let's see... the only person that could provide any more information about the crime three years ago came back dead.' He sighed again.

Constable Parker reappeared, breathless, and with a book in his hand, he asked the inspector,

'...and where in the Bible should I look, Sir?'

'Judgement Day, Apocalypse, anywhere near the end of the Bible, when Evil tries to steal other people's Christmas turkey,' the inspector replied sarcastically.

'This will take a while, Sir,' Parker informed him, a little concerned, flicking through the pages after licking his thumb.

'I was joking, Constable! Do you see? That is the problem – you are reading the Bible too much. Why the hell haven't they written a criminal code yet? It would be far more useful for us,' Inspector Parnell snapped.

'You should be more respectful of God's words, especially the Bible,' the vicar reproached him.

The vicar had hardly finished speaking when he was interrupted by Sir Christopher, who exclaimed,

'Ah... Andrew and Kate! How nice it is to see you both back safe and sound. You should be resting in your room, my dear, your face is very pale,' he observed.

'Thank you, Sir Christopher, but I can rest only after we have dealt with the murders that took place here in this hotel three years ago and now the death of Miss Eleanor,' Kate responded dejectedly.

Those words caught the attention of all the guests and staff, who were eager to know everything about the mysterious events since Sir Richard's accident, when the bodies of Adam Fairfax and his dog were found.

'However,' Kate continued, 'I need to talk to the hotel's owner first,' she said, but before she could say anything else, Mr Clark intervened, right behind her.

'I am here, Lady Katherine. What do you know about my daughter's death? Do you know how she died?' he asked in a hard, emotionless voice, completely resigned to the situation, which seemed rather strange to Kate for someone who had just lost his daughter.

'I am sorry, Mr Clark, I don't know how she died, but I can tell you everything she told me earlier today.' After a pause, she continued. 'She wanted to know where Miss Anna Fairfax was, because on the day she disappeared, Miss Eleanor stabbed Mrs Fairfax and her husband to death.' The gathered guests gasped in amazement at hearing this news. Kate continued. 'She stabbed Anna and the dog too, but the girl escaped, mortally wounded. Your daughter was seduced and betrayed by Mr Fairfax, Mr Clark, and in a moment of despair she killed the whole family. She thought that Anna had died somewhere, and animals did the rest during the night, leaving no remains. Miss Eleanor hid Mr Fairfax and his dog behind the wooden wall, where she used to meet Mr Fairfax, kept secret until today.' Another gasp went up from the guests and a flutter of whispering behind hands broke out. Kate paused due to her tiredness, then continued.

'Your daughter tried to kill me today, in the belief that I was hiding Miss Anna, but she didn't stab me deeply enough, so I escaped. I ran away and found a hole in the ground, which seemed to me a rabbit's house, but it was actually a stone chamber of sorts, where the ancient people buried their dead,' she explained; then Sir Richard interrupted her.

'You mean to say "skeletons and skulls"?' he asked inquisitively.

'Partially, and badly damaged; it is difficult to say as I did not have a lamp, and I don't have any specific knowledge about bones, really. However, I found something much more important than ancient bones – Miss Anna Fairfax's body; actually ,what's left of her.' Kate paused, due to a sad moan of pain that Lady Georgiana let out.

'Oh my dear Anna, lying out there! Are you sure that it was Anna?' she asked.

'I found this necklace with the owl pendant under the body, and only you, Lady Georgiana, can tell us for certain,' Kate said, offering the necklace to her. Lady Georgiana examined it closely then nodded, confirming that it did indeed belong to her goddaughter; then Kate explained the circumstances.

'Her body was near the entrance of the stone tomb. After being stabbed by Miss Eleanor, Anna must have somehow found that subterranean sepulchre then rested right there, near the entrance, hidden but mortally wounded. I was very lucky. When I was stabbed my waistcoat and corset deflected the knife so my wound is not deep, and I was able to hide until Andrew found me.' Kate finished, waiting for someone to say something, but the morbid silence was broken only by the solemn deep voice of Mr Clark,

'She was a good girl, Lady Katherine. I am the only one to blame, since I am the one who has been cursed all these years.' He paused, then added, 'We will have soup served soon.' Having said that, he left the lounge, walking with difficulty because of his distress and wooden leg. As soon as he had left, the guests started chattering amongst themselves at hearing about everything.

Kate couldn't help but feel sorry for Mr Clark who, despite having lost what was most dear to him, still had a sense of duty and obligation. Perhaps that was the only thing he could do in the tragic circumstances – keep moving forward, because going back was not an option, she supposed.

Kate watched the reaction of the guests and the police – sadness for some, joy for others, like Inspector Parnell, who turned to Constable Parker, quite relieved.

'Parker, forget the Bible, we don't need it anymore – our Christmas turkey is safe! However, Divine Providence may not give us another chance; therefore, finish your Scotch, and let's get out of this place as quickly as possible.'

'What about the bodies, Sir?' Constable Parker asked uncertainly.

'They cannot go anywhere, can they? There isn't a murderer to arrest, so the job now belongs to the vicar, who has to pray for their souls. We will send somebody to collect the bodies; hopefully by then the vicar will have finished saving those who were worth saving,' Inspector Parnell said coldly. Constable Parker nodded in agreement, leaving with his boss.

The atmosphere in the hotel gradually returned to some semblance of normality after the departure of the two police officers.

Diana's face was a good indicator of her terrible mood. She was annoyed because her husband's experiment was forgotten about. However, she was eager to make sure they were not completely obliterated, so she strove to give the guests a last glimpse of glamour, whilst her husband was not the sort of man to be downcast. Right after their sumptuous dinner, the guests were sipping their liqueurs, when Lord Henry addressed them with his prepared speech.

'My dear guests and friends, unfortunately we have had a small setback that momentarily drove us off our original course. I still have some cards hidden up my sleeve – good surprises for some, bitter disappointments for others, I am certain.' He looked around the room, smiling and making eye contact with everybody gathered around the tables before continuing.

'Therefore, tomorrow, after a hearty breakfast, we will head back to Tollemache Manor, where we will entertain ourselves for the next three days with some wonderful games – weather permitting – accompanied by an exquisite wine cellar, and a Christmas dinner fit for the Queen. It will be a perfect occasion for gifts and unexpected surprises. I will take the opportunity to extend the invitation to Sir Edmund Mulgrave and Lady Georgiana Larkhill, as they are part of our future plans.' Lord Henry raised his glass in a toast to the Queen, so everybody stood and joined him. His declaration created a much more cheerful atmosphere, and after the toast, the guests started chattering about what lay ahead.

'Chris, I'm worried about you, you know... you have been drinking rather a lot tonight; this is so unusual, not like you at all, especially before a long trip back tomorrow,' Sir Richard quietly mentioned to his friend, Sir Christopher, somewhat concerned for him.

'Henry is sometimes quite excessive when it comes to surprises,' the magistrate replied. 'He has a strange sense of humour that always appeals to some, but it is over the top for many others. I hope he knows exactly when to stop,' he said, worried about Lord Henry's plans.

'What do you think he has in mind, Edmund? He is being quite mysterious with his surprises, and I don't like it at all,' Lady Georgiana said in a whisper, intrigued.

'Keep your enemies close, especially when someone threatens to come between you and your Christmas pudding. I shall endeavour to discover what he is up to,' Sir Edmund whispered back to Lady Georgiana, so nobody would overhear.

'Please would you take care of the suitcases this time?' Kate asked. 'I am so very tired. I almost lost my life, you know?' Kate was trying to persuade Andrew to get everything prepared for their departure tomorrow.

'Next time I will have to chain you inside the bedroom to prevent you from getting into trouble.' Andrew laughed, offering his arm to Kate, who accepted it, and together they left the lounge to get their suitcases ready for the return to Diana's home.

'Peter, do you think that whilst we were here they put up a Christmas tree?' Ellen asked her husband, looking forward to the festive celebrations.

'Of course, darling, Diana would never forget such an important detail,' he reassured her, smiling, 'but don't expect a big one; after all, she would never accept anything that might outshine her...' Peter said.

'I have a bad feeling about this Christmas,' Charlotte confided to her husband Bernard and their friends.

'Diana is losing her touch, I must say. What a bizarre Christmas – ghosts, skulls, murders, religious fanatics,' Bernard said, lighting his pipe.

'Don't be so insensitive, Bernard; it is her husband's fault. He is the eccentric one here. I think that she is dealing with the "situation" with decorum and distinction, as a proper lady should,' Charlotte reproached her husband.

'I hope you are taking lessons about how to be a "lady", for when Her Majesty the Queen nominates me for one of her knighthoods,' Bernard teased his wife.

'Poor Diana, she must be mortified at having to restrain herself in the face of her husband's vanity; after all, one house cannot have two Christmas trees,' Peter added, laughing.

'Dr Turner, although you are British, you have been showing a certain common sense, somewhat in contrast to the others here. What do you think about Lord Henry's theory concerning Hyperborea?' Dr Gruber asked.

'What do you mean? This is a fantasy of those two lunatics – Lord Henry and Lady Katherine. It's a good thing that Cambridge got rid of her; and the other one, lord or not, I will not allow Tollemache to throw away hundreds of years of study; what are we going to do with all the research going on in Greece and Egypt led by our most renowned archaeologists and historians? I have to put an end to this once and for all. But don't think, Dr Gruber, that I forgot you copied one of my ideas in your last publication,' Dr Turner replied bitterly.

'We shall have a proper discussion about this small detail another time,' Dr Gruber replied. 'First of all we have to join forces to get rid of Tollemache, before he buys the Crown to support, as you said, "his fantasies". He is the imminent danger. Cambridge would lose funding for the archaeological sites in Egypt and Greece. If you leave Hyperborea for me, my government, which is investing in research into our Aryan heritage, will most certainly appreciate your contribution for our culture,' Dr Gruber said.

'I don't care about Hyperborea, Atlantis or Troy; you can have them all, as long we can get Tollemache out of our circle,' Dr Turner replied.

'It's not fair to leave these bodies without a proper burial. Would you like my assistance to pray for their souls?' Miss Abington asked the vicar.

'First, I need to know more about your Church; I mean, I need to know first if we fear the "same entity"?' He left the question in the air. 'I am not quite sure about this "God-Mind" you refer to. Has He anything to do with science? Because, I must say, I don't believe in any kind of evolution. What did you say yesterday about "men are evil"? Because women are evil, not men; don't forget the apple, I mean, the forbidden fruit.'

The vicar could not finish his statement, because Lord Henry's nephew, Albert, arrived to save his fiancée.

'Mary, we are leaving early tomorrow, so I will accompany you to your bedroom, and I advise you to do the same, Vicar,' Albert said, urging her to leave.

'St Clair! My name is Reverend St Clair! the vicar reminded Albert, with a frown.

Chapter 13

Kate felt relieved to leave the strange atmosphere of that hotel behind. Maybe she should give Dr Turner's opinion some credit. Perhaps the ghost dog was a hallucination. She didn't believe in the supernatural, but she had to admit that ghosts and murders had a certain appeal to the imagination.

Christmas was less than two days away, so Kate thought it would be better to join in the Christmas spirit and make a big effort to put aside whatever motivated people against those who had different opinions, beliefs or social status; it was not new to her that jealousy and hatred could take people to the edge, and sometimes end in tragedy.

Kate smiled, looking through the carriage window, prompting Andrew to ask,

'Why such a timid smile, Kate?'

'I suddenly remembered Emile in Paris, and his theory about gifts. At this time of the year we all expect gifts; some even think that God might send a special gift to each one of us. For some reason, though, other people's gifts always seem better than ours, which inevitably means that some people will never be satisfied,' she explained.

Andrew asked, 'What does Emile have to do with it?'

'If he was right in saying that gifts imply obligations, God may charge you twice for your greed, if you covet other people's gifts, leaving you with a bigger bill than you can afford at your death,' she said, smiling, attempting some humour.

'Indeed. Hopefully Henry will be cautious this time about his gifts and surprises,' Andrew replied, nodding.

Meanwhile, Sir Christopher could not stop thinking about his friend Lord Henry and his audacious and dangerous way of dealing with people. After a deep sigh, his face turned a little pale, then his friend, Richard, who was watching him asked, 'What happened, Chris? Why the sigh?'

'I don't know, Richard. All these people together, under the same roof, it doesn't feel quite right; it is a... provocation,' Sir Christopher replied.

'Don't be so miserable, Chris, there is a variety of moods here, I have to admit, but nothing too dramatic.' Getting out of his carriage, Sir Richard indicated some of the other guests, whispering to his friend,

'Look at them – they are happy for the return to comfort; and what about those, there?' He indicated the others. 'I can assure you, they are willing to have fun, whatever it is,' he said, waiting for his friend to agree.

'We see what we want to see, my dear fellow. In your case, you strategically forgot to mention those who received the unexpected invitation, and are possibly arming themselves for whatever surprise ahead. God knows what will happen when they arrive later on,' Sir Christopher confided to his friend, and without indicating anybody in particular, he added enigmatically, 'Most of all, there are those with an evil soul who will go to great lengths to achieve their goals at all costs.'

Diana desperately wanted to display the opulence of her wonderful new home, as well as the number of servants who, in a way, were also part of the property. Under her direction they were arrayed in front of the mansion; none of them, though, said anything, as silence was an essential requirement for those who worked in this line of business.

Communication, however, was effective amongst them through discreet looks, little movement of heads, and sighs of others, when they finally accepted that their little holiday was ended, and everything was about to start over again, as the master and his guests were back.

As part of an organised retinue, the servants knew precisely which carriage they would be assigned to, in order to unload the luggage and make their guests' arrival as stress free as possible after their tiring trip. The precarious roads, and the cold and powerful emotions still in effect, were unable to prevent the visitors from enjoying the longed-for afternoon tea with its inherent power to heal any mortal soul.

After tea, Andrew was asked to meet Lord Henry in the library to discuss an important subject, a private discussion which lasted all afternoon, leaving Kate with no option but to go to her room and prepare for dinner.

It was good to sit in a comfortable chair upstairs, listening to the quiet ticking of a wall clock, looking over her research. It also provided Kate the time to contemplate the harrowing circumstances surrounding her discovery of the statue of Asclepius in the little chamber she had taken refuge in. She hadn't had time to speak with anybody about her find, not even Andrew. Everybody was fascinated with the recent macabre events and the discovery of Anna's body, which made Kate want to avoid them all for the time being.

Whilst sitting in her chair, Kate heard the wheels of another carriage that had just arrived outside. The unmistakable voice of Sir Edmund Mulgrave, accompanied by Lady Georgiana Larkhill, shook everyone out of their strange lethargy, leaving no doubt that dinner would certainly be quite eventful.

Minutes later, Andrew entered the room, and when he saw Kate dressed and ready for dinner, he rushed to get changed. Kate was very curious about the meeting with Lord Henry, so she could not wait, and immediately began interrogating him.

'Whatever were you two talking about? That was such a long meeting.'

'I cannot tell you now, I promised Henry to wait until after dinner, when he will address everybody with his latest ruse; but don't worry, because it is all good news, for us at least,' Andrew answered with a little smile, knowing that Kate was dying from curiosity.

However, she was too proud to beg, so she decided to play the same game and replied,

'I also have a very important discovery to declare, which will make Lord Henry very excited.' She smiled sweetly.

'Hey, this is not fair. I am bound by a promise, you are not,' Andrew said, faking annoyance, certain that she would never give up until she knew his secret. Unable to resist the mystery, he capitulated and told her,

'Very well, but it is a secret, at least until after dinner.'

'I swear I won't tell anyone.' She giggled.

If the guests had entertained any sort of reservations about the forthcoming Christmas dinner, they were at once put aside by the sumptuous nine-course meal that was about to be revealed to them that evening.

An elegant assembly of finely attired servants brought canapés round the guests on little silver trays, myriad little dainty treats – quail eggs on toast triangles, caviar on crackers, pâté on miniature oatcakes, oysters on ice, Devil's-on-horseback, smoked Scottish salmon *vol-au-vents* with a lobster mayonnaise, and many other equally delectable light mouthfuls of happiness. The arrival of such a varied and exquisite array of *hor's d'oeuvres* was accompanied by an excited chatter as the gathered guests began their festive season in style in their sumptuous surroundings at Lord Henry's grand house, with its elegant dining room adorned with sparkling cut-crystal chandeliers, solid silver tableware and exquisite china service.

There followed a dazzling array of courses of plates of dainty fine food, starting with traditional London soup, which combined ham hock with onion, celery and carrots; line-caught whole salmon decorated with cucumber scales, quails cooked in an orange and cardamom sauce... but nothing could overshadow the main event, which consisted of a variety of roasted meats including huge fore-ribs of beef and a haunch of shot venison, accompanied by traditional duck-fat roast potatoes and vegetables. The meal was served with a range of splendid wines – each setting had seven distinctly different wine glasses, as well as one for iced water – little more could be said about the wines and liqueurs except that they were perfect, and accompanied the meal in complete harmony.

An army of servants brought Angels-on-Horseback (oysters wrapped in oak-smoked bacon) to bring the savoury courses to a close, after which a series of little desserts designed to amuse the jaded palate – chilled gooseberry fool, crystallised strawberries mixed with crumbled meringue and cream, miniature Bakewell tarts; Alexandretta Bombe and glazed ices shaped like fruit, then finally a medley of exotic imported fruits sliced and served with light cream; all deserts were accompanied by port and grenadine syrup.

The cheese board which followed the last sweet dish was an impeccable selection of British cheeses from counties near and far – there was crumbly Cheshire cheese, a sweet Lancashire, creamy cheese from a farm in Wensleydale, a variety of aged Somerset Cheddars, Blue Vinney from Dorset, Double Gloucester, Caerphilly from Wales, Scottish Caboc and the King of Cheese – white and blue Stilton from Melton Mowbray. These were accompanied by an elegant array of little crackers and biscuits from a variety of makers, yellow salted butter, grapes and celery. It was a magnificent end to a magnificent meal, and as soon as the last guest was presented with cheese, servants came round with silver plates of chocolates and coffee served from exquisitely decorated silver coffee pots. Everybody was entirely satisfied, enveloped by a warm, happy feeling generated by the delectable meal and their luxurious surroundings. If the evening meal they were digesting was anything to go by, their Christmas dinner would be magnificent.

After dinner, the guests were ushered to the drawing room to wait for Lord Henry and Lady Diana Tollemache, who had an important announcement to make before guests started drifting off to bed as many of them were tired from the travel. Everybody now had high expectations for the Christmas games the next day – a tradition in the Tollemache family in December, the games usually commencing after breakfast, stopping for lunch, then continuing throughout the afternoon until tea time.

It didn't take long for their hosts to appear, when a servant rang a little silver bell to bring conversation to a halt and attract the attention of their guests, who were deeply curious to know what was so important it demanded an announcement.

'My dear guests and friends,' began Lord Henry, 'I hope you have enjoyed your dinner and our company as much as we have enjoyed yours. I think that after our experiments and discussions about Stonehenge the last three days, it is time to let you know my conclusions, and my next steps for research. I have invited Sir Andrew Enfield to be in charge of my new project – the excavation of a group of barrows that we found by following the direction indicated by the astronomical event that we witnessed on the winter solstice.' He paused, then seeing Sir Edmund Mulgrave was about to interrupt him, the earl gave him no change to begin, and resumed.

'Tomorrow, at lunch time, my cousin Sir John Tollemache, who is employed by the Crown as the Commissioner of Woods, Forests and Land Revenues, will arrive to enjoy with us our traditional Christmas games and, of course, sumptuous dinners until New Year.' He beamed at his guests amiably. 'We shall discuss with Sir Edmund the importance of the stone circles and barrows around Amesbury – specifically Stonehenge – and the pressing need to make these archaeological sites pass to the tutelage of the Crown, in order to explore and research them scientifically, instead of letting them be used indiscriminately, for religious rituals,' he declared, at once infuriating Lady Georgiana and Sir Edmund who, again, were not allowed to interrupt him, as Lord Henry still had something to say.

'I would also like to inform you that Lady Diana Tollemache is from now on established as my heir, with one condition: to sponsor and continue my research, with the help of Andrew.'

Lord Henry had barely finished speaking when an excited chatter broke out amongst his guests – some were clearly pleased, others expressed surprise; some were indignant, and another group was simply too angry at what they had just heard, whilst others were nonplussed, as it didn't make any difference to them one way or the other as the food and wine were definitely more appealing.

Peter, with his habitual irony, said in a whisper to himself,

'Remarkable, Diana, always remarkable.'

In another corner of the drawing room, Sir Christopher whispered to his friend,

'Fascinating, Richard, just as I expected, Henry made a very dangerous move.'

One indignant voice stood out amongst the others.

'Uncle Henry, are you insane? What about me? I am supposed to be the next Earl Tollemache,' Albert complained, bitterly disappointed with his uncle.

'Indeed, the title is undoubtedly yours, my dear, but I have other plans for you,' Lord Henry reassured him. 'Our cousin, who will join us tomorrow, is going to retire soon, so we will appoint you to the position responsible for cataloguing the monuments of our English Heritage,' Henry Tollemache replied proudly, smiling.

'What? Are you out of your mind? I have my own plans with regard to Parliament, in which I have been investing for years, and that doesn't include cataloguing stones and poking around other people's country estates. Definitely not!' Albert shouted, very upset, and then he stomped out of the room.

Dr Turner, who was near to Sir Christopher and Sir Richard, was very surprised to hear all this, then with a pale face commented,

'That was going to be my job. I have been working for years to get that post. Tollemache has stabbed me in the back, but he'll pay for that.'

Then, Sir Edmund, who was beside Lady Georgiana, openly defied Lord Henry.

'How dare you try to prevent me from uttering the rites of my order on my own land? Over my dead body!' He was furious.

'Peter, if we're not quick, Dr Baker will collect Lord Henry and Sir Edmund's skulls before us.' Bernard grinned, lighting his pipe.

'We cannot let Sir Edmund fight this war to the death. How could we develop our tourism business without him?' Peter replied thoughtfully, lighting a cigarette.

'If you think that I will allow you to disturb the forests and balance of the cosmos, you will have to do it over my dead body as well!' Lady Georgiana declared furiously, getting up.

'Look, Peter, Dr Baker is writing something in his little book,' Bernard said. 'Do you think he is calculating the number of skulls he will collect from this quarrel?' Bernard laughed.

'It's possible, Bernard,' replied Peter, 'he seems to be a man of action, not words; he's always very quiet, perhaps measuring in his mind the size of the heads he can see. We have to talk with Sir Edmund before he loses his head and puts an end to our endeavour.'

At that point, Lord Henry turned to Kate and invited her to expose her new theory.

'Kate, my dear, your husband said that you have an interesting point to make about Stonehenge and the Greeks. Might you end our pleasant meeting in style, before we open space for port and sherry with mince pies – an exquisite recipe from the Tollemache family, I have to say, which has been passed down from generation to generation, since Medieval times.'

'If you allow me, Lord Henry, I would very much like to report an important discovery that I made the day after the solstice, when I found the body of Miss Anna Fairfax.' Kate stood to address the gathering who were, suddenly, attentive.

'Inside the underground chamber in which I hid, I found a stone statue holding in his hand a rod entwined with a serpent. I have no doubt that this statue is the personification of Asclepius, the god of Medicine,' she declared.

'Excuse me, Lady Enfield, but every classicist knows that the Greek god with the *caduceus* is the personification of Hermes Trimegistus – the Messenger,' Sir Richard interrupted knowledgably.

'Yes, the caduceus with two entwined snakes is traditionally associate to Hermes, the Messenger; however, one entwined serpent belongs unmistakably to Asclepius, and symbolises his power of healing,' Kate corrected him.

'Oh... I, err... didn't know that,' Sir Richard admitted.

'If Asclepius is in a chamber underground, what happened to your theory about the oracle at Stonehenge?' Dr Turner asked. 'As we all know, nobody ever said anything about oracles underground, did they?' he added.

Kate nodded, 'It confused me at first too, as it didn't make sense for Apollo's oracle to be in the middle of a stone circle, and Asclepius' statue to be underground. However, it definitely makes sense if we agree that the oracle at Stonehenge belonged to Apollo the Healer, and those who could not be healed and ultimately died were buried in that chamber – the domain of Asclepius, waiting for resurrection,' Kate explained.

'So they expected to be buried under those henges to be resurrected?' Lord Henry asked, enthralled.

'Why was his statue underground, and not worshipped in a normal shrine on the ground like the other Greek gods used to be?' Sir Richard interrupted. 'It seems implausible, especially for the son of Apollo, to be underground?' he insisted, incredulous.

'Because,' Kate replied, 'although Asclepius was his son, he was mortal. According to the myth, he began to resurrect the dead, which Zeus could not accept, so Zeus killed him with a lightning bolt. Later, Asclepius was transformed into a constellation. Some of his followers and disciples believed in resurrection, like Pythagoras believed in transmigration of the soul, so they used to think that they would come back from the dead one day,' Kate concluded.

'Like Jesus?' Ellen asked, fascinated.

'This is pure heresy! You cannot compare those pagan rituals with the Resurrection of Christ,' the vicar snapped.

'So, if we are all Christians, it means that we will all be resurrected too, doesn't it?' Ellen asked, excited.

'Only on Judgement Day, my darling; unfortunately, we have to die first and wait in the queue for while,' Peter explained to his wife.

'Fortunately, resurrection is only for those who were not condemned, which is not your case, Peter,' Diana sniped.

'I can testify in your favour on doomsday, Peter,' Bernard jokingly reassured his friend, laughing.

'No, thank you, Bernard, your testimony might throw us all to hell immediately,' Charlotte interjected, after she heard what her husband just said.

'Sir Christopher,' Bernard countered the magistrate, 'I am afraid that in our last conversation about who should be convicted, your point of view has just been weakened, because the Final Judgment is much more important than your mundane court,' he declared.

'I don't see why. Our law is part of God's jurisdiction. This is why testimonies must be confirmed by oath on the Bible. We merely help God in advance, instead of leave everybody to be judged on the Last Day,' Sir Christopher replied.

'I'm not going anywhere if I cannot enjoy good wine, an innocent card game, and smoke my cigarettes,' Peter announced.

'If you include Devon or Somerset Ciders I will join you, wherever you go,' Sir Richard told Peter, laughing.

'We, Hyperboreans, will never be refused anywhere, up or down,' Lord Henry declared. 'The doors will be always open for those who share knowledge and use it wisely,' he said, a little drunkenly, making Diana raise an angry eyebrow.

'You should be ashamed to utter such absurdities!' Dr Gruber laughed. 'You don't even have a basic knowledge of geography. Everyone knows that the Hyperboreans were from the north, and Britain is… northwest,' he insisted.

'Well, they didn't have compasses at that time, did they?' Lord Henry replied. 'Therefore, a few degrees in deviation is completely insignificant, and therefore acceptable, am I not right, Andrew?' He was indeed getting drunk.

'In fact, one cannot be precise when talking about time and space in antiquity,' Andrew agreed. 'Many elements have to be taken into account, whatever the position regarding the location of Hyperborea,' Andrew cautiously agreed.

'Further investigation will prove who is right.' Lord Henry wagged a finger at Dr Gruber, then addressed Kate and Andrew. 'I would like to show you tomorrow my little museum, my dearest place in this state, a little cottage where I keep all the archaeological artefacts that I have been collecting over the years; small jewels saved from their own ephemeral nature in order to give their testimony about our history; they will remain there for many generations, when we ephemeral beings, have already passed out.'

'That is wonderful, Lord Henry, I am honoured to have the opportunity to see your museum,' Kate exclaimed, very pleased to hear about his collection.

'You will be even more pleased when I show you a bronze *caduceus* with a serpent entwined around it; it was sold to me by a local hermit, who was supposedly descended from the ancient Order of the Druids.' He smiled, then added, 'Do not confuse it with these new orders that are out there. I am referring to the one which was here before the Romans. According to oral literature, only the highest priest walked with the *caduceus*, but when Christianity arrived, the old order was gradually set aside. I didn't know their *caduceus* had a link with Asclepius until just now, when you mentioned it.' He beamed at Kate.

'In my opinion, oral literature, due to its methodical process of memorisation and a lifetime dedicated to its practice, has more chance of preserving the integrity of the text than the written one which comes to us lost in repeated and tendentious translations in monasteries,' Kate replied.

'By the way, talking of monasteries, I have a book with a poem written by St Blathmac during the period of the Saxons, in which he called Jesus *"The perfect wise man – better than a prophet, with knowledge beyond the druids; a king and religious leader"*. It might be a copy of the original manuscript of course. Unfortunately, St Blathmac was killed, and cut into pieces in a church by the Scandinavians in 825AD,' Lord Henry informed them.

He paused, whilst everybody looked at Dr Gruber, who was quietly fuming; then the earl added, 'Tomorrow, after my cousin has arrived from London, and whilst everyone is entertained in their games, I will show you my archaeological treasures,' he said, smiling.

Kate could not be more excited about the possibility of proving the druids used the caduceus of Asclepius; an oral tradition which, as it goes further back in time, might be testimony that the Greek god of medicine was definitely older in Britain, and all his knowledge and healing rituals were passing orally from druid to druid over millennia.

The atmosphere in the drawing room was tense, excitement for a few and displeasure for others, like Sir Edmund and Lady Georgiana, who were outraged by the unworthiness to which their druidic orders were being subjected. However, the icy exchange of glances between the two aristocrats, and the significant way in which Sir Edmund raised his eyebrow whilst devising new strategies, left nobody in doubt that the two still had powerful cards to play.

Even though the majority of the guests were trying to resist the fatigue of such an intensely busy day, gradually they were dispersing, some in silence, while others could not avoid chattering, yet others talking in a whisper.

'I think, Richard, most of the souls here could never be less disappointed if they were promised surprises, mysteries and battles between egos,' Sir Christopher confided, whilst watching people leave the room.

'I will never complain about the boredom of my life again,' Sir Richard replied. 'Fortunately, we are safe here, away from the ghosts. Let's indulge our souls with the simplicity of life – good food, good company and a superb cellar,' he said, taking the last sip of wine from his glass.

'Simplicity? It sounds more like a "privilege for a few" to me,' Sir Christopher complained.

'Don't you think we are too old to support new ideas, Chris? Leave it to the younger ones; they have a lot of time ahead to make mistakes, like embracing liberal ideas, and we don't,' Sir Richard said with conviction.

'You might be right, my dear fellow, you might be right,' Sir Christopher replied, and they left the room together, very happy and content.

It was difficult for Diana to persuade her husband to end the celebrations that night. She wanted him to conserve his energy for the following day, as it was almost midnight and those last moments in the drawing room left no doubt that the next morning, a typical winter Christmas Eve, would start a little late.

The guests arrived at breakfast in waves, according to age and the amount of alcohol consumed the previous evening, an unchanging pattern since the first day at Tollemache Manor, with the exception of Lord Henry Tollemache himself, who surprisingly was the first to arrive at the breakfast room, followed by Andrew and Kate, whose expectations about the little treasures they would find in the cottage museum helped them rise early.

'Good morning, Henry.' Andrew announced their presence whilst pulling back the chair for Kate to sit. Lord Henry, then, stood up and greeted them.

'Good morning, Andrew, Lady Kate!' He beamed.

'Good morning, Lord Henry.' Kate smiled, admiring the beautiful and perfect buffet breakfast, arranged without any fault, which led Kate's mind to think of her little treasure upstairs, Mr Bear, in her bedroom, when she saw the scones on one side, with Devon cream to accompany them. She thought to herself with a smile,

'Don't worry, Mr Bear, I will save one for you, even knowing that you are very lazy and sleeping in our bed, snug and warm amongst the pillows.' Her thoughts were interrupted by Lord Henry.

'Tell me, Lady Kate, apart from Andrew's love, what else did you find in Greece that would be worth fighting for in these turbulent times in the Balkans?' he asked.

'I think that it would be worth fighting for words of wisdom, ensuring they remain buried, otherwise they might be silenced forever by those who don't understand their meaning,' Kate replied casually, whilst she was taking a gentle, delightful bite of a delicious scone.

'What are you two talking about?' Andrew asked, sipping his tea.

'My dear Andrew, let's say that we have to guard our history, especially the knowledge behind it. It is easy to be blinded by our ego and vanity, essential ingredients for man's fall,' Lord Henry replied, whilst eating his grilled bacon and eggs.

'I didn't know that you'd become a believer, Henry,' Sir Christopher interrupted, who upon entering the breakfast room had overheard their conversation.

'Oh, Chris, always on time – like a clock.' Lord Henry smiled. 'I think you have been waking up the last few years with the precision of your golden watch. I wonder if I will be like you when I am your age,' he joked.

'But we are the same age, Henry. Marriage might have invigorated you, but it was unable to perform a miracle,' Sir Christopher replied, whilst pouring a cup of tea.

'Time is so cruel. When we think we fooled time, it cruelly comes back to haunt us,' Lord Henry stated, with a deep sigh.

For the first time, Andrew realised that his suspicions were not unfounded. There was something in the air that was beyond his comprehension, and it was time to uncover the mystery.

'Is there anything I should know, Kate? They don't actually look hung over, whilst their talk is more like a riddle to me,' Andrew whispered to her.

Kate looked at him and into his eyes. She knew there was so much to tell him; things that he would not ever imagine. She knew, though, that he had been fighting for the same things as her over the years, just in a different way. Perhaps it was time to bring him into this secret and dangerous world, which some people would never tire of seeking to destroy. However, just when she was about to say something, Diana and Sir Richard appeared at the door.

'Oh... look at the weather! My dear Henry, it looks like it isn't going to rain,' Diana declared optimistically.

'Yes, indeed, my dear. Our guests will be over the moon,' Lord Henry replied.

'I will tell you later, Andrew,' Kate replied in a whisper, whilst looking at Sir Christopher, who was eating eggs and bacon with relish, and who had another plate next to it with a scone, jam and cream ready to conclude his delicious breakfast.

Lord Henry excused himself, as he had a job to do in his office. He told the guests who were gradually appearing for breakfast not to hurry, but to enjoy their meal as much and as long they wanted, because the Christmas games would start only when they were ready for it. Meanwhile, they were invited to explore the mansion, guided by Lady Diana Tollemache, who would introduce them to the long and illustrious history of the Tollemache family.

After Lord Henry left for his office alone, the guests split into small groups according to common interests. Today, most of them were speculating on the same subject – what would be the fate of Stonehenge? These groups had different agendas, with different views of how the situation should be dealt with.

The big attraction that morning, however, was the Christmas tree, which had been quietly erected by servants in the drawing room during the night, after the guests went to sleep. Diana was absolutely overjoyed at the superbly decorated tree, and very proud for giving her guests such a surprise, inculcating in them the sacred spirit of Christmas celebration, which had been overshadowed temporarily by the turbulent recent events.

'Look, Charlotte, I told you she would put a Christmas tree up,' Ellen whispered, delighted at the magnificent tree their host surprised them with.

'I think that it is bigger than the Queen's,' Charlotte exclaimed, equally impressed.

Everybody agreed it was the most excellent Christmas tree they had ever seen, whilst the lavish decorations that adorned the room – garlands and wreaths of holly with berries and ivy tied with burgundy-coloured silk ribbons – were truly wonderful; the aroma of frankincense and myrrh; Christmas spices permeated the room from a bronze incense burner shaped like a miniature wooden Anglo-Saxon church; dozens of large white pillar candles lent the room a peculiar feeling, much like one might encounter in an ancient Byzantine Church. Diana certainly knew how to impress. The room's nocturnal transformation gave the guests something splendid to talk about and admire.

Later, Diana invited the guests to see the rest of the house, showing them the paintings of the Tollemache family ancestors, which were distributed about the many rooms, as it would be impossible to concentrate four hundred years' worth of family portraits in one location. Whoever had decorated the rooms had taken great care to make the furniture and the decoration express in some way the tastes and style of the people portrayed in the paintings, and, if possible, a short narrative – spicy sometimes – if it was the case.

Sir Christopher and Sir Richard thoroughly enjoyed the tour around the mansion, and when most of the guests went outside for games, they decided to stay and enjoy the rest of the morning in their own way. Although it was not raining or snowing, it was winter, so the best pleasure in the world for those two and their arthritis was to sit next to a fireplace, with a warm cup of tea, until their bodies were ready for the first drinks of the day. After all, it was Christmas Eve, and according to these two old fellows, some sins were allowed in the hope that God would understand such a tiny slip at this time of year.

Even advanced age could not, though, resist the call of gossip, most of all disputes and threats, so it was imperative that the magistrate and his friend arranged to have their tea in their customary strategic place, from where they both could observe people coming and going; after all, nobody could blame them for listening to what people didn't bother to keep only to themselves.

Consequently, the two of them were sitting in one of the reception rooms, with the double doors wide open, in front of which it would be impossible not to pass whatever place of the house was your origin, and to whatever place you wished to go.

'It is a quiet day, I must say, and it looks like they are having fun,' Sir Richard said, smiling.

'We are very fortunate gentlemen, Richard, as we are able to have pleasure with simple things, like a good conversation and an excellent cup of tea,' Sir Christopher replied, enjoying his warm drink.

'I knew you would end up agreeing with me about the concept of "simplicity in life",' Sir Richard exclaimed, proudly.

'It's not worth being a hypocrite at our age. We proved what we could, and what we couldn't, stayed behind; there is no time to catch it up,' Sir Christopher agreed; however, he had barely finished his sentence when a deep and sonorous voice interrupted the quietness.

'I will go to the Queen if it is necessary, but I will not allow this to happen!' It was Sir Edmund, complaining to Lady Georgiana, who was waiting for him outside Lord Henry's office.

'Did you tell him that?' she asked.

'Yes... and more,' Sir Edmund replied; then he left the hall with her.

Later, the two friends watched Albert and Mary walking together, and heard her asking him in a worried voice,

'Did you tell him?'

'Yes, I did, but he is intransigent,' Albert replied, clearly upset.

Sir Christopher and Sir Richard exchanged glances in silence, then resumed their conversation, which included plans for next spring and a possible trip to Egypt.

'We should ask Andrew if he knows of any excavation projects in a place with easy access to hotels and reasonable wine cellars,' Sir Richard suggested.

'Don't be a pedant, Richard. You have to give up some comforts if you want to have action and adventure on vacation. It is part of the deal; it is not possible to have everything in one package,' Sir Christopher replied.

'As long as I am not chased by Kate's birds,' Sir Richard replied, and after he had finished his tea, he opened a bottle of white wine of exemplary vintage, which they had decided would be the best drink to start the day, with no doubt that the atmosphere in the house was getting warmer.

'Those birds are harmless, and besides, they have a refined taste. You are not the type of meat they like – too much fat,' Sir Christopher replied, trying to be cheerful as possible, as he was worried about his friend's health.

'But you agree with me that they are strange creatures, don't you? Eagle-owls don't follow people round like as they do with Kate; it is simply bizarre...' Sir Richard tried to garner some support, and continued. 'They just appear out of nowhere, when you least expect them.' He shook his head slightly in disapproval.

'You have been reading a lot of ghostly literature lately; why don't you start reading biographies?' Sir Christopher suggested.

'They are boring,' Sir Richard replied.

'When in doubt… write your own memoirs,' Sir Christopher insisted.

'I don't have exciting memories to write about, do you?' Sir Richard retorted.

'No, I am afraid not. Perhaps that's why we just watch other people, in an attempt to fill the empty spaces of our own memories.' He smiled.

'Indeed, my friend, indeed,' Sir Richard agreed, but their attention was diverted to yet another pair of dissatisfied guests, who crossed the hall and closed Lord Henry's office door behind them. As they passed by, their conversation was terse.

'If you had told him what I'd instructed you to tell, perhaps he would be more reasonable. He doesn't give us any other choice now,' Dr Gruber snarled, in a low voice.

'I don't have nerves for that. I told him what was going to happen if he insists in this nonsense,' Dr Turner replied, thinking about his next step.

'This is your problem – you should have more attitude and act immediately,' Dr Gruber stated.

'But we beat Napoleon, didn't we?' Dr Turner asked provocatively.

'Not without Prussian help,' Dr Gruber contested.

'We would win, with or without anybody's help,' Dr Turner responded.

'This is the problem with you British – you are so arrogant,' Dr Gruber declared.

'We… arrogant? How dare you say such a stupid and pretentious thing about us?' Dr Turner was outraged. Sir Richard and Sir Christopher could not make out any more of the conversation, as the two doctors left the hall, still arguing.

'Do you think it is possible to make so many enemies at Christmas?' Sir Richard asked his friend.

'If God is not able to protect him at Christmas, nobody else will be. I have warned Henry in the past about his excess of vanity, but we all have our weakness,' Sir Christopher replied, evidently quite worried about what lay ahead.

'I shall suggest that Diana asks the vicar to bless this house. If he could not save the man's soul, at least the house will be safe,' Sir Richard said, also concerned.

'You mean the cellar primarily...' Sir Christopher joked.

The old fellows laughed, then continued their conversation, enjoying the lovely atmosphere of the reception room, hoping that no one would come to disturb them with quarrelsome complaints.

Chapter 14

The good weather could not win the battle against the winter, and the heavy gathering clouds left no doubt that looking for shelter would be the most sensible thing to do before the coming of the rain or, perhaps, snow. The cold crept in like a stealthy cat, silently, and the guests shivered when it nipped them.

After inviting the visitors to the warmth and safety of the drawing room, Diana organised games to entertain everyone; even those who didn't really want to take part actively could enjoy watching the others playing and getting fooled – some more than others, it must be said.

To avoid creating any constraints for "Blind Man's Bluff", Diana offered herself up to be the first to be blindfolded, whilst the others circulated around her, trying to escape from her touch. When she asked for the participants to '"stop"' where they were, she had to locate by touch alone the closest then attempt to guess his or her identity.

If coincidence didn't exist, Peter should be the one to be blamed for pushing the situation when he intentionally put himself close enough to be first touched by her, who without any doubt or hesitation, said,

'There are only two possibilities – a ghost or the Devil – in both cases, though, it is someone from underground, who forgot the way back home. Peter, who else could it be?' Diana said sarcastically.

'I am afraid the underworld was overcrowded, and they sent me to Limbo, to see if there was any chance I might be accepted somewhere else. Perhaps, if I become a knight of the Queen, some doors, or windows, might be opened,' Peter said, laughing.

'It is your turn to be blindfolded, Peter!' Ellen exclaimed excitedly.

'Don't try to cheat, Peter, I'm watching you!' Bernard declared.

After walking around trying to catch somebody, Peter said "stop" and touched someone who was a little smaller than the average.

'You are not a knight, nor the queen, so you might be... the bishop: Reverend St Clair!' Peter announced loudly, taking the scarf off. Everybody laughed. The games continued in this fashion, with much gentile amusement and silliness appropriate for the season, a wonderful foil for the tense atmosphere of the past few days.

Later, before starting another game, Diana asked the butler to bring tea and biscuits. Meanwhile, Mary Abington approached Kate, who was alone close to the fireplace, whilst Andrew was having a chat with Sir Christopher and Sir Richard.

'I wondered when I would be able to speak with you privately. you are always very busy,' Mary said. 'It seems that everybody wants to know about your research, and I am no different from them. I really want to know more about what you do,' she asked, in a friendly tone.

'My husband and I work at the British School of Athens,' Kate explained. 'Next summer we will receive some post-graduate students from Britain for a short time. It will be interesting for their research to see some archaeological sites and learn some new techniques,' Kate said proudly.

'Do you believe in oracles?' Mary asked suddenly, taking Kate by surprise.

'Of course not!' Kate laughed, then she added, 'My research about ancient civilisations is scientific; it examines the way religion and politics were like two faces of the same coin. The Greeks, for example, didn't start a political debate without ritual sacrifices to the gods and goddesses; an earthquake could determine decisions related to war against their enemies, as if it was Poseidon's will,' she explained.

'I feel relieved to know that, because you seem to be so lovely yet simultaneously intelligent. I was raised within a religious household, so some people think that because I believe in God, and try to spread His word, I cannot have a public or academic life. Like you said, there was a perfect harmony between politics and religion amongst the Greeks,' Mary said, smiling a little.

'I noticed you defending your faith and your Church vehemently the other day. Did you study theology?' Kate asked, curious.

'Yes, indeed. But as you can see, the same thing happened to me – we never stop studying and researching when we like the subject; one topic leads to another... and another. It is simply fascinating,' Mary agreed.

'Exactly, some people even revive their faith when science and justice fail to provide them with the answers for their questions,' Kate encouraged her.

'I don't know, Kate, sometimes I feel so powerless when I hear about so many wars and conflicts around the world. I would like to be a Minister of my Church, perhaps set up a branch here in Britain, if Albert continues his political project. My worry is that I might not have the answers that my followers are looking for. It is much harder for a woman to embrace a public life, and if you intend to be a minister of God's Church, it is even harder, don't you think?' Mary asked, much more relaxed now.

'Yes, it is harder, but you can do it, trust me, especially if you like challenges,' Kate agreed, feeling some strange solidarity with this girl, who was trying to break down the same barriers that she had been trying to break for years.

'I became very interested when Lord Henry told us about St Blathmac and his beautiful poem. Do you think that he will allow me to see the manuscript? I might use it in my Church lectures,' Mary asked.

'I don't see why not. Lord Henry is a man ahead of his time. He has his weaknesses, but he is definitely an open mind, and I am sure that his objective is to use history to build a better new world. We shall use "knowledge" to build, not to destroy, and there is so much knowledge still hidden in the past... I have been asking myself if it is fair to allow such knowledge to remain hidden...' Kate replied thoughtfully.

'I don't understand, what you mean?' Mary asked, confused, when she was interrupted by an unmistakable voice.

'Knowledge... knowledge... is it a sin or a gift? Some will say gift, others sin.' Sir Christopher joined their conversation. 'We shall not blame knowledge, though, because it exists by itself. The real problem is we, humans, who don't know how to use it wisely.' Sir Christopher smiled amiably at the young ladies.

'Any knowledge that came from God is sacred, and we have to spread it over the Earth,' Mary replied politely.

'How do you know that it was sent by God and not by Evil?' Sir Christopher provoked her, whilst Kate listened.

'From Revelations; where else it could come from?' Mary replied confidently.

'You have to be careful with the source of the revelation – never open the packet without being sure about its origin.' Sir Richard joined them cheerfully, with a glass of wine in his hand followed by Andrew, giving Kate time to reflect upon her conversation with Mary. Perhaps she should have a break to analyse her own attitude, as it occurred to her that it might not be fair to be so quick to divulge her sacred knowledge without the consent of others. She pondered. Kate did not have the authority to decide whether the knowledge of Alexandria should become public or not. There were the other Guardians to consider, those like Professor Regina Davis, who gave her own life to prevent such knowledge from falling into the wrong hands. Taking this kind of decision without consulting those who protect this knowledge would be breaking a promise, destroying something that had been sacred for centuries.

Meanwhile, the guests looked to the tea and little bites that the servants brought, and the conversation moved on.

Having finished their teas, the guests were rejuvenated somewhat and eager to continue their games. Diana asked the butler to bring an ornate box with some archaeological artefacts that her husband had kindly donated to the games.

Flamboyantly, Diana opened the interesting box, then carefully took the artefacts out one by one, gently putting them on a large table with a red velvet cover; amongst them – the famous dagger discovered years ago in the Sun Barrow; an Anglo-Saxon cruciform brooch; two small pots with a Celtic design on them; some Roman coins; a bronze bracelet and a necklace with glass beads, both Viking; a Roman silver spoon, a small bronze horse statuette and a couple of Saxon glasses which were surprisingly intact. Then, she asked her guests to examine each artefact carefully, as they would be hidden in different places in the room.

A game is not a game if there isn't a prize to be won, so Diana displayed the prizes on another table. They would be awarded according to the number of objects that the guests located. There were prizes for men and women, and they could choose any of them; the most coveted prize seemed to be a bottle of champagne, which encouraged even the most disinterested and resistant to join to participate in the games – now people like Sir Richard, Sir Christopher, Dr Gruber and Dr Turner perked up and decided to have a go.

The other prizes would certainly meet the most demanding tastes, as they included a silver letter opener with a delicately carved handle; a French Limoges hand-painted porcelain; a silver-plated cigar case, a small fob-watch for a lady, a silver locket and other valuable little trinkets that were pleasing to the eye.

Whilst everyone admired the objects on display at the two tables, they couldn't resist the wines and whiskey being served. It would be remarkable if anybody would be sober enough to go in search of anything, including their hostess, whose task would be to hide the artefacts.

After about an hour of drink and chat, Diana finally asked everybody to leave the drawing room and enjoy some delicacies the cook had prepared which were set out as a little buffet in the dining room, whilst she hid the artefacts. Her task was not as simple as it seemed, since the fun of the game was to make it more difficult, or maybe impossible, to find them; but Diana did take into account the sobriety of her guests, otherwise some objects were at the risk of never being found again.

After returning to the drawing room, the guests' mood took a few minutes to thaw again. The game started cold, like all games, with people walking cautiously and silently around the large drawing room without touching anything – nobody wanted to be the first fool to make a mistake, but when they were warmed enough, some of them decided to take the risk and look under the tables, behind porcelain and furniture. Then Charlotte complained loudly,

'Ellen, you are cheating!'

'No, I am not,' Ellen replied, flushed. Everybody turned to look and she went redder still.

'Yes, you are! You are standing there watching us, memorising the places that we have already searched, then you go straight to the remaining places before we do,' Charlotte said, annoyed.

'This is a memorable day. I never thought that Ellen could cheat on you, Peter,' Diana said, laughing, a little giddy, having partaken of the wine rather more than anybody else.

'I found it! Here – a Roman coin!' Ellen cried. She was delighted with her find.

'Well done, Ellen, keep it away from Peter. I wouldn't be surprised if he tried to steal it,' Diana advised.

'I don't see why; after all, we are a team – a married team,' Peter retorted.

'Not at all! This is a game, and I am wining, and you are losing! So you can forget about the champagne,' Ellen said cheerfully.

'I didn't know you liked champagne so much,' Peter griped, then turning to Bernard, he added, 'As you said, Bernard, we do everything to make our wives happy, and in return they are ready to stab us, sometimes in the back.' He sighed.

'Don't start with your whining. This is typical of those who are losing a game, and hate to admit it,' Diana said, enjoying the situation.

'I found one of the Saxon glasses!' Dr Gruber declared. 'I must say, the Saxon tribe that immigrated to this island completely lost its Germanic essence, confirmed by the quality of this glass, which is inferior to the ones from the same period found in Europe,' he sniped, examining the glass very closely.

'They had to be different, Dr Gruber,' Kate interjected, 'because the immigrants had to adapt to a different climate, soil, and ways of living. Their priority was to produce food and interact with the natives, mostly through conflict initially, as we know.' She smiled and nodded her head at him politely, which shut him up, as the fire in her eyes betrayed an opponent he had no desire to cross swords with.

'Ah... ha! I found the Viking bracelet!' exclaimed Bernard very proudly, holding it up for everybody to see, then he asked Andrew, 'Clarify for me, Andrew, were the Vikings and the Christian Saxons both here at the same period of this bracelet?'

'Yes, they fought each other for a long time; surely you knew that. Why are you asking me?' Andrew asked, annoyed for have not found anything yet himself.

'You see, Reverend St Clair? If we hire a good bronzesmith, you can order some bracelets and ask him to engrave a Christian cross on it, as a reminder or souvenir of the time when Christians fought against Vikings,' Bernard suggested to the vicar.

'Nobody can use the Cross of Jesus as an adornment just to look pretty. This is an act of pure vanity and lust. The sacred Cross is not an ornament,' he lectured.

'What are you two talking about?' Sir Edmund asked, with a serious face.

'Sir Edmund, it is time for you, Bernard and me to have a very profitable conversation. We have the solution for your problems,' Peter intervened.

'What did you just say, Peter? Which side are you on?' Diana whispered angrily in his ear.

'I think that you are married to the wrong side, my dear. When the Queen hears about our tourism proposal for Stonehenge, she will be very tempted by the taxes and revenue. But you know how fond of you I am, so when you become a widow, you can join us as a business partner, what do you think?' Peter teased her, trying not to laugh at Diana's expression.

'Hmm... I see! I would prefer to kill you, before I knock on your door, begging for any help,' Diana retorted, then left him alone.

The game continued in a lively spirit, with innocent jokes from some, dangerous sarcasms from others, and pinpricks from the spiteful ones, who didn't find anything. However, gradually, some gave the game up due to an excess of wine, blaming the winter cold for their consumption; but, at that point, not everybody wanted to give up, and Ellen was one of the determined ones who was still searching high and low. She approached the place where Diana had hidden the dagger, but not finding it, Ellen gave up and sat beside Charlotte, completely frustrated.

Diana, who was sitting observing the scene whilst drinking her wine, stood up suddenly and went straight to the furniture behind which Ellen had just looked, and where the dagger was supposed to be. Astonished, she looked behind the furniture twice, then she looked at the guests who were standing watching her in silence, having noticed the strange attitude of their hostess, whilst waiting for an explanation for what was going on.

With a pale and a distressed expression, Diana, whilst trying to understand what had happened to the dagger, said in a flustered voice,

'It should be there... I don't understand.' She was genuinely confused and very upset.

Diana's perplexity was such that she began to doubt whether or not she was mistaken about the hiding place, thinking that perhaps she had drunk a little more than usual.

Those who could still find the energy started looking where she indicated to find the missing dagger, but they didn't trust Diana's sobriety, thinking that she probably had simply forgotten the place where she hid it. Shortly they gave the search up, as the butler announced the afternoon tea would be served; an invigorating pleasure to end a joyful and festive afternoon.

The entertainment could not have been more adequate, and everybody seemed happy. After tea, the guests retired to their rooms to recharge and get prepared for another evening of celebration. Meanwhile, Lord Henry's absence was not seriously noticed; in truth, it was very welcome for some, as his constant provocations and madcap ideas took some of the guests to the edge, creating an ambience of disagreement and animosity amongst them, which Diana found very irritating.

Diana thought about going to see her husband in his office, but after thinking twice she decided to not interrupt him, since his cousin Sir John should have arrived from London by now, no doubt directed to his office by the butler whilst the rest of them were playing games in the drawing room. She didn't think any more of it and went to her bedroom to recover a little from her tiredness, thinking that she would find the lost dagger later.

Kate was sitting in front of the dressing table, combing her long hair, whilst Andrew was lying on the bed with his arms crossed behind his head, watching her with a lazy smile, then he said,

'I love your hair. I wonder if we should send an excuse and stay here in the bedroom until tomorrow; after all, Christmas is not today, so the vicar cannot accuse us of not being good Christians, can he?' he said.

'Do you know what your problem is? You are a little drunk, but I cannot blame you as I am a little as well. Don't worry, though, we will feel better in a couple of hours. Knowing you, I am sure you will be able not to resist the appeal of the wonderful smell of roast beef in the oven for our dinner.' Kate smiled.

'Roast beef? How did you know that?' Andrew asked, sitting up in the bed.

'Mr Bear told me. He was behind the kitchen door watching the servants fetching the meat and vegetables. By the way, the dessert will be your favourite – Victoria sponge pudding, with double cream,' she teased, knowing he would love it all.

'Robert was right – you are a witch.' Andrew laughed, then continued to tease her. 'Did you bring food for your birds? They were out there watching us earlier, you know? Well, actually at the moment there is only one – can you see the eagle-owl? The other might have gone looking for food.' Andrew grinned.

'I will not answer this type of provocation anymore. If you think I have birds, it is your problem, not mine,' Kate said, pretending to be angry. Then she stood up and walked towards the bed to give him a cuddle, but couldn't resist first stopping in front of the window to look out at the eagle-owl, who was perched on one of the branches of the tree opposite the window. There he was, like a sentinel without rest, a silent guardian of the night, with the sole purpose of watching over Kate's dreams and life; a promise made a long time ago, so old that she no longer remembered herself, but the Guardians would never forget their promise.

Some people claim that old age gives people strength, and Sir Richard and Sir Christopher were prime examples of that theory, as after a quick rest, they met each other in their usual place in the reception room, from where they could watch the frenetic Christmas atmosphere of the manor house, happy for being spectators, without the heavy burden that falls on those who still have a lot of work to do until the celebration.

'I am intrigued about that dagger, Richard,' Sir Christopher said, and asked, 'How could Lady Diana forget where she hid it?'

'This is the problem with magistrates – they only think about murders, motives, poisons and daggers,' Sir Richard replied, trying to warm his hands and legs near the fireplace.

'Better than you professors of literature, who are obsessed about ghost dogs and bizarre eagle-owls,' Sir Christopher replied, faking annoyance.

'It has its appeal. We shouldn't be restricted to listening to those boring academic students,' Sir Richard replied, reclining in his comfy chair after his hands were warm; then he continued. 'It is very quiet now. They couldn't resist Morpheus; I wonder if they will come for dinner later.'

'Who is this *Morpheus*?' Sir Christopher asked, curious.

'Ah... ha! You should read more literature, Chris. Morpheus is the god of dreams,' Sir Richard explained, proud he knew something his friend did not.

'Fascinating, Richard. What I like most about you is that for good or bad you always surprise me,' Sir Christopher praised him.

'AHH!... AHH!'

A shrill scream of horror and anguish shattered the quiet of the house, making the two old fellows get up suddenly, without knowing what to do or where to turn.

'What was that?' Sir Richard asked in a panic.

'I don't know, but it seemed to me like Diana's voice... I mean... scream,' Sir Christopher replied, recovering from the shock then hurrying out of the reception room to the hall, to determine where the scream had come from.

Meanwhile, the sound of doors opening abruptly in different parts of the house could be heard, as well as people coming out of their bedrooms and asking each other what the source of that terrible sound could be.

Kate and Andrew quickly put their shoes on and ran to the bedroom door. When they opened it, they saw Peter running along the long corridor towards the stairs, pulling on his coat whilst running. Ellen, Charlotte and Mary were standing petrified in front of their respective doors looking at each other aghast, whilst Bernard had his pipe in his hand, in doubt whether he should light it or not. Meanwhile, Kate had no doubt that the screaming was Diana, who was not with them in the corridor.

'Help, help, somebody, help!' they heard her shout.

They worked out where the calls were coming from. Peter was the first to identify the location, running to the small dusty room where he'd found Diana a few days ago, with the small box containing the dagger.

Sir Christopher and Sir Richard followed Andrew and Kate, who were ahead, running after Peter, but when they all arrived at the room's door, they were astounded by the grotesque scene that unfolded in front of them – Peter was standing a couple of feet from Diana, who was kneeling on the floor, with a bloody hand, next to her husband's lifeless body, which was lying on the floor, with the missing dagger stuck in his chest.

Peter was pale and silent, looking at Diana, who in turn looked at Kate, then to Andrew. Shaking her head, she began babbling.

'I didn't do it... I didn't do it... I was looking for him in his office... but I couldn't find him... It's almost dinner time...

What should I tell my guests?' Diana was speaking very quickly; she was in shock, verging on a nervous collapse.

Sir Christopher, with his long experience of life, knew he had to take control of the situation, as the others were also in complete shock at the ghastly sight.

'Lady Tollemache, Kate will take you to your bedroom if you please, as we have a job to do here.' The magistrate spoke, gently and sadly for the death of his friend, then he turned to Kate and, knowing that only she could understand what he was about to say, asked enigmatically,

'Kate, would you take her to her bedroom, please? We have a dear Guardian of Words dead and, sadly, he and his words will be buried forever.' He grimaced and made a little signal with his hand.

Although Peter and Sir Richard didn't perceive the ambiguity of those words, Andrew on the other hand could not help noticing the mysterious ambience lurking in the atmosphere of that room. For some time he had suspected that his wife was part of a bigger secret, which so far he had been unable to unravel. However, much as he wanted, it was not the right time to try to investigate such a mystery, because there was in front of him a tragic situation calling urgently for answers.

Kate didn't hesitate or say anything because at that moment, Sir Christopher's words were the only thing that made sense for her. She promptly went over to Diana and silently helped her to stand, then very gently led her out of the ghastly room.

As they walked, they met some of the guests, who gradually descended from their rooms and stood lined up along the corridor, watching Diana and Kate walking through them, without understanding what had happened.

Sometimes, Kate thought, it is best not to jump to conclusions. Other people have sufficient knowledge and experience to deal with it, and Kate just didn't want to think about what had happened, because so much was at stake at that precise time. She knew that Lord Henry was a polarising person, but what could unleash such hatred as to kill a person? Heritage, prestige, jealousy, religion, passion, ideology?

Whatever the motive, none of them could justify such an act; even Diana, despite the remarkable differences between the two women, didn't seem to have a motive to kill Lord Henry. She was a woman of her time who would serve her husband without any question, if he provided what she wanted; and Diana knew how to play that game better than anyone else, as she was born with all the skills needed to be a persuasive and charming wife. Kate tried not to think about it.

Peter followed Diana's movements without saying anything; he walked to the room's door, watching her as she moved away; but the only thing he could think was that something was not quite right. However, everybody had to follow the protocol, and appearances, as always, were important.

'I always thought that he was too old for her. Maybe he committed suicide.' Ellen tried to defend her friend.

'Don't be silly, Ellen. Nobody commits suicide with a dagger in their chest; it would be more usual to use a pistol,' Charlotte corrected her friend.

'What do you think, Peter? Do you think that she wanted his money so desperately?' Bernard asked his friend.

'Something is not quite right, my dear; how long have we known Diana and Robert?' Peter responded with a question.

'For almost fifteen years, I suppose, long before we met Charlotte and Ellen anyway,' Bernard replied, finally finding the courage to light his pipe.

'Exactly, and she was the most clever and intelligent amongst us,' Peter interjected. 'I am sorry, but her actions were always calculated precisely. Poison or pistol fit her style more than a knife,' he stated categorically.

'Fascinating, Peter, we share the same deduction. I must say something does not fit properly in this situation – there is a lot of hatred and anger in that dagger's hilt,' Sir Christopher agreed, then from the door he looked at all the people lined up along the corridor: Sir Edmund, Lady Georgiana, Drs Gruber and Turner, as well as Dr Baker; on the other side, Albert, embracing Mary who was, at the same time, holding the vicar's hand; then Charlotte holding Ellen's arm.

After a few seconds in silence, Sir Christopher asked,

'Could somebody ask the butler, Mr Angus, to call the police?' His request fell like a bomb had exploded in the room.

'Do you think that is prudent, Chris?' Sir Richard whispered to his friend. 'I know this is not your jurisdiction; maybe we should wait a bit and make some inquiries, especially amongst the servants, to determine why Diana killed her husband.' He grimaced.

'I know what I am doing, my dear fellow. I need the police here to entertain... I mean... distract these people, leaving me free to observe everything and everyone. I need to hear and watch them slip up. The perpetrator may not make obvious mistakes, but he will certainly make some, when he does not feel himself under the scrutiny of the police,' the magistrate explained.

'Why do you always have to complicate things, Chris? Nothing could be more obvious than the scene we witnessed here,' Richard declared. 'Who else knew where the dagger was? Diana deceived us by pretending that she had hidden the dagger for the game, then implied that somebody stole the dagger to kill her husband, knowing that many of the people here had plenty of reasons to kill Lord Henry,' he suggested.

'I don't remember her saying anything about someone stealing the dagger. Actually, Diana was quite silent. She seemed confused about the place where the dagger might be; her behaviour was more likely of someone inclined to accept that she had forgotten the place because of the wine,' Sir Christopher said; then added, 'I am surprised at your obvious conclusion, Richard, because if this was the type of counsel you give Conan Doyle, his next book might be a very boring disaster,' Sir Christopher said, annoyed with his friend.

'You know that crimes are not my cup of tea. I don't have your talent. To be honest, as a professor of literature, I am a specialist in ghosts. I would not be surprised if Lord Henry took the dagger without saying anything to his wife, and later when he was examining the object, Kate's birds came in and give him a shock, so he fell on the dagger and died. Those ghost birds can't deceive me,' Sir Richard declared.

'I don't care if it is early, but I need a drink, Richard, urgently,' the magistrate said, incredulous at his friend's conclusion.

'That's it! Now you mentioned a drink, you've got me.' Sir Richard smiled.

'Of course, I would be even more in panic if you had refused a drink,' the magistrate replied sarcastically.

'No, you didn't understand. What I was trying to say is that I have been watching how much these people drink since we were in Greece last year,' Sir Richard replied. 'It is a fact that Diana likes to drink, as much as anybody else here, but I never saw her drink beyond her limit, and as far as I am concerned, she didn't drink enough to get drunk earlier, therefore we have two plausible hypotheses...' Sir Richard paused thoughtfully.

'Keep going, I'm very interested,' Sir Christopher urged his friend.

'She could be pretending to be drunk or... somebody put some kind of drug in her wine,' Sir Richard concluded proudly when he noticed Sir Christopher's nod denoting approval and interest in his theories.

'Come on, Richard, we cannot waste any more time.' The magistrate rushed his friend out of the room, then they encountered a crowd in the corridor, all talking loudly; all chattering about their own theory, because Christmas as a subject could not compete any longer.

Sir Richard did his best to keep up with his friend, promising to himself that he would lose weight next year. When he finally arrived at the drawing room, puffing and panting from exertion, he saw the magistrate standing in front of a velvet, comfortable and very expensive chair, which was Diana's favourite – she was never seen sitting anywhere else but on that particular chair.

'Richard, we are lucky the servants didn't clean the room yet. They might have left the cleaning for later, as they are probably all busy in the kitchen preparing the dinner, if there will actually be any this evening, which I doubt,' the magistrate said sadly.

'I know you were good friends, Chris, but don't be so pessimistic. We all have to eat, otherwise we cannot use our brains,' Sir Richard replied, trying to cheer his friend up.

'Tell me, Richard, if I am correct, this is her chair, and probably this is her glass, which has just a small sip of wine left in the bottom,' the magistrate said, taking the glass to smell its contents, then he added, 'If you are a good observer, as you said earlier, do you think that this bottle on this table here was the one which filled Lady Diana's glass? I think that this little table is the nearest to the chair, which make sense, eh? What do you think?' Sir Christopher asked.

'Would you allow me?' Sir Richard asked, then, taking the glass from Sir Christopher's hand, he smelled the contents, swirling them round the bottom of the glass to obtain the best aroma he could. After a moment in silence, he smelled it again, then he walked towards the table and sniffed the bottle, which still had wine enough for a half-glass in it.

Sir Christopher waited in silence, as this type of science was not precise, requiring specific skills, as well as an instinct, that only a few were gifted with. He was observing Sir Richard, who went to another table with different bottles of wine, and after a careful search he picked up one identical to the bottle that supposedly contained the wine which had filled Diana's glass. After minutes smelling the two bottles and the glass, he finally reached a conclusion.

'Chris, you might be right. I bet my title of Professor at Cambridge that this glass, which supposedly contained the wine drunk by Diana, contains the same wine from this bottle you found on the table next to her chair. However, this other Chardonnay lives up to its name, I have to say, and so remarkable a difference in smell is not acceptable,' Sir Richard explained categorically.

'Therefore, someone put something in this bottle next to her chair. Is this what you are trying to say?' Sir Christopher questioned his friend.

'We are not in the summer, and the servants had not yet replenished the fireplace for the night, as everybody decided to rest in their bedrooms; therefore, the room's temperature dropped since the last time we were here. I have no explanation for them to smell different,' Sir Richard re-affirmed.

'I might need you to taste the wine of the two bottles to see your reaction, my dear,' Sir Christopher suggested cautiously.

'What? Oh no! I don't want to miss the party,' Sir Richard complained loudly.

'Don't be silly. It is just a little sip to endorse our conclusion about the smell,' the magistrate insisted.

'And what happens if I fall unconscious and miss the dinner?' Sir Richard complained.

'I promise you, I will hire three servants to carry you to the dinner table and you will not miss anything. By the way, if you are right, Diana didn't fall asleep; she only got a little disorientated. I am only asking you to drink a little, to see if the taste changes from one bottle to another. It is very simple.' Sir Christopher used all his rhetoric to persuade his friend.

'Do you promise me you will wake me up for the dinner?' Sir Richard asked, not pleased to be the guinea pig.

'I swear to God.' Sir Christopher gave a kind smile.

'Only one sip, nothing more,' Sir Richard said resignedly.

After a brief hesitation, he took two empty clean glasses, smelled them, then poured a sip of wine from the different bottles into different glasses. Sir Richard didn't want to disappoint his friend, knowing how important finding the real murderer was to him, so he took a deep sigh and drank a sip from each glass, with a reasonable pause between the two, to have a proper separate taste of each wine.

With a disgusted face, Sir Richard pointed at the bottle and looked at his friend.

'Whoever did that to this Chardonnay should be arrested and hanged.' He grimaced.

'I know, my friend, I will, I promise you, and I am glad that you are alive,' Sir Christopher said jokingly, but he was happy to confirm what he'd suspected since the beginning.

The magistrate put the bottle on the table, and after a deep sigh he addressed his friend.

'Whoever adulterated this wine might not have worked alone, but the hate that guided the dagger is undeniable. We have a tough job here, Richard, a difficult task to save an innocent from being hanged,' Sir Christopher stated vehemently.

Chapter 15

Sir Christopher and Sir Richard stayed in the drawing room, trying to recall some particular details about the games earlier, discussing the behaviour of the guests.

'I think that Peter is very fond of Diana, have you noticed?' Sir Richard suggested acerbically.

'Don't be silly. Those two like to play cat and mouse. It is exciting for them; their lives must be very boring, trust me,' the magistrate said, trying to think of other possibilities.

'I don't think so. As you said, this might be a crime of passion,' Sir Richard insisted.

'I said there was too much hatred and anger involved, that is all. I think that he and Bernard were focusing on that business with Sir Edmund,' Sir Christopher replied.

'And what about Sir Edmund and Lady Georgiana? They seem very close since Amesbury,' Sir Richard asked.

'Quite plausible; both were furious and calling for blood.' Sir Christopher paused, then stood up as Angus the butler, accompanied by another man who was impeccably dressed, appeared at the door, waiting anxiously, so Sir Christopher asked,

'What happened, Angus, and who is this gentleman?'

'This is Sir John Tollemache, Lord… I am sorry… the Late Lord Henry Tollemache's cousin,' the butler replied, a little emotional given the state of affairs, and the murder of his employer.

'Oh… Sir John. It is a tragic circumstance to meet you, I am afraid. We expected you earlier. You have my condolences, it is an irreparable loss,' Sir Christopher said, with great sadness in his voice.

'Yes, indeed. I am in shock. I arrived earlier, Angus can confirm,' Sir John explained.

'Yes, Sir Christopher,' Angus responded, 'I myself took Sir John to Lord Henry's office, whilst Lady Tollemache and her guests were playing in the drawing room,' Angus confirmed.

'How long ago,' Sir Christopher asked.

'About four hours ago.' Sir John replied, embarrassed.

'Four hours? And where were you all this time?' Sir Christopher asked, astonished.

'Err... sleeping...' Sir John replied, extremely embarrassed.

'Henry was with you meanwhile?' Sir Christopher asked, trying to properly comprehend this bizarre twist.

'Hmm... maybe... I mean... for a while...' Sir John replied.

Sir Christopher looked at Sir Richard, then turned to Sir John, then quizzed him again.

'Could you be more precise please, Sir John?'

'As soon as I arrived, Angus took me to Henry's office, and there my cousin and I had a lovely conversation. We talked about his experiment and ideas, then he said he had something very special to show me and asked me to wait, whilst he went to get it. I don't know exactly what happened after. I remember I drank a cup of tea, which made me forget the long, cold journey here. I also noticed that Henry was taking too long to come back, but knowing about the games and the number of eminent guests, I relaxed, thinking he probably had to stop to talk with them. Therefore, I leaned back in that comfortable chair and fell fast asleep. I was exhausted, I have to admit – poor Henry, he seemed so happy,' Sir John said, clearly moved; then he added,

'I woke up about half an hour ago, when Angus opened the office door. He was very agitated, and told me what had happened. I spoke with some of the guests, and when I knew a magistrate was in charge of the investigation, I asked Angus to introduce me to you.'

'I am in charge only temporarily, as I have asked somebody to call the police, who, hopefully, might arrive tomorrow,' Sir Christopher explained. 'Meanwhile, I suggest you and Angus find Diana, and help her to proceed with the dinner, which I am sure would be Henry's will, and of course it will help to cheer people up. Richard and I will go to our rooms and get prepared for dinner, now.' The magistrate and his friend bid Sir John farewell and left the drawing room.

Kate and Andrew were informed by an elegantly dressed young servant that dinner would soon be served, at the usual time. They went downstairs in silence, wondering what people's mood would be after such a terrible event.

It transpired that they were the last to get to the dining room, and as they walked along the corridor, they could hear people talking noisily as they got closer.

Diana was beautiful, as usual. With a small handkerchief in one hand – probably to wipe away the tears that might come – she was talking to Ellen and Charlotte next to the empty honourable place in which the late Lord Henry used to sit.

Whilst Andrew left Kate to fetch wine, Mary approached Kate.

'I am very pleased that you came for dinner,' she said. 'I really need some advice about how to deal with Albert. He is inconsolable. He and his uncle always had their differences, but they really liked each other, and Lord Henry was Albert's closest relative.'

'It is very difficult to find words of comfort in a situation like this,' Kate replied, 'but I think your presence here beside him is already a great comfort. It will be a challenge tomorrow, I am afraid, a difficult day for everybody when the police arrive,' she said, without knowing what else to say.

'Thank you, Kate. Talking with you helps a lot. I don't have much in common with the other women here. They are probably talking about what they are going to wear at the funeral,' Mary said sadly.

'We deal with our losses the best way we can. Distracting our mind with other issues can be one of the best ways to deal with these matters.' Kate tried not to be hard on Diana.

'You may be right, and although Albert didn't want the position his uncle offered him, he admired Lord Henry's tenacity, and his experiments of course. He was even excited to show me his uncle's museum in the cottage, after you and I talked about it yesterday, you remember?' Mary asked.

'Yes, of course. However, my husband said that we shall leave as soon as the police allow us; he didn't take well his friend's death, and I am afraid that our visit to the cottage might have to wait for another time,' Kate said, disappointed.

'I understand,' Mary replied. 'As you said though, we will need something to do to distract our minds a little. It might take all day for this enquiry, and I am not so sure the police will be very kind when dealing with the people who really cared about Lord Henry, I am afraid.'

'You might be right,' Kate agreed, thinking that Mary really seemed to understand the heartache of those who were suffering.

'Let's wait until tomorrow, and see what the police say,' Mary said. 'I will let you know if we are going to the museum or not. I might ask Albert to take us whilst the police are interviewing the others. He told me it is not far,' Mary said with a timid smile.

'Thank you, Mary, you are very kind,' Kate replied, adding, 'It would help, I am sure.' Kate was pleased with the invitation, knowing the following day would be very awkward with the police asking questions and insinuating all sorts of things.

Their conversation was interrupted by Diana, who wanted the guests' attention.

'My dear friends,' she began, a little shakily, 'I imagine how affected you have been by my husband's unexpected death. But I also know how important this celebration was for him. So, we shall toast the Queen, then Henry.'

Everybody raised their glasses and toasted the Queen, then their missing host, Lord Henry Tollemache; emptying her glass, Diana continued emotionally.

'I am informed that the police will arrive early tomorrow, so none of us can leave the estate until we all talk with them. We shall cooperate with the inspector to solve the' her voice wavered slightly 'the... murder...' She wiped away a tear. 'Perhaps we might still have our Christmas dinner to honour my late husband because that would be his wish. But for now, let's enjoy our Christmas Eve dinner. I am going to retire a little earlier than usual, if you don't mind. However, feel free to stay longer, if you please.' She sat down again, visibly distraught, but determined to help her guests cope with the horrible situation, and at least keep them well fed and looked after.

There was not much to be said, especially with the prospect of having the police knocking on the door again the next day. This time, though, it was not about an old murder case. Several of the guests may have been motivated to murder Lord Henry, and all of those motives would no doubt come to light and be scrutinised by the police, leaving the guests in a very difficult position.

Dinner was an elegant affair, if somewhat subdued, but the food was delightful... It began with melon salad, followed by a light consommé, devilled crab, roast guinea-fowl with chestnut stuffing, a simple but beautifully decorated sherry trifle, followed by a cheese-board and crackers. Not many partook of the port or brandy offered towards the end of the meal, as the murder was not an inspiring topic after dinner; given the guests were tired after a long day of drinking, games and strong emotions caused by the murder itself, they all had good excuse to leave early for their rooms, to be ready and prepared for Christmas Day.

December 25th was a cloudy day with a leaden sky, and although a thunder storm was not likely, a storm inside might not be avoided. Everybody seemed to wake up very early and called their servants and maids to get their luggage ready to leave the estate, as soon as they were allowed to do so.

For the first time since the celebrations started a few days ago, all the guests had their breakfast at once, and gradually their usual strange sense of humour surfaced, with pinpricks and provocations, showing that life, in fact, goes on.

The vicar didn't waste any time, and whilst everyone was comfortably sitting, he took it upon himself to stand up and address them directly.

'Let's pray with contrition for Lord Henry's soul after breakfast...' The vicar could not finish his sentence because he was rudely interrupted by Bernard.

'We should check first to see if the body is still intact, Reverend.'

'What do you mean, Mr White?' the vicar asked, confused.

'I would not be surprised if we find Lord Henry's head is no longer attached to his body,' Bernard replied, standing up and getting his pipe out.

'Why wouldn't it be, Bernard?' Diana asked, astonished.

'It is well known that Dr Baker showed a very deep interest in taking his research to the next level, studying skulls with a brain still inside,' Bernard explained.

'How dare you insinuate such a thing?' Dr Baker stood up, outraged.

'This is heresy! God is not happy with you, Mr White.' the vicar interjected.

'Angus, go and check my husband's body immediately,' Diana ordered the butler.

'If you are not careful, Bernard, you are going to lose yours,' Charlotte warned her husband.

'Could we perhaps show a little more respect for the dead?' Andrew intervened, trying to calm the situation.

'Be careful, Sir Andrew, as far as I am concerned you would have much to gain from Lord Henry's death, being in charge of all his excavations and research,' Dr Gruber stated nastily.

'Over my dead body! I will curse you if you try to invade my land,' Sir Edmund warned Andrew.

'How dare you disrespect my husband's last wish whilst you are still a guest in my house?' Diana said to Sir Edmund, indignantly.

'Not only Sir Andrew, but you too, Lady Diana, are in a very good position since his death,' Dr Turner added to Dr Gruber's insinuation.

'If you repeat this outrage again...'

Kate could not finish because Andrew interrupted her, throwing cold water on the conversation by suggesting,

'Let's wait for the police to arrive...' in a very serious tone, daring anybody to disagree, or say anything else disrespectful.

'Excuse me. The inspector is here!' Angus announced from the door. The room first fell silent, then the guests began to leave the room towards the drawing room, which was determined by the police to be the appropriate place for the inquiry.

Inspector Parnell was standing in the entrance hall with Constable Parker, admiring the paintings on the walls, bedecked with expensive decorations, when he noticed the crowd leaving one of the rooms and heading in his direction. For a few moments the inspector seemed mute, as he thought he was experiencing some kind of hallucination; then he turned to Parker and said in a whisper,

'What the hell are all these people doing here? We left them in Amesbury.'

Then Constable Parker, after he too overcame his surprise, replied in a whisper,

'This is the deceased's house... I mean... estate.'

'I didn't ask you that. What I want to know is what are these people doing here?' the inspector insisted.

'Hmm... I think they are here to celebrate Christmas.' Constable Parker replied.

'When you took down the address, did you know it was Lord Henry's?' the inspector insisted, trying to get to the bottom of it.

'To be honest, Sir, I didn't know it, until I saw that crowd... I mean... these people, coming out of that room' Constable Parker replied, worried about the inspector's reaction.

'Who wrote the address, Constable, tell me?' The inspector's face was bright red.

'The new chap, Sir,' Parker said, very embarrassed.

'Why hadn't he written the name of the deceased along with the address?' the inspector demanded.

'Good question, Sir, perhaps he was in a hurry to catch the train for the Christmas holiday and forgot to write the name?' the constable responded, without conviction.

'You sacrificed my turkey, you know that, Parker?' the inspector said in a very strange, strained tone of voice.

'Sir, I don't see why... Sir... we could not find another deceased in time to escape from this one, Sir.' Parker's usually sober demeanour began to unravel.

'No, not another deceased, but we might have gotten the wrong address and arrive here only tomorrow, Parker. It is your fault only, did you know that?' the inspector declared.

Parker didn't have time to answer, as Diana approached them using a handkerchief to cover her mouth, as she was about to cry.

'Inspector Parnell, I don't know how to express my gratitude for your coming – a tragedy fell upon us! I count on you to discover the evil soul that deprived me so soon of my poor husband's company.' Diana paused, dabbing at a tear on her cheek.

'My condolences for your loss, Lady Tollemache,' Inspector Parnell said coldly, not prepared to spare anybody from his frustration.

'My husband had so many enemies, and some of them are still right here,' Diana confided in a whisper.

'I would not be surprised, Lady Diana. Tell me about your servants – does any one of them have a motive to kill your husband?'

'Not at all. They are all very busy, trying to cope with our loss and to prepare our Christmas dinner.' Then she added in a whisper,

'You knew my husband, and how much he valued a great celebration, especially after all his scientific achievements. Fortunately, his untamed spirit is giving me strength to proceed with our dinner. You and Constable Parker will have to dine with us and toast my husband's soul later.' She smiled timidly.

Inspector Parnell hadn't expected such an invitation, and his humour changed completely.

'You are most kind, my lady. Constable Parker and I will do our best to solve this heinous crime to guarantee you and your guests a lovely evening. By the way, who was the last person to see your husband alive?' he asked.

'Apart from the killer, Sir John Tollemache, his cousin, who arrived yesterday from London; he was the last one,' Diana replied, making an effort to be helpful.

'May I see the deceased?' the inspector asked.

'Of course, we didn't move his body yet,' Diana replied, then walked down the hall with the two police officers, and with Angus, the butler, following them waiting for instructions.

When they arrived at the small room where the body was found, Inspector Parnell asked Diana,

'Would you ask some servants to carefully remove the body, after we have finished analysing the scene please? I would like to interview the witnesses here in this very room. The place where he was killed could bring up some emotions, strong enough to make the killer reveal himself,' the inspector said confidently.

'Of course, Inspector, whatever you want,' Diana agreed, then after she had given Angus instructions, she covered her mouth with her handkerchief and left the room.

The inspector, with a hand on chin, quietly observed the body, walking around without saying anything, whilst Constable Parker stood attentively with his little black notebook and pencil in his hands, ready to take notes.

'Nice dagger, I must say,' Inspector Parnell said. 'Whoever killed him was not interested in opportunistic theft, or they would have taken this valuable knife; the dagger is the answer,' he inspector said thoughtfully.

'Well done, Inspector Parnell, we have reached the same conclusion,' the magistrate, followed by Sir Richard, announced from the door.

'Oh, Sir Christopher, Sir Richard,' the inspector greeted them. 'I wonder why they had to call me, if you are already here?' he said caustically

'This is not my jurisdiction, Inspector, as you well know.' Sir Christopher smiled. 'And I didn't want to undermine your authority, of course,' Sir Christopher said, hiding his little pleasure with the situation, as the exchange of looks between the inspector and the Constable didn't go unnoticed.

'Who found the body this time, Sir Richard? A ghost by any chance?' The inspector began his inquiry with a hint of dark humour.

'Even though the deceased was used to evoking celestial bodies, his death seems to have a very real and solid motive,' Sir Richard replied.

'What do you mean?' the inspector asked, surprised, but Sir Christopher urgently intervened.

'What he is trying to say, Inspector, is that we have a bunch of angry and vindictive guests who were dissatisfied with the endeavours of my dear, deceased friend.'

'Who benefits most from his death?' the inspector asked very directly.

'Hmm… hmm.' The magistrate cleared his throat.

'Lady Diana Tollemache,' Sir Richard replied suddenly, whilst Sir Christopher gave him a severe look, then tried to defend their hostess.

'This is a crime of passion, Inspector,' he said, 'committed by a perpetrator with an evil soul and a heart full of bitterness; someone not interested in profit, but with the purpose of preventing Lord Henry from going forward,' Sir Christopher stated in a dramatic tone.

'Instead of simplifying everything, you have complicated everything, Chris. Now we have a drawing room full of people who perfectly fit this profile you have created,' Sir Richard complained.

The inspector took a deep breath, then asked,

'You are trying to say that Lady Tollemache doesn't have anything to do with the murder? Why are you so sure?'

'Simple. Richard and I have evidence that Diana was drugged. We discovered that someone put something in her glass, causing her to become confused. I cannot say yet how the killer discovered the dagger and stole it, but you can be certain that once they had the dagger, it would be easy to leave the room without being noticed, and proceed with his or her intentions unknown,' Sir Christopher replied confidently.

'Well, let's see what we can discover from the interviews. Parker, bring the other Tollemache,' the inspector ordered.

'Which one, Sir?' Parker asked.

'Oh, no, how many do we have here?' the inspector complained, rubbing his brow, slightly discouraged.

'Two, Sir – a young one and an old one,' Parked promptly replied.

'How do you know that?' the inspector asked, surprised.

'From Amesbury, Sir. The deceased's nephew was there, and, according to Lady Diana Tollemache, the deceased's cousin – the old one – arrived from London yesterday,' Parker replied matter-of-factly.

'Very well, Parker. You might redeem yourself before the end of Christmas,' the inspector said. Constable Parker left the room, followed by Sir Richard and Sir Christopher, who wanted to mingle with the other guests with a very specific goal in mind.

Meanwhile, three servants entered and, although they seemed distressed with their master's death, in silence they gently covered him with a blanket and carried him out of the room.

Constable Parker was with Sir John Tollemache outside in the corridor, observing the scene, uncomfortable for being the first one to be interviewed; immediately after, he was asked in.

'Please, sit down, Sir John,' the inspector instructed, then proceeded, 'What has brought you here, Sir John?'

'Not "what", you mean "who",' Sir John replied seriously.

'No, I know "who", I want to know "what" was your reason for missing your Christmas turkey at home,' the inspector retorted impatiently.

'"Who" said I shall miss my Christmas turkey? I was invited to be here, which for me is a "what" most important,' Sir John replied, getting a bit upset.

'Yes, you're right – there isn't a "what" more important; but there is a "who", who is more important – Her Majesty the Queen is the "who" I am here acting as her representative,' Inspector Parnell informed him pointedly.

'...I am here representing Her Majesty the Queen, as well,' Sir John argued.

'Uhh... hmm.' Now look here, you're going to tell me what I want to know.' The inspector got him.

'Yes, indeed. But "why" weren't you clear since the beginning?' Sir John asked, and proceeded, without waiting for his reply, 'My cousin, Henry, wanted my approval for his project to excavate the Lunar Barrow near Amesbury. It seems that Sir Edmund has been reluctant to give his permission, so my cousin wanted the Queen's support,' Sir John explained.

'Are you favourable to the idea, hmm?' the inspector wondered.

'I don't know. He is dead now. To be honest, I don't think it's a good idea, really. We have been spending too much money on our borders, to maintain the empire.' Sir John was not very confident.

'Well, it seems that everybody has to change their plans. You can go for now, but don't you leave the estate; we may have to talk again later.' The inspector released him, and as soon as the gentleman had left, he asked Constable Parker,

'Did you check the kitchen?'

'Yes, Sir,' the constable replied.

'...and?' the inspector insisted.

'Turkey, and a beautiful suckling pig, Sir!' the constable replied with his eyes shining.

'Well done, Constable, well done.' The inspector nodded and smiled, whilst lighting his pipe.

'Right, Parker, ask the new widow to come here. We shall not keep her waiting; she is very busy organising the Christmas dinner.'

'Yes, Sir.' Parker disappeared to fetch the owner of the house.

Although Diana entered the room with a pale face and her little handkerchief covering her mouth, nothing could deny her natural exuberance.

'Thank you for calling me before the others, Inspector. I am extremely busy at the moment, with all these guests... I really don't know what to do with so many people around. If I could stay by my own in my bedroom, mourning my poor Henry... but I can't, you understand, don't you?' she pleaded with her eyes.

The inspector was about to reply when Diana interrupted him.

'I know... I know..., but my poor Henry would kill me if I didn't proceed with the celebrations, you do understand, don't you?' Diana asked, tilting her head a little and looking contrite.

'Well...' The inspector didn't manage to get any words out when she continued.

'Thank you, Inspector. I want you and Constable Parker to sit next to me, at dinner.' She didn't let him speak, and with some little excuse, she left the room, leaving the inspector and constable looking at each other without fully understanding what had just happened.

Ellen was the next to be interviewed, and she entered the room cheerfully, feeling important for being asked to provide her testimony.

'Merry Christmas, Inspector,' she said with a smile.

'Eh... Merry Christmas,' he replied reluctantly, then asked,

'How long have you known Lady Diana Tollemache?' Constable Parker licked his pencil, ready.

'A few years. Since I married Peter, actually. Peter and Bernard have known Diana since they were children. Now she is a Lady, and Peter promised me I will be a Lady as well. He is applying, did you know that?' She smiled.

'Yes, yes... Mrs White,' the inspector confirmed, then asked,

'What do you think about her?'

'She is so very distinctive. I am learning to be like her,' Ellen answered genuinely.

'Don't you think that Lady Diana could be, sometimes, imperious? Perhaps intimidating?' he asked.

'Oh, no! It is the complete opposite. Charlotte and I love it when Diana puts Bernard and Peter in their place; she often speaks for the three of us, if you know what I mean?' Ellen replied categorically.

'Indeed – the perfect marriage, I must say,' he inspector agreed, and stood up, saying,

'Thank you, Mrs White. By the way, you have a most beautiful dress.' He smiled, and bowed a little.

'Do you see? Peter is the best husband in the world. He lets me choose what I want and what I need,' she continued.

'God bless you, Mrs White... and your marriage,' the inspector replied with a sigh, watching as Ellen left the room in excellent spirits.

'Who shall I bring now, Sir?' the constable asked.

'Bring the knight, from Amesbury,' the inspector replied.

Meanwhile, hidden under the stairs next to the small interview room, Diana tried to hear what was being said through the wood panelled wall, when an unmistakable voice from behind surprised her.

'Still waiting for Father Christmas, my dear?' Peter asked quietly.

'Shhh... shut up, Peter,' Diana whispered. 'Why do you always have to be like a shadow, behind me?' she asked, pulling Peter under the stairs, so as not to be seen.

'You are so ungrateful,' Peter started. 'I am only trying to help. You should really be worried about your late husband, because he's going to come back later as a ghost, to haunt you.' Peter sighed.

'I didn't kill him, I told you that,' Diana fumed quietly, still whispering.

'I know it, but does he know you didn't have any role in his murder? He might think you were an accessory,' Peter said, laughing very quietly.

'Why don't you go away and take his ghost with you as well?' Diana strained to hear the interview behind the wall in the little office.

'I noticed that you forgot to hang some mistletoe and ivy up. If you had given us details of your macabre Christmas in advance, I would have brought some to hang on the doors, to hide your indomitable late husband's spirit until after Christmas,' Peter said, trying to light his cigarette.

But Diana didn't allow him, warning,

'No, don't, they will smell it and find us here.' Then she added, 'By the way, that proposal about the tourism business in Stonehenge, is it still on?' she wanted to know.

'I don't see why not. Sir Edmund might not resist the temptation to make money,' Peter replied, smiling when Diana raised her eyebrow.

Meanwhile, inside the interview room Inspector Parnell, surprised, asked the constable,

'I said the knight only, Parker. What is she doing here?'

'She wouldn't accept it, Sir,' the constable explained; then, Sir Edmund, accompanied by Lady Georgiana, who had a defiant look on her face, asked him,

'Why are we here? We have to return to Amesbury, as soon as possible.'

'You were not in a hurry earlier, and as far as I am concerned, you two came for the Christmas turkey, did you not?' the inspector suggested.

'Who cares about Christmas turkey? I came here because I wanted to find out what that vile scoundrel's next ruse would be,' Sir Edmund replied cattily.

'So, you had a motive to kill Lord Henry, didn't you? Perhaps a ritual of sacrifice in the parlance of your order, if I am not mistaken,' the inspector provoked them.

'How dare you insinuate such sacrilege? Stain the Mother Earth with the blood of that vile man?' Lady Georgiana was outraged.

'Do you think I would risk losing my knighthood, after Her Majesty threatened me?' Sir Edmund scowled.

At that exact moment, there was a knock on the door, and when Constable Parker opened it, Angus the butler was there.

'Excuse me, Sir, but the Lady of the house has invited you all for afternoon tea, er... which will be served now, at lunch time in the drawing room, due to the Christmas dinner later,' he explained.

The constable looked to the inspector, who, raising an eyebrow, responded,

'Hmm... we shall not leave Lady Diana Tollemache waiting for us; after all, she has to oversee the preparation of an important dinner today, don't you agree, Constable Parker?' the inspector asked.

'Indeed, Sir,' the constable replied, nodding.

'Consider this a break, Sir Edmund, so don't leave the house, as I may need to ask you a couple of questions later,' the inspector warned them, then the four of them left the interview room towards the drawing room, as even they could not resist an afternoon tea, especially in the Tollemache's' opulent mansion.

Chapter 16

The atmosphere in the drawing room could not be heavier. However, Sir Christopher was determined to conduct his own private investigation to find the murderer of his fellow Guardian. He first approached Mary and Kate to see what they were thinking, whilst Andrew was chatting with Sir Richard.

'I haven't seen your fiancé, Albert, since we discovered Henry's body?' he said.

'He went to the museum to open the windows and let some fresh air in,' Mary replied. 'It has been closed for months, and we are going to see some of the relics,' she said, with a little smile.

'I don't know if we should. I don't feel comfortable after his death,' Kate said sadly, but she was interrupted by Sir Christopher.

'I have to say – Henry was very proud of his little museum, and it would be a shame to deny those relics to those who care about the past.' He smiled reassuringly, then continued, 'By the way, Miss Abington, what is the name of your church, in America?' he asked.

'Science of Christ's Love. Did you hear about it?' Mary replied proudly.

'I am not sure, but I am quite concerned about the hostility that Catholics and Mormons have been subjected to by some radical groups over there,' he replied thoughtfully.

'God-Mind nourishes and guides our actions through a tortuous path, in order to ensure that the words of evil are buried forever,' Mary said fervently.

Kate found those words quite strange as they sounded like an echo from the past coming to the present to haunt them. She decided to find out more about this girl and her beliefs. Sir Christopher's attention, on the other hand, was distracted by the inspector and constable, who entered the drawing room accompanied by Lady Georgiana and Sir Edmund.

Diana was delighted that the two officers had accepted her invitation for an afternoon more like a lunch tea so early. Nobody could resist the exquisite delicacies which had been carefully arranged by her servants in the drawing room. She was certain the special treats would improve the inspector's mood and cheer up the guests up a little.

Meanwhile, Mary addressed Kate.

'I have to go to the little museum now. I don't want to leave Albert waiting for me too long. He needs my support. I'm very relieved he accepted the idea of showing me the relics. It will be nice to get away from this oppressive atmosphere; I can't wait for this all to end and then we can leave this place forever.'

Kate looked quizzically at Mary, then at the other guests, who were completely entertained by the beautiful '"lunch"' tea. She knew it was not a good idea to tell Andrew, as he was going to be interviewed by the inspector following tea, whilst the dramatic events of the past week made him both cautious and anxious about her; he certainly wouldn't want to lose sight of her. Kate also wanted to know more about Mary and Albert, who she found very intriguing. Consequently she agreed to go with Mary, and they quietly left the drawing room together, to visit the little museum.

The two girls went to the kitchen and asked one of the servants to ready two horses, so they could ride to the cottage. Kate thought that leaving the house for a while would do her good, so she decided to enjoy the little trip.

Although the tea and accompanying delicacies were wonderful, Inspector Parnell could not resist the opportunity to find out more about the guests. If he could take them to the edge, they might expose their real feelings, and, if he was lucky, they might inadvertently let slip something crucial. After considering who would be the best one to start with, he approached Dr Gruber.

'Refresh my mind, Doctor – are you the one who called the Queen's subjects monkeys? Hopefully you are not the one responsible for depriving me of my Christmas turkey.'

'The first one to say anything about monkeys was not me. It was one of your kind – that pseudo-scientist called Darwin,' Dr Gruber retaliated.

'Oh, yes, I remember, you have great plans for "your" kind – the Hyboreans.' Inspector Parnell didn't give up easily.

Constable Parker whispered to him,

'Sir, it is "Hyperboreans".'

'Ah, yes, exactly what I meant to say. I didn't finish with you yet, Dr Gruber. Your Hyperboreans didn't have an empire like ours.' The inspector sniffed, then with his cup of tea he walked away towards Peter, who was talking with his wife, Charlotte and Bernard.

'Ah... Mr Price! Good afternoon, I was told that you were the first to arrive at the murder scene. Did you see Lord Henry's wife with the dagger in her hand?' he asked.

'Diana is remarkable, Inspector, but daggers are not her style – too personal and too quiet. I have no doubt that she is capable of using dynamite to remove even small stones from her path, just for the pleasure of being heard or noticed. Great events with her in the lead role are more her kind of thing, I suppose,' Peter replied, smiling, whilst lighting his cigarette.

'You might agree with me, though, that Lord Henry was too old to play with dynamite, don't you think?' the inspector continued, but Charlotte replied,

'I don't think age was the problem, Inspector. It is better than having a husband without a brain.'

Then Bernard interjected, 'You should be grateful, Charlotte; at least I am alive. I have told you several times that I am worth more alive than dead, am I right, Peter?' He looked to his friend for support.

Inspector Parnell and Constable Parker didn't want to get involved in domestic quarrels, and hastily moved away from them, approaching their next victim – Dr Baker.

'Ah... I remember you, you and your skulls. Last time you were thinking of collecting skulls with brains still inside; a fresh one would be ideal, I suppose?' the inspector taunted him.

'I didn't steal his skull; you can check. It is still there. Anyway, a brain is useless after twenty four hours,' Dr Baker replied.

'How do you know that? Have you tried fresh brains before?' the inspector insisted.

'How dare you?' Dr Baker replied, glowering.

'I don't want you out of my sight, Dr Baker.' the inspector declared, then went away to speak with Dr Turner, but on the way he whispered to Constable Parker,

'Thank goodness Christmas turkey doesn't have a head, otherwise it would be gone by now too,' and Constable Parker nodded, then smiled discreetly.

'Dr Turner, you seem to know a lot about poison, especially gas, and the hallucinations it can cause,' the inspector stated, then Constable Parker whispered in his ear,

'Sir, the deceased was stabbed, not poisoned.'

'Hmm... I might have forgotten my spectacles in the other room.' The inspector tried to read his notes in his little notebook, then confided to Parker, 'I don't deserve this. Well, well, at least I had a good Christmas Eve,' then Parker added,

'And a good malt whisky, Sir.'

Inspector Parnell looked at the constable a little too seriously and raised his eyebrow, whilst addressing Dr Turner again.

'Were you trying to disprove the existence of ghosts with the murder of Lord Henry?' the inspector asked pointedly, but the vicar interrupted.

'Inspector, you cannot continue with this line of inquiry without clarifying first your own beliefs in this respect.'

'What do you mean?' the inspector asked, surprised.

'Are you a Christian soul or not?' The vicar insisted.

'What does my belief have to do with this inquiry?' the inspector asked, confused.

'If you are a Christian you cannot mention the word "ghost",' the vicar admonished him.

'Ask him if you can use it in a metaphorical way,' Constable Parker whispered to the inspector, but the vicar continued with his haranguing.

'Anyway, now that he is dead, he belongs to God, and these heretics don't have the right to bring his soul back,' the vicar replied spitefully.

'Who said anything about bring the deceased's soul back? We were talking about the deceased's ghost,' the inspector argued.

'Now I am confused; aren't they the same?' Bernard interjected, as he had been listening to their conversation, whilst trying to light his pipe.

'Did you hear him? I told you, my husband doesn't have brain,' Charlotte intervened, referring to Bernard, but she was interrupted by Dr Baker, who stated,

'Lord Henry was a brilliant scientist, and an atheist. He would be disgusted to hear you talking about his… his…'

'You mean his soul?' the inspector suggested.

'I think it would be better you call it existence,' Dr Baker intervened.

'Bravo, Dr Baker, a body with mind, ghost and soul is too heavy to be lifted to heaven; it would be impossible with all those sins attached.' Sir Richard quipped, then added, 'On the other hand, if he only existed, he didn't have to worry about the weight to carry, after dying.'

'He cannot enter heaven if he is… I mean… "was" an atheist.' Dr Turner stated.

'How dare you insinuate that my poor Henry cannot enter heaven?' Diana fumed.

'Don't worry, Lady Tollemache, my prayers will be sufficient to guarantee his place in heaven,' the vicar assured her, whilst glowering at Dr Turner.

'I would not be surprised if God gives Henry an authorised return to haunt you all,' Andrew stated, disgusted with the discussion.

'Are you talking about resurrection, Andrew?' Ellen asked, genuinely curious.

'Hmm… wait a moment, I can pray for him to go to heaven, but an atheist cannot be resurrected,' the vicar announced angrily.

' "An authorised return" doesn't mean resurrection, which implies mind and soul. He can return, though, without authorisation, as a ghost, which is still not the same thing; actually, I think it is quite acceptable, don't you think, Diana?' Peter suggested.

'What are you trying to say, Peter?' Diana demanded. 'My dear husband would never come back to haunt me. He wanted the best for me, and for Britain, which meant putting Stonehenge on the map as one of the Wonders of the World,' she stated.

'What are you trying to say, Lady Diana?' Sir Edmund questioned. 'I will not allow you to put your feet on my land ever again,' he said bitterly, then, addressing Parker, he said, 'You can write in your notebook if you want, Constable, I can see you didn't miss any of my words. Stonehenge belongs to me, and only over my dead body… ' then Peter interrupted him.

'Sir Edmund, you have no idea how much you can profit from an enterprise authorised by the Queen,' he said, immediately taking the wind out of Sir Edmund's sails.

'What do you mean?' Sir Edmund asked.

'Let's have a proper chat, sir – you, me and Bernard,' Peter suggested.

Then, whilst Sir Edmund and Lady Georgiana clustered with Peter and Bernard, the inspector looked at Parker and said,

'I think murder isn't the main subject anymore. People get bored very easily these days; they cry out for new things all the time. I wonder if we would do any good for society if we arrested them all. What do you think, Parker?' the inspector asked, sighing.

'I agree, Sir, they don't seem to care about the dead, as long as their interests are preserved. No wonder scientists think we descend from apes,' he said.

'Indeed, Parker, indeed.'

The inspector nodded; and after a brief pause, the constable asked,

'Who should I call for the next interview, Sir?'

'Let's follow the protocols, Parker; bring Sir Andrew, since he is one of the beneficiaries of the death of Lord Henry,' the inspector replied.

Whilst the constable headed off to get Andrew, the inspector went to the interview room, annoyed by the lack of progress in his inquiry. Solving this murder case might make his career, whilst failure was not an option he could contemplate.

In the drawing room, whilst Andrew was having a chat with Sir Christopher and Sir Richard, the constable approached them and interrupted.

'Sir Andrew, Inspector Parnell wants to speak with you now.'

'Chris, would you mind finding Kate? She might be in the kitchen, looking for more scones,' Andrew asked.

'Of course, Andrew, don't worry, I will find her,' Sir Christopher reassured him; then Andrew left with Parker.

Riding across the field towards the cottage, Kate admired the landscape and smiled to herself, thinking that England should not be remembered for the spring and summer only. The beauty of the English winter reflected the tenacity of its people and their "latent" life, almost like they were asleep; ready to rise, though, when the first ray of sunshine returned.

The two girls spotted the museum from a distance as they approached, and Kate's breath was taken away whilst admiring the large medieval cottage, which certainly would be holding precious testimonies of the past; perhaps more distant in time than she could ever have imagined.

They left their horses under a big tree next to the cottage, then entered the reception, from where Kate had her first great impression. Lord Henry could not have been more correct in calling it a museum in *stricto sensu*. She really felt as she was at the entrance of a great museum, with its relics and artefacts carefully placed to invite guests to each corner of the hall for a different journey back into the past.

Kate had to admit that Lord Henry was not only an antiquarian; he could certainly called be an artist, seducing whoever came to the entrance to not be frightened of the past, but to embrace it, not only as part of your history, but also part of your soul.

Why was the past so important for people like her? Kate wondered. But suddenly any wondering was blurry when she recognised the caduceus with the twisted serpent that Lord Henry had mentioned. She had no doubt that strange forces of nature actually attracted her there, in order to witness what others, in turn, would never be able to.

'Look, Mary, the caduceus with the twisted serpent! The presence of Asclepius here in Hyperborea is irrefutable,' Kate exclaimed. 'The ancient druids knew about him. The oral tradition must go even further into the past, as the Romans mentioned the druids amongst the Celts. Sir Joshua was right, the myth of Apollo and Asclepius came from the northwest, long before the Greeks had built their temples in Delphi,' Kate said excitedly; then she turned to Mary and added,

'If we follow the oral tradition and the alignment between the sun, the moon and the stone circles, we may be able to find the right places to dig, and who can imagine what we might find there?'

Mary looked at the caduceus with a cold face, then, with a frosty voice she said,

'You will not show anything to anybody.'

'What do you mean?' Kate said, taken by surprise, then she suddenly realised that all the windows were locked, and there was no sign of Albert.

'I will not let you do what you want,' Mary told her, very calmly, and turning to the door, she locked it behind her, put the key in her pocket, and walked over to a mannequin dressed in a Saxon warrior's costume, with a shield in one hand and a sword in the other.

Mary grasped the heavy sword and flourished it, making a swishing noise in the air in front of Kate.

'You will do what I say now,' she commanded.

'Where is Albert?' asked an incredulous Kate.

'He was not invited to our great event, Kate. Now, go up those stairs to the upper hall and don't try any tricks, because I have this sword in my hand, right behind you,' Mary ordered, and watched as Kate ascended the stairs.

When the two women arrived on the first floor, Kate looked round examining the large hall, trying to think of a way to escape Mary. The walls were relatively featureless, and there were just two windows which, unfortunately, were locked. There was a small skylight, though, with a brass handle.

The hall was full of antiquities, and Kate knew that some of them might be very valuable. There was a table and its chairs in front of a bookshelf with codices, old books and manuscripts; some of them were on the table, and a particular medieval codex with its sheets made of vellum and adorned with illuminations captured her attention.

Kate approached the table to get a better look at the codex, whose words were written in beautiful calligraphy. However, when she read the name "Jesus", a new discovery was revealed – the Saxon poem of St Blathmac. Kate looked at Mary and said,

'You knew about the codex and the poem about Jesus. So why did you bring me here?'

'Because I needed to get rid of you more than anything else too. I wanted, though, you to see it first, so you would understand what I have to do,' Mary replied.

'Why don't you just stop with your riddles, and tell me once and for all what you want from me?' Kate said angrily. She was fed up of Mary's games.

'We knew about your "Guardians". Don't try to deny it, we have been tracing this order for a long time,' Mary replied, enjoying the suspense. 'I confess that we lost you for a while, when you became Lady Kate Enfield, and stopped using your family name, Miss Tiverton,' Mary said.

'What do you think you know about us?' Kate needled her.

'We know enough to want to silence you and the evil words forever. Alexandria was burned for the purpose of making way for the Son of God-Mind,' Mary replied, agitated.

'But Alexandria was burned decades before Christ, don't you see?' Kate said.

'The Messiah was due hundreds of years before, and all those papyri from the Greeks, Egyptians and Babylonians only served to confuse people's minds with this nonsense promoted by what you call science,' Mary snarled.

'But it is knowledge, and to deny it to people is tyranny. We made so many achievements over the millennia, are you so blind that you cannot see?' Kate argued.

'So what you and your Guardians are doing is not tyranny? When do you intend to reveal the place, the secret place, where the remains of your beloved Library of Alexandria are hidden?' Mary asked.

'I don't know; nobody knows, to be honest,' Kate replied honestly 'We have been waiting for the right moment in this world, when people will understand that knowledge should be used to build things, and not to destroy anything. We are waiting when people like you will finally understand that faith in science and faith in God don't exclude each other, but possibly complement each other, don't you see? We don't know how to do it yet, but we have to find a way, like St Blathmac in his poem here.' Kate pointed at the codex on the table, then continued.

'Although he was surrounded by war and death, he didn't lose his faith in Jesus, calling him a prophet, king and a religious leader; St Blathmac even acknowledged other people's faiths, without claiming for a war against them,' Kate explained.

'Do you actually agree with this absurdity?' Mary snapped. 'This "saint", as you call him, called the Son of God-Mind the perfect wise man. How did he dare identify Christ as a man? Jesus could not be anything other than a pure and sacred extension of God-Mind,' Mary replied, upset at Kate's words.

It was at this point that Kate realised she was wasting her time, as she was dealing with a religious fanatic. She also recalled Mary's words when Sir Christopher had asked HER if she was aware of the religious massacres in the United States. Kate had been too selfish during that conversation, thinking only about visiting the museum. She was blind and selfish enough not to pay attention to Mary's words, when she said that "*tortuous paths were needed to ensure that evil words would be buried forever*". Why hadn't she seen the signs from the outset? She would never be like Professor Regina Davis, who gave her life to save Alexandria. Kate realised she was not prepared for such an important duty, but it was too late now.

Mary seemed to be proud of her own achievements, looking from Kate to the antiquities in the museum, saying,

'Is this what you think that life is about: old tools, colourful sheets of vellum, and some pieces of furniture? We should not think about the past, but the future, and how to spread the word of God-Mind,' Mary declared.

'Perhaps God is also waiting for us to add to His words,' Kate interjected, 'words we learned from the mistakes of the past. History is here to guide us. We never stopped learning, don't you know that?' Kate replied.

'I'm sorry, but God will be the one who will decide if your soul is worth saving or not,' Mary responded enigmatically.

'What do you mean?' Kate asked.

'It is not in my hands now. You will burn here to the ground,' Mary said, looking around her, and she added, 'You and this evil place. It is a shame that Lord Henry died without knowing the destiny of his precious little museum.'

'Did you kill him? My God, you are actually evil,' Kate replied, disgusted.

'We certainly have different points of view, Kate. Your death will be an accident, one that nobody could ever prove was anything other than an accidental death. However, as I planned, Lord Henry's death will be blamed on your husband and, most of all, on his own wife, Diana, the first two beneficiaries of his death. His wife's greed could never be denied, especially after the death of the only heir that could contest Lord Henry's will – his nephew,' Mary told her, proud of her complex plan.

'Are you going to kill Albert?' Kate asked, aghast. 'Please, stop! You cannot keep killing people in the name of God. I assure you, this wasn't His plan. We have to learn to overcome our differences, otherwise this is not a God who is worth worshipping.'

Kate tried the last argument in vain, however, as after taking one last look around, Mary went to the door and said, 'Enjoy your reading, Kate.' Then she closed and locked the heavy wooden door behind her, whilst Kate tried to think of a way of escaping her prison.

Chapter 17

Sir Christopher hurried to the kitchen to find Kate, and as he approached along a corridor he could smell the delicious aroma of Christmas roasts, mixed with the intoxicating fragrance of breads and spiced cakes that were also being baked; and for a brief moment he forgot about the tragedy that had engulfed that house.

When he entered the kitchen, though, after a quick look round he could see no sign of Kate, so he asked one of the servants,

'I was told that Lady Katherine Enfield was here, do you know where she is?'

'Lady Katherine and Miss Abington went for a ride, sir,' the servant answered, a little annoyed at having her busy day interrupted. Servants didn't have any time to waste in the kitchen due to the frantic preparations for the Christmas dinner.

Sir Christopher, though, joked, 'Oh, these young ones change their minds all the time and, as usual, they don't tell us.' He smiled kindly. 'They make us guess and I'm quite certain that they decided to go to the little museum after all. Your cooking smells wonderful, I'm sure the guests will be delighted,' he reassured her, and with that, Sir Christopher excused himself and left.

Back in the corridor, he could not escape a bad feeling in his gut which had been bothering him since the beginning of his journey. Having experienced so many morbid incidents, he had the impression that the surprises were not over just yet.

Sir Christopher found Sir Richard next to the drawing room door, talking with Peter and Bernard, who welcomed him with a smile, leaving the magistrate in no doubt that the three of them were planning something to cheer everybody up later.

'Chris, we decided to have a last game of cards after dinner, in that exquisite cellar, to honour our late Lord Henry. What do you think?' Sir Richard asked enthusiastically.

'As long as we have brought his killer to Justice by then,' Sir Christopher agreed, not entirely enthusiastically, though.

'Don't be pessimistic, Chris, at least...' Sir Richard was unable to finish what he was saying, as everybody looked at each other in amazement when they heard a deafening scream from their host, Diana. After the initial shock, they ran out of the drawing room to see what it was about.

Peter called out,

'Diana?'

'Not again!' Bernard exclaimed, before running after Peter, who had set off at break-neck speed to find out what else could have happened to add to this macabre Christmas.

In the hall they were joined by Inspector Parnell, followed by Andrew, then Constable Parker.

'It was Diana! Where is she?' Andrew asked, especially worried as he still hadn't found Kate amongst the crowd that huddled in the hall.

'Please, somebody help,' they heard Diana shout.

'It's from upstairs!' Peter shouted, then bounded up the stairs, followed by the inspector and the constable.

'Chris, where is Kate?' Andrew asked the magistrate, grabbing his friend's arm.

'She went to the cottage, with Miss Abington,' Sir Christopher replied, upset and feeling he had failed in some respect. They set off after the other men, who were making their way quickly upstairs.

When they reached the room from where the noise was coming, they found Diana standing next to Albert's bedroom door, very upset.

'Somebody is trying to frame me, and I know exactly who she is. Where is that vile witch who came to poison my house and ruin my Christmas? Where is Mary?' Diana shouted.

When Andrew looked inside the bedroom, he saw Albert, stone-cold and lifeless on the floor, with a large wound to his skull and a broken glass vase covered in blood next to him.

'Diana, what happened?' Andrew asked, incredulous at what he was seeing.

'It was not me. It was that vile woman, and I will kill her when I find her,' Diana raged.

'I would not like to be in Miss Abington's skin, would you?' Bernard whispered to Peter.

'I knew the title of Lady Tollemache was too much for her. She might need more than prayers to get rid of this curse,' Peter replied, in a half-hearted joke.

'Do you think her husband was cursed?' Bernard asked, lighting his pipe.

'The whole family, my dear,' Peter replied, lighting a cigarette.

'Do you think the Christmas turkey can wait, sir?' the constable asked the inspector, feeling hopeless at the situation and believing his dinner would be cancelled for sure now.

'Quiet, Parker, and write down what I am about to say: neither the old nor the newly dead will get between me and my Christmas turkey,' the inspector stated adamantly. He turned to Diana and asked impatiently, 'My dear lady, could you tell us, please, what is going on here?' He tried to be kind, but stern at the same time.

'Don't worry, Inspector, because this time I have witnesses, and if you don't arrest her, I will kill her!' Diana exclaimed furiously.

However, the inspector waved his hand and interrupted her.

'Calm down, my lady, calm down. Let us do our job. Take a deep breath and start at the beginning.' He smiled, to reassure her.

'Andrew, we have to go,' Sir Christopher declared, starting to panic.

'Why? What do you mean?' Andrew said, confused.

'I know where Kate is, and she is in terrible danger,' Sir Christopher replied. He made off, and was followed by Andrew to the hall where they instructed servants to fetch two fresh horses immediately.

Meanwhile, upstairs, Diana started telling her version of events leading to Albert's demise.

'I was in the kitchen, checking to see if everything was being prepared according to my late husband's wishes,' she said. 'I know how very important this celebration was to him. Mary appeared from nowhere, and in her usual sweet voice, which I have to say never convinced me, she told me that Albert was upstairs, and that he regretted being rude to me and his uncle last night. Then she said that my poor Henry's soul would be in peace if Albert and I worked our differences out.' Diana paused and seemed about to faint, but Constable Parker caught her arm to support her, and she continued.

'Thank you, Constable. All these murders... It's too much for me.' Her voice was shaking. 'Although that vile serpent was speaking to me quietly so no one else would hear what she was saying, she didn't know that Angus, our handyman, was fixing the tap behind the wall where we were. When she had left the kitchen, Angus came and told me that he was very pleased that Albert had come to terms with the situation. Angus has been working for the Tollemache family for thirty years, and he was sure that Henry loved his nephew very much,' Diana explained.

'... and?' the inspector asked.

'... and... what?' Diana asked.

'Why are you here, in the deceased's bedroom?' The inspector wanted more details.

'Oh! I had to make some arrangements. I am very busy today. I decided to have a word with Albert and, perhaps, we might have a peaceful Christmas dinner, exactly how my poor Henry imagined it would be.' Diana paused to get her handkerchief out of her sleeve to dry a tear from her eye; she sniffed, then continued.

'I was about to knock on his door, but it was not completely closed, then I called his name, and you can imagine the shock I had when I saw his body lifeless surrounded by a pool of blood. Oh my God, how could that serpent be so cruel to me. She has ruined what should be the best Christmas of my life. Now I don't have my poor Henry,' Diana complained, then she started crying.

'Don't worry, my darling, you have us, and we will not abandon you during this difficult time.' Charlotte hugged Diana, then insisted,

'Let's go downstairs and have something to drink. You'll be fine.' Charlotte then turned to her husband.

'Don't just stand there doing nothing, Bernard. Ask the butler to bring us some wine to cheer us up. Come on, Diana, let's go to the drawing room.' She left with Diana.

'I will speak with the butler, Mrs White, and order wine for all of us. I think we all need one,' Sir Richard promised.

'Hmm… Sir Richard, could you ask the butler to come? I need to speak with him,' the inspector asked, and stood at the bedroom door, looking at the body on the floor.

'What are you thinking, Sir?' Constable Parker asked once they were alone.

'Motive, Parker, motive. Why the hell would that sweet lady want to get rid of those two?' the inspector growled.

'Whatever her motive, Sir, it was sufficient to make her extremely angry,' the constable replied.

'Indeed, Parker, although it is difficult to believe she is responsible,' the inspector agreed.

Meanwhile, in the cottage museum, Kate was trying to open the heavy door in vain. After searching desperately for another means of escape, she noticed the small skylight in the ceiling, and an idea blossomed in her mind, but she would have to find something to help her reach the window. Looking round, she saw a small table in the back of the room, and at that moment Kate had a glimmer of hope.

She pulled the table and placed it under the skylight, but although she could reach the window, she couldn't get it open. She didn't realise how much her life was at risk until the smell of smoke crept under the door. She could hear a crackling noise and she realised that Mary had apparently set the building alight downstairs. Being of wooden construction, it would not take long to for the fire to reach the first floor.

To make things even worse, whilst contemplating the fire engulfing the cottage, from outside Mary saw the skylight being forced open. Without any hesitation, she ran back inside and climbed the stairs, not without a little difficulty though, as the fire was destroying history faster than the course of time itself.

Kate knew she had to find something to reach higher so she could open the skylight fully. If she could escape onto the roof, it would be relatively easy to get down. When she heard Mary's voice on the stairs, screeching and full of hatred, she didn't waste any time; she put a wooden chair on top of the table and climbed up. With joy, Kate breathed the cold air from outside once she opened the skylight.

Steadying her arms on the sill, Kate pulled herself up and supported her body on the bottom of the window frame for a second, straining. When she got one of her knees on the frame, and was about to pull the other up, she felt two hands pulling her back in – it was Mary. She had grabbed Kate's leg and wouldn't let go.

There was nothing that Kate could do at that moment. It was her life or Mary's. Some survival instinct gave her strength, and Kate kicked Mary full in the face with her booted foot, knocking her unconscious; Mary fell, limp to the wooden floor, knocking over the chair, which fell onto her.

There was no time to find out what would happen to Mary. Smoke was enveloping Kate, making it difficult to breathe, whilst the intolerable heat from the fire was growing in intensity. Kate couldn't stay on the thatched roof for long as it would soon be consumed by the flames, but the roof was too high to jump off, so she had to find another way to get down, but could not see how.

Smiling in despair to herself, Kate thought: 'I always have to do everything by myself, and you, Mr Bear, might be sleeping comfortably in a warm bed, in this freezing night.' However, she was not entirely alone – the hoot of an owl came from the tree next to the cottage where she and Mary had left their horses. Kate could not see the owl indeed, didn't even hear it again – but her instinct told her there was no other chance to survive. She had to reach that tree.

Riding as quickly as they safely could, Andrew and Sir Christopher didn't have time to talk. For Andrew there was only one thing to do – follow his friend and trust that he would take him to Kate. Sir Christopher reined in his horse and looked in the direction of a large blaze. When Andrew asked him what was going on, he let out an urgent cry to hurry.

'Come on, Andrew. Quick!' The two of them rode hard in the direction of the fire.

As they approached that dazzling light, a terrible scene unfolded in front of them. Andrew's heart seemed about to burst when he realised the cottage was on fire, and there was nothing they could do to save it.

'Oh no, Kate cannot be in there. Where is she, Chris, please, where is she?' Andrew jumped off his horse and fell to his knees, and with glistening eyes, he stared at the intense fire that had engulfed the roof in great flames.

Sir Christopher, without saying anything, knew there was nothing they could do. He stood watching, speechless, sickened with the sound of wood burning and crackling, breaking into burning pieces that fell in piles inside the red-hot interior of the building. The noise of the inferno prevented them from hearing a plaintive voice, muffled by the smoke that was flowing around the tree.

'Andrew...!' Kate shouted again, almost breathless; this time, though, he heard her, and quickly stood up. He ran wildly to the tree next to the house, shouting,

'Kate, Kate... I'm coming...'

Andrew could see she was in danger, the branch that she was clutching was very close to the burning roof, so whilst Sir Christopher released the horses tied to the tree, Andrew scrambled up the tree until he got very close to where Kate was holding on for her life.

He knew her branch would not support the weight of the two of them, so he reached out his hand for her to hold. They started to climb down, a task made more difficult because of the long skirt of her dress, but the worst was passed, and after some tricky slips, the couple finally reached the safety of the ground.

Sir Christopher hugged both of them, laughing, knowing how close he had been to losing them. When they were walking back towards the horses, he suddenly turned to Kate and asked quietly,

'Where is Mary?'

Kate turned towards the burning cottage, then explained.

'She died, trying to silence the words forever.'

'Did she kill Henry?' Sir Christopher asked. Kate nodded her head in the affirmative.

'A powerful woman with an evil soul, I am afraid,' Sir Christopher said. 'She was prevented from achieving her goals, but not before causing a deep and painful wound to our order,' Sir Christopher continued, looking at Andrew, who stopped walking and said,

'I cannot protect her without knowing exactly what "order" is putting her life in constant danger. It is time for you to stop with your riddles and tell me once and for all what is going on, Chris,' Andrew begged of his friend.

Kate looked at Andrew, then to Sir Christopher, waiting for him to take the lead.

'You are right, Andrew,' Sir Christopher replied, sighing. 'It is time for you to know about us "Guardians". We are an order whose members, allied with "Kore", Lady Katherine, vowed to protect the papyri and manuscripts that Didymus Chalcenterus saved from the library in Alexandria, just before the Romans set it on fire. Kate's father was one of us, and her mother was "Kore" before her, and so was Professor Regina Davis,' Sir Christopher explained, but Andrew interrupted him, addressing Kate.

'Did you know this all the time... I mean... long before we went to Greece?'

Kate was about to answer, but Sir Christopher intervened.

'She only knew when she got to Eleusis and met Professor Davis, who died protecting Alexandria. She was Kore before the earthquake. After her death, Kate took her place. John, Kate's tutor, was one of us, as well as Henry, our dear friend who was murdered by Mary Abington.'

'Do you want Kate to risk her life to protect the Library of Alexandria with all these religious fanatics around?' Andrew asked angrily.

'It was my choice, Andrew,' Kate interjected. 'If we don't protect it, who else will? Shall we leave the past unprotected, and all that knowledge buried forever?' Kate replied. 'You were the first person to tell me about Alexandria, when I was ten years old, and I could see your eyes shining when you mentioned it,' Kate argued, reminding him.

'That was before I had you back in my life again. I cannot lose you.' Andrew spoke in almost a whisper, distressed and struggling to comprehend.

'Therefore, you have good reason never to lose sight of her again, Andrew,' Sir Christopher explained, in a kindly voice.

'Wait a moment,' Kate said. 'I cannot walk with "Guardians" all around me; after all, it's not me you have to protect – what about the library? It's thousands of miles away. Who is protecting those papyri and manuscripts now?' she asked.

'What about our honeymoon, Kate?' Andrew asked.

'Well, my dear fellows, our Christmas dinner is waiting...' Sir Christopher tried to change the subject.

'Don't forget about Henry's barrows to excavate near Stonehenge,' Andrew added.

'Enough! Could we please sit down and make a plan? This is getting out of control,' Kate interrupted them, annoyed.

'My dear, age is the big secret – with it comes wisdom, reminding us to take one step at a time,' Sir Christopher said eloquently. 'It is still Christmas... I mean... at least we didn't have our dinner yet, so I suggest, before any plan, a good old Scotch, as we all deserve it.'

'We cannot disappoint Diana, I suppose. This celebration means too much to her,' Kate added with a small smile.

'Indeed, my dear, indeed; and we shall be quick, before the Christmas turkey gets cold,' Sir Christopher agreed.

'We mustn't upset Inspector Parnell right now. This turkey means a lot to him,' Kate added, trying to be cheerful, whilst her heart was crushed, like those of her husband and Sir

Christopher, who were looking at the burning cottage for the last time, knowing that part of British history had disappeared with it, never to be seen or heard of again.

Chapter 18

Angus, the butler, entered the drawing room where an agitated crowd was gathered, eager to anticipate the inspector's next move, which could decide the fate of that macabre Christmas and its long-awaited dinner.

Inspector Parnell commenced the interview of Angus.

'Angus, thank you for coming. Tell me, please, what did you hear from Miss Abington and Lady Diana Tollemache's conversation?' he asked, but vouchsafed, 'By the way, I don't think it is appropriate to eavesdrop on other people's conversation from behind closed doors.'

'I do beg your pardon, Sir. I was called to solve a hydraulic problem next to the kitchen, since it might delay the Christmas dinner. As you can see today, the servants are extremely busy, and also very upset with the tragedy that has befallen this unlucky house,' Angus replied politely.

'Yes, yes… hopefully the Christmas dinner has not been badly affected by misfortune?' the inspector asked.

'Not at all, Sir! I would never allow the late Lord Henry's last wish to go neglected, or his good lady wife's express orders,' Angus replied, ever so slightly offended.

'May I also deduce that such efficiency is an indication of your good judgement regarding the conversation between the two ladies you heard?' The inspector looked intently over his wire-rimmed spectacles at the butler.

'Inspector, I can assure you, Miss Abington made it very clear that Lady Diana should go and see Mr Albert, to make peace and thus allow Lord Henry's soul to rest in peace,' Angus stated categorically.

'What about Lady Diana's and Albert's relationship? What have you to say about that?' the inspector pressed.

'It was quite normal and peaceful, until Miss Abington was introduced to this house, Sir,' Angus replied, without a jot of sympathy for the girl.

'I told you, that vile serpent poisoned my house. I have no doubt that she devised this entire plan with the intention of killing Albert, and incriminating me,' Diana declared from where she was sitting – in a beautiful blue velvet chair, between her two friends, who were holding her hands.

'That woman never fooled me – *Christ's Science*, huh!' interrupted the vicar sarcastically.

'Actually, that's wrong. It is *Love of Christ' Science*,' Sir Richard corrected.

'I am sorry, Sir Richard, but Christ didn't have any "science"; not that I know,' Bernard disagreed.

'Miss Abington's Church does, though,' Sir Richard insisted.

'What about *Christ Lovely Science*? Everything about Christ is lovely, don't you think, Peter?' Ellen suggested.

'I think, my darling, we should forget the "science". It is a long title,' Peter suggested.

'I don't see why we have to cut off "science". If you religious fanatics think that God created man, and man created science, by deduction, science was in God's plan since the very beginning,' Dr Turner interjected.

'Angus, could you please fetch a good Scotch for both of us, as I feel Constable Parker and I will have a hard time until dinner is served,' the inspector begged of the butler, who left hurriedly to get their whisky.

'No, you will not, Inspector!' Sir Christopher's voice echoed eloquently and theatrically from the drawing room door, followed by a silence, whilst everybody tried to work out what had happened to Kate, whose dress had some small rips and tears, and was stained with soot.

'Kate, why don't you try to be, well, normal sometimes?' Diana asked her, disgusted with her appearance.

'I have been trying to explain from the very beginning that academia is not a suitable place for women,' Sir Richard declared.

'Indeed, women should never be scientists. They don't know how to play with fire, I am afraid,' Dr Turner agreed, somewhat ambiguously.

'This could only happen in Britain, I assure you. We Austrians keep our wives out of trouble and under our sight,' Dr Gruber added disdainfully.

'Show more respect for my wife, you wretched little man,' Andrew snarled, and was about to punch the Austrian doctor, but was stopped by Sir Christopher, Bernard and Peter, who had to make an enormous effort to constrain him.

'That's enough! If you don't behave like civilised people I will arrest you all, and take you to the police station right now!' the inspector shouted, then Constable Parker whispered in his ear,

'What about the dinner, Sir?'

'Shut up, Parker! Wherever I go, this turkey goes with me,' the inspector announced categorically.

'...as evidence, Sir?' Constable Parker asked, smiling.

'Any more jokes from you and I will roast "you" as well; and don't drink anything else until dinner, Parker,' the inspector ordered, then continued. 'Sir Christopher, why did you leave in such a hurry? Can anybody tell me where Miss Mary Abington is? I have some questions she must answer,' he demanded.

'Andrew, take Kate upstairs, as you two need rest, and compose yourselves for later,' Sir Christopher said, then turned to address the inspector.

'You will be pleased to know, Inspector, that two murders have just been solved,' he said, proud of himself.

'What do you mean?' the inspector asked.

'Miss Abington tried to kill Kate, setting fire to Lord Henry's cottage museum with her locked in it,' Sir Christopher began, but he was interrupted by Diana.'

'Oh, my God! Henry's little treasures! Now I really will kill that witch. Where is she?' Diana shouted, getting up from her chair.

'Dead, I am afraid,' Sir Christopher replied quietly.

'What do you mean, "dead"?' Diana asked, incredulous.

'Oh no, another body?' the inspector exclaimed, throwing himself disconsolately into one of the chairs, at the very moment that the butler arrived with the Scotch.

'Earlier in this very room, Miss Abington told us that Albert was in the cottage opening the windows to air the rooms. Then later, when I looked for Kate, the two had already gone,' Sir Christopher explained. 'When I saw Albert's body, the pieces of the puzzle came together for me as if by magic, and I suddenly realised that she had lied to us from the beginning.' The magistrate paused, letting people absorb this information, before continuing.

'Her words earlier were quite familiar, but I couldn't remember when or where I had heard them *"God will bury evil words forever"*. However, after the deaths of Henry and Albert, knowing that Henry was an atheist, and how much of his life he'd dedicated to science, my doubts dissipated, because the hilt of that dagger was raised by a fanatical religious hatred.'

Sir Christopher was interrupted by the inspector's exclamation.

'Motive, Parker, now we have a motive!' He perked up; however, Sir Christopher took the advantage and added,

'Indeed, Inspector, a strong motive, which not only reaped Henry and Albert's lives, but also the lives of dozens of Catholics and Mormons, years ago in America. Whilst the fire was burning a Catholic church there, they found in the grass outside a note written in blood *"God will bury evil words forever"*.

'Hopefully she is burning in hell,' Diana cursed Mary loudly.

'That is not very Christian, Diana,' Ellen reproached her friend.

'My darling, the only hell with fire is the Christian one, I assure you,' Peter corrected his wife.

'Thank God we can finally put my poor Henry's soul to rest in peace, and prepare to enjoy our Christmas dinner, the way he wanted it so much,' Diana declared. 'Therefore if you, my guests, will allow me, I will go to my bedroom for a while to get ready.' Diana then left the drawing room.

'Remarkable, Diana, this is how life should be led – with such heart and feeling, the best way to overcome adversity. Actually, to be honest, this is the part that I like the most, I have to admit,' Peter said, smiling ironically, whilst lighting his cigarette.

'Indeed, my friend,' Bernard agreed, lighting his pipe; then he addressed his wife. 'Don't even think about it, Charlotte; you will be a very poor widow, trust me.' His wife looked at him, up and down, with a frown.

The long-awaited dinner was finally about to begin, and all the guests and friends, who were glamorously dressed and reunited in the drawing room, stopped talking when the butler appeared at the door, bowed, and announced,

'Dinner is served.'

The guests gradually walked elegantly to the dining room, and once everyone was sat in their chairs around the table, Diana stood up, with Inspector Parnell and Constable Parker beside her, as promised, and asked for everybody's attention.

'My dear friends, we don't have my poor Henry with us…' She paused, and after glowering at Peter defiantly, she continued. 'Nor in any other "immaterial" form…' Suddenly, though, one of the two crossed swords hanging on the wall of the dining hall behind her, which composed part of the Tollemache family coat of arms, fell loudly to the floor in a clatter, making the guests gasp in amazement and look at each other in wide-eyed fear.

Diana was not somebody to give up, so whilst the butler quickly brought a servant to remove the sword and, as a precaution, removed the other one from the wall, Diana, after raising an eyebrow and glancing at Peter, continued.

'As I was saying, my poor Henry is not "materially" amongst us, but he is definitely in our memories, thoughts, consciousness and unconsciousness, wherever there is a space for him to be remembered…'

When Diana said that, Ellen whispered to Charlotte,

'Do you think he will be resurrected like Jesus?'

'Don't be silly, Ellen, Jesus was not a ghost.' Charlotte shook her head.

'Do you think it was his soul or his mind?' Bernard asked Peter, trying to hold back his laughter.

'That is a very good question, my dear, and whatever the answer, nobody would like to be in Diana's bed tonight, not with that sword flying around,' Peter answered, trying hard not to laugh.

'Excuse me, Sir, would it be possible we go home after dinner?' Constable Parker asked the inspector.

'What? Not at all! I will not miss a good full English breakfast,' replied the inspector, then asked, 'Why, Parker? What is your problem?'

'Err... I don't like this place. These people are weird,' Parker replied nervously; then Sir Christopher, who was paying attention to their conversation, intervened.

'Don't worry, Constable, there are two servants looking after the two bodies.'

'I would not be worried about the bodies, Chris; "ghosts" are my real concern,' Sir Richard interjected.

'Is anybody looking after the "skulls"?' Dr Baker, who was usually very quiet, asked.

'Yes, why?' the inspector asked him.

'Just asking. That's all...' Dr Baker apologised.

'We will leave tomorrow at dawn, before breakfast, and before the snow falls and blocks our way. I cannot take another day around here,' Andrew said quietly to Kate.

'What about the excavations at Stonehenge?' Kate asked, disappointed.

'Don't be silly, Kate, we are in the middle of winter. Leave it to me. We have something called "letters". We will deal with everything by letter; even if I have to send a pigeon post to deal with Diana and Sir Edmund.'

'Over my dead body!' Sir Edmund exclaimed, more drunk than he should be, when he heard his name.

'Don't worry, Andrew, we are negotiating a profitable venture ahead,' Peter assured him.

'Yes, we are, so let's toast to Lady Diana Tollemache, our most generous hostess!' Sir Edmund, really drunk now, raised his glass, but Lady Georgiana, who was next to him, whispered in his ear,

'What did you promise them?'

'Don't worry, Georgiana, the birds, the trees, the moon and the sun are safe, but I cannot guarantee the rest,' Sir Edmund replied, with difficulty.

'What do you mean?' Lady Georgiana insisted, agitated.

'Don't worry, Lady Georgiana, he cannot remember the details of our proposal at the moment, as you can see,' Bernard informed her, and continued. 'However, in our partnership we can guarantee the birds' health, the stones' integrity, and the certainty that the sun and the moon will always return, if we put up a small stall with appropriate souvenirs to seal the pact between Mother Nature, and those who seek peace of mind,' Bernard explained in a rhetorical way.

'Hmm...' Lady Georgiana agreed, without understanding exactly what he had just said.

At that point, the conversation was interrupted by the butler, who opened the double doors wide, to allow a vast array of servants to carry large silver trays with the most exquisite imaginable Christmas delicacies through to the waiting guests.

There was salmon, duck and goose, as well as turkey and pork; platters of roast vegetables and great towers of Yorkshire puddings; a fleet of silver gravy boats, Cumberland relish, and three different types of stuffing; everything one could imagine at the most indulgent Christmas feast.

The desserts were not so much of an afterthought as an exquisite array of perfections, each magnificently composed and grand in presentation. There was sherry trifle, decorated with little sugar fancies and piped cream; Christmas puddings with gold half-sovereign coins hidden in each bowl, which certainly aroused the guests' curiosity about the ability to make such a thing; there was a huge Yule log, made with a delicious and very fine dark chocolate sponge, decorated with edible holly berries and ivy, showered with icing sugar and tiny little flakes of edible gold-leaf; something for every palette, followed by cheese and biscuits, as well as petit-fours with coffee and cream; brandy for the gentlemen and exotic liquors for the ladies, or anybody who fancied something a little different. Even freshly made soft chocolate coated peppermints and spearmints to refresh the mouth were not forgotten. Everybody was completely satisfied, as things seemed so sensible and sane as Christmas worked her charm.

Andrew was right, though; it was time to go, and Kate was very happy to head home. They had explained their intentions and said their goodbyes the night before; so, although a feeling of nostalgia overcame her momentarily, Kate knew in her heart it was time to follow the way home.

Kate was sitting inside their carriage, watching the first light winter snow begin to fall, whilst Andrew was giving the last instructions to the coachman. She smiled and hugged Mr Bear tight, thinking about home – would her home be in England, or in Greece? she wondered. However, she already knew the answer – none of them or, perhaps, both. Who cared about geography, when the heart is where the home is? She would follow that man she loved wherever he went. Kate closed her eyes and hugged Mr Bear even more tightly, saying,

'I think you may rest, Mr Bear. He is going to look after us both forever.'

When Andrew entered the carriage, he smiled at her and Mr Bear, saying, 'Don't worry, we are finally going home, so you may rest, Mr Bear, as I will look after you two forever, especially now that I am officially a "Guardian",' Andrew announced.

There were no delays at first. The snow had stopped, and a cheerful atmosphere enveloped the couple whilst they made their plans for the next few days.

'I'm very excited about New Year's Eve, aren't you?' Andrew asked, smiling, then he added, 'Finally, we will have a few days just for us. If it keeps snowing, we could make a huge snowman. That would be fun, eh?' He laughed.

'I would love to,' Kate replied, then Andrew explained,

'My father died years ago, but I remember that the last New Year I spent at the in Enfield estate I was alone, because I had just arrived from Greece and it was snowing a lot, so I couldn't leave the house, although I had some invitations. The butler and the housekeeper always organised a small party together with the other employees, and they invited me to join them – it was the best New Year of my life. You and I could join them again this year, if you wish?' Andrew asked cheerfully.

'That would be fun. I can help in the kitchen, perhaps bake some cakes,' Kate replied happily. The couple was entertained with their plans for the New Year when the carriage stopped.

'The coachman probably wants to rest the horses, I suppose,' Kate explained, noticing Andrew's suddenly serious face. They were taken by surprise when an unexpected and ruddy face appeared at their carriage window, cheerfully announcing,

'Happy New Year! Andrew, Kate!'

'What the hell are you doing here, Anthony? And where is Myra?' Andrew asked, not entirely pleased at the surprise.

'I am here!' a cheerful familiar voice announced. 'Happy New Year!' Myra greeted from the opposite window, and Kate started to laugh, observing the look on Andrew's face.

'Is she alright, Andrew? She seems... a bit dazed,' Anthony asked, worried about Kate.

'She is happy to see us, silly. May I enter? I am freezing,' Myra begged.

'Of course, climb in. We thought you two were in... Greece?' Kate replied after she managed to stop laughing.

Anthony noticed Andrew's silence, and immediately he tried to reassure his friend.

'Don't worry, Andrew, there is no mission this time.' He grinned.

'So, why are you here? You were supposed to be in Greece, holding the fort there, at the British school. I know you... what do you have in mind?' Andrew asked, suspicious.

'Oh, don't be so miserable. We are here to celebrate New Year with both of you. We don't have anybody else, and Myra's father is not entirely happy with our marriage. For some obscure reason he doesn't like me,' Anthony replied naively.

'I wonder why?' Andrew asked sarcastically.

'We have to be honest with them, Anthony; after all, they will have to know sooner or later,' Myra pressured her husband.

'I knew it! What's going on, Anthony? Tell me or I will not let you in,' Andrew stated, whilst the snow started to fall heavily again.

'At least let us get inside. It's freezing here, did you not notice?' Anthony asked.

Once Anthony and Myra were comfortably sitting inside the carriage, the coachman came to the window asking for instructions.

'Shall we go, Sir Andrew?' he asked.

When Anthony saw Andrew's hesitation, he took advantage.

'Yes, we are all going to Enfield Manor.'

'Wait a moment... what about your carriage?' Andrew argued.

'He will follow us, don't worry, we have to make plans for New Year's Eve,' Anthony replied cheerfully.

'What do you mean "plans"?' Andrew wanted to know.

'Calm down, Andrew,' Anthony reassured him, then Myra intervened.

'I will tell you. I was helping Thomas to catalogue the books that Sir Joshua donated to our library, then I found a book written by Sir John Evans, about prehistoric stone implements, and I read about these carved stone balls in Aberdeenshire,' she explained.

'Yes, I read his book, but what is the point?' Andrew asked impatiently.

'Well, we all know Sir Joshua Egerton was a specialist in Greek culture, but, although Sir John Evans is a brilliant antiquarian, his work is about Britain, not Greece. Therefore, I began to read his book very carefully, and I found a little note inside, marking the chapters where Sir John wrote about those carved stone balls in Britain. Did you know about them?' Myra asked Andrew.

'Yes, I know about them of course, but I didn't have the opportunity to see many yet; just a couple in Edinburgh one time. We have been very busy...' Andrew said, curious about the note, but he didn't want to show his interest.

'For some reason, Sir Joshua's research about Apollo and the Hyperboreans has a connection with these carved stone balls from Scotland,' Myra explained, excited.

Kate found Myra's excitement a little strange, so she asked her about the note.

'How do you know the note inside the book was written by Sir Joshua?'

'I recognised his hand writing. I have been reading his manuscripts,' Myra replied.

'Have you brought the note?' Kate asked.

'Of course; it is here in my bag.' Myra looked inside, pulled out a book, opened it and gave the note to Kate, who realised that it was not a text that made any sense. Sir Joshua had written some random words in Greek, underlining some letters as they were disposed as a code, for himself perhaps, five in total.

ο φοιβος Απολλων οι Υπερβορεοι πολυεδρον και
η χρυση γλαύξ Πυθαγορας τον μεμαθηκα

Kate's face blanched, and she looked at Myra, then to Andrew after, however it was Myra who took the initiative to speak.

'I know, I tried to match those letters and compose words with them, and I found "*phylax*" – "Guardian" in Greek – but I don't know why this word is important,' Myra explained.

But Kate noticed something else, and said,

'Myra, I am not stupid, and I think you two are here because Sir Joshua also wrote "the golden owl" in Greek, and you think that the owl is here, in Hyperborea.'

'I knew it! You are after trouble!' Andrew growled at Anthony, who was a little annoyed at the insinuation and replied,

'Hmm... not really... you hurt my feelings, do you know that? We don't have anybody else, only you two, so it sounded a good excuse to wish you both "Happy New Year",' Anthony said, looking from Andrew to Kate.

'Oh... don't worry about him. You are very welcome.' Kate laughed, not entirely successful in calming the situation though, as her husband grimaced at her, and said,

'I know you as well, and don't look at me with that sweet face, Kate, because I know you are thinking of going after "the golden owl".'

He felt completely hopeless in the face of such combined opposition, whilst Kate opened her eyes wide and exclaimed, embracing Mr Bear in an attitude of defiance, as if he was her only ally,

'How dare you say that? Would you throw our friends in the snow? Deny them warmth and shelter, a hot cup of tea, a warm cuddle, a...' Kate could not finish, as Andrew interrupted.

'Yes, yes, I know... I will not frustrate their plans, but you and I will have a serious conversation later, without Mr Bear,' Andrew said, then crossed his arms in front of his chest in a huff, glaring out of the window in a bad humour, while Kate addressed Anthony and Myra, excited by the news.

'Happy New Year to you two as well. By the way, Myra, in what chapter did you find that note?' and they started chartering excitedly about her find.

A few days later, at Stonehenge, a solemn procession of druids, dressed in hooded white cloaks, with candles cupped in their hands, slowly walked towards the centre of the stone circle. Meanwhile, another group, dressed in their hooded black cloaks, came from the opposite direction, moving simultaneously, to the same centre.

One of the women dressed in black, who was following the procession, was called to by one of the men in white, who headed in her direction.

'Hello, my dear, what are you doing here in this freezing weather? Would you like me to warm your feet?' Peter asked in a loud whisper.

'What are you doing here dressed like a... druid? I remember hearing you say you would never put your feet in this county again,' Diana said incredulously.

'Indeed, my darling, but someone had to calculate the risk for our great partnership with Sir Edmund,' he replied, with a provocative smile.

'Oh… and where is your twin shadow?' Diana asked, looking round, a little disappointed she was not the main reason for the reunion.

'Don't be so disappointed, Diana. Knowing you how I do, I knew you would love to be informed about the progress of our business enterprise. By the way, Bernard is not a shadow, he is doing a crucial accounting job for us. Poor lad, with all that paperwork in Sir Edmund's house.' Peter laughed, having fun with Diana's disappointment.

'Edmund's house? What about Ellen?' Diana asked, surprised.

'Oh, she is there as well, of course, with Charlotte and Bernard. She is quite scared of one of those recently departed spirits taking possession of her apparently. Anyway, Sir Edmund's procession is only for men, so she could not attend,' he explained.

'What are you saying? You four traitors accepted Edmund's invitation for New Year's Eve, and nobody invited me?' Diana declared in a hoarse whisper, very upset.

'We thought that you were an inconsolable grieving widow, and would want to mourn your late husband alone,' Peter replied, trying to refrain from laughing.

'What did you say? Me? Completely alone in that mausoleum?' Diana asked, irritated and very upset for being neglected.

'I knew you could not resist knocking on old Peter's door again,' Peter joked.

'I am not knocking, I am "begging", and I want to kill you for that,' Diana replied in a whisper, furious.

'You cannot kill me, my dear, we are not married,' he replied, enjoying Diana's exasperation; then he continued, 'However, I am not an insensitive man. I have to be honest with you. I interceded in your favour, and Sir Edmund agreed to include you in our partnership as well.' He smiled.

'You are not Bernard's twin shadow, you are "half" a shadow; you aren't even a shadow. You knew, and waited to see me beg,' Diana complained, even more furious.

'Hopefully you won't decide to marry Sir Edmund in revenge. He is quite… "ancient".' Peter tried to soothe her, still in a whisper.

'This is not a bad idea. What do you think about *Lady Diana Beckwith-Tollemache-Mulgrave of Wiltshire*, she retorted.

'Remarkable, Diana. You don't have any limits. Are you sure that you want to own the whole county, maybe be a countess? You may not have time for entertainment, and time passes very quickly, my dear.' Peter paused, then continued in an ironic tone when he noticed that Diana was thoughtful. 'Thank goodness we didn't marry years ago or I would be just a surname by now.'

'What do you mean?' Diana asked.

'Because you prefer to be a widow, and I would be dead by now. Perhaps this is the reason why you didn't accept my proposals in the past, so you can always knock on old Peter's door when you are bored, or if Tollemache's ghost comes back to haunt you,' Peter replied, laughing, though discreetly.

'He will haunt you, not me,' Diana retorted. 'Anyway, do you think that Andrew will find any treasure when he excavates the barrows?' Diana asked, but they were interrupted by Sir Edmund's voice,

'OVER MY DEAD BODY!' he yelled.

'Don't be silly, old man! If my order of druidesses comes on moonlit nights our profits will be higher, instead of reduced,' Lady Georgiana tried to reason with him.

'What do you mean by "reduced"?' Sir Edmund asked, annoyed.

'How many wives will allow their husbands to come out in a procession, if they could not do the same?' Lady Georgiana replied defiantly.

'What happens if the day is cloudy and there isn't any sun, then the clouds disappear in the night, and your moon comes out bright and shining – they will think the moon is more powerful than the sun?' Sir Edmund declared pugnaciously.

'I have an idea,' Georgiana exclaimed. 'If this happens, we close the stall with the moon's souvenirs that night, and leave only the stall with the sun's souvenirs open, to attest to the sun's presence in our hearts and thoughts, even during the night,' Lady Georgiana suggested, but she was interrupted by another angry voice.

'Nobody has any authority to close the Christian stall! We will be open all of the time,' declared the vicar. As due to the cold everyone was using hooded cloaks and scarves, nobody was able to identify anybody properly, therefore Diana and Peter looked at each other in astonishment, then, discreetly, Peter asked her,

'Did he see you?'

'No. What about you?' Diana asked.

'I don't think so,' Peter replied, temped to light a cigarette, but Diana stopped him.

'Don't even think about it; he will see us. Let's leave, whilst they are arguing, because if he sees me here in this procession, in these pagan clothes, I will have to pray on my knees, in contrition, until next year.'

So it was that Diana and Peter left the stone circle as discreetly as possible, whilst Sir Edmund yelled,

'Christian stall? Who said anything about crosses and Bibles! Are you mad?'

The last day of the year finally came around and found everyone at Enfield Manor very busy. In the kitchen, Kate, under the cook's supervision, was working on a medieval bread recipe, which included spices, dried fruits and honey. The cook was used to working by herself, without interference, so she didn't think it was a good idea give such an important task for the Lady of the House, but Kate, with flour all over her, including in her hair, insisted on it.

Meanwhile, Myra was filling Victoria sponge sandwich cake with cream and preserved raspberries, when Andrew and Anthony came into the kitchen carrying wood for the stove and the fireplace. After they stacked the wood, Andrew brought a few bottles of cider from the cellar and declared,

'Now we have plenty of wood for the whole year, I think.' He smiled. 'We shall celebrate the fire, the winter, the owls...' Kate, white as a ghost due the flour, intervened, and addressed Anthony.

'What happened to him... he seems... unnaturally cheerful?' She raised her eyebrows.

'I'm sorry, but we drank some port out the back; it was very cold,' Anthony apologised, then Andrew said, in a very cheerful mood,

'But there is always space for a good old English cider.'

'Good. Because I will save this champagne for the end of the party then,' Anthony said, suddenly flourishing a bottle of champagne which had been hidden in one of the cupboards.

'This was my first champagne, when I...' Myra happily began to say, but then she stopped and cleared her throat.

'Hmm... hmm... I mean... it was a few years ago; it doesn't matter really.'

They laughed without any proper reason as, apart from the New Year itself, nothing else would defy that freezing weather and knock on their door, except when the butler interrupted them, and announced,

'I am sorry, Sir Andrew, but a couple of gentlemen have arrived and they want to see you.'

The butler hardly finished the introduction, when those very two gentlemen appeared at the kitchen door, and the first one said, without any hint of embarrassment, 'Andrew! Kate! You have no idea how glad I am to see you healthy and... white?' Sir Christopher exclaimed, looking at Kate, showered with flour; then he asked, 'Anthony, Myra... what happened with Greece?'

'It might have been invaded by Turkey again,' Sir Richard replied, smiling, when he saw the bottles of cider Andrew was still holding.

'Sir Richard, what an... unexpected visit!' Kate greeted him cordially and a little hesitantly, with her shield ready for whatever battle was ahead.

Andrew smiled a self-satisfied smile to himself, given he finally had his revenge, knowing Kate's feelings towards Sir Richard, then he said,

'Indeed, Chris, Richard… where did you come from, by the way?' Andrew asked, a little confused at their sudden appearance without notice.

'Hmm… we got stuck in the snow on our way to Devon, and there were only two options – stay on the road and freeze to death, or to come back; however, the nearest house was yours,' Sir Christopher replied calmly, with authority derived and learned from mature age.

'Well, we are stuck together until next year, I suppose, so let's have something to warm our… frozen bodies,' Anthony interjected cheerfully, serving the cook and her assistants first, trying to be diplomatic with the employees, who didn't seem to like the acquisition of two new guests to accommodate for the party.

'Well said, Anthony,' Sir Christopher praised him. 'Come on, Richard, get that chair and let's sit here in front of this warm fire – it sounds like heaven to me.' However, Andrew intervened.

'Oh, no! If you want to eat and drink, you have to work, and there is plenty of work to do, trust me. By the way, dinner will not be in the dining room tonight. We are invited to the employees' dinner – a tradition of this house from now on.'

'Fair enough!' Sir Richard agreed, after a quick look to his annoyed friend, Chris, who had to get up from the chair to lend a hand, then Sir Richard tied a small and disproportionate apron around his waist, and exclaimed,

'My grandmother taught me how to make an oat ginger biscuit with chocolate ganache.'

'Oh… that sounds delicious,' Myra said enthusiastically, whilst Sir Richard pushed aside Kate, and the cook, whose humour became even more sinister with such a crowd in her kitchen.

'Thank God birds migrate in the winter,' Sir Richard provoked Kate, who raised an eyebrow, denoting disapproval.

'Who said that? Certainly not Kate's birds,' Anthony said, sitting on one of the chairs to enjoy his cider.

'What do you mean?' Sir Richard asked, worried.

'Look at those two owls, up there, hidden quietly in that gap in the wall,' Anthony replied, teasing him.

Kate looked triumphantly at Sir Richard, and said with disdain,

'I don't have any birds!'

Andrew could no longer contain his laughter and began to fill everyone's glasses, inviting them to toast.

'To Queen Victoria and… to the owls!' and everyone raised their glasses to toast.

'To Queen Victoria and… to the owls.'

www.ingramcontent.com/pod-product-compliance
Lightning Source LLC
LaVergne TN
LVHW010254260326
834688LV00044B/1282